In Motion

By Andy Piascik

ISBN 978-0-692-51620-1

2016 Sunshine Publishers

Cover Art by Dennis Irwin

ONE

The sky that began blue in the morning before quickly turning white grew increasingly gray as the day wore on. A moist breeze that foretold rain was doing tricks with Jackie's hair as she strode up the driveway to the garage door. Jackie didn't fear the rain. She had cut out of school early despite the ominous clouds, determined to get a full afternoon of gardening in. The garden was one of her favorite places and this would be her first big day of work.

Her life in recent weeks was much like the sky. Amidst brief stretches of blue and the occasional bit of gray, there was mostly dull white. Uncertainty reigned and the happiness she longed for remained elusive. There were moments of joy that she could not prolong and long periods of anxiety over unknown things she was sure she was missing. Perhaps getting back to the soil on a regular basis would help.

She slipped out of her shoes and uniform and stood solemnly before the floor length mirror. After an agonizingly long time, her breasts had finally blossomed. They weren't the greatest shape and she wasn't happy with the size of her aureoles, but at least they were no longer simply bumps on her chest. She turned sideways and ran her hand along her thin waist. She saw mostly flab. After a winter of eating that terrified her, she had lost the weight she had gained, plus a few pounds. Her waist was smaller but it wasn't small enough – there was no *small enough*. She had to be vigilant. When school ended, she would discipline herself to eat a late breakfast so she could do without lunch.

She turned to face the mirror straight on and stroked her stomach fondly. Then the flab that had momentarily slipped from view reappeared and her stroke became apprehensive. She pinched her flesh with both hands in the vain hope she could forego all the discipline and instead tear the imaginary excess away. She turned sideways and fingered her outie belly button as if she might discover a way to push it in permanently. The little protrusion was one of the few things about her body she had liked until Dan made a point of remarking what a turn-off it was. Since then, the sense of being part of a select group was gone and her belly button became instead one more thing to worry over.

She let her eyes wander from her stomach. She studied her face, her legs, her breasts and the secret place at the top of her thighs that was hidden from view. She fingered the birthmark on her neck that she hated and stood on her toes to see what it was like to be taller than sixty-one inches. It was a jumbled maze of an image distorted by confusion and of always wanting to be something better. She saw herself mostly through a filter of how she thought others saw her, yet it was not as they really saw her. If she could have seen herself as others did, she would have believed them when they told her she was beautiful. She knew she wasn't beautiful. That was just people condescending to a young girl. She knew what beautiful women looked like and she did not look like them.

There were things to like such as finally having breasts, but complacency would be deadly. She must never again allow herself to balloon as she had when she gained four pounds in December and January. She would accept having an ugly belly button and being the third shortest girl in the senior class if she could obtain a thin waist and keep it. She couldn't say in advance what thin was, but she would know when she saw it. She would show them beautiful, with a waist so small the other girls would die to keep up.

Jackie was forever being compared to her sisters. She liked that they were beautiful, but their beauty made it difficult for her to feel that way. She sometimes wished she could skip all the in-between stuff and instantly be twenty-five, but she knew even that wouldn't do, for she would still be the youngest and thus still less a woman. So she put her confusion away in a dark place and stumbled along, smiling as best she could so no one would suspect that anything was amiss.

Her oldest sister Susan was the only person who no longer treated her like a kid. Susan listened and advised only when she knew Jackie wanted her to. Best of all, she talked about herself honestly. She knew what it was to be slotted as Beautiful rather than acknowledged for what she really was. She was thirty-one and still dealing with it. She was dealing with it by being brilliant and dedicating herself to the things she cared most about. And Susan was good at so much of what she did. That's what Jackie thought made her sister truly beautiful. She *was* beautiful to look at but the work she did, together with her brilliance and the dedication she brought to it – that's what really made her dazzle.

Though Susan assured her that one day she, too, would dazzle, Jackie wasn't sure. Amidst the dullness and confusion that surrounded her, however, she had come to the wonderful realization that each new day was the smartest day of her life. She was constantly chasing new ideas and soaking up knowledge. In addition to a steady stream of books, Jackie read pamphlets and magazines and newspapers she got from Susan. Best of all were the hours she spent on the phone with Susan asking questions, clarifying and formulating opinions. She learned more that way than in any of her classes and marveled at times that she could *feel* her mind growing.

Downstairs, she grabbed the mail. Immediately she spotted the envelope from NYU addressed to her father. For months, the tension in the house over school had been palpable. It had not eased a bit even though a decision had been made – on the contrary, her father could barely hide his resentment that she would not be going to Harvard. Everything with her father, it seemed, was about winning and losing and on those rare occasions when he did not get his way, he was a terrible loser.

The night of the showdown about school had been something. Jackie was not one to cry, but she was so upset talking on the phone with Susan that she couldn't get through more than a sentence without breaking down. She eventually handed the phone to her mother in surrender, her father's decision apparently final. Three hours later, Susan was there and Jackie awoke from depressed slumber to the sound of raised voices. For as long as she could remember, she had loved and admired Susan more than anyone in the world.

Never had she loved or admired her as much as that night when Susan refused to back down from their father. The pivotal point was when Susan declared that she would pay Jackie's way at NYU herself if she had to. Listening through the door, Jackie shed tears of gratitude and love that washed away all the heartache.

Since that night, she saw her parents less frequently. They were three in the large house where they had once been eight and avoidance was easy. She moved more of her things to the third floor and began to sleep there regularly. Her parents barely noticed.

She had big plans for the garden. Despite the cool air, she wore shorts, a short-sleeved shirt, and the breeze and the soil felt good against her skin. She worked diligently and the rain held, perhaps taken aback by her defiance. In no time she was absorbed in thought as she worked beyond the tyrannical reach of clock and calendar.

There were big doings brewing for the coming summer. Already her mother was talking excitedly about the Queen of England's visit to New York, though it was six weeks away. Then there were Operation Sail, the Olympics in Montreal that Jackie and two of her friends had talked about attending, and all of the great summer concerts within easy driving distance. Biggest of all was the Bicentennial, the Fourth of July that promised to be the Fourth of July to top all others.

Guys? They were everywhere. God, were they everywhere. *You're the prettiest girl in the whole school, Jackie. You can get any guy you want. Lucky stiff.* Too many of them were like Dan, though. Instead of grudgingly accepting the lines she drew as in the past, they were pushing harder, certain they were finally entitled to sex. A few she even tried hard to like, but none of it felt lucky. Mostly it felt like someone uninteresting who loved talking about himself trying to cop a feel every five minutes.

She was more than willing to put a bit of work into making

something happen with the right guy. But too often she found herself settling, as with Jim, who she somehow went out with for five months. Or she found herself saying Yes because of other people's expectations when No was the better answer, like with Dan and the prom. *You of all people can't not go to the prom, Jackie.* She had finally agreed to see Dan for the first time since prom. They would go to the library together. No matter how hard he pushed, that would be all.

She dug on, sifting through the months of apple cores, grapefruit rinds, lettuce stems and banana peels that she had assiduously collected. Everything she touched, every stray twig and every decayed bit of fruit, was alive. She rejoiced in the soil that collected under her fingernails and dug her bare feet deeper. Whenever she disturbed an ant, a spider or a worm, she guided it to safety. They were sacred all, the worms especially for being wholly at one with – literally of – the earth. She smiled and contemplated the highly evolved simplicity of a worm's life.

It was just past five when she felt a rain drop on her arm. She gathered the gardening tools and set them on the ground near the cellar door. From a distance, she looked over the fruits of her efforts. She had extended the garden while also enhancing the aesthetics and the ecology of the space.

"Alright," she said aloud in honor of an afternoon well spent.

Inside, she washed up and poured a glass of water. It would be another hour before either of her parents arrived home and the house was quiet. Though the sky appeared about to burst, there were no more raindrops. Perhaps the rain would hold until dinner. Deciding to chance it, she went outside. She stretched out on a lounge chair and took up with her current amante, John Keats. She read aloud to better hear the texture of each word and the rhythm of each line. Occasionally, she went back and re-read a phrase to better understand. Other times she repeated fragments that sounded too right to simply be enunciated once and discarded.

For a while, Keats' verse, like gardening, kept thoughts of the friction with her parents away. She was a distracted lover, however, and after thirty minutes Keats no longer held her attention. She leaned back and her mind grew groggy. Hazy scenes danced before her. One moment she saw herself from a distance, the next she was herself, straining hard to see something that wouldn't come into focus. She was at the lake where she had gone frequently the previous September. She was in love with William Carlos Williams at the time and saw her book of his poems lying in the sand.

A raindrop on her forehead woke her. When she opened her eyes, it was May again.

The rain that had teased all day from its lofty perch descended with a vengeance. She could not recall ever having seen rain go from the first innocent drops to a heavy torrent so quickly. Back inside, she scurried about closing windows. Then she stood for a moment in the kitchen listening as the rain made a slapping sound against the driveway, its power drawing her in. There was something all wrong about being indoors, cut off from such unbound energy. Venturing out to commiserate might help to leave bad things behind. If not, it would at least be good for a laugh.

The rain was cool and hard on her skin and in no time she was drenched. She walked across the grass to the exposed soil where she had been working. Puddles had formed and her feet sank into the earth. She had a sudden urge to fly. Just like that, the rain slackened, as though it had read her thoughts. She knew her moment of opportunity would be brief. There was the work of watering the planet to do and the rain could only dally so long.

She measured off a short distance, ran four steps and did a cartwheel into a back flip. Despite the wet grass, her execution was flawless, right down to the skid-free landing. Feeling invincible, she did another and again stuck it. Before she had time to line up again, the rain began falling as hard as before. It was impossible to even consider a third. Two were enough.

"I love all of it." Though she spoke loudly, her voice was as small as a single raindrop against the storm's power. She stretched her arms out, threw back her head and stood completely still except for the blinking of her eyes. No one had ever written words that fully expressed what rain felt like or created a painting that captured rain's beauty.

"Can you hear me? I love all of it." She raised her arms straight up. "All of it."

TWO

The library was busy for Monday night. People were lined up on both sides of Jackie along the long card catalogue as she wrote down the call numbers of the books she was looking for. She rarely got to go downtown to the main library, so she was actually glad Dan had called and asked her to join him.

The small branch library close to home was a special place for Jackie when she was younger, but it did not have many of the kinds of books she was interested in now. The main library had plenty, plus it was easy to wander around and get lost in. The city's past was also much alive there, most visibly through the photographs on the walls.

Dan had drifted off to the newspaper room so Jackie reacquainted herself with some of the photos on the walls as she waited. One from 1934 showed a group of men pausing from digging out of a massive snowfall. Another was of a robust 1946 picket line. Four photos from the turn of the century captured vibrant activity in the harbor, with dozens of vessels of various sizes moored just off land. She studied the photos, lost in the past and unaware of the male figure who approached until he spoke.

"Jackie? It is you. Jack Simmons."

"Oh my God, Jack. Hi. How are you?"

They had gone to grade school together but to different high schools. Though he had been a year ahead of her, they got to know each other the way people can in a small school. They had also lived just a few blocks from each other and so took the same route every day. Shortly after he graduated from the eighth grade, his family moved and they hadn't seen each other since.

"I'm good," he replied.

There was so much she wanted to say and, more, to ask, yet she was flummoxed and unable to come up with anything more than, "How've you been?"

She was used to having to look up to guys, but at six-four Jack was in a whole different category. The shadows of the younger Jack Simmons were there in his face, yet he had changed in a way she couldn't pinpoint at first. It wasn't the brown hair that was longer, nor was it his easy grace. It was something about his eyes. They were alive in a way she had rarely seen in anyone. He had always been bright and eager to learn and for that reason it seemed fitting that it was at the library that she had run into him after all this time.

"I've been good," he said. "God, it's so great to see you. Are you cramming for finals yet, or is it too early for that?"

"No, it's not too early," she replied. "I'm actually done with three of my classes already."

Soon they were talking familiarly, as if five days had passed rather than five years. She talked about NYU and her tentative plan to work another summer as a swimming instructor. She was surprised to discover he had spent the year since high school working rather than attending college and delighted when he said he would be starting at Keene State in September.

"You'll like New Hampshire," she said. "It's lovely there."

"It's pretty lovely right here all of a sudden."

She smiled and looked away, hoping against hope that Dan was deeply immersed in newspapers. They reminisced about good times and kids they had gone to school with. She was pleasantly surprised that he knew a number of girls from her high school and puzzled when he said he knew them from the library.

"Wow, NYU. Are you excited?"

"Yeah, I am," she said. "It'll probably hit me more come August but, yeah, I am."

"Well, graduate and enjoy the summer. Maybe get back to teaching little guppies and polliwogs how to swim. I bet a lotta little boy polliwogs fell madly in love with their teacher." He laughed effortlessly so she couldn't help but laugh along. "God, NYU. That is so great."

"You sound more excited about it than I am," she said. "I can't believe we haven't run into each other all this time."

"You look great, by the way. Just like always, only – only better."

"Thanks," she said. His stammering was a nice contrast to the smooth talkers. "It would be nice if we could – "

"Hey, sweetie." Dan sidled up and put his arm around Jackie's waist. her. "Got your books?"

She attempted to pull away but Dan held fast and she introduced them.

"Nice to meet you," Jack said.

"Ready to go, babe?" Dan said, ignoring the hand Jack offered. "Almost closing time."

"My books are all in the stacks." She was annoyed at Dan for holding fast to her, for going out of his way to be rude and for acting like he was her boyfriend. Him acting that way confirmed, if confirming was needed, that she had been right to give him the slip since prom.

Jack held out a handful of call slips. "I guess some of these are yours."

"You work here?" her voice was so serious that Jack couldn't help but smile as a woman approached. It was Becky the reference librarian.

"There are a few people waiting, Jack." She handed him more call slips and looked at the clock.

"Yeah, Jack, people are waiting," Dan said. "You don't wanna get fired from such a prestigious job, now do you?"

"I'll get yours first," Jack said, looking at Jackie and refusing to take the bait.

"No rush."

"Hey, come on, babe," Dan said. "We got to get to the Point."

Jackie glared. The Point was a spot along the Sound popular for, among other things, backseat sex.

"They'll be in the pick-up box in a minute," Jack said. "Great seeing you again, Jackie. Nice meeting you."

"Yeah," Dan said.

"Great seeing you, Jack." He was gone before she could figure out a way to say that she and Dan absolutely, positively were not going to the Point.

Jack fingered Jackie's call slip for *Far From the Madding Crowd*. It was the others that caught his eye, though: three volumes of Rimbaud. He smiled and peaked back to where she was standing. *Little Jackie Gendron, all grown up. In more ways than one.*

THREE

Mrs. Gendron was home when Lynn dropped Jackie off. That was a common enough occurrence, for Jackie's mother liked to get away from the office each afternoon and she wasn't one to go out for lunch. Her mother was on the phone and Jackie gave a quick wave on her way upstairs to change. The windows were up and her room smelled like fresh flowers. It was a wonderful smell, a scent that for Jackie brought to mind rebirth, creativity and love. Love? She smiled to herself. Dan was history. He had been an inadequate insurance policy for prom and definitely no boyfriend – not hers anyway. If Dan was the alternative, she would stick with Thoreau and Rimbaud.

"Mom?" She couldn't understand why her mother didn't answer the door. Downstairs, the house was still and the car was gone. On the table was a note: *Late for Appointment. See You Around 6:30. Happy Gardening, Mom.* After the bell rang a fourth time, she saw a form move toward the driveway through the window next to the front door. When she opened the door, Jack Simmons appeared from around the shrubbery.

"Jack. Hi." They were both wearing blue jeans that had been cut into shorts and bright orange shirts. She was barefoot, he sockless with sneakers.

"Hi. I rang the bell but there was no answer. It seemed weird that the garage door would be up with nobody home." He was unsure of himself in a way he had not been the night before at the library. "If you're not busy, I thought maybe we could hang out."

"No, I'm not – "

"I don't have my car," he went on, "otherwise we could go for a ride. I was riding my bike around the old neighborhood and the next thing I knew I was heading this way. I wasn't really planning to drop in like this."

"Come in." How charming that he should be nervous.

"Is there somewhere I can put my bike?"

"The garage," she said, pointing. "Go around and I'll let you in that way."

She got them each a glass of lemonade and they went upstairs to the deck on the second floor. Within minutes, it was smooth like the night before. She looked at the garden, content suddenly to let it go for a day.

She was surprised when he mentioned that, in addition to the library, he was employed at the brass factory that sat in the middle of the city. She imagined it a difficult place and the people who worked there as old beyond their years. Jack did not fit that picture. He was youthful and there was a delicateness about him despite his size. She could easily picture him on a dance floor or a basketball court or studying the Romance Languages he said he was going to major in, but it was difficult to imagine him working in a hellhole like the Brass.

He spoke very precisely and didn't stumble for words the way so many their age did. It made for good listening. He also smiled frequently and was quick to poke fun at himself. When he turned in either direction, she could see acne scars on the sides of his face.

"Looks like you've got a little tan goin' already," he said.

"From working in the yard, I guess." She wanted to talk about the garden but she had never met a guy yet who cared about flowers other than as an obligatory thing to bring along on a date. Instead she talked about social studies and poetry and the interview project she did for her history class. His eyebrows went up at the mention of Latin, and he smiled at the passion in her voice as she spoke of class trips to the Museum of Modern Art. When he asked about the interview project, she explained that it was an effort to tell the history of the city through the stories of everyday people. Most people thought it boring so she didn't mention that it was the most interesting and rewarding thing she had ever done in thirteen years of school. Instead she went on to something else while noting again how alive his eyes were.

He didn't let her drift very far from the interview project before bringing her back with several questions that revealed that he knew a lot about the subject, and she began to wonder if he had read the background material and listened to the interview tapes. Never, though, did he make it his show. The only other person she had talked that way about the project and her interest in it was Susan.

She noticed whenever he spoke that the fire in his eyes had spread to his voice and she tried several times to ask him questions just so she could listen to him talk. Before long, though, he asked about her sisters and surprised her by rattling off all of their names.

She loved talking about her sisters. It was easy going and she studied him further as she spoke. The shirt he wore was too large and his arms were thin. His brown hair was long and appealing, though he did not put much effort into maintaining it. The chair he was in was much too small for him, but he sat as easily as he had moved about at the library.

She knew she was talking too much but each time she arrived at a good place to ask him a question, he beat her to the punch. And she hadn't even gotten to Susan yet. Finally she just stopped.

"Jack, this is embarrassing. I'm doing all the talking."

"I like listening to you," he said simply. "But I'll talk if you want." And then it was he who brought up Susan, specifically articles of hers he'd read in both *Radical America* and the local free weekly the *Advocate*.

"Did you read the one she wrote about the Bicentennial?" she asked, unable to stop herself from interrupting.

"Yeah, that was great." Thinking of another one, he smiled.

"What's so funny?"

"Whatever It Is, I'm Against It," he said, citing the title of an article of Susan's he'd read just a few weeks before.

Jackie laughed. "Yeah, I think that's my all-time favorite."

With some effort she was finally able to rein in her enthusiasm about Susan and listen. The sound of his voice was soothing and the fact that he actually kept up rather closely with her favorite sister's writing drew her in all the more deeply. She snapped out of it with a sudden unpleasant thought about Dan. What could Jack have thought after seeing her with him? He probably figured they were a couple and that – oh, God.

At once she saw something change in his expression that she took to mean he knew what she was thinking. Then he stopped talking altogether and she knew that he knew she was thinking about Dan. Unnerved, she stammered out something about how nice it had been seeing him at the library the night before.

"Yeah, it was." He smiled. "But you do know that you said that two or three times already, don't you? Not that it's not nice to hear again or that it wasn't nice last night but – "

"Dan's not my boyfriend," she blurted out. "And we didn't go to the Point last night. Not last night or ever."

She couldn't believe how stupid she sounded and waited for him to burst out laughing. She was all wrong, though, and instead a look of concern for her embarrassment and understanding for her need to explain came on his face. He could have made her feel foolish and small with any number of words and she desperately wanted to keep talking to spare herself. No words came, however, and she was about to give up and make matters worse by standing up on the pretext of getting more lemonade.

"Jackie, how's about we forget about Dan and talk about Susan." With the barest movement, he put his hand on her arm, firm and soft at the same time. All of the tension of the moment dissolved away and she felt like she could take his hand and kiss it. Instead he patted her hand with his and, true to his word, asked what it was she liked about Whatever It Is, I'm Against It, the one about the Bicentennial and several others she had forgotten about.

She lightened thereafter and the laughter and talk came even easier. Previously discordant ideas cohered and she spoke about any number of things from the American Revolution to the smug cynicism of Eugene O'Neill with a passion that surprised her. She talked in a way she never talked outside a classroom but it was different from school in its mutuality and its honesty. No one was trying to score points or show off nor did they have to worry about a teacher trying to maintain a position of superiority. They talked on and on, finishing one another's sentences and interrupting each other without it mattering.

When it got so the sun was shining in her face, they shifted their chairs. There was more spring in the air than summer and it was pleasantly warm. Not once did Jackie think about the gardening she wasn't doing.

"Maybe we could save the rest of the Gendron saga and talk about your family," she said finally.

"Just one more thing." He smiled. "It's fascinating that even though you're the youngest, you're closest to your oldest sister. Most people are tighter with whoever's closest to them in age, don't you think?"

No one, not even in her family, had ever remarked upon Susan and her that way. "I don't know."

"Well, anyway. I think it's great."

For as long as Jackie could remember, Susan had been her favorite. She had never thought about why. She had to force herself back. "So how is everybody?"

"I figured you knew." He looked at her closely for a moment. "My folks split up."

"No," she said. "I'm so sorry."

"Well, they're split up now. Supposedly they're talking about getting back together. I don't know."

She was stunned to hear that both of his parents had cheated. Though he smiled, there was unmistakable bitterness in his voice as he related the basics. Then casually, he mentioned he'd been living on his own for the last two years.

"On Skidmore Street," he said. "It's three rooms in the back of a store owned by this very cool guy from India, Bandu. He used to live there with his wife before their kids were born. It's great. I get up when I want, eat when I want and go to bed when I want."

Though there was something admirable about him choosing to

16

live on his own, she knew it wasn't great. He didn't go into detail and she didn't press. Arguments about college were one thing; confronting the fallibility of one's parents the way he had was something else again. Two years! That meant he'd been on his own since before his senior year. And here she was concerned whether she would hold up without crying during graduation.

She was interested to know more, but she saw that it was easier for him if she talked. Hoping to help him forget his troubles, she went on enthusiastically about Latin, rolled her eyes at her mother's excitement over the Queen's visit, and joked about Gerald Ford and Jimmy Carter. When they were done laughing, a twinkle came into his eyes.

"What?"

"For some reason," he said, "I just remembered what some of the guys in school used to call you."

"Jacqueline Jack-o-Lantern," she said immediately.

"You must've hated that."

"Actually, I didn't," she said, "because I love Jack-o-lanterns. I just hated the way they would say it."

He let his eyes run the breadth of the spacious yard. "I love your garden, by the way. Will you show it to me?"

"What do you do when you're not working?" she asked when they were back on the deck.

"Well, tomorrow at one-thirty, I'm going swimming at the lake," he said.

"Are you serious? What is it, a Polar Bears Club? The water will be freezing."

"A little chilly maybe, but not freezing. Anyway, no polar bears. Just one little polliwog." Peter Frampton's voice wafted over from a radio next door. "Gee, my favorite."

"Come on," she said. "You can't not like this record."

"I like it, but I'd like it more if I didn't hear it six times a day."

"Oh, my God," she said suddenly. "Did you see the list of concerts they're having at Colt Park in Hartford?" Before he could answer, she dashed into the house and returned with a page torn from a newspaper. She read aloud from the list, skipping some and emphasizing Fleetwood Mac, Frampton, Neil Young and several others.

He let out an exaggerated squeal when she handed him the clipping. "Fleetwood Mac *and* Jefferson Starship on the same bill? Golly gee. Now if it was Jefferson *Airplane* – "

"You didn't actually see them when they were still Airplane, did you?"

"Four summers ago," he said. "Dillon Stadium."

"Well, anyway, *I'm* looking forward to going even if you're not."

He squealed again. "Fleetwood Cadillac *and* Jefferson Plane-crash."

"That's right. Stevie Slick and Grace Nicks."

"Good one," Jack said. "And despite what you think, I'll definitely be going."

She thought he might say something about the two of them going together. Instead he asked about *Far From the Madding Crowd* and she was off again. Just like with Susan's articles, Jackie put forward an analysis of books she loved dearly and had been dying to talk about that was so sharp that she had to stop at several points and wonder where all the ideas were coming from. It was as thrilling as when she first dove into the books themselves. Heartened by his quiet encouragement, she nonetheless forced herself to stop after twenty minutes.

"So how did the big football player get interested in literature and Romance Languages?"

It didn't come out the way she intended and she noticed him pull back slightly, though he quickly covered it up with a smile. All of her noble thoughts about how people should get past her physical appearance to see something more, to not pigeonhole her, and here she was doing exactly the same to him. He was easy, though, and before she could even begin to formulate an apology, he explained matter of factly about a day in senior year English when he suddenly fell in love with learning. She pictured him in a classroom with a light as bright as the brightest star going off in his head, a star that had been increasing in luminosity ever since.

"Don't you think?" He said all of a sudden.

She had said something about *The Return of the Native* and then fell behind, lost again in his voice and his eyes and his passion.

"You didn't like it?" he said, misreading her distractedness. "The heath, the – "

"No, I did," she said. "It's one of my favorites. The beautiful but doomed Eustacia Vye. I bet you fell in love with her."

"Yeah, sure," he said, "that was part of it. I'm sure I wasn't the first."

"Tell me one of your favorite parts."

"One part I really liked," he said immediately, "was when she dresses like a guy so she can get in on the action with the mummers, which leads to her meeting Clym. He, of course, is intrigued the way any guy would be by this beautiful girl dressed up as a guy who he just *knows* is a girl."

"That *was* good," she said. He was quick. She'd show him she was, too. "So you like girls who dress up as guys."

He smiled. "Depends on the girl."

He accepted an offer of a second glass of lemonade and watched as she moved about the deck and into and out of the house with the grace of a gazelle in flight, every motion just right. As fluid as it looked, he knew from his martial arts classes that it wasn't instinctive or even natural. There was discipline and design in the way she moved.

"You're birthday is soon," he said once she was back seated, "isn't it?"

A mouthful of lemonade almost went down the wrong way. "June ninth. Yours too, right?"

"May twenty-fourth," he said.

"That was yesterday," she said, her voice excited as if it warranted a national holiday. "Are you kidding? Yesterday really was your birthday? Well, happy birthday. Susan's was Sunday."

"You're way more of an Aquarius than a Gemini."

She smiled. "Really? Why?"

"I guess it's the way you always were," he said. "Creative, friendly, open to new things. You care a lot about other people. Plus – "

"Wow. There's more?"

"Plus," he continued, "you always had the hippie thing going on."

"Said the guy with the orange sunshine shirt."

"My shirt's the same color as yours," he said.

"It's almost as nice as the lilac one you had on last night."

"Purple," he said mock defensively.

She shook her head. "You think I don't know the difference between purple and lilac? And rich lilac, no less. Very sweet."

"I'm glad you're enjoying yourself so much," he said.

"Probably listen to Sergeant Pepper at least once a day, with flowers in your hair and bare feet. "

"Said the girl in bare feet."

She laughed. She was enjoying herself. "What'd you do for your birthday?"

"You saw the sum total of the whole thing at the library," he said. "I worked my one job, worked my second job and then went home to bed."

That was sad. Jackie loved birthdays. She let it go, knowing it would likely lead back to his family. He needed someone to talk to about his parents but she knew better than to push. Another time.

The afternoon was fading and her mother would soon be home.

Four hours had passed since his arrival. Fifteen minutes in, Jackie anticipated that he would, when the time was right, ask her out. Memorial Day weekend was approaching and he had to have some time off where they could do something together. She couldn't fathom that he had come by merely to see how she was doing. She had never asked a guy out. If it came to that, it couldn't be so hard.

He seemed as aware of the time and what it meant as she was. The day had been perfect so far and the best way to end it was by leaving while it was still just the two of them. Their conversation had finally run out of steam. He stood up, looked around admiringly at the yard and said something about it being time to go.

Jackie never found the right words, certain to the very end that she wouldn't have to. She was missing something. He apparently had no attachment and had enjoyed the afternoon as much as she had, yet he got on his bike and rode away as if he had indeed stopped by just to check on how she was. An hour later, she was still buzzed by the visit and the stimulating talk. Two hours later, she was going back and forth between the buzz and the disappointment. It made studying for Latin complicated.

By bedtime, she was dreaming up scenarios. The best were variations of him showing up at the house again, declaring himself. She would accept his proclamations of love while keeping her feelings to herself. That was easy enough, for she wasn't sure what they were. She'd make him want her and deal with it however felt right.

FOUR

Far from the Gendron home in a neighborhood Jackie had never been to, a house was on fire. Though the fire department was on the scene in a flash, it was a professional job and the firefighters fought desperately against the flames. All the residents were evacuated and the fire was confined to the one building, but no one would ever live there again.

A fire in a three-apartment house inhabited exclusively by black people warranted some space in the next day's newspaper, but not much. The fire chief was sufficiently worried that he expressed his concerns off the record to the reporter on the scene. Professional jobs rarely came in ones, he knew.

The chief went way back with the reporter and had never deceived him. Together they would monitor the situation without raising any undue alarm. Neither was about to whitewash what happened and so agreed on the word "suspicious." Perhaps this might be the time when the chief was wrong and there would be no more. They would see. Though six people were now without a home, no one was injured so no names were included in the reporter's account of the fire.

Fires on the East Side were common enough so that Jackie skipped over the four-paragraph story. The thing was, she knew Miss Adele Williams, the woman who lived in the immaculate apartment on the third floor. They sat together for three hours one winter morning at the senior center so Jackie could interview her for her school project. Fortunately, Miss Williams was visiting her sister in Virginia at the time of the fire. It wasn't until the taxi pulled up to the house that she found out her home was gone.

The morning of the interview, it had not occurred to Jackie that meeting at the senior center was arranged for her convenience. Miss Williams's apartment was warm and spacious and Jackie would have loved it, but someone decided it wouldn't do. Miss Williams navigated her way through the streets of her neighborhood and up two flights of stairs every day at seventy-seven years young, plus she rode the long bus on a freezing winter's day just to get to the center for the interview. But send a seventeen-year old white girl from a private school to those same streets and up those same stairs? Are you stone cold crazy?

Miss Williams was Jackie's favorite interview. What a memory. The best year of her life was 1919 and she remembered all of it. And such a flair for detail. Like the IWW organizer named Angelo whose eyes were "brown as roasting chestnuts." Jackie even dug that Miss Williams was born in 1899. Such a cool number, so much better than 1900.

"Be sure to come see me in the year 2000, Jacqueline, and we'll celebrate three centuries."

The best part was how happy she was. Before, Jackie could not imagine that seventy-seven could be happy. But Miss Williams was so happy that Jackie came away happy. That made for a better paper. The teacher had Miss Williams' address and she mailed a copy of the paper along with Jackie's handwritten note. *Dear Miss Williams. Thank you so much. I hope you like the paper. Drop me a line some time. Sincerely, Jacqueline Gendron.* But Jackie hadn't made note of the address and so the mention of Pulaski Street in the newspaper story about the fire that destroyed Miss Williams' home made no impression.

Jackie's paper and the note were gone, along with everything else Miss Williams owned. Miss Williams's sister urged her to come to Virginia to live but she didn't want to. Though her pastor helped her find a new apartment, it wasn't the same. The new place was smaller and the street wasn't as nice, plus all her stuff was gone. And it wasn't home. It could never be home, not after forty-one years on Pulaski Street. Three days after she moved in, there was a fire a block away and for the first time in a long while Miss Williams was afraid.

FIVE

The woods were alive with birds as Jackie turned onto a gravel road that was the last leg of the drive. The parking area was set higher than the lake and when it came into view, so, too, did the dark blue water in the distance. In Octobers past, Jackie stood in the same spot and took in the oaks and maples ablaze with red, orange and purple leaves. She recalled one chilly day when a solitary figure was in the water and smiled, wondering if maybe it had been Jack.

There was a magical sense of isolation in the woods. It was a special place even in the bitter winter cold, as she discovered one afternoon the previous January. Depressed, she had gone that day intending to drive around the circumference of the forest, only to be captivated by the strength of the bare trees. Barren of leaves, the trees took on a new character and she had walked amongst them until her gloom lifted.

Winter was far away as Jackie parked her mother's car and walked down the path. Three quarters of the way, she saw his bike and then after a few more steps she saw him in the water. She smiled to herself that he really was crazy enough to be swimming in water that had to be freezing. Only his head was above the surface and he had goggles pulled up onto his brow.

"Hi," he said with great enthusiasm before she could speak. "You're looking gorgeous, gorgeous. Did you bring your bathing suit?

"No way." That he was unashamedly happy to see her lessened Jackie's fear that it looked like she had come chasing after him. "How long – "

"Jackie, it's great." He swept his arm around at the green foliage and the powder blue sky. "What else could you ask for?"

"Aren't you freezing?"

"Are you sure you didn't bring your bathing suit? He slipped entirely under water and emerged with his arms flailing about.

"There's a little polliwog drowning. Help."

"Jack, don't even joke about that."

"I never did learn the backstroke and I'd love for you to be the one to teach me," he said. "I know that was your best event."

That was a shocker, that he knew she swam the backstroke for her school swim team. None of the guys she knew cared about girls sports nor did the people who ran the sports page of the local daily newspaper. If he'd read anything about her accomplishments, he must have had a mighty powerful magnifying glass. Or the ability to read invisible ink. He went under again and came up twenty feet closer to shore.

"I don't know if you'd prefer to go back up the trail, but I'm not wearing a bathing suit."

"Yeah, right," she replied. "Very funny."

He shrugged nonchalantly and breast-stroked forward. When he rose out of the water, she saw that he was indeed wearing nothing but the goggles. He slugged slowly through the water, looking off toward the woods. Her eyes, meanwhile, were drawn to his penis. There wasn't much to it but it was most definitely a penis. Though Jackie was not inexperienced sexually, her experiences were mostly hurried ones in dark places and she had never before gotten a good look at a naked boy. Now here under bright sunlight was Jack as raw as the moment he was born. She had often thought about how great it would be to study a guy in the nude in some relaxed setting, like an artist painting from a model. This wasn't like that, however, and she was uncomfortable for reasons she couldn't pinpoint. It was even more disconcerting because he seemed quite comfortable though he came nowhere near measuring up to the naked guys she'd seen in magazines.

"God, Jack. It's the middle of the day and you're out here ... out here – "

"Having the time of my life?"

"Naked as a jaybird." She was angry at him but mostly she was angry at herself for behaving like she was eleven.

"I told you I was," he said.

"I didn't think you *meant* it."

He shrugged. "You know, that's such a strange expression, 'naked as a jaybird.' Aren't all birds naked? Why single out jays? Why not 'naked as a barn owl?'"

As he stood with his back to her drying himself, she turned so she could both have a good view of him and be able to turn away quickly if he looked at her. His body was red from the cold, but what she noticed most of all was that he was tight and not at all delicate the way he seemed the day before. Though lean, he was coiled in his upper back and upper legs, more like a sprinter or gymnast than the football player she knew he had been.

"And what exactly is a jaybird?" He went on as casually as if they were back on her deck sipping lemonade. "It's a jay, not a jaybird. It's understood that it's a *bird*."

"You know," she said, "not only are you swimming buck naked, you also don't live in town, which is like a twenty dollar fine, plus there are 'No Swimming' signs all around. That's probably another twenty – "

"Oh, is that what that says?" He squinted toward one of the signs. "I thought it said 'Walk In Like You Own The Place.'"

"Jack, will you please put your clothes on before somebody sees you?"

"Alright." Without bothering with underwear, he slipped into a pair of jeans. "But the day will come when some girl begs me to take my clothes *off*."

"Good luck with *that*." His body was nice and the banter was nice but her anger had not entirely dissipated. "What in the world possessed you to go swimming without a bathing suit?"

"I don't know," he replied apologetically. "It's such a lovely place, something about it just felt right. I wouldn't have if I knew you were gonna be here. You know that, don't you?"

That was honest enough. When she cut through the contradictory feelings, she remembered she wanted to be there, with him. And he was right, it was a lovely spot. She thought about them swimming there together on some unbearably hot July night.

"I can't believe you're not cold."

"Well, I did start to feel cold until ... " He stopped, pretending to be preoccupied with his shirt. She walked right in.

"Until when?"

"Until I felt this unbelievable warmth radiating down," he replied, "and I looked up and there you were."

"Liar," she said, unable not to smile.

"It was as though you and the sunshine and the blue sky were as one."

"You're such a liar." He seemed about ready to go and she moved toward him.

"Guess I'll have to work harder to break through the very transparent fake coat of protective armor you pretend to wear," he said. "I figure another day, maybe two at the most."

"Pretty confident, aren't you?"

"No, not at all," he said. "I hate confidence. It's for bosses and bullies and people who like to run other people over. What I am is hopeful. Hope is great. Hope is beautiful." They fell in step as he pushed his bike along between them. "Now getting back to that protective coat of armor we were talking about."

"I only hear you."

"And she's funny, too," he said. "Is that a smile I see?"

She looked away so he wouldn't see her smile as the car came into view. He popped the front tire off his bike and put it and the rest of the bike in the trunk. When she started the car and got back to the main road, an awkward silence descended. She was drawn to him more powerfully than was comfortable, yet he seemed oblivious. Had he put his hand on her leg, Jackie was convinced she would have melted on the spot. She fumbled for something to say in fear he might read what she was thinking, but he spoke before she was able.

"Jackie, I'm sorry," he said quietly. "About swimming naked ...

being naked in front of you. I should've been more clear about that before I got out of the water. I ... I'm sorry."

His embarrassment only made him more desirable. How silly she felt at having been angry. She would make a game of it, certain she could get him to blush. It had been a long time since a guy had blushed because of her. It was something she found irresistible.

"That's alright. I didn't mind." If she could get him to blush, they were on their way. If not, they were done. "You know, once I get the word around, there are lots of girls at my school who will beg you to take your clothes off. Whatta you say?"

Sure enough, he blushed. She waited for him to meet her gaze but all he did was laugh weakly and look away as his face reddened. Jackie struggled to hide her elation. They were off to the races. She composed herself, struck by something he had said.

"That bit about confidence was interesting," she said. "What you said is true, but what about people who aren't bosses or bullies but are the ones who get pushed around? Aren't they better off if they have confidence? It's definitely good to not wanna be a bully or a boss, but – "

"Makes sense," he said agreeably. "I guess I was thinking too much about guys I know who swagger around and get off on intimidating people."

"But that's not confidence, is it?"

"No, I guess not," he said slowly, as though he was confused about something. "I suppose that's why you're going to NYU and I'm going to Keene State."

She turned hard toward him but he was leaning out the window doing his best to soak up sunshine.

When they crossed the town line into the city, the surroundings became less green and more compressed. Many of the houses were in need of work and yards were cluttered and untidy, like the one with the clothes dryer near the cellar door that nobody had gotten around to disposing of. Kids just out of school gathered on corners, on church lawns and in a small park where most of the grass had been worn away. He asked if they could stop at the bank and then at his mother's and gave her directions on how to get there.

She appreciated the chance to drive with him, both because she enjoyed his company and because it was an opportunity to traverse parts of the city she might not have gone through alone. Hardscrabble as it was, the city was full of interesting architecture she could never get enough of, like the beautiful building that had housed the dance school she attended for years. Though it was now a credit union, the building would be a part of her for as long as it stood. Other places with a less direct connection like the old sewing machine factory were also nonetheless linked to her life. She couldn't drive past it without remembering reading aloud while her grandmother worked at her Singer sewing machine making beautiful outfits for Jackie and her sisters.

She was proud that people in her hometown made sewing machines and adding machines and drill presses and lots of other stuff that people all over the world used. The city's manufacturing history made it all the more distressing that so much of it had ground to a halt. The sewing machine factory had been one of the first to shut down and, as with virtually all of the other closings, the plant's demise was not the result of any downturn in business. Sewing machines were being manufactured in record numbers, in fact, yet someone had decided after all this time that they could be better made ... somewhere else?

Many of the abandoned plants were situated along the railroad tracks that ran the breadth of town and they passed them as they drove. Incredibly durable but now abandoned buildings deteriorated quickly once no one bothered to keep them up. Windows by the score were broken, paint was peeling, and gaping wounds showed where accoutrements of any value had been stripped. Perhaps most ominously, the abandoned factories were a sort of threat to the workers at the remaining plants that no one's job was safe as well as a taunting reminder to everybody else that maybe the best times had come and gone.

Regardless, the Chamber of Commerce, the regional business association, spokespeople for specific plants, the mayor, and officials from the unions all spoke of the present and the future with great enthusiasm. It was made clear they spoke for everyone including the recently laid off who, it was said, would be given every opportunity to receive training for other employment. The displaced were rarely allowed a voice of their own and then only in the controlled confines of a newspaper story. For that reason, they seemed oddly invisible even though most everybody in town knew somebody whose place of work had recently closed.

The business community's cheerleading had taken on a decidedly Bicentennial tone as summer approached. Announcements of anything from an upgraded model of jig grinder to the signing of a new collective bargaining agreement were made out to be analogous to the crossing of the Delaware. To a greater extent than ever, the nation's past was marketed until it became hopelessly entwined with the goals of its modern day industrial captains. Anything that could be sold was promoted with a nationalistic fervor and the legacies of everyone from Tom Paine to Helen Keller were tapped to pitch consumption and profit-taking as the obligation of all good patriots. The most extreme of the optimists went so far as to guarantee that the city's industry would soon bustle as it had during two world wars, though none went so far as to suggest another world war as the best way of achieving that end. Not out loud, anyway.

She sidetracked slightly and drew a bead on the factory where he worked. Previously, it had been a formidable steel mass where anonymous people worked. Now it had meaning. Her jobs shuffling papers at her father's law firm and as a swimming instructor were one thing. Working in a brass factory was something else altogether and she wanted to better understand it.

"You don't mind, do you?"

"Not at all," he said. "I was wondering where you were going."

The plant consisted of two large buildings that looked like airplane hangars and a smaller brick office building. The two larger structures were scarred badly and emitted noises loud enough to hear a hundred yards away. As they drew closer, Jackie could feel the car vibrate. Behind the plant, a passenger train of the New Haven Railroad was passing on the elevated tracks. Just beyond the railroad viaduct was a river that flowed from the north to Long Island Sound. A cornerstone of the city's development, the river was now blocked from view by the very steel and brick monstrosities it had helped make possible and fenced off from residents who barely knew of its existence.

She slowed as they passed over long-abandoned railroad tracks that protruded through the pavement. Weeds overran sections of road where few vehicles besides large trucks ventured. A threatening cloud of gray smoke hovered over the entire area, though it was difficult to tell which of the hulking structures was the source. They were stopped on a deserted street and she studied the buildings as though seeing them for the first time.

Jack had a smile on his face that was more puzzled than amused. No one cared that he worked there. For a year, it had simply been a not very pleasant job. Unbeknownst to Jackie, he was quitting soon so he wouldn't have to spend the summer before starting college working seventy hours a week. He would continue working at the library because he had to have some money coming in, but he desperately wanted something good to happen in his life and there was definitely nothing good about the prospect of another long hot summer working in a godforsaken brass factory. For all that, though, the place had become a part of him.

Still, as he approached his final day of employment, wistfulness was not one of the sensations he was experiencing. Never once had he punched in to start his shift without feeling he was surrendering a part of himself. To whom or what he wasn't sure, but surrender it was and he was convinced that every single person who worked there felt the same way whether they would admit it or not. Many of those with the hardest jobs, the ones his age especially, dealt with it by fortifying themselves before, during and after work with whiskey, pot, amphetamine and who knew what else. He had done so many times himself and it helped, but there is only so much pain and alienation one can anesthetize away.

The collective brains and brawn of the four thousand men and women who worked at the plant was something he would remember. Perhaps that, anyway, was something to be wistful about. What weighed so heavily was that they had no say over any of it. That was the one absolute on which those who held title of ownership would not give ground, ever.

In the employ of the owners were intermediaries – people with lots of degrees and clean clothes whose job description was to convince those who did the work that they didn't know anything. Every day, day after day, though collectively they understood every intricacy of every machine in every department in the place, three shifts of human beings drove, bussed and carpooled home at the end of a long day or night of work convinced that they didn't know anything. For if they knew anything, how could it be that they had no say over how any of it should be done?

In many ways, the worst of the intermediaries were those who ostensibly represented the workers. The time managers and efficiency experts were employed by the company so there was never any question about whose interests they served. As unfortunate as it was that they chose to use the knowledge they collected at prestigious institutions that way, there was nothing duplicitous about it. In a begrudging way, some of the workers even came to like some of them.

Those from the union, on the other hand, were not to be excused. They were as opposed to workers control as those who held the deed to ownership, and that included the ones who cited Lenin, Trotsky and Marx when doing so. To many of those working in the plant, it often seemed the union guys were the more vicious of the two in making it stick.

"Where do you work?"

He pointed to the closest of the two large buildings. "Here, go this way."

She rolled slowly forward, uncertain but trusting him, until they came upon another part of the factory. Trucks rumbled, forklifts scooted about, and there was even another fairly large building tucked in near the railroad viaduct. The road was beat to hell and she slowed almost to a complete stop after one rocky bounce.

"Who knew this was even here?"

"There's gonna be a quiz later," he said as she shifted into park.

He had no idea what she saw as she looked at the plant, no idea what she was seeking. Trying to understand it from her point of view, he was suddenly sorry they had come this way and glad he would soon be done with his job here forever. It couldn't possibly be making a good impression, this ugly place where he sold his soul forty, fifty, sometimes sixty hours a week. He thought of how beat and dirty and smelly he was at the end of his shift and he thought of NYU and how smart and sophisticated and beautiful she was, and of how deluded he was to hope that he might be able to get her to want him as much as he wanted her.

His shame that this was his life grew as they sat, each looking straight ahead, through a long silence. She was fascinated but she couldn't help but pick up on his discomfort. Finally, slightly embarrassed for having lingered so long and for making him uncomfortable, she turned the radio on and drove carefully away from the plant.

"Sorry, I know you wanna get to your mother's house," she said, desperate for something to say.

Up above was a confluence of highways and most of the rush hour traffic was traveling north away from town. It was the reverse of what had been expected when the expansion of the highway had been announced, with great fanfare, fifteen years before. Then, the whole justification for the destruction of hundreds of homes and dozens of businesses was that the highways would bring many more people into downtown. Instead, it became easier for people to leave, to live and shop elsewhere, and that they did in great numbers, so much so that many businesses that were spared the wrecking ball died prematurely anyway of neglect.

Jackie turned the radio off. Music was fine when she was with her friends and essential on more dates than she cared to remember, turned up loud to make conversation impossible, but they were not so far from his mother's and she wanted to get back to the way they were on her deck the day before. She felt she was blowing an important opportunity and she felt the need to make amends. She wasn't sure what for exactly, only that she had pushed hard enough for an understanding of who he was to make him uneasy.

"Jack, would you say you liked high school?" She sidetracked away from the direction of his mother's, hoping he wouldn't mind. When he began to speak, she was happy that all traces of his uneasiness were gone.

All in all, while he hadn't much liked it, high school was an experience worth having. He talked about his studies but mostly he talked about what he called the sociological education he got. It was a rough school with a heterogeneous student body in which white, middle class kids like him were a minority. That was a far cry from their grammar school, her high school and the high schools of all the boys she dated.

The other thing he talked about was the more difficult lives the students had, the blacks and Puerto Ricans mainly but the whites, too. Most were working class and many of the whites were immigrants from Romania, Greece, Portugal and Hungary and he described how in the halls between periods, there were conversations in many languages as well as in English heavy with accents of many more.

Many of the kids were nowhere near ready for high school academically and many floundered, caught in a system that was

34

as inflexible as it was lacking in imagination. The academically unprepared and the immigrants were aggressively tracked, the boys into shop and the girls into Home Ec. Many disappeared. Others persevered but were unable to finish in four years. From a freshman class of four hundred and twenty-five, just under three hundred graduated.

"Do you ever wish you had gone to a different school?" It was kind of a reversal from the day before. She asked questions and he talked. He was easy to listen to. He wasn't working at being funny like at the lake, yet touches of humor popped up at just the right moments.

He was also conscious to avoid framing his experience as in any way superior to hers or of making her guilty by association for having gone to an elite school that cost more than UConn. Instead, he said some things about her that she liked to believe were true, such as how well-attuned she was to the difficulties of other people. Why he worked that into a long exchange about his high school she didn't know, and he moved on so fluidly that she didn't have time to figure it out. But he had, and the fact that he had warmed her. She figured it was his way of encouraging her to embrace that part of herself more deeply. She also wanted to believe that it meant he really did like her.

At times as she listened, Jackie thought of Susan. Susan, too, spent most of her time amidst the people and issues Jack spoke so perceptively about – tenants in conflict with landlords, workers in conflict with employers, blacks in conflict with the police. To most of Jackie's classmates, such people were abstractions and their lives mildly interesting only when they burst onto the TV news. With Susan and Jack, they were three dimensional and as worthy of knowing as any character in Shakespeare.

"No, I really don't think I would've liked to have gone any-where else." And then he was off at length about things he could not have learned elsewhere, at least not in the same way: black music, black speech, black culture, Tito Puente, class distinctions, and the rage of so many of the guys in particular that would eventually be reined in by the assembly line, the legal system or the morgue.

She wondered why his sister Lisa went to a Catholic high school instead of the school he had gone to. He took a long time before replying.

"It didn't seem like a good fit."

She waited until it was obvious he was not going to go on. "What about your other sisters?"

"Same plan," he said. "Since they're all way smarter than me, this way, they'll have a better chance to get into a good college."

"So it was your idea."

He didn't answer. Jackie was proud she had gone to one of the best high schools in the state, but she saw more than ever a part she was not proud of. The flip side of *exclusive* was *excluded* and, the generous scholarship programs at her school notwithstanding, exclusive was about who could pay.

Then *he* brought up Susan, just as he had the day before. And as if he was reading her thoughts, he brought up Susan to illustrate that what she was thinking wasn't entirely right. Susan was bright, brilliant even, and she had gone to the same high school as Jackie as well as a college that was every bit as elite as NYU. She could easily have lived very comfortably by creating a life exclusively for herself but instead she used her skills in service of people who didn't have her privileges. Jack understood the rightness of that better than any of Jackie's friends, her other sisters, her parents, even, much as she admired Susan, herself. Many were the times she had passionately defended Susan without being able to adequately explain why it was right that Susan lived the way she did, and here he was stating Susan's case about as well as it could be stated. And more than understanding, there was obvious admiration in his voice.

"Damn. My mother's home from work early." He had said he had little to do with his folks but there was still something jarring about such a bold expression of displeasure.

"Is that her car?" A 1964 Falcon Spirit was parked in the driveway.

"No, it's my car. Let's make this as short and sweet as possible." He hesitated before getting out and looked at her hopefully. "You wanna just wait here?"

"No, I'll say hello."

Inside, Jack presented her to his mother and disappeared. Having heard nothing from Jack about her, Mrs. Simmons was surprised to see Jackie at all, and taken aback at the beautiful woman she had grown into. It was a refrain Jackie heard constantly, and once in a while it was nice. This was one of those times.

She had forgotten how much younger Mrs. Simmons was than her own mother. Mrs. Simmons was not particularly attractive but she had smooth skin and soft features, and her physical appearance was accentuated by her vivaciousness. Jackie sensed she was someone who could love heartily if given half a chance and though she didn't know how that squared with the end of her marriage, she was more than willing to give Mrs. Simmons the benefit of the doubt.

They shared a laugh remembering the time Jack fell into a pond showing off and had to walk home soaking wet. Though Mrs. Simmons had never been close with Jackie's mother, she spoke fondly about her. What Jackie remembered with some embarrassment was her mother once dismissing Mrs. Simmons as a mere *secretary*, enunciating the word secretary the same way she did *Republican*.

"If you give me your keys, I'll move your mom's car into the driveway," Jack said when he returned. Mrs. Simmons looked at her son but he refused to reciprocate.

"Jack – "

"I figured it out," he said as he walked away. "You need my car tomorrow, too."

"He's helped us all so much." Mrs. Simmons whispered once he was gone. "Working two jobs. I'm so proud of him."

"You should be."

When he returned, Mrs. Simmons said, "Wouldn't you like to stay for lunch?"

"We already ate." He went past them to the driveway.

As they talked on about the Gendron family, Jackie knew Mrs. Simmons was holding her tongue, that she really wanted to talk about Jack. But she also sensed that Mrs. Simmons was embarrassed about having revealed too much.

"He wouldn't want you to know," Mrs. Simmons couldn't help saying. "You understand, don't you Jackie?"

"I understand."

After Jack pulled Mrs. Gendron's car up to the top of the driveway, his mother tried one last time. "Are you sure you can't stay? Nature Boy?"

He rolled his eyes. "I'm gonna get gas. We'll be back later."

"Jack?" As much as Mrs. Simmons didn't want to speak openly in front of Jackie again, pride was a luxury she could no longer afford.

"It's on the table," he said of the money she had asked for on short notice.

"I guess we're ready to go," Jackie said awkwardly after he again exited and left the two women to themselves. "Maybe the three of us can have lunch another time."

"I'd like that very much," Mrs. Simmons replied with great feeling. "I'd like that more than anything I can think of."

"Bye, Mrs. Simmons."

"Good-bye, Jacqueline."

It wasn't the time to say anything, she knew. Everything she had seen the last two days had earned him that much. As difficult as it was to observe how he treated his mother, Mrs. Simmons' own words had been as good a tribute to him as anything anyone could have said. There was something hard about this part of him, however, hard enough that Jackie knew to proceed with caution. There was more here than just cheating and the end of his parents' marriage. In time she might come to know, perhaps from him, perhaps from his mother. What was clear and a little disorienting was that she wanted to know. It was more than the possibility they might become girlfriend and boyfriend, though it was definitely that; she wanted to help him. All of that after just two days. She laughed. Then she shuddered. So there it was.

"You wanna drive?" He said.

"Your car?"

"Why not." He tossed her his keys. "You were having such a good time before."

"Fine by me," she said. "Anything I need to know about your car?"

"You might have to move the seat up a little," he said, laughing.

"Any place special you wanna go besides to get gas?"

She saw that troubled look come over his face again. "Any-where far, far from here."

SIX

Jack was piling up overtime and they didn't see each other the rest of the week. Instead, they talked on the phone at all hours night and day, laughing about the jingoistic Memorial Day hooplah, the presidential primaries, and her father's desperate hope that Ted Kennedy might still ride in on a white horse and save the day. She talked about songs she loved and poems newly discovered and couldn't help but think about how smooth they were together. Old stuff wasn't so important anymore. How could it be, with so much that was new opening up.

They didn't have to bother with getting to know each other and several times Jackie found herself thinking it was like falling in love with a friend. Then she'd shake her head. It was that word again, love. Not if she could help it. She would go with the flow and enjoy wherever this thing that wasn't love took her. Too much was against them. Her parents for one, or her father anyway. She would see.

More importantly, time was against them. In three months, she would be in New York and he would be in New Hampshire. That couldn't possibly work. She had seen it with her sisters and several friends. They could have a fun summer together and then go their separate ways. That was a far more likely outcome than staying together beyond Labor Day. Perhaps it might be enough. It would have to be.

Still, there was something peculiar about her and Jack. They were destined for different places, yet they were moving in the same direction. He was the only person her age she knew who spoke about poverty, inequality, and environmental destruction as things to do something about rather than as immutable laws of life. Sometimes when he spoke, she heard her own thoughts in his voice. Unlike her friends who rolled their eyes at the thought of sit-ins, marches and strikes, Jack's face brightened. His interest didn't sound like thrill-seeking, either. He was serious about it, as though changing the world was something to make a life of, as Susan had. Funny, Jackie wanted more than anything to be like Susan and here was Jack talking about his life in much the same way. People not much older than they were, people Susan's age and younger, had radically transformed the United States. Why couldn't they carry it on and do as much?

Though Jack sometimes expressed himself forthrightly, he generally didn't speak as if he knew exactly where he was going. He had begun a journey and had far more questions than answers. He evaluated information and events as best he could while studying the work of those with more experience and greater knowledge, just like she did. When he asked her what a better world might look like, it was not a test but an honest question. That he asked made her think. That he cared what she thought made her want to be with him.

She found herself driving by his place when she knew he wasn't home. There wasn't much to see from the outside and she wished for the day when he would have her over. He talked elliptically about other girls he had known as if it was understood and hardly worth discussing, and she thought about how advantageous it was to have his own apartment. No need to worry about backseats of cars, after all, or sneaking someone in when mom and dad were out.

She went to bed at night thinking of him. She dreamt about seeing him naked at the lake and woke up wanting to touch him. Best of all was the sound of his voice on the telephone. He figured out the better times to call and set his sleeping schedule accordingly. Better were the times she called him. No matter how groggy he was, he was always willing to talk. They'd talk for hours, sometimes more than once in a day.

Sometimes she called full of enthusiasm immediately after having spoken with Susan or after reading something Susan had written. Then they would talk passionately about Emma Goldman, the Paris Commune and so much more. When she got back her final paper for her American Drama class, she gushed about 'A Raisin in the Sun' and was delighted to hear he had also once written a paper about it. He was reluctant to talk about his so as not to steal her thunder, she knew, but she prodded him until he told her about it.

She was astonished to discover that he had translated *The Stranger* from French to English just for practice and was working on translating *Open Veins of Latin America* from Spanish. Astonished that he had somehow found the time but even more at his proficiency.

She so wanted him to go to New York with her for Memorial Day that she didn't dare say anything to her parents. When he said yes, she concocted a plan where one of her friends would pick her up under cover of taking her to the train station and drop her at his place. Her folks nixed that possibility, however, by insisting on taking her to the station themselves, which she knew would include waiting on the platform with her. Jack smiled when she said she would get off after one stop to meet him.

"I like it," he said. "It's like sneaking across the border into enemy territory, rescuing the damsel in distress, and then sneaking back to freedom together. Should I wear a trench coat? Maybe you should wear a blonde wig. No one will ever recognize you as a blonde."

"Meet me by the clock," she said, his absurdist sense of drama infectious. "I'll buy the *Times* and the *News* but not the *Telegram*. That'll be our signal. If I buy the *Telegram*, too, it means I'm being followed."

"Right. And if I'm already holding a copy of the *News*, that means I'm a double agent and about to betray you."

She laughed. She couldn't wait for Monday.

SEVEN

It had been a while since Jack had run and he pushed on, lost in the surroundings. Nothing around them was familiar other than the Hudson River. Many of the buildings reminded him of black and white movies he'd seen on television. He was unaware that Susan's boyfriend Walt was struggling to keep up and thus surprised when Walt stopped not long after they turned back. They were a good two miles from Susan's place and he estimated it would take at least thirty minutes if they walked the whole way.

"Good thing I brought a change of clothes," Jack said after they'd gone a while in silence. "I'd hate to have to go on a picnic all sweaty like this."

"Jackie certainly is a sweet kid," Walt said.

"Yeah, she's great," Jack said. "Susan's great, too."

"Yeah. She really is."

The conviction in Walt's response was easy to understand. In addition to Jackie's glowing words, Jack had read a dozen of Susan's articles in the past week in preparation for meeting her. He was struck again and again by her intelligence, her optimism, her deft touch with words and her conviction that only everyday people can be the agents if society is to be changed in any meaningful way. It was quite something, then, to discover that Susan in person exceeded his expectations.

"Are you and Jackie boyfriend and girlfriend?"

"No," Jack said. "I'd like it but I don't think she's interested."

Walt smiled and let it drop. Soon they were talking of other things, with Jack mostly listening, for not only did Walt know his stuff, he was good at explaining things. Though Jack couldn't keep up with everything he said, it was refreshing to listen to someone who knew so much about how the world worked. So many guys he knew, especially the ones who were the least informed, spoke endlessly and with no sense of embarrassment of things they knew little about.

Like so many who lived in New York City, Walt was from somewhere else, which in his case was Michigan. He taught in the Sociology department at Hunter College and was taking it easy during the time between the end of the spring semester and the beginning of summer session. He liked Jack and respected his intelligence. It was difficult to cultivate young minds, what with students focused so greatly on getting the right grade rather than on learning. After just a few hours together, Walt suspected with some confidence that Jack was not like that.

Walt was equally confident that Jackie was one of those who wanted the knowledge but definitely wanted the highest grades, too. She was an excellent student who knew how to learn and utilize knowledge but who also never lost sight of the materialistic goals. She couldn't help herself, Walt knew. It was her background and the culture at the high school she attended. He saw the same things in Susan. So far Susan had not succumbed to the pursuit of the materialistic goals and maybe she never would. Perhaps Jackie never would, either. But the likelihood that she would was greater than with Jack, Walt was certain. Jack might come to know about living on the fringe, as Walt had for a while, but neither Jackie or Susan ever would.

"How did you and Susan meet?"

"At a meeting." Walt laughed. "We met at a meeting."

Jack tried to imagine himself approaching Susan, the difference in their ages notwithstanding. Not only was she incredibly attractive, she seemed approachable in a way most women that attractive weren't. It was difficult for him to picture. The odds that he would be able to make time with a worldly, beautiful woman like Susan were nonexistent. She would never regard him as a man the way she did Walt.

"Did you start going out right away?"

"No, she was with someone else at the time," Walt explained. "Then some time went by where we didn't see each other. Maybe six months. Somehow I found out she was no longer attached."

"So you asked her out?"

Walt smiled. "No. I … it's hard to explain."

They walked in silence for a while. The further downtown they went to Susan's, the quieter the streets became. Jack had utilized his maps to figure out how to drive to Susan's, but he had no idea what Lower West Side meant or what it was like. So as they walked, he studied the cool architecture and grew increasingly amazed that a Manhattan neighborhood could be so quiet and deserted.

"I guess I felt a need to pretend I wasn't interested." Walt had never talked about the beginning of his relationship with Susan before, not even with her, not really, yet here he was letting go with a nineteen-year old kid he had just met that morning. He recognized himself in Jack's need to understand and because of Jack's need, he knew nothing he confided would ever be repeated. Not that that was an issue; everybody, Susan included, employed games of all kinds. Susan had practically admitted as much.

"So we circled each other for a while," Walt went on. "I had a feeling she was interested in me and I knew I was interested in her but I wanted to make her wait because she had been with someone else when we first met. I guess I was supposed to be flattered but I didn't like her assuming she could go from the other guy to me in one easy step, like it was her God-given right to get what she wanted." They stopped to let a couple of bicyclists go by. "Is any of this making sense?"

"Yeah, absolutely," Jack replied. In fact, it sounded all too familiar.

"So I didn't do anything. Just to kinda put her on edge a little."

Jack was intrigued. "Did she ask you out?"

"No," Walt said with some force. "That would have ruined everything. See, I didn't want her to make a move. I wanted her to *think* about making a move while being unable to do so because she wasn't sure what answer she would get. I also wanted her to be unsure of whether I was interested to cut her confidence down a little. I suspected she was used to getting who she wanted. That's fine. Were it so we all could. I just felt the need to refuse to be one more easy pushover melting at the feet of this beautiful woman."

"Wow. And it actually worked." Jack was duly impressed. "So you eventually asked her out."

"Eventually," Walt said, somewhat impressed himself. "And you know, she never once has said anything or asked me about why I waited the way I did. It's almost like it's still hard for her to accept that that's the way it went."

There was one part of it that didn't fit. "Didn't you worry that you'd wait too long and miss your chance?"

"Yeah," Walt replied, his respect for Jack growing. "And that would have been a drag. I hope it doesn't sound sinister. And I didn't really mean that Susan always gets exactly who she wants."

Despite Walt's disavowal, Jack saw that it could be true. "I don't really know but I bet probably she could."

"Jackie, too." Walt made it more a question than a statement so as to spare Jack.

"Yeah." Jack had thought the same thing more times than he cared to remember. Walt knew Jack was intentionally playing it low key. He had seen the exuberant way he was with Jackie and it saddened him. It reminded him too much of himself, of how he had always been the more ardent of every coupling he had been a part of until Susan. It was a fate he wouldn't wish on any guy.

"Well," Walt said, "she hasn't told you to get lost so that's a start anyway."

Jack wanted to believe that was true. He just didn't know. He had been certain with other girls that he was doing alright, only to find out otherwise the hard way. Jackie was far and away the prettiest girl he had been out with and everybody said the prettiest girls were the hardest to make and the hardest to keep. He didn't much like the idea of having to make anybody to begin with, and knowing there were guys always on the make was something he tried not to think about. Maybe what he'd needed more than anything was a guy with a brain in his head like Walt to talk to. Maybe in a week or a month, if need be, they could talk about it some more.

Jackie and her oldest sister were busy at work on the feast the four of them would eat at the park. The vegetable market had opened a half day despite the holiday and they had gotten a bounty of fresh produce markedly superior to that at the nearby grocery store. As they prepared food, Susan watched in amusement as Jackie danced in place to the song on the radio.

"So who's hot that I should know about?"

"Peter Frampton," Jackie replied immediately. "His record's everywhere. And Fleetwood Mac. You've probably heard songs from their record. 'Rhiannon' maybe?"

Susan was making potato salad. "Do you and Jack like the same music?"

"Yeah." Optimistically, Jackie added, "We're talking about going to some of the outdoor concerts they're having for the summer at Colt Park in Hartford."

"That sounds nice," Susan said. "So you do see the two of you becoming something more."

"Yeah. That's what I hope, anyway. And I think it's what he wants. This is sort of our first date, if you can call it a date. Mostly we've just hung out driving around and stuff."

"That can be a nice way to get to know each other," Susan said helpfully.

"Plus we talk on the phone for hours. I mean literally for hours."

"Wow. A guy who likes talking on the phone."

"I know," Jackie gushed. "You probably don't remember but we actually knew each other pretty well in school."

"Really?" Susan said. "Tell me about him."

Once she got going, Jackie discovered there was a lot to tell. Partly it was because he had lived fairly close by before his family moved. Partly it was that Jackie preferred boys games to girls. And partly, she suspected, it was because he secretly liked her all along. It was he, after all, who insisted that she be included in the boys games, even football. The other boys' payback for acquiescing was that Jack had to have her on his team, which was a pretty stiff price because not only was she a girl, she was small. Really small. Plus they always lost. She knew they lost because of her but he never complained and never failed to stick up for her the next time somebody made a thing about her playing.

She talked about the end-of-school party the seventh grade threw for the eighth grade when he asked her to dance. From then on, neither of them danced with anyone else the rest of the afternoon. She talked about walking home from school together. It wasn't many times in all but enough so she remembered doing so with fondness. And she remembered the time in the school basement when they were alone and she thought he might kiss her.

Susan worked as she listened, smiling occasionally. It had never been easy for her with guys. They always wrote their own dreams onto her rather than seeing her for what she was. Falling in love with a friend was one of the best things she had ever known and she hoped Jackie might know that experience as well. Perhaps with Jack, perhaps not, although why not Jack, since in many ways he seemed so right for her.

Jackie also spoke about her uncertainties, though they were not as easy to articulate. Jack was both more and less serious than any guy she knew – more serious about the world beyond and less serious about himself. While he was in a hurry like her, he wasn't fixed to a specific plan. He was in a hurry to live in a general way, confident he would find his place in due time. The important thing to him was to be hooked into something bigger, some collective force that was taking on the general barrenness of the human landscape.

Though only a year older than her, he was already a part of that human force. In small ways perhaps and haltingly but engaged nonetheless. Susan's encouragement notwithstanding, Jackie had not made that leap yet. She thought of it as something people did when they were older. From Jack she saw that it wasn't necessary to wait, that now was as good a time as any and wherever she was a perfect place to begin.

Jackie's other uncertainties had to do with her folks. She had always gone along with their idea of a boyfriend, trying to please them and never being satisfied herself. All but Rob had been someone she knew they would unfailingly approve of. Not so Jack, regardless of how long they had known each other or how nice a guy he might be. It would be a fight and she was willing to try.

As always, there was also a voice of caution within. She thought back to the previous summer and the crush she had on Rob. He was gorgeous beyond endurance and she could barely take her eyes off him as they worked together day after day in the pool. No sooner had she given herself to him than she discovered she was just one of a rather extensive collection. It was hard to think of Jack doing something like that, but she hadn't thought it possible that Rob would, either. Until he did.

Jack and Walt joined them at three-thirty. While Walt hit the shower, Jack joined the conversation. Though Susan had treated him with great warmth all day, Jackie was certain she was even friendlier now. She knew how highly he thought of Susan and it brightened her greatly that Susan approved so completely of him.

Jack took his turn in the shower when Walt was done and then they set out for the small stretch of green between Greenwich Street and the West Side Highway for their picnic. They were pleasantly surprised at how deserted the small park was, for that allowed them plenty of space and relaxation. A cloudless sky and gentle breezes made it an ideal day for relaxing, too, and they had a beautiful view of the sun as it made its inexorable way down beyond the Hudson.

Though he was quitting in little more than a week, Jack had chosen not to take the night off. It was still possible to call in but he could not shake his loyalty to the rest of the crew. They would already be short-handed big-time because of the holiday, and the graveyard shift was especially difficult when they were short of help. In fact, the foreman had practically begged him to come in early for eight o'clock. There was nothing anybody could do if he didn't show but it was crazy to pass up all that premium overtime, especially now that he was on the verge of having to live only on what he made working at the library.

Once Jack put his plate down for the last time, he and Jackie set out to explore the neighborhood. They set off aimlessly to the south and east, turning and investigating as they discovered streets and alleyways along the way. There was something exotic about how sparsely populated the area was, though wherever they went the towers of the World Trade Center hovered over them menacingly, like Godzilla and Gigantor.

"What are you thinking about?' She asked after thirty minutes of walking.

"I have to go to work, Jackie," he said. "I don't want to but I have to."

"There'll be other times," she said. Rather than being disappointed, she was impressed, knowing from his mother that his dedication wasn't just to his co-workers but to financially helping to support her and his sisters.

"Other times," he said as they stopped and faced each other, "when you and I will stand right here on this very spot, with no commitments and nothing to do except whatever we want?" He was good at making her laugh and at creating abstract romantic scenery, but intimacy or anything close to it was another matter. Everything – the skyscrapers in the distance, the streets he had never heard of, the setting sun, and most of all, her – was magnificent, yet he could not draw strength from any of it.

"Scout's honor," she said.

He hesitated for all the wrong reasons, wishing he knew what she wanted him to do, what she expected of him. He knew what *he* wanted to do but things always went awry when he acted on that impulse. He doubted she would slap his face, but he had made that mistake before. He began to feel foolish, so long after the moment passed he clumsily leaned forward and kissed the top of her head. He looked away and tried to think of a time to come when things might be better, when *he* might be better. Without meeting her gaze, he turned and they resumed walking.

"Thanks," she said. "That was nice." It was nice but it was difficult to figure. She tried not to think too much, yet she couldn't help but feel there was something about her he didn't like. Perhaps it would be easier for them if they got high.

"I have pot," she said. They had double backed and were on Warren Street heading west toward the river. There was no one else in sight.

"Yeah, me too." He laughed but there was an edge to his laugh. He didn't want it to be like that. He wanted to be unstoned and smooth and in charge when he took her in his arms the way he had envisioned doing so many times, just as Walt was with Susan.

"If you want to, that is," she said.

But the moment for smoking had also passed, he knew, at least with her. He would get stoned later by himself so he could make it through a night's work without dwelling too much on how weak he was.

"It's almost time to go," he said. He could make it by eight if he left right away and he tried to pretend to himself that it was about how nice the extra money would look in his check. He would smoke on the drive back and at coffee break and again at dinner time so he would have other things to think about besides her.

"We could just leave now if you want."

"You don't have to go," he insisted. "Stay over. I know you want to and you said before there's absolutely no reason to go to school tomorrow. Or you could catch an early train in the morning."

"Yeah," she said, overpowered by how determined he was for her to stay. "I can catch an early train in the morning."

51

"I'll call you tomorrow."

It all sounded perfectly logical but it wasn't what she wanted. She wanted to be with him, but she couldn't help but again think there was something about her that he found objectionable, objectionable enough that he wanted to leave her behind and get away.

"Okay," she said halfheartedly. "You've rescued the damsel in distress. You may go."

He laughed again and this time his laugh was hollow. He hated being weak, yet weak he was.

EIGHT

In the three years they had been together, Susan had come to understand many things about Walt. She was unable to understand the depth of his anger, however, and his anger was the foundation of the wall that had grown between them. It had not always been that way and the feeling that she somehow was its cause gnawed ever deeper. Were he as angry at the time they met, she would not have been interested in a relationship. She was more turned off than most by anger and she certainly would have noticed. That was not to say she didn't understand anger in general or that she was incapable of it herself. In the heady, terrible days when the Movement seemed so ineffectual in the face of endless killing and overwhelming injustice, anger was a regular and not necessarily negative presence.

But one of the heartening things Susan had learned with a bit of distance was that the work she and millions of others had done was far from ineffectual. The genocidal war in Southeast Asia was over, apartheid in the United States was at an end, a women's movement that hadn't existed ten years before was flourishing, and many other radical roots that had been planted were bearing glorious fruit. They certainly had been right to be angry, yet Susan would never be angry to the same degree or in the same way again.

She had learned a valuable lesson that many missed. Rather than being angry or even discouraged that they were not as strong as even five years ago, she was proud of all they had done, more optimistic each day, and as committed as ever to the long haul.

Neither the first or the second of those three things was true of Walt, and Susan doubted if the third was, either. Though he was frequently funny and sometimes fun to be with, the anger had moved disturbingly close to the center of his being. In to and out from his anger flowed gloom and an inability to enjoy even the best of things. What sustained their relationship more than anything was her belief that he could change. Or, rather, that she could change him. That was the hope that kept her loving him even as they were more far apart than ever.

She had come to know Walt's parents and there was nothing about them or his relationship with them that explained his anger. His relationships with his siblings also offered no clues. Such clues weren't always evident and many people were masters of hiding what they didn't want others to see, but she was good at delving below the surface. To date she had found nothing, though, so she remained frustrated by his anger, frustrated that she increasingly bore its brunt, and frustrated that the loving relationship she wanted so much remained ever elusive.

Walt was far from alone among people she knew in being angry. Not only did injustice flourish, the Movement's momentum had receded. Or rather, as Susan saw and lived it, the Movement had taken a different shape. Walt didn't see it that way nor did he live it that way. He didn't see it that way *because* he didn't live it that way. As far as he was concerned, they had lost their way and he took that personally. In his worst moments, it looked much like defeat. So much remained to do, yet so many who just a few years before spoke passionately about revolution were nowhere to be found. Burn-out, earning a living, starting a family – Walt had heard all the explanations and they all sounded like surrender. Worst of all were those who prettied up surrendering as some kind of continuation of what they had done before.

He certainly was a brilliant guy. His quick, agile mind was the characteristic Susan was drawn to most at first. He wasn't arrogant about it, either. His self-effacing manner was one of the other things that most appealed to her. Unlike Walt, however, she was wholly sympathetic to those whose lives were different at thirty-one than they had been at twenty-one, and not only because she was one of them. Her life was richer and her understanding of what to do and how to do it was deeper. So were the lives and understandings of many of the people Walt derided. Where he saw a straight road to be navigated as quickly and efficiently as possible, Susan, many of her friends, and people she admired saw that change was built every day in how one lived. There were other differences as well besides the routes they were on. They increasingly had different destinations in mind, so much so that his There often didn't seem so different from Here.

It puzzled Susan that no one they knew saw the depth to Walt's anger that she did. That was true even of her women friends. They found him serious – sometimes unbearably so – and they disagreed with him often, but none of the women in their crowd found his anger or anything else about him more excessive than the other men they knew. Their male friends got along with him very well; some were quite forthcoming in their admiration. Such sentiments by people she respected sometimes caused Susan to second guess herself. They all disagreed with each other regularly, after all. Disagreement didn't mean they couldn't love and work and build a new society together.

In good moments, Walt talked about his anger as though sincerely trying to understand it himself. When he did, he often spoke of the guilt he felt about choosing academia while so many of his friends struggled. In response, she emphasized that he was making a contribution he would not be able to make working in a warehouse or factory. Besides, there was no reason he couldn't maintain those friendships. Some of Susan's best relationships were with women and men whose lives and work were very different from hers.

For whatever reason, Walt was unable to do so. He said it was because he couldn't but Susan suspected it was because he chose not to. Many of his friends had left college behind and gone into auto and steel factories. Others had gotten jobs as dockworkers and truck drivers. Yet here was Walt, the most vociferous anti-intellectual of the lot, still on campus, just as he had been the past twelve years. He half-hoped to be denied tenure so he could get away from back-stabbing colleagues and twenty-year olds who didn't know Bobby Seale from Soupy Sales and didn't care to.

The undercurrent to Walt's displeasure with his situation was that he did not respect the work Susan did any more than he respected his own. In bad moments, he openly voiced his disrespect. She had settled comfortably into her career confident of her ability to stand beside the working class and make a contribution to its cause, and nothing had happened to shake that confidence. On the contrary, she was surer than ever. Try as she did, she could not get him to see the rich variety of experiences that could expand the boundaries of a liberated society. He saw mostly the ugliness of now and the need for all of them to fight as vigorously as possible. She, meanwhile, saw the awful dangers of a new world built on a foundation of hate.

The affluence of New York's elites weighed heavily on Walt and made it difficult for him to enjoy much of anything about New York. Early on, he assumed the weight would lighten. Instead it had grown suffocating. In a place with so much to see, he saw mostly ostentatious displays of wealth. Even when in vibrant neighborhoods of the working class and the poor, his vision was clouded by the wealth that was never far away. The poverty and despair he had seen in the years he lived in Detroit was often depressing but it was nowhere near as depressing as the opulence of Manhattan. There was no make-believe in Detroit. Manhattan, on the other hand, seemed to contain endless swaths of rich people, every one of them and everything about them make-believe. Walt had come to hate not only the titans of business and finance the city housed, but the hordes who worked in advertising, fashion, television and academia and did so well peddling lies and phoniness.

When he was honest with himself, Walt knew he was lucky to have Susan in his life. Most of the time, though, he was haunted by all the women he had wanted and not gotten. They were present always. By contrast, men and sex in large quantities had come easily to her. No matter that she was fiercely monogamous, the men from her past were also always present. She was smart, beautiful, passionate and dying to bring all of herself to him, yet he couldn't get past his horrible need to make their relationship a contest of wills that neither of them – him least of all – could ever win. He had waited years for someone to help him free himself, only to discover that it was too late. He had waited too long.

And though Walt never failed to give more of himself to those he cheated with than he did to Susan, the affairs were no more fulfilling than his life with her. As long as he stayed the present course, he would never know peace no matter how large his collection of conquests grew, and he couldn't leave because that road led only to the terrible loneliness he knew too well. The only way forward was to fight through all the garbage that was cluttering up his life and making him so miserable, to accept and love Susan as she was, yet he refused to do so. He had been in his comfortable, terrifying trap for too long. Even more terrifying than the trap itself was the realization that it was tightening to a point of no return and that it was he who was doing the tightening.

NINE

It wasn't often that thoughts of Jack were far from Jackie's mind. She thought about the way he spoke, the things he said, and the luster of his hair. In so many ways they were right on the cusp except for that thing she was sure he didn't like about her, whatever it was. She knew she wanted to be his girlfriend and she used that to overcome her doubts.

He met her at school the only time they saw each other that week. She cut out early and changed out of her uniform in one of the locker rooms off the gym. Though he had worked all the previous night as well as half a day at the library, he was full of energy. Just when she was about to suggest they go toward the Sound, she realized he was making his way in that very direction. As they passed the Nathan Hale housing project and the factory where people made adding machines, she began venting about the final in history she had taken that morning. Though history had become her favorite subject, the teacher was terrible and it was the class she worried about the most. Though she was confident she had done a great job on her final, she knew the teacher wouldn't like what she had chosen to write about. Choosing a different topic would have meant a better shot at an A and she couldn't get past second guessing herself.

He nudged her toward the content of her essay as the huge park, with the Sound in the distance, opened up before them. As she hoped it would be, the park and the beach were deserted. The only sign of human activity was way off in the distance where a man drove a lawn mower over the lush spread of grass that seemed to go on for miles.

Finally, she became aware that she was the only one talking. Or rather, she came to be certain that he couldn't possibly still be listening, not with any interest anyway, and that it was rude and selfish of her to keep going. But he loved that she had tapped Susan's experiences and written about Freedom Summer. So much of what he had been forced to study in history was insufferably dull, and so much of the wonderful, tumultuous history of the past fifteen years that he was dying to know more about was paved over or left out altogether. It was when Jackie stopped and looked at him that she realized he had selected the day of her hardest final to pick her up precisely because it was the day she would most need someone to talk to.

"You really are a sly one, aren't you?"

"What?" He was lost with Susan and a car full of others somewhere in Mississippi just days after the murders of Chaney, Goodman and Schwerner. "You didn't finish."

"Jack, I – "

"You can't tell ninety percent of the story and not finish," he insisted.

"Alright," and she went on, noting as she did that he listened to every word.

In the distance was the historic Seaside Lighthouse, long abandoned but still resplendent. No longer a nautical beacon, it stood instead as a reminder of how things once had been. Her eyes were drawn to it and she knew intuitively they would walk to it.

"When was the last time you were out there?" His eyes were on it, too, so that it wasn't necessary that she specify what she meant.

"It's been a while," he replied.

It was windy at that spot and he grabbed a sweatshirt from the backseat and gave it to her. Though it was farcically big on her, she wore it gladly, not so much because it warmed her but because it was his. Even better were the hands and arms and shoulders he offered as they made their way on the rock path. Though she didn't really need assistance, she gladly accepted because it allowed them to touch again and again. Touching was easier for him that way and she allowed herself to believe that maybe that other thing was a figment of her imagination.

They were in no hurry and they stopped often along the way to read fifty-year old graffiti carved into the rocks and to investigate tide pools teeming with life. Horseshoe crabs were scattered about that isolated stretch of beach and they caught a quick glimpse of a very well-fed raccoon before it became aware of their presence and scurried for cover. Even the sand was alive and its color vivid, as though the water had come up overnight and washed it clean just for them.

The rock path ended a hundred yards from the lighthouse and they walked the rest of the way on hard sand amidst a cluster of sturdy trees that seemed out of place so close to the Sound. The lighthouse and lightkeeper's residence had not been occupied for decades, but they were made of sturdy stone and still in good shape. The Sound from that vantage point was more intimidating, less a place for leisurely swimming than one to be careful around. In the distance were oil tankers and other vessels of commerce and beyond that the gray outline of Long Island. The peninsula on which the lighthouse stood was so infrequently visited by humans that the land birds and insects that called it home stopped as they passed and considered the two of them for a bit before going on their way.

They made faster time on the way back, acclimated as they were to walking on the rocks. The tide was coming in and the stretch of sand with the horseshoe crabs was slowly being overtaken. At several points some disturbance in the water caused the tide to jolt and spray them with a cold, salty mist. As she was wearing his sweatshirt, he got the worst of it but he went on effortlessly as though walking along slippery boulders was a part of his daily routine.

"Jack, why does your mother call you Nature Boy?" From the safety of the car, the Sound again seemed peaceful.

"It's just some dumb song." He looked away and she was sure

she heard him laugh. "Actually, it's a nice song. My mother just has this dumb idea … "

She looked at him hopefully but he said no more and she let it go. "Susan's having a party Friday. We're invited, if you'd like to go."

"Love to," he said.

"Can we stop by your place before you drop me off?"

"Sure," he said. "As long as you're not expecting much. It's kinda Early Minimalist."

The books and records were what she noticed right off. More records than she'd seen anywhere except in a record store were stacked along one whole wall several rows high and several rows deep. Seven hundred, a thousand, probably more, all arranged quite neatly.

The books were another matter. They were everywhere and they were not stacked neatly. They were not stacked at all, really, but piled, dropped and put wherever there was a place. There were hundreds of those, too, perhaps more books than albums: thick hard covers, flimsy paperbacks, oversized art and photography books, and just about any other type in between. Nowhere did she see a bookcase. The closest approximations were several wooden crates piled so high with books that a number had toppled over to the floor. In all, it was a thorough disgrace to library pages and book shelvers everywhere.

There may have been furniture under the books, Jackie wasn't sure. The only place to sit was a very sturdy rocking chair that was much larger than any she'd seen before, almost twice the size of her grandmother's. It, too, was piled with books. In the middle of the room was a large cable spool turned on its side that served as a table. On it were more books, notepads and several pens. One corner of the room was a repository for an assortment of athletic gear: weights and a bench, a basketball, a pair of hockey skates, a baseball glove, a football, and a tennis racket. Behind the bench against the wall was his bike and hanging from one of the handlebars were his swimming goggles.

"Sorry, I haven't had time to straighten up."

She almost answered *You mean since 1974?* but held her tongue, in part because two kittens joined them when he pushed open a door. They rubbed against her legs and she ran her hand along the coat of each.

"Have a seat." Since he had gone through the trouble of clearing off the rocker, she felt obligated to sit. When she did, she found she could only touch the floor with her feet if she leaned all the way forward.

"Rocking chairs and kittens? Isn't that a bad combination?"

"So far so good," he answered from the kitchen.

Jackie wasn't up for chancing it, though, so she stood and picked up the black kitten with green eyes. "What're their names?"

"The white one's Ornette," he said as he passed through and went into the bedroom. "The black one's Jorma."

"I guess I should've known they wouldn't be Tabby and Frisky."

"They may be Tabby and Frisky soon," he said. "They're a birthday present for my sister Penelope. She's more the Tabby and Frisky type. They were abandoned in that alley next door."

"Cool present," she said. "You call your sister Penelope and not Penny?"

"I call her Penny to her face," he said. "She doesn't like Penelope. Don't ask me why. It's such a pretty name."

"Yeah." She watched as he moved about, trying still to pin him down. She remembered him walking home from school with his four little sisters and wondered if having to do so embarrassed him. She wished she had offered some word of encouragement at the time, to have told him it was a good thing.

"You have fish, too?" Amidst all the books and records was a huge fish tank against the longest wall.

"Turtles," he answered. "Not at the moment, though."

She lifted the cover off the top of the tank and put two fingers in the green water. Unlike any fish tank she had ever seen, it was alive with rocks and soil and plant life, like a place turtles would enjoy living. It even had the feel that a turtle or two had been there recently and would soon return.

While he was in the bathroom tending to the litter box, she wandered around. The bedroom was as neat as the living room was messy, though there were still more books stacked in piles in one corner. The kitchen was small but perfectly serviceable. A table was pressed against one wall and a chair was positioned not so much for someone to sit and eat but because that's where it was most out of the way. There weren't many visible signs of sustenance, just a bowl of onions on the table, a bag of rice on the counter and a few canned goods in an open cupboard. The only items in the refrigerator were a very large jar of applesauce and a carton of grapefruit juice. She went back to the living room and, curious as to what he had listened to that morning or the previous night or whenever it was that he had last listened, put the needle to the record on the turntable just as he re-appeared looking set to go.

"Ready?"

"No way," he replied. "We can't walk out on Trane."

Once she realized he was serious, she sat on a pillow and listened. She had never heard anything like 'Afro-Blue' and she followed it, transfixed, as she stroked the kittens. It was serious, especially the sax, but not at all somber. The early break to piano was a surprise and the sound opened up as the piano player glided majestically over the keys, stretching, building, cooking, swooping, diving, a sound both to think over and move to. It went on elegant- ly and a bit teasingly, the way she imagined being made love to in just the right way would be, on and on and on, then a big rush of drums until the sax came back in and the room was filled with the sound of hundreds of years of agonized, heroic history. It was joyous and heartbreaking in a way she had never thought anything could be both joyous and heartbreaking simultaneously, this tale of love and anguish and liberation blown by a mad griot with a direct line to God. She looked at him in search of a clue as to what he was feeling, of what the sound was doing to him, certain he was feeling *something* to the depth of his soul just as she was, or at least that he had the first time he heard the record, something that could never adequately be put into words but could only be felt and experienced the way a lover's touch or the winds of a hurricane could only be felt and experienced, never explained, not adequately. He didn't look at her – intentionally, she knew somehow – but she could tell by the expression on his face and the way he was standing that he was absorbed and she wondered if it was possible for two people to be absorbed by the very same thing at precisely the same time in exactly the same way. It was more than wondering, she wanted to know definitively, and she wanted to find out definitively somehow someway sometime with him. The prospect of doing so exhilarated her as much as the record and she felt a need to look away, lest she expose a part of herself she wasn't yet sure she wanted him to see, though she *knew* that if the day ever came when she was able to open herself to him without reservation that it would absolutely positively be the best experience of her life.

Outside, the colors of the sun and the leaves on the trees were sharper like after a storm and the sky seemed to have expanded toward infinity.

"Can I borrow that record some time?"

TEN

"It's nobody's fault," Walt was saying. "It's capitalism. Capitalism infects everything with the imperative of the market, including personal relationships. *Especially* personal relations. Maybe it's going a little far to say that most men are johns and most women hookers, but as long as you reduce everything to the market, isn't that basically true?"

Jack sat for a few minutes on the loading dock that jutted out from the building next to Susan's for a few minutes after Walt had gone inside, then set out walking toward the Hudson. After a few minutes, he lit up and held the smoke in his lungs for a long time before exhaling, hoping the pot would set him straight.

There was so much he had wanted to say to Walt. Mostly he wanted to tell him he was full of it and that what he and Jackie had going on would prove him wrong. Instead he had held his tongue. Partly that was because he knew he was overmatched. Walt was far more experienced than him and Jack was sure he would have exposed himself as a fool had he said anything. He also held his tongue, he had to admit, because some of what Walt said seemed uncomfortably accurate.

What exactly was it that he and Jackie had going on, anyway? So far, it wasn't much more than lots of talking on the phone and platonic hanging-out that confirmed everything Walt said. In some ways, he didn't know anything about her at all. He knew her favorite bands and what classes she liked best and that she was in love with the prospect of living in New York, but he had no idea what she felt about him or what it was he had to do to get her to like him the way he liked her. Like? It was so far past that it wasn't funny. He thought about her all the time, so much that it sometimes made his stomach ache. He longed to tell her his fears and hoped that she was afraid, too, and that they might talk about their fears as honestly as they talked about books and music and changing the world. She seemed not to possess a fearful bone in her body, however, so he went on pretending he didn't, either.

He looked across the water at New Jersey and wondered how many people there were reveling in the beauty of twilight and how many were weighed down by worries. For as long as he could remember, he had fought against being a predator. Now here was Walt saying that, when it came to girls, he'd better learn to prey damn quick or risk being left in the dust. Jack shook his head as he exhaled: he was already in the dust and he hadn't even known it. He had always been certain he hated the predators because of the way they treated girls. Now he saw he hated them because they got what they wanted, what *he* wanted and didn't know how to get and maybe would never get until he learned to take. What had Walt said? Make sure you take what you want because ain't nobody giving.

He lit another joint and looked at Ellis Island in the distance. He tried to think sweet things about Jackie but the images were blurry. More of Walt's words intruded – something about the terrible necessity to play on a woman's insecurities. It was a topic of endless conversation among guys Jack knew, yet it was disconcerting to hear a man as worldly as Walt own to it in regards to someone as great as Susan. Whenever Jack fantasized about what it would be like to make time with Susan, he thought about the things that made her strong, the things that made her unique, how smart and dedicated she was to her work, how on fire she was. Was it possible that all those things, the very things that made her so desirable, were the same things that made her unobtainable and that the only way she could be had was to exploit her weaknesses? If that was true of Susan, it almost certainly had to be true of Jackie as well.

He laughed. All this time he thought his fumbling about was just confusion that would clear up in time. Now he began to feel he was in some cosmically determined battle and that the only way forward was to arm himself. He hated that thought and was heartened to discover that he was stoned enough for it not to matter. He drew in one more time and headed back.

Susan's street was a small, intimate one and most of the buildings were the same as hers: three story jobs of brick and stone pressed one against another, each with a fire escape attached to the upper two floors. It was a tiny sliver of the city and none of the many landmarks that surrounded it were in view, yet Jack had the distinct impression there was something uniquely New York about it.

"There you are," Jackie said as she came through the door. "Where'd you go, the river?"

"Yeah."

She studied the tightness of his face. "I would've joined you, you know."

"I just went for a smoke."

"And to think?"

He forced out a laugh. "Sometimes the less of that the better."

She was standing on the loading dock so that she towered over him. She wanted to put her arms around him and tell him everything was alright but this troubled side of him that she had seen that day at his mother's was a bit intimidating. She didn't know that everything *was* alright, but she knew that if they could just get going that everything *would be* alright. Yet for all the things she did so well, she couldn't get past her uncertainty, her fear, so instead she waited, hoping *he* would take *her* in his arms, for surely there was nothing about her that he could possibly fear or find intimidating.

"I need a soda," he said.

She hesitated before going in as he held the door, trying to understand what it was she had done this time.

ELEVEN

No sooner had Jackie filled the birdbath than birds descended from all around. Mostly they were starlings and sparrows, with a robin or two mixed in, and they flocked to the water enthusiastically. Beyond the birdbath streaks of yellow from the late afternoon sun cut through a clump of trees and the Kelly green leaves swayed softly from side to side like seagulls hovering above the Sound. The yellow and green and the soft blue of a cloudless sky made quite a scene, a scene all the more remarkable because of the way it just was. Mother Nature never had to call attention to herself, She just was.

In no time, the large crowd of birds had diminished to three and there was not enough water remaining even for that small number to bathe. Jackie stopped what she was doing and went outside to refill the bowl. Before she was even back in the kitchen, the bath was again full of birds. She could only hope that sparrows and starlings had some sense of sharing.

It was her birthday. Finals were done and all that remained of school was graduation on Monday. Her parents were having a barbecue with some of their friends and she had agreed to stick around in exchange for being allowed to stay out late with two of her friends. Not much of a bargain, really, for birthday or not, what was there to do on a Wednesday night? Worst of all, there would be no Jack.

"Such a nice evening." Mrs. Gendron had come in and begun gathering plates and dishes and glasses. "I'll take it from here, honey."

Jackie started to speak but checked herself and headed toward the stairs.

"Jackie? I didn't mean you had to leave the room the way you do whenever I come in."

She could tell her mother wanted to talk. Her mother didn't know that she wanted to talk, too. No, the problem wasn't that she didn't want to talk. The problem was that she was so unhappy and there was so much she wanted to talk about that she had no idea how or where to start. She would let her mother decide and take it from there. In the meantime, she grabbed a towel and silently dried dishes.

"I hope you're not still angry about the to-do we had about school," her mother said of the most recent conversation she, her husband and Jackie had had about Jackie's plans for college. "It's worked out the way you wanted in the end."

Mrs. Gendron opened the refrigerator and began lifting out the food she had taken the afternoon off to prepare. She could do marvelous things in the kitchen. One by one she laid out deviled eggs, potato salad, hummus sprinkled with raw garlic that Jackie loved and could never quite make as well, and plenty of broccoli crowns and celery and carrot sticks, also for Jackie, since she wouldn't eat the steak or swordfish they'd grill. Mrs. Gendron had also prepared peppers, tomatoes, onions and mushrooms for shish kebab as well as pastries and a birthday cake that in all likelihood hardly anyone would eat because by dessert time the Scotch and martinis would be flowing so freely that no one would want anything so sweet.

"It used to be better between us, didn't it?" Mrs. Gendron said. "What happened?"

"I don't know. You're the mother. Seems like if either of us should know, it should be you."

"Sometimes, when you say things like that, I get the feeling you think I intentionally do things to hurt you." Mrs. Gendron glanced across the room at her daughter, but Jackie was looking out at the birdbath. "Are things so bad that you don't even want to talk to me?"

Jackie spread a section of newspaper out and began shucking corn. "No, I want to talk. It just doesn't seem worth it."

"It's worth it to me if it means we might be closer again."

Jackie took a breath and began hesitantly about how difficult it had been as her five sisters moved away, one by one, struggling as she did to find the right words. She never struggled during discussions in school, yet she was unable to tap that skill as she spoke to her mother. The big showdown that had been building, her big chance to finally make her mother hear her, and she couldn't even get herself to make sense.

"I wanna live the way *I* wanna live," she said finally, "not according to some prefabricated plan that somebody else has for me."

"Of course you do," Mrs. Gendron said, taken aback by the intensity in her daughter's voice. "What should we have done that we didn't do?"

Jackie wasn't sure. Since getting to know Jack again, she saw more clearly the privileges she enjoyed and that her problems were small. Still, she couldn't help but think that the things that went wrong were so often the most important ones. Like with Jack.

"There was never any way around dad and his rules," Jackie said. "Sometimes I thought I was gonna die from being caged in."

When her mother returned again to the ongoing disagreement about college, Jackie laughed bitterly to herself. It was almost as though her mother was oblivious to the way that subject represented the gap between them better than anything she could think of.

"I just wish you could understand how much he wanted you to go to Harvard."

"Oh, I understand," Jackie countered. "What I don't get is how nobody except Susan gets how important it is to *me* to go to school where *I* wanna go. She gets that my life is my life, not dad's life."

"I guess it wouldn't do any good to try and convince you that I believe that, too." Mrs. Gendron smiled sadly. "It always seems to come down to Susan whenever we talk, doesn't it?"

Susan was a topic they had argued about before and Jackie steered clear. Susan was her sister but she was more her parents' peer than hers. In fact, Jackie was certain Susan knew more about how the world really worked than either of her parents ever would. Then her mother mentioned Jack and Jackie slid back into a morass of confusion. She wished he was there to take her away. They had argued on Saturday and she hadn't seen or heard from him since. Or rather, she had argued. He had said something about her talking too much about Susan, about wanting too much to be like Susan, to a point where it was getting in the way of being herself. It angered her and she told him off. Four days later her words sounded worse each time she remembered them. *We spend a little time together and already you're trying to change me?* Which was not what he was trying to do at all, she knew. She had come to the very same realization about herself, yet she still saw fit to skewer him for voicing it.

Not only that, but after all the waiting and wondering, she had slipped away from him when he tried to kiss her that night. So many times she had wanted to do that, and she had done it with the one guy she never should have. But there was Jack, after treating her better than ever to make amends for saying something that he was actually right about, leaning in at the end of what had otherwise been a nice night, and she gave him the slip. Why would he call? Perhaps after a few more days she could convince herself he wasn't such a great guy after all.

"Is that what this is really about, honey? Jack Simmons?"

Still Jackie said nothing. It was all slipping away. Jack. Her hopes of making peace with her folks. The plans for a fun summer. She might just as well enroll in some courses and spend what could have been a great three months in a bunch of dreary classrooms.

"He didn't take what he wanted from you and disappear, did he?"

Jackie turned from the window and looked hard at her mother. "How dare you say that." Her tone startled both of them but she went on. "That shows how much you don't get it. Jim Dorn of the Yale University Dorns, that's what he would've done. And Jerry Marshall, the good Doctor Marshall's son? He *did* do that."

"Jackie."

"Oh, mom. You don't really think – " It was worse that she

thought. "Jack is an absolute gentleman. He's worked seventy hours a week in a crummy factory and at the library for the last year because his father lost his job to make sure his sisters can go to a better high school. If anything, it's *me* who doesn't deserve *him*."

She wasn't about to leave now. She loved a good argument with her mother. Conflict was so much easier than peace.

"He's a better guy than anybody I know," she went on. "I haven't even told you about the very respectable boy whose parents are very respectable friends of yours who basically tried to rape me."

Mrs. Gendron had long since stopped with the food preparation. She stared at her daughter in desperation, but Jackie looked away, diligently shucking corn

"See, we can't talk about anything without it getting like this," Jackie went on. "You should be thrilled if Jack would have me for his girlfriend. And if I should be lucky enough that he calls me, that he still wants me, I'm going to give myself to him. And yes, I do mean what you think I mean."

"So you have been ... with boys."

She didn't even bother to look at her mother. "I can't believe this."

"Well, it's a little startling to hear."

"That's because you haven't been listening. All these years, you haven't listened once, not when I really tried talking to you. God, mom." Jackie knew she should stop but she couldn't help herself. "There are six of us so I know you've had sex at least six times. Didn't you like it just a little?"

There was just no way forward. She didn't want to try and solve everything herself, she *wanted* to talk to her mother the way she talked to Susan, to get guidance and advice from her. But if her mother was going to insist on going back to some great time in their lives that never existed – had her mother really thought all this time that she'd never been with a boy?

"I don't think anyone has ever said anything that harsh to me in my entire life," Mrs. Gendron said.

She knew she was hitting her mother hard because she was also hitting herself. She could feel the pain of the blows in her heart and especially in her stomach.

"I just thought you would've figured out there's more to it than making a baby," Jackie said. "You know, that it might be fun. Or better than fun. Did you really think I'd get to where I'm about to start college without wanting to know what all the fuss is about?"

"What is all this, Jackie?" Mrs. Gendron knew it would do no good to simply try, one more time, to one-up her daughter. To lose for winning. "Why are you doing this?"

Jackie started to speak but her throat caught. She thought for a moment she might be sick.

"Honey?"

"I don't know." Jackie's voice was a whisper. Slowly and with great difficulty, she forced out something she had wanted to say for a long time. "You should've stuck up for me." Then, painfully, the hardest part. "You should've helped me. Why didn't you help me?"

"Jackie." Mrs. Gendron spoke as if she had been punched in the stomach.

"Why didn't you help me?" For a moment the anger was gone, pushed out by an unbearable sadness. She turned so her mother wouldn't see the tears welling in her eyes.

For several years, Mrs. Gendron had been telling anyone who would listen that her youngest daughter was all grown up and that she couldn't be prouder. It was mostly words, she could see now, because Jackie *was* grown up, only being grown up wasn't about accomplishments in school or going off to college. It was about anguish, the anguish that could not be avoided by anyone who really lived. It was about loneliness and abandonment and aching over elusive, undefinable things and all the other perils Mrs. Gendron had worked so hard to keep from her children. But there was no way to keep any of it away and here it all was for her to see and hear in the accusations and the agonized tone of her daughter's voice. And pretending not to see or wishing it was otherwise wouldn't make any of it go away.

"How much of what we're talking about has to do with Jack?"

Jackie watched two sparrows frolicking in the birdbath, beautiful little sparrows that didn't care that everyone took them for granted. So much better to be a bird.

"Does he feel the same way about you?"

No, it wasn't better to be a bird. The gnawing emptiness in her stomach that she was dying to fill told her that. It was better to try. She was tired of fighting. Most of all she was tired of fighting with herself.

"I think so. At least he did. Except – " Her voice cracked ever so slightly. "Except I pushed him away."

For the first time, Mrs. Gendron was seeing the corrosive affect her inattention was having on her bright, beautiful child. It had been years since she had held her daughter, almost as long since she had touched her in any meaningful way. She hesitated too long, though, and Jackie moved so the table was between them. If she was going to cry, she would do so upstairs when she was alone and not on the shoulder of her mother.

"Honey, what can I do?"

Jackie struggled to keep it together. "There's nothing to do."

"No, there is," Mrs. Gendron insisted. "You said that I should help you. It's not too late. I still can."

"Why?"

"Do you actually have to ask me that?"

The hurt in her mother's voice gave Jackie a glimmer of hope. "It doesn't matter."

"Of course it matters."

She moved close to the window and resumed shucking corn, the good girl as always, doing more than asked. It was like the care she gave the garden and all the extra reading she did. Maybe if she just kept busy enough, all the trouble would go away.

"Jackie, I'm on your side. We can help each other. One way you can help me is by telling me how I can help you."

"It doesn't matter," Jackie said. "About Jack, I mean. It doesn't matter because he's gone."

"You don't know that, honey. The good ones rarely give up that easily. Based on what you've said, I bet he'll be back."

Jackie looked at her mother, certain she was being humored. Certain Jack was a lost cause. "Except he doesn't want to be."

Her mother's eyes were on her but it was different from before. Her mother was stronger than she was and Jackie was humbled. It was a strength she didn't think her mother still possessed, a strength she had forgotten she needed her mother to possess.

"Don't give up hope," Mrs. Gendron said.

That was Jack's word. Hope. It reminded her of what a good thing she'd almost had. He had given up, though. His elaborate plans to break through to her – gone. Done. She had joked that he never would and here in a well of loneliness as deep as any she had ever been, and on her birthday no less, she saw that the joke was on her.

"Honey, there's so much I want to say and so much more I want to hear from you about Jack. About NYU, too. About every-thing." Mrs. Gendron had been through all this with her five other daughters and it had driven each of them away – why had not she learned? The rules she had grown up with had been exposed as fraudulent and she had come to see that it was women who had suffered most under them. Not only could she no longer deny that the new ways were better, she could see clearly that they opened up the possibility that things might be *much* better. Careers. Inde-pendence. Love. And, yes, sex. For Susan, for her other daughters, but most of all for Jackie, her youngest and brightest star, with her whole life before her. Nothing about it would be easy – nothing about it *was* easy – but it was the only way. Looking at her young-est and wanting so desperately to connect with her, Mrs. Gendron wondered, as she had more times than was comfortable, if the reason for her resistance was that it had happened for them but not for her.

Her resistance to change and her unwillingness to challenge her husband had even destroyed most vestiges of sisterly togetherness among her daughters. For the most part, except for Jackie and Susan, they had little contact with each other. If not for Susan's unflagging efforts, they might have had no contact whatsoever. That was why Jackie worshipped Susan. She worshipped her because of all of her accomplishments, but she also worshipped her because Susan unfailingly supported her and their sisters and everyone else who was in her life. Susan, Mrs. Gendron had come to see, was everything to Jackie that she was not. Maybe she could make that into a good thing for once rather than a jealous thing.

"There's dad," Jackie said as her father pulled into the driveway in his car.

"Honey, what you said earlier." Mrs. Gendron looked longingly at her daughter, hoping Jackie would turn and face her. There was so much more to say but her husband was home and they were out of time. "Has sex ... has it been fun?"

A solitary sparrow bathed in the little water that remained. Jackie watched her father take a bag of groceries from the trunk and then retrieve what she suspected was a birthday gift for her from the backseat. Though she could not bring herself to look at her mother, she was compelled to answer honestly.

"No."

"I'm sorry." They weren't out of time at all, Mrs. Gendron decided. They were only just beginning. "Honey, let's continue this soon. Not tonight, of course, but soon. We should make time to talk with Susan when she's here for your graduation."

Jackie could not recall her mother ever having said anything like that regarding Susan. She turned half-expecting it to be a joke but her mother's face was bright with determination. "I should get ready."

"Jackie, I'm sorry." The room suddenly turned heavy and they were oblivious to the sound of the door from the garage opening. "I hope you can find it in your heart to forgive me. And please don't get down on yourself. I promise to be there for you from now on."

A chill ran through her. "Alright."

"I know I've said it so many times that you're probably tired of hearing it, but we're so proud of you. And happy birthday."

Jackie was relieved by what she had revealed about herself and heartened by her mother's words. Because her mother had been a spectator to her life for so long, she was also a little skeptical. She was surprised at how powerful her need to have things right between them was and she had to caution herself that there was only so much that could change in one evening. She caught herself paying close attention to everything her mother said and did, especially to how her mother interacted with her in front of their guests. Within thirty minutes time, there was no denying that her mother was making a great effort at least for one evening.

The food was sensational. The roasted corn on the cob and vegetable shish kebab were so good she didn't even get to the hummus. That was fine. There was so much of it, there was bound to be plenty left over. They might throw away enough food to feed a village but Jackie would eat hummus for lunch every day until it was gone.

At eight-thirty Mrs. Gendron said, "Honey, anytime you wanna go is okay. Thanks for everything. Thanks especially for being here."

"Mom." Jackie looked around to make sure no one could hear. "I'm sorry about the things I said before."

"No, you were right to say them. We'll talk more. And don't worry about curfew."

Awkwardly, Jackie reciprocated the smile her mother flashed. "Mom, do you know a song 'Nature Boy?'"

"Of course." Mrs. Gendron looked at her daughter curiously.

"Why?"

"No reason. I read something about it the other day."

"It's there in the living room, on one of the Nat King Cole records," Mrs. Gendron said. "It's quite beautiful. But go. Go have some fun. And happy birthday."

Jackie couldn't tear herself away just yet, though, because her father and his friend Professor Ed May were, as they often did, talking about Susan. Although she was in many ways the most accomplished of his daughters, Susan was also the one most troubling to Mr. Gendron. He got more than a bit of ribbing from his friends about her, and it was May who frequently led the charge. Whenever an article of hers got published in one of the local alternative newspapers or her name popped up locally for leading a session for rank and file workers, Mr. Gendron was sure to hear from May.

Mr. Gendron hadn't much enjoyed Susan's years as an undergraduate, yet he chalked that period of her life up to youth and being caught up in the times. He was proud when she went to Mississippi twelve summers before but his pride had waned long ago as radicalism became her life's calling. Susan was thirty-one and it was her choice of callings as well as the embarrassment it occasionally caused her father that the distinguished political scientist May found endlessly amusing.

Jackie listened to May's latest teasing of her father while pretending to be busy with something else. Not that it was difficult to keep up, for as was his wont May was speaking loudly enough for all to hear. Never once had she cut in on one of her father's friends but then May casually referred to Susan as a Communist. Jackie had heard that one many times but there was something about the smug way that May said it and the fact that her father simply sipped his scotch and said nothing that got her.

"She's not a Communist." Jackie's quiet voice cut sharply through the some peripheral chatter.

"Ah, yes, Jacqueline," May said after an awkward bit of silence.

"I stand corrected."

"Susan is an exceptional young woman, Ed." Lucy Green was inspired by Jackie to speak up. "You have to admit that regardless of what you think of her political views."

"Some day you might walk into one of your faculty meetings and find her there sitting across from you," Joan Walters said.

"Yeah, as your new department head," Clark Green added to laughter all around.

"I wonder if you're not secretly in love with her, Ed," said Joan Walters. "I know at minimum you'd like to sleep with her." There was more laughter, some of it uncomfortable.

They continued to talk but Jackie wanted nothing more to do with it. She gathered some plates and went inside. No matter what anyone might say, the air was sullied. Jackie just could not abide anyone saying anything against Susan. What really galled her was that none of her parents' friends would ever speak that way to Susan's face, for if they did Jackie knew Susan would slice and dice the New Deal, the Great Society and all that Kennedy shit to pieces with the same aplomb Jackie had seen on so many occasions.

Her mother followed her into the kitchen and gave her a big hug for standing up to May, then Mrs. Green came in after her mother left and did likewise. Mrs. Green wasn't her favorite of her mother's friends, but she was appreciative of what Mrs. Green had said. Jackie waited expectantly, as it appeared that behind her smile Mrs. Green desired to re-visit the subject, but she said nothing and left.

She hadn't told her mother but she had called her friends and cancelled their plans. She was glad she had because she suddenly felt depressed. When she was sure she was alone, she went into the living room and found 'Nature Boy.' She stood by the huge console stereo she loved so much and listened. The song certainly was beautiful but it was no substitute for a real boy, at least not the boy she couldn't stop thinking about. If only she could get up the nerve to call him. Just five days before it would have been a snap. They had talked so much on the phone and calling him had been so easy. No more.

She played it again and had just begun washing dishes when she became aware of someone in the doorway. She didn't much want to talk to Mrs. Green so she worked on, hoping the older woman would go away. Instead, the blurry figure came nearer.

When she turned, Jack stepped forward. She had just enough time to see it was him before he took her in his arms and pressed his lips to hers. Tense at first, she quickly relaxed. He let them come up for air ever so briefly and kissed her again. She pressed against him and put her hands behind his neck.

They stood for a long time, motionless except for the slow, synchronous movement of their heads and their mouths. With her eyes closed and her body afloat in his arms, she let the smell of his skin and the taste of his lips consume her. He was dressed in something other than his usual summer garb and the material of his shirt was soft to the touch of her hands.

"I thought I heard 'Nature Boy,'" he said, smiling.

"And look what happened. It brought me you."

The sound of voices and laughter from outside brought her back. She took his hand and led him to the front of the house. They stood in a secluded corner and she kissed him. She moved so she was on the first step of the staircase and she kissed him again. They had both been storing something up and Jackie was overwhelmed by the flood of passion in his kissing as well as by how his hands found all the right spots.

"Oh my God, you cut your hair," she said.

"Yeah, you know. Summertime. You think it's too short?"

"I think it looks great." Right then, everything about him looked great.

"Jack, I'm so glad to see you."

"You know," he said, "I'm kinda getting that."

She laughed. She had never kissed anyone with such abandon, yet there was no sense of it being risky or dangerous.

"Sorry I've been out of touch," he said in a low, serious tone.

"Well, you're here now." She touched his face just to be sure.

"All I think about is you."

His words lingered between them for a moment, then he poked her playfully in the stomach and said something about birthday presents and having something lined up if she wanted to go out. When she couldn't get anything out of him about the presents, she suggested he bring them to the den away from the crowd while she went up to change.

"I'm okay with seeing your folks and meeting their friends," he said. "I mean, how could they not love me?"

"Let us count the ways, handsome." She bounded halfway up the stairs, came back and kissed him, then took off to go change.

First up among the gifts was a Jack-o'-lantern with a lit candle inside. Jackie squealed with delight and carefully picked it up to see that it was complete with eyes, nose and a smiling mouth carved out of one side. She was beside herself with happiness that he was there. And not only was he there but he, the same Jack who had spent his own birthday alone doing nothing more exciting than work, was making hers into a wonderful spectacle.

The next box contained another Jack-o'-lantern, this one with a battery-powered strobe light inside instead of a candle that he activated by pressing a small button. Jackie held it up to get the full effect. It was even better than the first.

In the last box was a turtle in a tank of water. When Jack had told her he helped rehabilitate turtles, she asked about getting set up to do likewise. He explained that it had been sick and was a few days away from being fully recovered. He handed her a small vial of medicine and a sheet of paper with instructions. Taking the bowl from her, he mentioned that it would be better to transfer the turtle to a large space sooner rather than later.

"Let's do it right now. I cleaned out the fish tank we have."
She was looking intently through the glass. "Turtles are so cool. They're like these great surviving relics of prehistoric times."

His plans were still a surprise when they drove off. He pointed to the glove compartment and she took out a bag of pot. They rode in silence toward the Sound as she rolled and as he tried to figure out how to begin. He hadn't been joking – he had thought of her every waking minute since Saturday, certain he had blown it. He had tried hiding in work during his last days at the Brass, to no avail. Work wasn't real. Nothing was real. Only she was real.

He wanted to get it out before they smoked. Holding her and kissing her had been as good as he hoped but he had to tell her how he felt. He began by explaining that he had been out of touch because of his friend Steve at the University of Buffalo who broke his leg at a keg party celebrating the end of freshman year. He was laid up in the school infirmary for a weekend that turned into a week and then two weeks because his mother didn't drive and couldn't leave the younger kids anyway. So Jack went.

"You drove all the way to Buffalo and back the same day and then went to work?"

"Yeah, but … " He stopped. He had to make it honest but this was the hardest thing he had ever tried to be honest about. "No, that's not it. That's a lie. Forget I said that."

"Alright."

"I don't mean it's a lie like it didn't happen," he went on. "It did. I mean my friend really did break his leg and I did go to Buffalo. That's not the part that's a lie."

She struck a match to fire up, thinking that's what she wanted him to do.

"Wait." He felt her eyes on him and he drove on without turning to look at her. "Going to Buffalo, that's not the reason. The real reason I didn't call is that I was afraid."

"Jack, when two people care about each other, there are certain things they don't have to say."

"But I wanna say this." It took all the will he possessed but finally he looked at her. "I wanna be with you, Jackie. I wanna be with you more than anything in the world."

"And so you are." She put her hand on his. "And so you shall be."

The park by the Sound was crowded and loud and traffic was moving at a snail's pace. In the rear Jack spied a familiar Coronet close behind.

"Could you do me a favor and roll another one of those? Extra thick? And then put the bag in the glove compartment."

When she finished, he pulled over and the Coronet pulled alongside. Sitting on the front passenger side was Manny, the twenty-two year old leader of a group of Portuguese guys Jack knew. They weren't a gang exactly and they were nowhere near the biggest or most dangerous ethnic clan in town, but they were not people to be on the outs with. Mess with any of them in any way and there was an unpleasant price to be paid. Stand with them in a tough spot, as Jack had accidentally once done, and they were tenaciously loyal. Without turning the engine off, Jack started in on introductions.

"You know Jackie, don't you?"

"No, I don't," Manny replied. "Believe me, if I ever met her, I'd remember. And now that I met her, I won't forget."

She sensed that Jack was tense. She had no idea what her role was, whether she should talk or lay back. "Hi."

"That's Antonio in back," Jack continued on to the two other guys in the Coronet. "And you remember Fernando from school."

"Hi, Fernando."

"You get any of that red that's around?" Manny asked hopefully. Jack took the joint from Jackie and passed it through the window. "Hey, solid, man. You hook me up with some more?"

Jack promised to do what he could. And to make a quick get-away easier, he mentioned they were going out for Jackie's birth-day.

"Happy birthday," Manny said. "You're a very pretty lady. And this brother here is solid. Nobody messes with him and nobody'll mess with you if you're ever out by yourself."

"Thank you," was all she could think to say.

"You got my word on that, bro."

"I appreciate it," Jack said. "Lotsa wild stuff happening in Portugal. On the serious side."

Manny prided himself on never being caught off guard but a look of surprise crept over his face. "How you know about all that?"

Jack smiled. "I get around a little."

"I'm serious about that red."

"Tomorrow." Jack turned the radio on and let the car roll forward. "Round this time."

"You seem pretty tight with those guys," she said as they drove along the water. She had been impressed since they reconnected by the code of loyalty he lived by. It was so far beyond anyone else their age she knew that he might as well have been thirty-nine as nineteen. But there was an unmistakable loneliness behind it, as if in living that way he had sacrificed his youth.

He didn't reply so she tried again more directly. "It's very impressive how you make sure to take care of the people you know."

"Jackie, it was just a joint."

"I don't mean just that." She knew he was deflecting her away from thinking of him that way and it made her more determined. "I mean me, with all the fuss you've made about my birthday, driving all the way to Buffalo for your friend, and what you do for your family."

"My family?"

"Well, you had to bike to work for two days so your mother could use your car," she said. "And you care about where your sisters go to high school."

He laughed. "Why is that a big deal, exactly?"

"I think it's nice that you care."

She wanted to tell him she knew from his mother that he was

giving her all the money he could and that he was feeling guilty about quitting the Brass. It wasn't the time, though. They were together and the surge of happiness she had felt earlier when he told her how she felt had not abated one bit. She took his hand and put it on hers.

"I was reading about Portugal in *Radical America*," she said. "Is that what – "

"Yeah," he said. "Exciting stuff. Exciting times. And it was revolution in Africa that *caused* the revolution in Portugal."

"Exciting times," she said, his enthusiasm infectious.

"Sorry, I interrupted you. You were saying something about the article you read."

She loved listening to him and the sound of his voice but she loved more that he was always encouraging her to talk. "Well – "

"Is it okay if I interrupt you again?"

She laughed. "Only if it's important."

"You think maybe we could smoke that joint?"

"Sorry, I forgot."

He reached to turn the radio off but 'Show Me The Way' had come on and she beat him to it and turned the volume up. He rolled his eyes but smiled as he did. Right then, even Frampton sounded great.

"When did you say he comes to Colt Park?"

"July first," she said.

"We should go. Wanna go? Together, I mean."

A mile from the Sound, they were stoned and still talking for all they were worth about how the people might still prevail in Portugal when they passed under the railroad viaduct and came upon water surging from an open hydrant that had them scrambling to get the windows up. They did so just in time as the car got blasted with a deluge of water. Instinctively, Jackie put her arms up. She shrieked, then laughed, startled but completely dry.

Things quieted when they reached an upscale residential neighborhood and died completely as they exited the city. Jack turned off the road into a parking lot beside the best ice cream place in the area and she was still wondering about the surprise as they approached a bar she had driven by a number of times without noticing.

"I seem to recall you're a really good dancer," he said.

"Yeah?" She took his arm. "How about you? Are you still good?"

"I don't know," he replied, "but I'd love to dance with you again."

There were about thirty people inside. Jack had given Fred the manager twenty dollars the night before in exchange for which Fred would play music from his special collection for Jackie's birthday. Jack knew Fred well enough to know he would take care of the rest, except Fred was nowhere in sight. Jackie sat at a small table near the door as Jack walked up to the bar and ordered two Cokes.

"Girlfriend have I.D.?"

"I.D.? To drink Coke?"

"To be in here, period," the bartender said. "Look man, she's got to be eighteen to be in here and as far I'm concerned, she could be fourteen."

Jack went back and asked for her driver's license.

"Where'd she get this, a Cracker Jack box?"

"It's the same as mine or yours or anybody else's," Jack said. "Look at the birthdate. She turned eighteen today. That's why we're here, to celebrate."

Slowly, the man handed over Jackie's license and filled two tall glasses with ice and Coke. He took Jack's bill and lay his change on the bar.

"Fred around?"

"He'll be back."

After she took her glass, Jackie said, "So did you hear from somebody that this is a dancing place?"

He began to wonder. It wasn't always easy to get a straight story from Fred. While explaining his treasure trove of bootleg music one time, he said he had worked at the Fillmore East. Next time, he said he worked at a hotspot recording studio in Los Angeles and another time for RCA Records, and that he'd been a roadie for this group and that group. He claimed to know Pennebaker and Wadleigh and Spector. Even George Martin.

What was undeniable was that he had music that Jack had never heard or seen anywhere: complete sets from Monterey and Woodstock, concert tapes that had never been released as albums, alternative takes of well-known records from original sessions, studio tapes of songs by big name bands that had never appeared on any album. Once they got to know each other, Fred gave him incredible reel-to-reel tapes of some of his favorite groups. The only proviso was that he could never say where he had gotten them.

They took their Cokes and walked to the jukebox. "Well, we've gotta hear this," she said as she pointed to 'School's Out' and they laughed.

While they pooled their quarters, a medium sized man in his mid-thirties snuck up from behind and slapped Jack on the back. "Play some music while I do one thing." It was Fred. He gave Jackie the once-over, winked approvingly at Jack and headed around the bar.

When the last of the songs they selected ended, they stood in anticipation sipping Coke as Fred worked to get the tape he had ready into place. Once he got it going, he turned the volume up even louder than the jukebox had been so music filled the space.

It began with drums and combustible shards of guitar. Then thunder ran through the floor in the form of bass guitar as Jackie had never heard it played before, sonic and irresistible, as though the one creating it had done a long apprenticeship at the feet of Thor himself. When she heard the unmistakable voice of Marty Balin, she knew it was Jefferson Airplane and that Jack was having his little fun and that he couldn't have been more right about how good it was. It enveloped her instantly and she caught his eye and smiled.

It wasn't just the relentless drive of the sound, the lyrics were good, too, alternately thoughtful and playful, funny even, like the one about china breaking, leaves falling and laughing/laughing, laughing/laughing – *laughing*. As more and more people began dancing, Fred cranked the volume so that if they had closed their eyes they might have believed they really were at the Fillmore East. The playing was raw, with lots of improvisation, and Jackie was further seized by the music.

Then she really found a groove. The sound, Jack, the pot, some line she crossed into just letting go – it was all of those and a few other things. Once she got going, she really went. At first it was tinged with a bit of look at me. She was performing for all the people in her life who didn't really know her, presenting herself as she wanted to be seen, no matter that it might not be how they wanted to see her. *Especially* because it might not be how they wanted to see her.

It was better, though, when she got past that. Then it was just Jack, her, the music, and her body moving. Before long she was incandescent all over, down to the depth of her soul. There was a naturalness to the way she moved as well as a part of it she controlled. It was a wonderful combination, naturalness and control and the sensuousness of movement, exactly how she imagined lovemaking could be. How lovemaking might be with Jack.

But she was too in the moment to be concerned about lovemaking or what anyone saw when they looked at her. All that mattered was the unbridled exuberance of now. She had experienced the sensation of her body in motion before and she knew she had more than she'd ever called on, but she had no idea she could dance as she was there with him. She moved without having to think it or plan it. She felt a new place and went. There was nothing to remember or any coherent way to explain what she was doing. It was the first ever confluence of what she wanted to be and what she was. But even that was too reflective, for this was all id. She was deep in some primal place she'd never been before and going deeper.

He was an essential part of what was happening, beautiful and sexy, far enough away so she could check him out and close enough so that she could feel his heat. He moved gracefully, yet with such passion that she couldn't hide her delight. Sometimes when he caught her eye, her delight tipped over to a big smile. As they were taken further and further away by the sound and the pleasure of moving together, she felt the unmistakable vibe of love radiating out from him.

The music rolled seamlessly from song to song and pushed her still higher. It was full, with flashing fireworks out front grounded by the thump, thump, thumping of the underbeat. The recording was of a live performance and the sound was volcanic. There was no playing around, no tricks, and all sense of limits was gone. Once they and everyone around them surrendered, the music became a part of them. It was a wonderful synchronicity where the power of the sound was a perfect match for the energy and the emotion in the room.

Unbeknownst to either of them, people in the bar were riveted by the whirling young girl with the lustrous brown hair and the short skirt. Women as well as men could not take their eyes off her. It was as though she tapped ten thousand years of human movement and fused the very best parts for one night. Years of listening to music, years of dance lessons, years of waiting for the chance to let all that was beautiful inside of her fly free, all came together including, she knew, the right person to light a spark.

The lights were about as low as they could be without being off and the darkness added an erotic touch. It was hard to know how long they danced. Because of the pot, the kinetic energy between them, but most of all because of the music, time didn't matter. When the beat finally changed and Jack slowed, they stopped. It was when she sat down that Jackie became aware of the power pulsating through her body.

"Jackie, I gotta say," he yelled above the music, "you're incredible."

"You're pretty incredible yourself," she shouted.

"How about something to drink?"

"Wine?"

He bought a glass for each of them. Unable to sit still, they gulped the wine and got back to it. The music was still Airplane, still some hellacious live performance, just as good as before. The longer they went, the more she was physically drawn to him. She could feel his eyes on her and every move she made was as much for him as for herself. Eventually, they relaxed and let themselves play a little. They joked physically, moving while in contact with each other and laughing as they tried new moves. Then something with the music would click and away they'd fly.

They were back sitting near the open door with more wine when he took a joint out and lit it. In a flash they were re-buzzed and they danced on for what seemed like hours. More people than before were dancing, like-minded souls who made it even more fun. Soon, though, Jackie was again aware only of herself and of Jack and she could tell it was the same for him. There were occasional breaks and slowdowns but then the music would roll once more and they would be off, lost again in a sound so strong and full that several times she was sure the floor and walls were vibrating.

When they sat down again, they were both breathing hard. After she swallowed some wine, she tucked her hair behind her ear. That was enough to get him going and he leaned in and kissed her. They were up against closing so with the music as fresh as when they started, they danced some more. There would be plenty of time later for kissing. Now, there was just enough time for them to expend themselves in one more extended burst of exhilarated movement.

Fred eased them all to the finish line. After the music stopped, he shook Jack's hand and stuck a twenty-dollar bill in it.

"Fred, I can't take this," Jack said low enough so Jackie couldn't hear.

"Look," Fred said, leaning in close, "this was the best Wednesday we've had since we opened. Believe me, I made way more than twenty dollars. Besides, if you don't take it, I'll never let you or your girlfriend in here again. How's that?"

They made out against the side of the building, the night quiet other than the ringing in their ears. They leaned against his car and made out in the warm night air without another soul in sight. Then they made out some more in the front seat before they even got started on the chocolate ice cream cones they bought just before the ice cream place closed for the night.

"Susan's having people over for Walt's birthday Friday if you wanna go," she said as best she could while he ran his mouth along her neck to her throat.

"What are you doing tomorrow night?"

"I kinda owe it to my friends to hang out after baling tonight," she said, still with some difficulty between breaths, "but we could meet up later. How about if I call you?"

He didn't answer, preferring to concentrate on what he was doing. She was sure she felt good in every single way it was possible to feel good but then he did something with his hands that was even better.

"Remember you have to meet Manny," she said, her eyes closed. "Nine o'clock."

"Uh-huh."

"We should probably go," she said, though it was the last thing in the world she wanted.

For part of the way home, she sat with her bare feet dangling out the window. There was no way to do that and be close, however, so she slid next to him and propped her feet up on the dashboard. Everything along the way was closed and there were hardly any cars on the road. When they got to her street, every house was dark.

"You taste chocolate," she said as they made out in front of her house.

"*You* taste like chocolate wine."

She laughed and thought about a night to come when he would take her home to his place. That he hadn't tried or even suggested it this time made her want him all the more.

If you feel like love making/if you feel like flying/Make love flying/make love flying, flying, flying.

But not yet.

TWELVE

Jackie could tell Susan was upset so she kept her company through most of the party. Though the roof of Susan's building was a great setting, the party itself was a dud. Walt began celebrating his 30th birthday early and by the time he arrived at five, he was very drunk. With him were two friends no one else knew who were also very drunk. After a few hours, the three of them went back to the bar.

Despite her disappointment, Susan knew something good was up with Jackie. There was no time during the party when they were alone long enough for her to draw Jackie out, however, so she took strength from her sister's happiness and used it to help forget about Walt and his friends.

As the party broke up, Jack started in on the dishes. Thirty minutes later, he was still going.

"Jack," Susan said, "you don't have to do that." When he kept to it, she grabbed a towel and started drying. "I saw you talking to James. I'm sure he was delighted you knew who he was."

"Yeah, what a cool guy." James was a fifty-ish poet friend of Susan's whose work was published regularly in some of the magazines she wrote for. "So smart and very funny."

"Jackie and I are going over to the river to see the sunset," Susan said as Jackie came in with an armful of plates. "Would you like to join us?"

"Yeah, sure. James is still here, isn't he?"

"He's the last one," Jackie said. "He's not exactly passed out but he's close."

"I told him we'd give him a ride to Queens," Jack said. "You don't mind, do you?"

"No, it'll be fun," Jackie replied.

"Lemme go check in on him and tell him we'll be back," Jack said and he went into the hallway and up the stairs to the roof.

"We'll meet you outside," Susan said as she smiled at Jackie. "I see what you mean about the way he moves."

The street was quiet and the sky was graying. Casually, the two sisters crossed the street and Jackie hopped onto the hood of Jack's car.

"You know, I forgot that Walt was a Gemini," Jackie said. "That makes all four of us. You and Walt and me and Jack. Isn't that weird?"

"There's some deep significance there," Susan said, "but what it is I don't know."

"Me either," Jackie laughed. "And don't worry. Walt's probably just a little freaked about turning thirty."

"I guess." Susan's face lit up. "Hey, I just had a thought. You can work at the Center for the summer. Jack, too, if he's looking to make extra money."

She went on to explain that The Center for Working Class Studies where she worked had just received a grant to interview retired union members about their experiences, with a special focus on the 1930's. As Jackie listened, she saw immediately that it was a great opportunity. Still, she wondered aloud if they were qualified.

"Jackie, believe me, you'll be great," Susan replied. "You worked a whole school year on an oral history project with exactly the kind of people you'll be interviewing and did a great job. As enthusiastic as you are, people will be delighted to talk to you. And Jack, with his background working in a factory and being involved in his union and the rank and file network he told me about? That's perfect."

"I'd love to do it," Jackie said, "but I want us to get hired because we're good enough and not because you're my sister. We'll have to go through an interview and everything, won't we?"

"The two of you are so far ahead of the other people we're likely to hire it isn't funny," Susan said with great confidence. "But you're more than welcome to go to an interview as Jackie X so no one knows you're my sister. How's that sound?"

Jackie laughed again and hopped off the car. "I'm sure Jack will go for it."

"Good, then it's settled," Susan said.

They fell silent and Jackie saw her chance. Susan was far and away Jackie's main confidant when it came to boys and sex but the questions never came easily. She dreaded the day Susan might react like their parents and scold rather than guide. There was also the matter of intruding.

"What is it?" Susan asked as they went back across the street.

"Well," Jackie said hesitantly , "if Jack and I are ever in the city together and mom and dad don't know he's with me, would it be alright if … you know, if … "

"Would it be alright if what, little sister?"

For one who was a highly skilled teaser, Jackie wasn't good at recognizing when she was getting it. "You know ... if we could stay at your place."

"Tonight?"

"No, dad nixed that as soon as he found out Jack was coming."

"Of course it's okay. As long as you don't make too much noise." Susan put her arm around Jackie's waist. "Did you make much noise last night?"

"God, Susan."

Susan squeezed her close. "Oh, my God. You did, didn't you? Do you usually?"

"No, never." In a flash, Jackie went from embarrassed to thrilled. She had been dying to tell and Susan's knack for making it easy never failed. "It was … I … never – "

"Oh, my God. Look at you."

"Oh, my God, Susan, it was *so* good." Jackie looped her arm around her sister's waist and lowered her voice to a whisper. "Can you believe he went down on me on our very first time together? And then we made love the regular way and it was just as good."

"Wow, look at you," Susan said again. "You know how old I was the first time a guy ever went … never mind."

"How old?"

"Never mind. Well, congratulations. He must be pretty experienced."

"Yeah." Jackie figured there were lots of girls. She tried not to think about it.

"Quarterbacks usually do pretty well, plus you said he was the only white guy on the basketball team. That probably got him a lotta girls." Susan felt Jackie tense. "Is that a problem, if there were lots of other girls?"

"No," Jackie said as convincingly as she could. "Of course not."

Susan squeezed Jackie close and congratulated her again as Jack came through the door. Susan was smiling broadly and Jackie felt a moment of trepidation that her sister might inadvertently spill the beans.

"What?" he asked.

"Jackie and I are very happy she invited you," Susan replied, "and that she persisted so tenaciously with our folks about you coming today."

"That makes three of us," he said. "Wow. I didn't realize it was like that."

"Well, I'm exaggerating a little," Susan said. "But don't worry. It'll get better. After all, how could they not love thee?"

He laughed. "Let us count the ways."

"Let us count the ways, indeed," Jackie said as she took his hand. "Hey, we have great news."

"Do you realize," he said excitedly, "that all four of us are Geminis? The three of us, plus Walt? Isn't that weird?"

"Isn't it, now?" Jackie said as she and Susan laughed. "And Penelope, too."

"Right," he said. "Penelope, too. So what's the great news?"

"Susan wants us to interview for jobs where she works."

Jackie had never been across the Brooklyn Bridge. It was a splendid night for a drive and the majesty of the bridge, so superior to its mates further up the East River, added a touch of romance. Even at that hour, the harbor to the south throbbed with life. Overseeing it all was Lady Liberty, frozen in what Susan in one of her articles called her All Power to the People salute.

James was drunk when they departed and he drank the whole way. Listening to him as he performed from the backseat, Jack thought of his Lenny Bruce records. James was no help with directions but Jack had used his maps to cipher the best route, though he didn't know until they pulled up in front of the place that they were looking for a motel. James sobered some upon arriving home and insisted they join him for a nightcap.

Room 119 was neat and relatively bare, given that it housed most everything James owned in the world. Its visible contents were a bed, a bureau, a TV, a radio, a small refrigerator, a hot plate, a line of liquor bottles, a chair, and a table on which sat a Royal typewriter. A small collection of books rested alongside the typewriter and a stack of magazines were piled neatly on the other.

James took two folding chairs from a closet for them. There was cold beer in the fridge and whatever was in all the liquor bottles, but Jackie opted for orange juice and Jack for Pepsi. Without speaking, James passed them their drinks, a large bag of peanuts and a bowl. The air conditioner was not in top form so James propped the door open with an extra chair. Occasionally people passed and the sound of their voices in the moment when they were directly in front made for a weird audio effect. Twice somebody stopped to say hello. Each time, he introduced his new friends.

James didn't feel the need to entertain as he had on the ride over. Instead he asked questions about their lives and their plans for the future. He liked the sound of the interview project, was unimpressed by their plans for college, and suggested as an alternative getting union cards at the maritime hall so they could sign on to work the high seas.

"You'll learn more than you'll ever learn at New York University," he said in a way that made it sound like it had to be true. He would not be deterred from questioning them even when they asked him about his work. He gave them magazines with his poems and thin volumes of his work but forbade them from reading them.

"Read them out loud at the top of a mountain," he said as he swallowed a mouthful of whatever it was he was drinking. "That's what I had in mind when I wrote 'em. Now tell me more about yourselves."

They set the books down as he poured himself another drink. He liked that Jack had worked in a brass factory. Honest work, he called it. And he liked what they said about home.

"Honest blue collar town," he said. "A real place full of real people. Not like this temple of commerce and accumulation inhabited by zombies."

He offered refills that they accepted on the condition he talk about his poetry. He agreed unenthusiastically and closed the door. It was fascinating listening as he talked with hilarious brilliance about the superiority of play to work, the beauty of nature and the inevitable death of industrialism.

They were a good audience full of good questions and he rewarded them by reading a few poems. As soon as he began, he sobered. The themes he spoke of were all there and the rhythm fluctuated effortlessly between harsh, staccato fragments and extended stretches of reflective quietude. His command was impressive, too, as if he had been born to fill the world with the sound of his ideas.

When he would do no more, Jack asked if he could pick up. He selected a short one and James applauded when he finished so he read another. Jackie applauded so he read a longer piece that was the best one so far. Then she read one. When she finished, she looked at James and saw that he had tears in his eyes.

They would have liked to go on all night but the unfortunate matter of her curfew was staring them down. Jack took one last Pepsi for the road and ducked into the bathroom to roll a joint. James insisted that he had boxes full of all of his the books and that they were free to take whatever they wanted. They took one of everything and between them came up with fifteen dollars.

"You think because I live in a place like this that I need the money?" Knowing his situation from Susan, they pressed until he pocketed the bills.

"Susan said she's organizing a reading," Jackie said as they stood awkwardly in the doorway. "We'll definitely be there."

"Wonderful. Your sister is my biggest booster." James couldn't pass up the opportunity to kiss a young woman so he pressed his lips to Jackie's cheek. "Be sure to come armed with tales of the high seas."

"Too bad Walt decided to tie one on," Jackie said. They were going through New Rochelle and making good time. "I think you've talked more with him in the last two weeks than I ever have. Do the two of you ever talk about Susan?"

"Not really."

"Not really? Jack, you must."

"Well, he said he's really lucky they're together." He looked at her and realized she was fishing as a concerned sister. "Overall, I'd say he's really happy to be with her."

"You sure there's not more to it than that?"

"Well, you know how smart he is." She was suspicious of Walt and he knew she was right to be. He had found himself alone with Walt again and gotten another sophisticated dose of the inherently poisoned and poisonous nature of relations between men and women.

"Yeah, so?"

"Sometimes I have a hard time keeping up," he said. "Mostly

it's stuff about how hard it was for him with girls when he was younger."

"What does that have to do with Susan?"

"I don't know." Jack had successfully put the talk with Walt out of his mind and just like that, it all came flooding back. "It probably doesn't have anything to do with Susan."

She looked out the window. "Is there any of it you'd like to share?"

"It really has nothing to do with Susan so you don't have to worry," he said.

They lit up once they crossed into Connecticut. The pot felt nice but Jack couldn't get out from under Walt and his theories. Here he thought himself lucky to be winning the heart of the girl he had always wanted, yet the things Walt had said wouldn't go away.

"What are you thinking about?"

Her sweet voice brought him back. "Me?" He stalled, disgusted with himself, wanting a way to make it all right. "Nothing."

"Really? Nothing?"

"I was thinking how great it's gonna be if we both get hired for the job Susan told us about." He was crazy in love and he desperately wanted that to be enough. "The two of us spending all kinds of time in New York. Together."

THIRTEEN

By every standard that once had mattered as well as by some that still did, Maurice Francis Gendron had a good life. His law practice was prospering, his home was resplendent and valued at eight times what it was when he bought it, his wife loved him, and he still began most days with a spring in his step. His golf game was at eighty-four, he always took a week off at Christmas, and he had a timetable to travel to those parts of the world that he wanted to visit but hadn't gotten to yet. He weighed exactly what he was supposed to weigh, he had never smoked a cigarette in his life even during the twenty-nine months he'd spent in the army during the war, and he'd developed a taste for many of the kinds of fish his wife insisted he eat in place of pork chops and roast beef.

Still, Mr. Gendron could not quell the notion that he had less than he wanted. Troubling him most were the arcs of the lives of his five oldest daughters. His plans for them had been so big that they allowed him to withstand the jokes he knew people cracked behind his back about not producing a son because of some flaw in his sperm. After all the hard work and planning, however, his daughters' lives little resembled the pictures he had drawn up years before. Worse still was the realization that it was too late.

There was a time when he would write the years the five oldest were born on a piece of paper, they were so neat and orderly: 1945, 1947, 1949, 1951, 1953. Then there was Jacqueline, born in 1958. Although he and his wife denied it every time Jacqueline asked, Mrs. Gendron's sixth pregnancy had most definitely been an accident. No matter. It wasn't like they were digging ditches and scrubbing floors to make do. Besides, as the summer of 1976 approached, Mr. Gendron was glad more than ever that he had Jacqueline. She was his last hope. She had broken the pattern once before and she could do so again.

The last thing Jack expected was a call from Jackie's father. In no time, he found himself agreeing to go to the Gendron house early so they could get better acquainted. He knew Jackie was out with her mother and that she would be pissed at her father when she found out, but she would have to take that up with him. He had long since stopped expecting the things parents did to make sense.

From what Jackie had told him, her father was much like his own. The tension between Jack and his folks had begun years before. It built and built until finally, at seventeen, he began down the lonely road that had taken him so far from home. The realization that he was on his own was jarring at first, but eventually it became liberating.

For one thing, there were no shades of gray about where anyone stood. His father, and his mother, too, to a lesser extent, were fighting against the very changes in the society Jack enthusiastically embraced. Well before he went his own way, Jack knew he would get no guidance from either of them. By the time he did leave, the thought of seeking advice from them was laughable. He didn't particularly like having to work so much to make ends meet, but it was worth it because it made it possible for him to live on his own.

"Come in, Jack, come in." Mr. Gendron was above average height and the summer clothes he wore revealed a solid build. The time on the golf course had also allowed him to get an early tan. "Glad you were able to come on such short notice."

"No problem, Mr. Gendron, especially since I was coming over anyway."

"My thoughts exactly."

He accepted an offer of lemonade and followed Mr. Gendron to the den. He hadn't noticed much about the room the night of Jackie's birthday and he saw that it was a handsome, impeccably organized room. Hundreds of hardcover books filled shelves that were set into the walls along two sides. The entire room was paneled with beautiful wood and a large console television sat at the far end.

Jack sat on a sofa that was perpendicular to Mr. Gendron's

chair. Though the summer solstice was just days away, a supply of logs was stacked neatly in front of the fireplace. In three of the four corners of the room were vases with flowers, while along the windowsills and hanging from the ceiling were plants of all kinds. Mr. Gendron handed Jack a glass of lemonade and sat down with a .glass of his own that contained mostly Johnny Walker Black.

One of the reasons Mr. Gendron was so successful profession-ally was his ability to seize opportunity by the throat. Since the intricacies of his family life were as demanding as those at the firm, he saw no reason why he shouldn't approach the business of Home the same way. What better way, then, to get to know Jackie's new beau than to invite him over while Jackie was out with her mother.

He began leisurely, with small talk and soft questions about Jack's job at the library. He grew more serious when he asked about the year Jack had worked at the brass factory, pointing out as he did that many of the guys he'd grown up with worked there. It was a bit intimidating talking to an accomplished attorney about two jobs that didn't add up to much, but Jack fielded the ques-tions as best he could. He emphasized that the job at the Brass paid about as well as any that somebody with just a high school diploma could find. He also declined to make working as many as seventy hours a week sound burdensome and almost apologized at having quit with three months remaining before the start of school.

"Working two jobs, that's very admirable." Mr. Gendron shift-ed so he faced Jack more directly. "Beyond that, however, do you have an idea of what you'd like to be?"

Jack hesitated, then decided to chance it. "Well, for a long time I wanted to be Bobby Orr. Now I just wanna be myself, though I'm not sure who exactly that is yet."

"Jackie mentioned that you have a sense of humor." The older man sipped his drink. "Well said. As long as it doesn't take too long to figure it out."

"Yes, sir," Jack agreed. "I'm starting school in September at Keene State. Maybe Jackie told you?"

Mr. Gendron ignored the question at the end. "Interesting choice. Do they have a program there that interests you that no one else has? Or perhaps you have a special interest in the state of New Hampshire?"

"No, neither." For the first time, he felt Jackie's father bearing down on him. "I know you're a man who appreciates honesty, Mr. Gendron, and the truth is, Keene State is the only school I got into."

"I guess that's as good a reason as any."

Jack laughed nervously. "I'm sure you're excited about Jackie going to NYU."

Mr. Gendron didn't say anything for several seconds that seemed far longer. "I don't suppose she told you she got into Harvard."

"No," Jack said in a surprised tone that he immediately tried to catch and take back.

"Of course not." Mr. Gendron took a long swig of his drink. "I'm surprised, given your accomplishments in sports, that you didn't have an opportunity to attend college on an athletic scholarship."

Though Jack had expected it might come, it was a subject that was still sensitive, one that his own father still brought up with obvious disappointment whenever they saw each other. He tried for the next fifteen minutes to answer, first by downplaying his athletic abilities and then by emphasizing how valuable a year away from school had been. Mr. Gendron surprised him by mentioning that he had seen him play both football and basketball a number of times, pointing out along the way that he had gone to the same high school and played the same sports. Jack was certainly good enough to get any number of basketball scholarships, he insisted, and might have drawn comparable attention for football except for the curious fact that he had not played his senior year.

That was a surprise, too, that Mr. Gendron knew he had quit the football team his senior year. As he listened, Jack tried to think of something to say that would make him seem like something other than a quitter. Quitting was about the worst thing one could do in the world of athletics, a world that Mr. Gendron emphasized had shaped him through law school, the war, and thirty years as an attorney.

"You were definitely good enough," Mr. Gendron said in a way that precluded further debate on the point. "Jacqueline is quite the athlete, if you don't mind a father singing the praises of his daughter. Or at least she is when she keeps at it."

Jack was relieved that he wasn't required to explain himself further. "She is. You might not remember but she even played football with us."

"I had forgotten that," Mr. Gendron said after he sipped from his drink. "She was a bit of a tomboy, wasn't she?"

"And I know how well she did this year on the swim team." Jack's enthusiasm was genuine no matter that it was received rather cautiously. "And ice skating? Forget it. She was the fastest skater of all of us, including all the boys."

Mr. Gendron's expression softened slightly. "It so happens we were talking about that just the other night. Only she said you were the fastest and she the second fastest."

"That's because she used to let me win." Jack thought he saw a smile on the older man's face but he wasn't sure.

"Excuse me if I'm not entirely convinced, although it certainly is a nice thing to say to a young girl's father." Mr. Gendron stood up and turned the TV on to the Mets game. "Sure looks like another long year for these guys. And it couldn't be worse timing, what with the Yankees in first place."

"I don't think you should worry too much about the Yankees, Mr. Gendron," Jack said. "The Reds are too good. If the Yankees get that far, it'll be like men against boys."

For the first time since Jack's arrival, a look of respect took hold of Mr. Gendron's face.

"It's just an uninformed opinion," Jack clarified.

"Nonsense. It's very informed." Mr. Gendron drained the last of his drink. "What time were you originally supposed to come by?'

"Eight-thirty, "Jack replied. "Jackie told me she was going out to dinner with your wife. I know they're trying to spend more time together before Jackie goes off to school."

Mr. Gendron stood up and carefully placed three ice cubes in his glass. He filled it three quarters of the way with scotch, topped it with just the slightest bit of water, and swirled the combination of ingredients as that last bit hung between them. Several times Jack thought he'd come up with something good to say, and each time he chose instead to remain silent.

"I'm not sure you can appreciate the situation I'm in, Jack, as the father of six daughters." Mr. Gendron studied his watch intently for a moment. "I've had suitors such as yourself beating a path to my door since my oldest daughter was fourteen. That was seventeen years ago. Almost as long as Jacqueline has been alive."

Mr. Gendron walked to the TV and turned it off. After briefly looking out a window, he began pacing.

"It's more than the time. It's a thousand arguments, three arrests, two high speed automobile accidents including one daughter hospitalized and one car totaled, three premarital pregnancies two of which resulted in abortions and the other of which resulted in a beautiful child whose father's whereabouts are currently unknown, other pregnancies and abortions that I may not be aware of, oceans of tears over guys who suddenly decided not to call anymore – would you like more lemonade while I'm up?"

"No, sir." Jack knew they were at the purpose of their talk.

"A certain amount of aggravation and trouble, heartache even, can be well worth it if the end result is rewarding enough. I would be the last person in the world to speak against any of my daughters, Jacqueline least of all. She's our youngest and great things await her. But much of whether those great things happen depends on the choices she makes. And I have to say, the end result with her sisters has not been entirely satisfying."

He sat down, took a long sip from his drink, and began a

106

concise and occasionally hilarious synopsis of the lives of his five oldest daughters. Jack had heard a great deal about each of them in recent weeks but he listened with rapt interest, captivated by the undercurrent of weariness in Mr. Gendron's voice that was in such striking contrast to Jackie's bubbly enthusiasm when she spoke of them. Like Jackie, he also began with the second oldest Diane, went on to the others in order of their ages and saved Susan for last, just as Jackie had that day on the deck. His synopsis of Susan went on as long as the others combined, also just as Jackie's had.

"She's the smartest person I've ever met," Jack said helpfully of Susan.

"Yes, I forgot that you've met her. I'm surprised she hasn't sat you down for a long interview for one of her books or an article. You're of the proletariat. All the tedium of your job that probably drove you crazy would interest her no end." Mr. Gendron sipped his drink. "I'm glad you said what you said earlier about my appreciation of honesty, Jack, because that way we don't have to play games with each other. So as one honest man to another, I'm going to come out and say that I know you're fucking my daughter. I'm also going to tell you that I don't like very much that you're fucking my daughter."

Jack started to speak but Mr. Gendron cut him off by raising his hand.

"Don't worry. I'm as aware as you are that there's nothing much I can do about it. I mean, there's a great deal I *could* do about it, but there's not much I *choose* to do about it because anything I might do would probably drive Jacqueline and you closer together." He paused. "The fact that I don't like things as they stand is not because I don't like you, Jack. It's just that it doesn't make sense that Jacqueline would take on a boyfriend when she knows she's about to go off to a whole new world at college, not to mention that you'll be quite far from each other. You see how that doesn't make sense, don't you?"

There was no right answer that Jack could see and he bit his tongue even though it seemed for a moment that the older man expected him to speak.

"Assuming that whatever it is that exists between the two of you lasts through the summer," Mr. Gendron went on, "do you envision any way that you can continue seeing Jacqueline after the two of you go your separate ways to school?"

"We haven't been going out very long," Jack said tentatively, "but I'd like to keep it going come September, depending on what Jackie wanted."

"And perhaps to some extent what Jackie's mother and I want."

As it was a statement and not a question, Jack let it go. It was important that he say something about how he felt, however. As he gathered himself, he couldn't help but be impressed that Mr. Gendron gave no indication that the scotch was having any affect.

"The biggest thing I'd like you to understand, sir," he said with as much confidence as he could muster, "is that I would never, ever do anything to hurt Jackie. I enjoy being with her and I look forward to continuing to see her no matter how long it lasts. I'd like it to be with your approval and I'd like to demonstrate to you that I deserve your approval. I don't know what I can say that would get you to trust me, sir, but I will say that you can trust me."

The sound of the garage door closing echoed through the house. "Seems like we're wrapping this up just in time," Mr. Gendron said. "Perhaps that's a foundation we can build on. And, Jack, I don't want to leave the impression that I'm angry about you and Jacqueline. I may not be entirely pleased about it, but I'm not angry. In fact, I feel a little better about things than I did before tonight."

"Maurice?" It was Mrs. Gendron.

"We're in here," Mr. Gendron said. "I'll give some thought to how you might gain more of my approval, Jack."

The good feelings engendered by a pleasant two hours spent with her mother were obliterated by her father's subterfuge and

108

Jackie was fuming as they walked to the car. Not only had he invited Jack over without her knowledge, he had gone into her room to fish out his phone number. The only saving grace was that he had apparently not figured out that Jack was living on his own and not with his mother.

"Is Susan really thirty-one?" Jack asked as they walked toward his car. For one of the few times since they'd been together, he was oblivious to her Jackie's mood.

"Why, what did he say about her?" She was struggling to compose herself.

"He was just reminiscing with great fondness about the many years his six lovely daughters have been dating. He seemed especially delighted that you had nailed it so well. You know, with me."

"What else did you talk about?"

"The usual guy stuff: baseball, work, are you screwing my daughter." She stopped and glared but still he didn't see how upset she was. "I'm joking. Although he was very happy to hear we're using rubbers."

"God, that is not funny," she said.

"It's sorta funny, isn't it?"

As they got in the car she vowed to try and go along, hoping that with his help she could force her way out of her funk. Then he mentioned Harvard.

"That is so great," he said. "The best part is that you get to blow them off. How great is that? How many people get to blow off Harvard?"

"Very funny. Did he tell you that he went to Harvard and about how desperately he wants me to go there? Did he tell you how disappointed he is that none of my sisters could go there and about all the letters he wrote over the years urging them to start admitting women? And did he tell you how excited he was when they decided to accept women and how it happened just in time so I ... not that he would've bothered with any of that if he'd had even one son who could've gone there. Then he wouldn't have cared."

She looked at him but he was looking straight ahead in embarrassment, having finally grasped the depth of her anger.

"And did you get to the part," she went on, "about how disappointed he is that none of my sisters is a lawyer and how many times he's said that he would love for me to go to law school? That he expects me to? That he plans to keep it hanging over my head for the next four years even though he knows I have absolutely no interest? You might want to keep that in mind the next time the two of you get together for another chat about my future."

When he finally turned to her, she looked straight into his eyes.

"Are we done?"

They drove in silence until he swerved unexpectedly into the huge parking lot of the A&P and she eyed him suspiciously as he made his way to a deserted corner. When he parked and shut the engine off, he turned so his right leg rested on the seat between them. His eyes were on her and she did what she could to avoid them. She wanted to fight back against the silence he was forcing on her but she had to be careful because she knew she was in danger of breaking.

"Why exactly are we parked here?" It was the same parking lot where the local drum corps used to practice on long ago summer evenings just like this one. The two of them had talked once about the thrill of hearing the music through open windows as little kids, delighted at having finally found someone else who remembered. Just about any other time, the memory of that would have brought great comfort. On this occasion, however, she could draw no strength from it.

"Well?" She shot him a quick glance, still determined to drive the bad feelings out by directing her anger at him. She was shivering despite the heat and she held herself to make it stop, lest he see. When he stretched his arms toward her she ignored them and tried to say something mean, but the words caught somewhere even lower than her throat. A tear rolled down her cheek.

"Why does everything have to be so hard?" She began to sob.

It was stronger than she was and she couldn't have checked it had she wanted to. She slid over and pressed herself close as he put his arms around her. She sobbed some more and when the sobbing stopped she cried quietly and for a longer time than she had in years. As she did a heavy weight disattached itself from her shoulders and vanished through the window into the warm air. She held fast for many minutes even after the tears stopped and soon she became aware that all of the oppressive thoughts were gone out the window as well.

She insisted they stick to their plan to see 'The Reincarnation of Peter Proud' at the ninety-nine cent theater that specialized in year old movies. She had wanted to see it when it came out the previous spring and could think of nothing better than losing herself in a love story with him. They were behind schedule and he wove effortlessly from lane to lane, faster than usual but carefully. Jackie studied the side of his face for a moment, aware as never before of how safe she always felt when she was with him. Then 'Jackie Blue' came on and she laughed quietly.

"No, leave it," she said as he reached to change it. "I should hate it by now but I don't."

"Why should you hate it?"

"People used to sing it to me," she said. "Or *at* me, I should say."

"Guys you said no to, I bet," he said. "I mean, come on. You have to know you're nothing like the girl in this song."

Had it been only guys she said no to, it might have been okay. But there was also Jim. He sang it while they were going together and at first it was funny. Then he began singing it when he was mad at her and continued long after she asked him not to. Each time, his singing got more hostile. After they broke up, he called several times a week for a month just to sing the part he knew she disliked most at her through the phone.

"Not even tonight?" she asked.

"You were upset because you had a good reason to be upset."

They were at a red light and she felt him looking at her. She sensed they weren't through, that he wanted to know all of it, but for her sake. It was dangerous ground she was approaching, what with the crying, the rant about her father, some stupid song on the radio. Great way to get a guy to fall in love, by letting him see all your weaknesses.

"Jackie?" His voice was as comforting as his arms had been. "Tell me?"

She began with some hesitation. Once she got going, it flowed easily and she was aware only of what she wanted to say and of him. The truth was that she had come to hate the song. Not the song exactly, but that anybody would think she was like that. Jackie Blue. Jackie was not that common a name and she knew some people sang it at her simply because she was convenient. With Jim, it was all mixed up. She liked him very much and was always happy to see him. There was nothing blue about that, yet he had insisted on turning something good into something nasty.

He made it easier by mostly keeping his eyes straight ahead. She didn't mind it the few times their eyes met, it was simply easier when she was able to study the side of his face as she talked. She had grown used to his acne scars and even found them oddly ennobling. He didn't smile unless she laughed first and he never probed. He simply nodded when she emphasized a point and kept his eyes on the road. Other times when she told the sad tale of Jim and 'Jackie Blue', it seemed quite silly. It wasn't that way this time.

"Well, I'll say it again," he said. "You're the most vivacious person I know and anybody who thinks you're like that song is crazy."

At the theater, they discovered they had thirty minutes to kill because the starting times for the movie had been listed incorrectly in the newspaper. They were on their way back to the car to smoke when he suddenly took hold of her arm and steered them around the corner of the theater up a long driveway. He didn't slow down until they turned another corner at the back of the building.

"Who are those people?"

He ignored her and produced a pack of rolling papers. They each peeled one off and she scooped pot into the sheets with her thumb and forefinger. It was a good, safe spot with long sightlines.

"Jack?"

"The Whittakers," he said. "Married couple from school. He's a math teacher. Nice guy. She was my guidance counselor. Let's just say we didn't get along."

She sensed vulnerability, something she could help him with, but he looked away. Other times, she had let it go. But she wanted to be in, not out, so she touched his arm and used the same words he had.

"Tell me?" Other than the last leap with her heart that she was not sure she could make, she trusted him unequivocally. She wished he would do likewise. Every secret she could get him to share brought them nearer. "Please, Jack?"

"She was always giving me a hard time because I was taking both Spanish and French," he said, "even though they were my two best subjects. She kept reminding me that in all her years as a guidance counselor, she'd never had a kid who took two languages for four years. Then she'd start in about me not having any plans for college and all this time my parents are cheating on each other, the football coach is hassling me about pot, plus

I'm working all these hours so I can afford my own place. So one day when she brought up college for the millionth time, I told her I was gonna spend four years in college and four years in grad school making an up-close, intensive, personal study of female sexual behavior and become the world's foremost expert on female sexuality, and did she have suggestions about which schools to apply to and anything else at all to say that might be helpful."

"You didn't." She laughed awkwardly at first, then really let go. "You *didn't*."

"I did." He laughed, too. "She tried to have me suspended but the principal shot that down. As it turned out, a lotta parents had complained about her and eventually they forced her back into teaching. Business, I think it is."

"Well, good. It worked out perfectly." She laughed again. "That is so funny."

He was sure it was the pot but it didn't matter. There was a brilliant glow about her and he couldn't take his eyes away. He loved that he could make her laugh and that she wanted to know what was inside of him. As they smoked on, they barely talked. Instead they smiled and giggled and reveled in their closeness.

"They have birch beer here, you know" she said in the lobby of the movie theater. "The red kind."

He stopped on his way to the bathroom and went for his wallet. "Get me one?"

"I think I can afford to buy you a soda," she said.

"Extra large?"

"Boop boop-a-doop."

No sooner was he out of the bathroom than he ran smack into the Whittakers. This time there was nowhere to hide. Mrs. Whittaker was gleeful to learn that he had spent the year since graduation working in a factory rather than in college and was expressing her doubts about how long he would last at Keene State when Jackie ambled over and handed him his soda.

"Well, we better go inside," Jack said. He couldn't imagine they would suggest sitting together but he wanted out fast just in case.

"I'm Jackie. And you're Mrs. Whittaker, Jack's guidance counselor. He's told me so much about you. That must be such a great job, helping young people." Jack moved toward the theater and she put her am around his waist to stop him. "Oh, by the way –

that business the two of you talked about? You know, his plans for college and a career? The mysteries of the female heart, you might call it?"

The Whittakers shuffled uncomfortably.

"He's getting nothing but A-pluses." She tiptoed up and gave Jack a peck on the cheek as he pulled her toward the theater. While allowing herself to be moved, she gave them a thumbs up and a wink. "A-pluses across the board."

Though he had flushed red, Jack was struggling to hold back laughter. When they went through the door, they laughed loudly enough so that most of the twenty people in the theater looked at them.

"I bet he's getting nothing but F's," she said as they took seats in a secluded spot.

"Or just getting nothing, period," he said and she laughed still more loudly. "No one's ever had my back like that. Thanks."

"You really mean that, don't you?"

"Yeah, I do," he said.

"Well, it was my pleasure," she said as she moved closer.

"Yeah, she's beautiful," he said when she asked about Jennifer O'Neill. "They're all beautiful. I think that's the whole point, isn't it?"

Jackie didn't know what to make of that. "Did you like 'The Summer of '42?"

"No," he said without hesitating.

"I thought every guy liked that. Maybe you didn't like it because she ditches him?"

"Maybe." After a moment, he continued. "It seemed fake. Not fake like it could never happen, but fake for some reason I can't put my finger on. Orchestrated. More orchestrated than your average Hollywood movie."

They were driving with no particular destination. Jackie hadn't started it as a test but his thinking intrigued her. She crossed her fingers and asked if he had liked 'The Godfather.'

"No. Actually, I disliked it so much I walked out. I never got into that Mafia stuff."

"But you did like the movie tonight."

"I thought it was great," he said.

"Yeah, me too." Then urgently, she said, "Turn here. We used to live on this street. My mother grew up here."

In her mother's youth, the neighborhood had been the oldest and best-known Italian enclave in the city. Now it was a rundown mix of warehouses, two-family houses, vacant lots, abandoned machine shops – and most definitely no Italians. Close by was the Lincoln housing project that opened the year the Gendrons moved away, on one corner was a long closed Catholic grammar school, and looming over the area was the smokestack of the massive power plant that began operating the year Jackie was born.

He slowed to a stop when she pointed to a green house as a black boy about sixteen stared at them. Though she had said *we*, her family had moved six years before Jackie was born. That gave the house a romantic quality it might not have held had she ever actually lived there. For her, it was a place where her sisters and even her mother would forever be young.

The last time she had been on the street, it had made her sad. Not so this time and she knew it was because of him. She felt strong by his side and images of the past didn't seem so important so she let go and focused on the present. Though it was past midnight, it was quite warm and she thought they might go swimming at the lake together for the first time. There was something magical about first times.

"How's about we go to the observatory?" he said. "It's clear so there'll be a lot to look at."

She had been wanting to check out the observatory for years. "You mean the – "

"I've got the keys."

She laughed in disbelief. "You've got the keys to your high school? How is that possible?"

"I turned the astronomy teacher on," he said. "And don't worry. He told me if I ever get caught that I should have the cops call him at home and he'd take care of it. Whatta you say?"

Another first time. The two of them. Together. "I'd love to."

FOURTEEN

Summertime. Strawberries, blueberries and cherries, too. Rise up singing and spread your wings. A city dying - somebody *killing* it. Dancing in the Streets on the real side and pool-hopping in the moonlight. Asteroids and jelly beans, Tall Ships and BUYcentennial Blues. Getting high every day – Do You Feel Like I Do?

On the East Side, it was already the Summer of Fire, though summer had not even officially begun yet. Everyone who had resided there for any length of time knew that, come the warm weather, there would be fires. What was different this time was the frequency. Houses and stores were disappearing in flames every night. With the fire came a relentless sense of fear, fear that could not easily find expression, for no one knew who or where or when. The fear was all the more oppressive because the hottest months – the months when there were always far and away the most fires – were still ahead.

No residents or firefighters had died thus far, a circumstance the mayor declared "sheer luck." Those who had been hospitalized with burns or for smoke inhalation didn't feel lucky, nor did the far larger number of people who had been displaced. The staff at the Red Cross was overwhelmed by the demand for emergency shelter and scurrying to plan for what they would do if the fires kept coming at the same pace. The city, meanwhile, suddenly had a number of vacant buildings that were in danger of collapsing and vulnerable to being set ablaze again.

Set ablaze. Every single fire of any consequence had been set and that was what frightened people most. Someone was burning the city, or parts of it anyway, and the mayor and the fire department seemed powerless. The scourge could not be kept quiet, either, the way the contaminated land in the same part of town from the factory that had been liberally spreading toxic waste for

118

decades had thus far been kept quiet. Not with the sky alive with flames and the piercing sound of sirens every night.

Sometimes the sirens came in waves, beginning not long after sunset and lasting all night. Other times most of the night would be quiet, only to erupt into sound at some point before sun-up. Several fires had raged for hours and required the attention of firefighters from several miles around. On those occasions, the sirens had begun in divergent locations with no rhythm or order to them, only to draw closer and closer until they converged in one giant mass of terrifying sound.

Not many years before, the Black Panthers and Young Lords had been a force in that part of town and some residents wondered if things might have been different had they still been. Even the skeptical in the community had to admit they were organizations of action. During that time, if the powers-that-be had to be confronted until answers were forthcoming, the Panthers and Lords were the ones who led the way. Only shadows of the Panthers and Lords remained, however, their memberships having been harassed and jailed into silence. People did what they could to carry on, most notably a group of loosely organized women, but their efforts were thus far isolated cries of protest lacking the kind of organization that might have made a difference.

So as the days got longer and the drumbeat of the Bicentennial grew louder, people tried as best they could to put the specter of fire out of their minds. Neighborhood reunions, Juneteenth celebrations, school graduations, and the Puerto Rican Day Parade all went on as they had in the past. More informal were the street parties to celebrate the coming of summer. Still, as good as the parties were, they could not quell the dread that ran through East Side neighborhoods each evening as sunset neared.

FIFTEEN

They got off the 6 train at Bleecker Street for the simple reason that Jackie loved the sound of the word Bleecker. There was something so very New York about it. She was guessing there wasn't a Bleecker Street anywhere in the entire state of Connecticut, and maybe not anywhere else, either.

They set out in the opposite direction of the club, east by northeast, not at all daunted by the distance their exploring would take them from their ultimate destination. Jackie had always been drawn to New York as an idea but, lacking a kindred spirit, exploration had never been all that rewarding. When she mentioned the club, Jack was as enthusiastic as she was. It was a new place and the fact that it was downtown appealed to her more than the bands. *Downtown* brought to mind images of sharply-dressed, serious, smart people like Susan and her friends.

They successfully navigated several blocks without once breaking stride while paying attention to everything around them. They passed bars whose loud talk blew out into the street and restaurants whose outdoor seating was filled to capacity. From a second floor window, a saxophone and drums could be heard. All about them people walked in every direction and cars sped along narrow, one-way streets. The words **PEOPLE STARVE ON THIS BLOCK** were scrawled in bold script on a wall between two fancy eateries.

A group of children played kick ball on one street, dodging and staring down the cars that had the audacity to interrupt their game. People sat on stoops and hung out in front of tattoo parlors and other businesses that were not only open at that late hour, but doing a brisk business. As the two of them took it all in, they drew a bit of attention themselves. That was largely because of how radiant she was but it was also because of the disparity in their respective heights. Four weeks into whatever was happening between them, it was old news and they barely noticed those who did double takes.

"Everything okay, Jacqueline?"

"Never better," she said. "You?"

"Well, I'll tell you. I'm walking through the most exciting city in the world on a beautiful summer night with a scorchingly fine girl by my side – I'd say I'm doin' alright." He turned her way with a smile but she successfully suppressed the urge to reciprocate. "Great shoes, by the way." She was wearing one of her pairs of black flats. "Simple but stylish. Minimalist, yet elegant. Attractive and comfortable."

She laughed and rolled her hip into him. "They should hire you to do their ads."

The sound of her laughter was a constant backbeat to their time together and it was a sound Jackie had come to like. She also liked that he was able to adore her without in any way boxing her in. And unlike so many guys she knew who were already bitter about life, Jack rarely had a negative word to say about anything. There was nothing naïve about it, either, for he was more aware of the world and the sometimes ugly way that it worked than anyone their age she knew.

"The best thing about you, Jackie," he said as they wound their way past everyone in their midst, "is how fast you walk."

In addition to the sounds and sights, they were surrounded by a potpourri of powerful scents. In that part of town, that mostly meant food. One block was sautéed garlic and smoky barbecue, the next chocolate and pastries, and everywhere the aroma of rich, high grade coffee. At no point were they tempted to stop, yet it was delightful to know such a wide range of pleasures could be indulged virtually around the clock.

They turned around and set back to the south and west, fluidly blowing by everyone who was moving too slowly. They made a point of taking an entirely different route and absorbed the sights just as intently. In all they had been walking for over an hour when, just after crossing Canal Street, they arrived at the club. A large crowd was milling about out front.

"Whatta you think?"

"Not sure," she replied, "but I know one thing: I'm not waiting in any line."

They gathered from snippets of conversation that only women flying solo were being allowed in by the very large bouncer who stood behind a rope that stretched before the entrance. His hair was pulled tight in a ponytail and he wore an expensive black suit jacket that he left unbuttoned to better show off his weightlifter's torso. The sarcastic smile he wore was not going over well with those gathered on the sidewalk.

"I'm ready for Prescott's," Jack said after a few minutes, referring to their fallback destination.

"I hate to come all this way and split without trying." She looked around. "How about if I get his attention and see if I can get us in?"

"I bet if you bat those beautiful brown eyes the way I know you can – the way you never have for me, I might add – that he'll give you the keys to the place." When she turned and, with great exaggeration, batted her eyes, he clutched his heart. "Help me, I'm melting."

She had to wait only a few minutes before an opportunity arose. As she and the bouncer talked, the expression on the guy's face went from bemused condescension to annoyance.

"Look, sweetie," the guy said finally, apparently unconcerned that arguing with a young woman less than half his size might not be good for business. "You want in, leave your scrawny boyfriend home."

"Hey Bluto," she said, angered that he had brought insulting Jack into it, "since apparently no one's told you yet: That pony tail? Very corny."

"This is the hottest spot in town, sweetie." The guy glared as Jack moved within earshot. "Maybe you should stick with the junior prom."

She glared back. "Go fuck yourself."

Jack moved to her side. It was the first time he had ever heard her curse.

"You shouldn't let your little lesbian friend go round talkin' like that." He was as tall as Jack and fifty pounds heavier.

Sensing danger, she stepped between them. "Come on, Jack. Forget this."

"Listen to the little lesbian, bud."

Jack allowed himself to be pushed, but there was something about this that was too over the top. "You heard what she said. Go fuck yourself."

When the guy charged, Jack moved away from Jackie, took a long, quick step forward and got as low as he could. Before anyone knew what was happening, the bouncer flipped over and landed on a pile of garbage. As soon as Jack was sure the guy's neck wasn't broken, he grabbed her hand.

"Let's go."

They walked quickly across the street past startled onlookers as another club employee emerged from inside to tend to his colleague. When Jack put his arm around her, Jackie surrendered as he led her back the way they had come. He seemed to sense, as she did, that they would be safer if they could get back across Canal Street.

Cars were zipping along at great speeds in both directions as they started across in the middle of the block. It was his deal now and she closed her eyes and held on. She did not need an NYU education to know that mis-stepping while jaywalking across Canal Street against a red light at that hour on a Friday night was a good way to end up in the back of an ambulance. It took some timing, some moxie and some fancy footwork but he was able to maneuver them through eight lanes of maniacally speeding traffic without them ever being in any serious danger.

She opened her eyes when they hit the other side and sagged as soon as he loosened his grip. He immediately took a firm hold again and pulled her close. Her heart was racing and visions of a crazed carload of pissed-off bouncers clouded her brain.

"I'm so sorry," she said.

"Are you kidding?" He was providing practically all of their combined propulsion, yet he was neither sweating or breathing hard. "That was way better than any band we could've seen at that stupid club."

"Do you think he'll come after us?"

"Not us, Kemo Sabe. Me." He took a quick look over his shoulder. "Little Jacqueline Gendron."

It was oddly comforting that he should call her that just then. "Jack, I'm so – "

"You were so great. 'Go fuck yourself, Bluto. You and your corny ponytail.'"

She squeezed him tight. They never once thought of hailing a cab and riding away to a safe distance. It would have been too much like surrender. Instead they made their way west and eventually back down to Canal Street close to the chaotic entrance to the Holland Tunnel. Though the light was green, Jackie stopped.

"Lemme guess." He was as composed as she was uncertain. "We're waiting for the light to turn red and then we'll cross, just because it was so much fun the first time."

"Right."

"Uncanny how we so frequently think alike."

She knew what he was doing and it was working. "Good luck with *that*."

He laughed. "No matter how much you fight it, I remain, as always, undeterred."

She laughed, too, glad that he remained, as always, undeterred. "Jack, you have to let me say this. I'm so sorry."

"Alright. Even though you are in no way responsible for anything that happened, apology accepted." When they reached the south side of Canal Street, he stopped and looked at her. "Ready to have the best night of our lives?"

They were in a part of the city that was theirs for the taking. There were no restaurants or bars in sight, no crowds to get lost in, nothing but silent warehouses and small indeterminate businesses that had closed hours before. Even taxi cabs, the one omnipresent part of the Manhattan tableau - not a one. She saw that he was as alert to everything around them as she was. Partly it was his curiosity but she knew it was also for her sake. It was clear he could handle himself in just about any situation and that any trouble he might have would be because she was along slowing him down. It was a good trade-off for her, not so good for him, not walking the streets at that hour with a girl, though he would never say so. For both the better part of the bargain and the fact that he would never acknowledge it, she was grateful. She also made a silent vow to be smarter.

"It should only be about six or seven blocks," she said of Prescott's,feeling a need to reassure him that she knew what she was doing.

"Hey, Jackie, I can do this all night as long as I get to do it with you."

"Well," she said, smiling to herself at how open he was about how much he dug her, "hopefully it won't come to that."

The quiet and the solitude were refreshing. She had carefully studied her maps so she knew the names of the streets, but those were just words and lines on paper and did not capture the area's charm. They had stumbled into a secret place that even most New Yorkers didn't know about and along with the still, warm air she thought she detected a hint of honeysuckle – was that even possible?

"Hard to believe we're even in Manhattan," he said. "I mean, Desbrosses Street? Who's ever even heard of that? And that other one, Lispenard Street. Where *are* we?"

His enthusiasm was infectious. "I know. Isn't it great?" When they came face to face with the abandoned hulk of the West Side Highway, however, she knew they had made a wrong turn somewhere.

"You know," he said as they backtracked, "you're all self-conscious that maybe you're not sure exactly where we are but I'm amazed at how well you know this place."

"I just go by what a very wise man told me once: Walk in like you own the place."

"You're gonna love living here," he said in that bubbly tone he used whenever he spoke about her future. "I can see you in some cool old New York apartment somewhere roller skating from room to room."

She laughed. "Roller skating?"

"The first time I ever saw you when I was six years old, you were roller skating," he said. "You were smooth as Peggy Fleming."

"Wow." She looked at him keenly. "To tell you the truth, I'll be happy with a little room somewhere, a typewriter, some music and a library card."

"And maybe a guy coming in from the sticks of New Hampshire once in a while to visit?"

For the first time, she detected some hurt in his voice. "I said that, didn't I? A sophisticated scholar who beats up bullies and can handle himself in any situation imaginable." She took his hand. "You were great back there. That guy probably weighs way over two hundred pounds. How in the world did you flip him?"

"Same way I lost my virginity, I guess."

"Whatever that means." And then sensing he was going to leave her hanging, "What does it mean?"

"I closed my eyes and tried not to make a mess." After she laughed obligingly, he went on. "I studied martial arts for a few years to help me with sports. You know, balance, movement, positioning, all that cool stuff."

"Well, I'm glad you did." She tiptoed up and kissed his cheek.

They backtracked, zigzagged, turned a corner and laughed in unison when they came upon – "Horses?" It was a stable full of police horses. They stopped for a moment, as a radio blared through the stale air. The guard dozing at the far end was the first person they'd seen since crossing back to the south of Canal Street.

They entered a block with clear signs that much commerce was transacted on its premises by day, with waste containers and stacks of skids on both sides of the street and vegetable boxes strewn about. It was as silent as a street in the smallest town in the world at that hour, however, and full of the scent of cheese. Up ahead she spied a building she and Susan had passed on a recent walk.

"I know exactly where we are," she said confidently.

"Oh, do you now, little Jacqueline?" He put his arm around her waist and they both inhaled, aware of a new scent.

"Bubble gum."

"Not bubble gum," he clarified. "Gumballs."

She inhaled again. "Gumballs. Exactly. Maybe there's a big gumball factory hidden around here somewhere."

They sat on a loading dock on Franklin Street and he took out his stash. They sat close and looked at the stars as they smoked, enjoying the quiet and the solitude.

"I still can't believe that guy at the club," she said after a while. "Whatta you think his deal was?"

"Roid Rage, maybe."

She looked at him, puzzled, and exhaled. "What about all that lesbian stuff? I mean, he knew I was with you. Is there something about me that would make him think - "

"No, not all," he said. "It's probably because he's on a very long losing streak."

It was such a surprising answer that she had to make sure she understood. "You mean with girls?"

"That's what guys do. They take that frustration out on girls. With a beautiful girl like you, it's worse because you represent everything he wants but can't get."

He rarely spoke so declaratively. When he did, he was never wrong. Her hope that he would elaborate without prompting slipped away, however, so instead she embraced the impact the pot was having. They were out to have fun and it was a night made for it. Besides, there was a more important matter she wanted to ask about.

He sat with both feet flat on the ground as she stepped onto the tips of his sneakers in her bare feet. After taking a toke and exhaling, she leaned forward and lifted her right leg back so his right foot bore all of her weight, though there was no more pressure than before because she had positioned herself perfectly. Reflexively, he put his hands up but there was no need. She stood that way with her leg extended behind her and her arms outstretched for far longer than seemed possible without once coming close to tipping in any direction. Then, in one motion, she brought her leg down and hopped back.

He clapped and then for the second time that she'd noticed, he rubbed his right shoulder. After mashing out the last of the joint, she got up on the loading dock behind him and began working his neck and clavicle with both hands. When he closed his eyes, she knew she was close and pressed harder. The pot was the best so far and she felt great. Her worries about the bouncer were gone and she was dying to see if Prescott's was as good as Susan said. Most of all, she was happy the two of them were together and maybe in the middle of the best night of their lives. That thought emboldened her to go forward.

"Can I ask you something?"

"Alright." He smiled without opening his eyes. "I'll stop calling you Little Jacqueline."

She had found the tender spot and was working it firmly with both hands. "Do you really think that bothers me?"

"Well, if it ever does, let me know and I'll stop. Maybe say something like, How's the weather up there?"

"I would never say that. That's completely stupid." She slapped his shoulder and hopped down.

"Good as new." He put his arm around her and they set out toward Greenwich Street. "Thanks."

"But that's not what I was gonna ask you. What you said before

… who was the lucky girl to whom you gave your virginity?"

He stopped and let his arm drop from her waist. "I figured you were gonna ask me that eventually but I didn't think it was gonna be tonight."

"I'm interested, that's all," she said. "I told you about myself because I thought you'd wanna know. You didn't say anything about yourself so … wait … do you mean – "

"Look, do me a favor," he said. "Don't say it out loud, okay? Whatever you do, don't say it out loud."

"But what about the girlfriends you told me about?"

He shrugged. She hadn't dreamt in a million years that she was his first girl. That together with him not being her first, she knew, was a potentially lethal combination. She looked at him intently.

"The funny thing is, I would've told you eventually," he said.

"Then what difference does it make?"

"Forget it," he said, unable to bring himself to look at her. "It doesn't matter."

She would have loved for him to talk to her about it but he simply drifted away in silence. That left it to her. There were so many things she could say that might be all wrong, she knew, yet still she tried.

"It's kind of thrilling for me, now that I know."

"Great. I'm glad you're thrilled." He laughed. "I'm thrilled that you're thrilled."

He lit another joint and inhaled as if to take the whole thing in at once. Though she didn't much want to smoke any more, she took it when he offered in the hope that doing so might help reverse the chasm she could feel opening between them.

She wanted to understand. She *did* understand. Why didn't *he* understand? Waiting for the right guy got tired because every guy thought he was The Right Guy. Every single one. There was no way to win. She lost Jim because she hadn't told him and he found out on his own. Now Jack was upset because she *had* told him. But the telling or not telling wasn't even it, she knew. What it really came down to was that she had been his first and he hadn't been her first.

"You know, before you, it was never any good." She was willing to keep trying, that's how far along she was.

He laughed bitterly. "Look, I know you're trying to make things better but do you think maybe you could stop talking about it? I listened that night at my place and that was fine but I really don't wanna hear any more about all the other guys you – "

"God, Jack. You make it sound … don't you understand that it doesn't matter?"

"I know it doesn't matter," he said sharply. "That's what *I* keep telling *you*."

It was the first time he had ever spoken to her that way. She had let herself believe he was different from the others, yet in a matter of moments he had metamorphosed into someone she didn't entirely recognize. Wanting him for everything he was is what made the lovemaking so great. Suddenly, that desire felt cheap.

She understood the ways it was easier for her. Guys had been sniffing around since she was eleven. Her first time had been important but it was hardly some big accomplishment to finally say Yes instead of No. She knew the pressure he was under, but he obviously didn't get the pressure *she* had been under. And whatever it was she had with those other guys hadn't added up to anything close to what she had with him. What she and Jack had was authentic. Or so she thought. Just like that, she wasn't sure.

He casually flipped the last of the joint away and stood for a long time with his back to her. She was confused by the feeling she had betrayed him and that it was up to her to make it right. If only she could find the right words, everything would be okay. But none of her words had worked thus far so she waited, wanting him to hold her tight but fearing that if she went to him he would reject her. Finally, he looked at her.

"Look, Jackie. I'm in love with you and I hate for things to be like this between us. I don't want to be acting like this but there's something about it I can't help." He stepped close and took her hands in his. "All I want is for us to be together. Right now, I wanna go listen to music and drink wine and dance up a storm and have fun. With you. Do you think we can never, ever talk about this again and just go have some fun?"

"Yeah," she said, wanting to believe.

Twenty people were outside Prescott's dancing, drinking and laughing as they approached. The little corner structure had long, high windows that ran along two sides and the doors were jammed open. Inside, the crowd was five-deep from the door to the bar and at least seventy-five people were packed into the small space. Fifteen feet from the door was a beautifully crafted bar behind which one male and one female bartender were humping drinks. Deeper in and to the left, people were dancing.

It was a diverse crowd of working class bikers, college students, neighborhood artists, tourists in town for the Bicentennial celebration, and blacks drawn by the best jukebox south of 122nd Street. The fluidity with which people from each of the groups overlapped and intermingled amidst what seemed an entirely genuine live-and-let-live vibe was striking.

Jack shouted an order to the female bartender. The chairs at four small tables were all taken but there was room on a ledge that ran the entire length of the bottom of the window and once Jack squeezed in, Jackie sat on his knee. The sound was deafening so they drank in silence and checked out the scene. It was apparent they were the two youngest people there and that those around them were better looking, better dressed, better dancers and just plain hipper than any gathering either of them had ever been in.

Jackie was surprised that almost half the crowd was female and she studied the hairstyles, earrings, and clothes they wore. More striking, though, was the confident manner in which so many of them comported themselves. It was partly alcohol, partly the music and partly just old-fashioned fun, but there was also a defiant assertiveness she keenly appreciated, perhaps because she had never quite been able to muster it herself.

She put her mouth to his ear when 'Love Hangover' came on. "Whatta you say?"

He gulped down the last of his wine. She swallowed as much of hers as she could, then handed the rest to him to finish. The wine on top of the pot was nice but that was just for starters. What really took them away was the energy of the place and the music and they went to it through three more songs. When they made their way back to the window, he again slid in while Jackie positioned herself between his legs.

The music was all over the place and Jack knew them all. Every single one. The black ones, the San Francisco ones, the Detroit ones, the Mersey ones, the ones released before he was born, the Troggs, the Undisputed Truth, the Zombies, the Impressions, Little Stevie Wonder, little Steve Winwood, Norman Greenbaum, Junior Walker and the All-Stars, Sly and the Family, Shocking Blue – he knew them all. A guy sitting next to them asked about 'Who Do You Love' just as it was ending.

"Jack knows," Jackie said, certain she wasn't wrong.

"Bo Diddley," he said.

She shot him a glance. She was smiling because he was never wrong, he because she had so deftly set him up. Unable to sit still, they got back to it. As good a time as Jackie was having, she couldn't entirely escape the thought that maybe Jack was just another guy destined to fall by the wayside. If so, too bad. Too bad for both of them but mostly, too bad for him. Realistically, they only had until Labor Day anyway – why did she care so much?

Her mind drifted and she was absorbed in the music when it hit her that the reason she cared so much was that she was in love with him. She missed a step and shot a quick look to make sure he hadn't noticed, then got back to it, concentrating hard so it wouldn't happen again while searching desperately for reasons it couldn't be true. She had fought so hard against it, it *couldn't* be true. It was, though, there was no doubt about it. Suddenly, all that mattered was keeping him. She struggled to gather herself.

"You're a really good dancer, you know that?" She leaned close between songs, her voice strained from having to shout.

"You saying that is like Doctor J telling me I can play some ball."

She laughed and nodded toward the door. The party was going strong outside as sound filled the streets through the open doors and they easily fell into conversation with people around them. Jack knew it was because people were drawn to her and he was fine with that. She always included him.

As she talked and listened and laughed, Jackie searched again for ways that it couldn't be true. She couldn't be in love, not now, not when for the first time he had shown that he might not be in love with her after all. That would be so typical, to fall for a guy just when he had one foot out the door. But there was no way around it. However it had happened, there was no going back. The only thing to do was to make herself irresistible. Frequently he had said he found her irresistible. She would help him rediscover why.

He lit a joint, handed it to her and she passed it along. He lit another and passed it the opposite way and, to the warm air, the camaraderie and the music was added the sweet smell of marijuana. One last one he kept for them and a woman Jackie was talking to.

"This is Margie." She was around twenty-four, pretty, and had about her the sad look of too many one-night stands.

"Hi. I'm Jack."

"Jack and Jackie? I love it. Do you ever get mixed up?"

"We were both born mixed up," he said, "so it comes naturally."

"He's constantly talking to himself. That gets real confusing. Half the time, I don't know if he's talking to me or to himself."

Margie laughed. "You guys are good together. You should hold on for dear life."

"Hear that?" Jackie said after Margie had drifted off. "Can't forget the Motor City."

"Definitely the right song for tonight," he said.

He did just what she was hoping he would do and led her by the hand to a spot alongside the bar. He sat on a low wall and pulled her down onto his lap. His mouth on hers felt wonderful. She was weightless, completely dependent on him to keep her up and that, too, felt wonderful. Maybe it was the best night of their lives, maybe not, but there was nowhere Jackie would rather have been and no one she'd rather have been with.

"Nice hands," she said after they pulled their faces apart.

"Nice ass."

She laughed and ran a finger along his face. He pressed his mouth to hers and went to it with his hands again as every part of her that he explored came more fully to life. With his tongue around hers and his hand between her legs she didn't think it could get much better, but when he slid his hand under her skirt and along her ass as he ran his lips along her neck, wow, it did. No longer was she thinking about how she might entice him back. Instead she wondered whether anyone would mind very much if they went at it right there on the sidewalk.

Bright light intruded and they looked up to see a police car with its spot trained on them. He knew what she was thinking as soon as she recoiled sharply and looked at him.

"Don't worry, I'm clean."

He pulled her head to his chest so her eyes were shielded from the glare. They waited. Finally, he said, "Anything wrong, officers?"

There was no reply. Still the light wouldn't quit so the two of them sat motionless until it finally went out and the car moved slowly down the street. Music from inside continued to fill the street and the party outside showed no signs of slowing. Their personal magic had been broken, though, so they got up and went back toward the crowd.

"Whatta you suppose that was all about?"

"Cops justifying their existence, I'd say," he replied as they sat on the curb.

More than ever, he seemed much older than nineteen. Even what she had taken as the last remnants of boyhood like his candid declarations of love for her were, she now understood, a refreshingly mature openness. Until the last few hours, she had regarded that openness as a little game between them. Now she saw that she could go higher with him at her side than she had ever gone before and she vowed to pull them through their trouble. She put her hand on his arm, appreciating anew the importance he placed on touch.

Words could be faked in ways that touch couldn't.

"What?"

"Nothing." She ran her hand over his arm until he blushed and looked away. The color in his face was as beautiful as that day at the lake. "Handsome."

The Bicentennial build-up had made its way even to bohemian New York. There were notices of events in the coming week wheatpasted to walls and lots of red, white and blue. Atop one building a Bennington flag flew, the distinctive 76 in the blue field looking very sharp.

"Looks like you've got some New York grime on your new sneakers," she said.

"Looks like you've got a little New York grime of your own." She had slipped out of her left shoe to reveal a thin black streak on the top of her big toe. He put his finger in his glass and wiped the mark away and she wiggled her toe until they both laughed.

"I love this cobblestone road," he said of the stretch of Harrison Street where they sat. "Aren't we pretty close to where the big celebration will be on the Fourth?"

"Yes," she said, looking south in the general direction of Battery Park.

"I guess this place will really be hopping," he said, meaning the bar, although he might as well have been talking about the neighborhood or the entire city.

"I'm really looking forward to the Counter Bicentennial rally in Philadelphia you told me about," she said. "And you don't mind rushing back up here for the fireworks?"

"Of course not," he said enthusiastically. "They're both gonna be great."

"You don't think the fireworks thing is lame?"

He sipped wine from her glass. "Nothing I get to do with you could ever be lame."

She felt a rush of excitement in her chest. She wanted more than anything to go back to Susan's spare bedroom, but she wanted it to be his idea.

"Jackie, I'm sorry," he said. "About before. I acted like a jerk. I – "

She put a finger to his lips and forced him to meet her eyes. The effort he was making was as good as making love. "What would you like to do now?"

"How's about one more dance? Then we'll see if maybe they'll sell us a bottle of wine."

"Sounds great," she said. "We can find a good spot to watch the sun come up. And woe be to anyone who messes with us."

"I like that. Woe be to anyone who messes with us." He looked past her and his eyes got big. "Oh, my God. No, don't look. I just saw that guy Bluto. He's hiding behind a car, making his way down the street like he's on a commando mission."

"You better be joking." She was fairly sure he was but his poker face was good. "Help, help. Somebody save me."

"He says he'll let me go if he can have you."

"Oh, that's nice."

He put his arm around her. "Over my dead body."

"Why don't we go inside so it won't come to that?" She ran her hand through his hair. His light was definitely on but it was in need of brightening. Still work to do. "Besides, you owe me one more dance."

They made their way to the end of the bar. One more dance turned into an hour and a half of high voltage fun and she provided most of the fire. Of all the dancing done by all the people there that night, nobody could touch what she did for a stretch that went on right to closing time. People around them danced better because of her.

Jackie was oblivious to that. She gave herself to the music and moved with greater passion than ever, even more than on her birthday, for herself and for him. He made her feel beautiful and if he needed re-captivating, she would show him how beautiful she was so it would be impossible for him to not love her back.

Whenever she looked at him, he was watching her. Each time she smiled and kept going. They could make love later or not – it no longer mattered. She danced so dancing was as good as making love, grooving on until she lost herself in that primal place again and there was nothing but the exhilaration of her body in motion and the gorgeous guy who was always close by. She was in love with him, and as never before with herself, and while the music lasted that and the exultation of movement were the only things that mattered.

SIXTEEN

Nobody at Jefferson Park cared that he had played in the state tournament at the New Haven Coliseum. To those he didn't know, he was just one more white boy. What happened there on their court and not some newspaper clippings about long ago games would determine who could play and who couldn't. That was fine by Jack. It played well with his distaste for people riding on their reputations or bragging about the stuff their parents could afford. He knew there were plenty of guys in town better than he was who had never so much as tried out for their high school team. Talent and dedication and determination mattered, but those were items that could be purchased and not everyone had sufficient scratch, like with the rest of life. Why would basketball be different?

Set where it was in a tough stretch of the East Side, the park was intimidating even by the last hours of daylight. That was part of the drill, for it kept away the meek and rattled newcomers. Jack felt its affects at first but after a few times up and down the court, he found his game. It wasn't his A game; he had left that behind at the high school gym the last time he played seriously – what was that, fifteen months now? A-/B+ wasn't so bad, though. Besides, he wasn't out to prove anything. Or at least that's what he told himself.

He looked around at the black faces. He wondered what they thought of him or if they thought of him. They said nothing and interacted not at all beyond the game. That left him with little more than the awareness that they knew him better than he knew them, and that was about as uncomfortable as it got.

It helped that he a few of them had been teammates. Others he had played against. Several he went all the way back to Little League with including Gene, the one of the group he knew best. Most he didn't know but that was okay. The game was what mattered and it was nice to be flying through the air again. Most stimulating of all was the challenge of bringing it with guys who could play and of finding a groove with his four teammates. Finding a groove and a way to win.

His team kept winning and played on. There were no lights in the park so they started up right away each time. When his team finally lost, Jack got a drink from the fountain and sat on the grass. The sun was about gone and most everybody who wasn't playing had drifted off. He was thinking about doing likewise when Al Armstrong, one of those he knew from Little League, passed him the last of a bottle of cheap wine.

"Wish I had more." Al was skinny as hell but a good player.

"Yeah, too bad it's past eight o'clock," Jack said.

"Time ain't the problem. There's a place right down the street where we can cop." Al took several crumpled bills out of his pocket. "Just a little light."

The prospect of passing a couple of bottles around was suddenly appealing and Jack dug out a five-dollar bill.

"Yo, Taylor." Al called to the far end of the court to his main man Taylor, who had stopped momentarily along with everyone else in the game while Gene chased the ball down. "You good for five?"

"Yeah."

"He's good for it," Al said and Jack produced another five. "Be right back."

The last game went to twenty-six and ended in darkness before Gene's team won. Five minutes later, it was just Jack and Gene. Taylor had gone for the bathroom and never come back.

"You know where this place is Al was goin' to buy wine?"

Gene looked away. "There ain't no place, man. There ain't no wine. He went to cop but it wasn't at no after hours liquor establishment. How much you give him?"

"Doesn't matter." Jack snickered. "Call me naïve."

"You ever see anybody play hoops wearin' long sleeves and it's eighty somethin' degrees out?"

"Like I said," Jack said as he rolled a joint. "Call me naïve."

"Sorry, man. I shoulda said somethin'." Gene had seen so many lose their way to drugs, he sometimes forgot that not everybody knew of that world. Plus he was sick and tired of watching it. So many he knew thought they could navigate it safely but none ever did. No one ever won. Not against scag, the undefeated heavyweight champeen of the world.

Jack would miss the ten bucks but Al was gone and that was that. He asked Gene about a serious ballplayer the two of them had known named Leon.

"He's upstate."

Jack was stunned. "In the joint?"

"Wasn't talkin' 'bout UConn."

"How much was he carrying?"

"Two years' worth." Gene drew in and held the smoke in his lungs. "Went down for a second time. Got lucky the first. Not so lucky the second."

Last Jack knew, Leon was playing hoops for the community college. From there, people who acted like they knew said the next step was somewhere big. Syracuse, somebody said. It could just as well have been baseball, Leon was that good, going all the way back to the four years of Little League they played together.

"Last time I saw him he was going to school."

Gene turned away and rolled his eyes. "That was a scam by somebody. He was a ballplayer, man. Couldn't read and couldn't write. That shit can fly in high school, maybe even college, but not for him. Too much pride." He took the joint back. "He had enough of sittin' in classrooms pretending he knew what was going on."

Jack had never dealt with Leon at that level. Instead he was used to being told what he wanted to hear because he couldn't see. Wouldn't see. A guy with a chance to get out – why? Because he had a serious game of basketball? Call him naïve and smack him upside his white head. *You will never know. Can never know. You think you know? You don't know. Play all the Coltrane you want and maybe even get some of it but you will never know.*

140

"You don't wanna be here this late, man." Gene took one last hit. "There's games every night. Come run whenever you want."

Jack looked around. It was very dark. Very black. "You need a ride?"

"No, I'm good." They exchanged a soul shake. Black Gene smiled and disappeared into the black. "Next time, bring your own wine."

SEVENTEEN

Jackie lay with her head on a pillow, watching. Jack was looking out the bedroom window of his apartment, stiff and remote, staring vacantly through the open blinds, though there was nothing to see except the building next door. The air had cooled since a brief shower just before sunset and a soft breeze filled the room.

He was waiting for her to fall asleep. He knew she would try to find the right thing to say and he didn't want to be bothered. Bad enough to fail so miserably at something he so desperately wanted to be good at; he would not compound matters by politely talking about it. Instead he would look out into the night until she fell asleep.

She was struck far more profoundly by how he was acting than by the fact that he had been unable to perform. He had allowed her to see him vulnerable on several occasions, after all, and it was one of the things she liked most about him. It was a testament to the weird thing called masculinity that he was reacting as he was. She knew it was related to the trouble that had surfaced that night in New York and that it could get out of control very fast.

Three weeks before, she would have closed her eyes and gone to sleep. Three weeks before, she wouldn't have known what else to do. She would have believed unfailingly that some guy not being able to get it up was somehow about her. But Jack wasn't some guy. He was the one who made her laugh on every occasion they were together, the one who always found the right thing to say when she most needed to hear just the right thing.

She got up and moved across the room so quietly that he turned his head abruptly when she touched him. Instantly she felt the tension in his body. As though pretending she wasn't there, he returned his gaze to the darkness as she took a deep, silent breath.

Setting her sight on a point on his back, she slid both of her feet so she was almost directly behind him. Slowly she ran her hand up his back and then down, up and then down, up and then

142

down. She turned her hand over and ran the back of it the whole length of his back the same way. She did the same with the tip of her right forefinger and then with the tips of all five fingers. At first touch, his back had relaxed. Now it was tightening again. She thought for a moment about taking a different tact, that for whatever reason he still wasn't willing to come to meet her. She was willing to go as far to him as necessary so she focused greater energy on the tips of her fingers.

When she moved so her hair brushed ever so lightly against his back, she felt his body stiffen. Through her fingers, she knew it was an entirely different kind of tension. When he turned slowly to face her, she let her hand run along his skin until it rested on his chest. She could see in his eyes that he was ready.

He dipped to pick her up, but he didn't pick her up to carry her as she anticipated. Instead he took hold of both sides of the bottom of her ass and lifted her straight up so she had to grab quickly for his shoulders. She opened her legs and he guided her down with one hand while taking hold of himself with the other. She wasn't quite as ready as he was and she let out a gasp when he went inside. By the time he turned them so her back was to the wall, however, she was ready.

Up and down, slowly at first, and more gasps. They both gasped and grunted and moaned as they went from slow to medium and then fast. Before long they crossed over to a frenzy of movement. On previous occasions, he had demonstrated a willingness to shift gears and coax her to climax. She was having none of that this time. She was in a hurry and she urged him on.

His back and every other part of him was full of the tension she had detected through her fingers. She locked her hands and wrists behind him, squeezed her legs tight against him and pumped back as hard as she could while they propelled themselves frantically but in perfect rhythm toward a magical oneness. She couldn't get there fast enough. She was so deep in it that all awareness of being vertical slipped away, nor did it much register when her ass slammed against the wall several times. They could have driven themselves through to the ground outside for all she cared.

"Go, go."

Her face tightened and her eyes closed hard. She wasn't going to miss, that was certain well before she reached the point of no return, yet for longer than ever before she dangled in a state of uncertainty that was as tantalizing as it was delicious. As fast as the torrent of pleasure flowed to her brain, it couldn't flow fast enough. There was no way she could thrust any harder, but still she couldn't get to the end that was so clearly within reach. It was a wonderful, helpless, exquisite feeling.

When she finally came, she buried her face in his skin. All of the waiting and teasing had been worth it and waves of pleasure rolled over her. He was emitting all kinds of beautiful sounds and the fact that it was happening to him made it better for her. When she absolutely, positively thought he had to be through, he kept bringing it and she squeezed her arms against his back as hard as she could to let it flow over her. Even as he softened he pressed close and currents of pleasure pulsated through her.

They remained frozen for a long time as they both slowly went limp. She felt as light as a feather wrapped around him that way. Her breaths were shallow, yet with each one she took in the raw smell emanating from his pores. It was an intoxicating scent with a dash of danger about it. He rubbed his face through her hair as if grateful, as she too was, that just the slightest touch from it had helped him get in gear. She loved that he dug her hair, that he dug more and more things about her all the time, little things they never spoke about and that she had never thought much about prior to realizing they drew him closer to her. That power, too, was intoxicating.

They let themselves down and lay on the floor for a long time. It was dark and quiet and there was nothing to say or do. She was entering new ground. He joked about the spell she had over him and there was so much in how he acted to indicate it was true. That in itself was powerful, the combination of him being in love with her as well as being so open about it. But now she was in love with him and not only was there little to do about it, she had no desire to do anything about it other than keep going. On all counts it was different from the other guys she had crushed on.

She was on new ground in other ways besides with him. Doors were opening and new ways of living were within reach. Her life was better than it ever had been and the future was full of promise. All of the confusing, frustrating days didn't seem so bad anymore because each, in their way, had brought her to where she was. She wasn't sure where that was exactly, but it was definitely a great place and it made all the confusion and frustration worth it.

Still, there was something in the way, something she couldn't yet get past. There was a need to keep something all for herself, to not let him know how she felt. She wouldn't deceive him and it was possible he would pick up on how she felt even without her verbalizing it, but for some reason she didn't entirely understand she wasn't ready to say how she felt. He said he didn't care, that he was in love with her even if she wasn't with him. Maybe it was true. She would see.

"You have such a musical name, you know that? Jacqueline Elaine Gendron." He was running his fingers along her stomach. "And a great belly button."

"Jacqueline Elaine *Marie* Gendron," she said.

"Even better. Jacqueline Elaine *Marie* Gendron."

There was something he wanted to say, she could sense it. Was that more evidence of love taking hold, the knowing that someone is going to do or say something before they do or say it? It was a daunting thought that would have to wait for another time because she felt too good to be daunted by anything.

"So much for not being able to get it up," he said finally.

She tried but she could not hold in a giggle. He got back by tickling her furiously. Resistance was futile so she gave herself over and laughed until her sides ached. When at last she was able to say "That's not fair," he stretched out on his stomach and let her do it to him. She wasn't sure at first but he kept his hands away and she worked his sides until he laughed as heartily as she had. Straddling him, she grew ever friskier as she poked and probed with her fingers. When she rolled him over, she was delighted to discover that he was hard again.

EIGHTEEN

Jackie's friend Janet picked the flyer for the march and rally in Philadelphia on July 4th up from the table as if doing so would help her better understand. They had gone around twice and Janet still didn't get what the big deal was. She looked intently at the bold words in large type before her.

Jobs and a Decent Standard of Living
Democracy and Equality
A Bicentennial Without Colonies

It all seemed reasonable enough. Though Janet wasn't sure about the colonies part, why would anybody have to go marching for any of it? Didn't most everybody have those other things already? And wasn't all that marching stuff over with?

Jackie hadn't expected Janet to decide to come along. She had, however, hoped to get her to understand why she was going. It sounded so straightforward when she talked about it with Susan and Jack. Like Jack, she was excited by the prospect of being part of a huge throng of like-minded people for the first time. It would be a way to put into practice things that so far existed only in her head and her heart. What those things were wasn't so easy to pinpoint, though, and that's why she wasn't getting through to Janet.

Janet drove through the same city streets and saw the same people with hard lives that she did. She even had a hilarious knee-jerk animus for their spoiled high school classmates from wealthy families. There was a connection between those two, Jackie knew, the difficult lives of the many and the comfortable lives of a few. Susan had a way of making that connection clear. As young as he was, Jack did, too. It wasn't as easy for Jackie. She wasn't ready to give up, however.

"What better way to honor the American Revolution than with a march for democracy and equality?"

Janet remained unconvinced. "I don't know. Sure seems like a weird way to spend the Fourth of July. I mean, Jackie, this is gonna be the biggest Fourth ever."

"I know," Jackie said. "And we should celebrate. But there's more to it than that. Some people have everything and lots of people have nothing. That's not right."

"I know blacks still have it bad, but what can you do about it?" Janet wasn't arguing, she sincerely wanted to know. "Is going to a march going to change that?"

Jackie believed it was everyone's responsibility that everybody be free.

Democracy and freedom were without meaning unless they applied to all. None of it was given, it had to be worked at and worked for.

"It could," Jackie said.

"And all the way to Philadelphia?" Janet looked at the flyer again. "Why don't you just come with us to the beach to watch the fireworks? There'll be kegs and hundreds of people."

A classless society, people living cooperatively, no hierarchies. It was real and it was doable. As Susan said, that was pretty much how humans lived for most of history.

"We could do both," Jackie insisted. "March and celebrate."

The other part of it was love. More than anything, Jackie believed in love. The kind of love she felt for Jack, the love she had for Susan, her love of all the people in the world, a love of life. People lived to be loved. If they missed love, they missed living. So many people did, too, and it didn't have to be that way. Somewhere, amidst all the hurrying and all the work, there had to be a way to make sure everyone was loved. And in a better world where there wasn't any hurrying or all that much work, it would come naturally. People would love each other as naturally as they slept and ate.

"Was Jack really in Jefferson Park with that guy who got shot by the police?" Janet had given up on trying to understand.

"Not when it happened," Jackie replied. "They were playing basketball a few hours earlier."

148

It was past eleven when Janet left. At midnight, when her parents went to bed, Jackie went to the window overlooking the yard. Below was the garden, subdued in the moonlight but beautiful nonetheless. When it called to her, she responded.

She slid the screen up, stepped onto the deck and went down the steps onto the moist grass. Amidst the stars she spied the lights of a jet six miles above the earth moving across the sky. The soil was cooler than the grass and she hesitated for a moment before lowering her bare backside down to the earth. She lay with her legs apart and rubbed her thighs against some of the plants. The soft ground was as comfortable as any bed.

She moved her arms and legs the way she did to make angels in the snow, then rolled over and rested her forehead and the tip of her nose to the ground. She had thought many times of sleeping in the yard naked as she was, but anyone finding her there wouldn't understand. They never understood and she had never been comfortable enough to relax and sleep without worrying about being discovered.

She was relaxed this time. She was relaxed because she was happy, and she was happy because of Jack. She thought of a time when they would make love in the garden and lie the night through with the earth as their mattress. He was so at ease with himself that she couldn't help but be at ease with herself just from knowing him.

She lay on her back and listened to the sounds of night: leaves rustling softly, the music of early summer insects, the late train coming in from Grand Central. The skin of her stomach and thighs was sensitized and acutely alive to the gentle touch of her fingers. The scent of skunk spray filled the air and she opened her legs and let that inside as well.

She wanted to call Jack right then and have him come to her. He would come, she knew, and she loved him for that. Better still would be a time when she could go to him whenever she desired, a time she would show up at his door and wake him out of a sound sleep knowing he would love her in just the right way. For now, she dreamt of him.

She awoke not knowing how long she slept. It couldn't have been very long, for everything was as it was before, including the wonderful smell of skunk. She wished she could find the exact spot and roll around in skunk spray until it became a part of her in the same way the earth and the night air were a part of her.

As she climbed the stairs, her body speckled with soil and mulch, she looked again for a moment at the garden. Then she showered as she often did before bed, though she had no intention of sleeping. She was burning to live and love and do even at that hour and sleep was such an awful waste of time.

After an hour with her journal, she was unable to concentrate any longer because of the sirens. She hadn't minded at first. There was a musical beauty to the distant sound that was just the right backdrop to the words of love she wrote about purple bellflowers and Jack's kisses. No matter the delicacy of the sound, though, sirens weren't beautiful. Had they stopped, she might have been able to continue. But the sound went on and she knew that somewhere not very far away someone's life was on fire.

NINETEEN

"We might be the only white people there, you know," Jack said on the way across town. They were.

The gathering on July 3rd was originally planned as the beginning of the East Side's weekend long Bicentennial celebration. When Officer Brian Donohue shot Al Armstrong in Jefferson Park, however, the event was changed to include a speak-out on police violence. People were singing along to the Gil Scott-Heron record that was playing over a loudspeaker when they arrived. *America is like Johannesburg.*

Some in the crowd glared at the two of them. Others welcomed them with smiles and friendly looks. As they slowly made their way through the throng, Jack kept an eye out for familiar faces. Amidst the overwhelmingly black gathering was a group of Puerto Ricans. Ringed around the outer edges of the park were a large number of police officers, one black, one Puerto Rican, all the rest white.

The MC introduced himself as a one-time member of the Black Panther Party for Self-Defense. An experienced, razor sharp speaker, he alternately had the crowd cheering, laughing and clamoring for action. He ridiculed and taunted the cops and compared the ongoing state violence in the city's black neighborhoods to recent events in Soweto. Others who addressed the crowd echoed that theme.

The speakers were good at saying what they had to say quickly and the MC kept things moving. In between, he had everybody chanting. Along the way, he interjected more lightning fast jabs at the chief of police, President Ford, the board of Gulf Oil and the NAACP. Some in the crowd cried out for them to march to the nearest police station. Then Al Armstrong's mother was introduced. She announced that plans were in the works for a march later in the month and the crowd let out a collective yell. She exhorted each of them to talk to their neighbors and garner support for both the march and the creation of a committee of everyday people to oversee the police.

The MC then led the crowd in an even longer round of spirited chanting. Many people turned so they faced the cops rather than the stage as the rage at the dramatic spike in police violence in recent years spilled over. The chanting grew louder as it progressed and a number of people punctuated the chants by throwing their fists in the air. Though the sun was relentless, people yelled on in unison and cries that they go to the police station were again heard. Even after the MC brought that portion of the day's activities to a formal end, people continued to give spirited voice to their anger.

'Johannesburg' came on again and people shifted from chanting to singing. Though the song rang out as powerfully as ever, it had the effect of disarming the crowd. Gradually people stopped singing. When the song ended, a few left. Most began slowly to move in the direction of the picnic tables for the scheduled barbecue. Others set out rounding up kids for the organized games scheduled to begin at one-thirty. The guy Lawrence who had told Jack about the event one day at the library approached. They exchanged a soul shake and Jack introduced Jackie. He was one of the event organizers and it was obvious he had more important things to do than chat with them but chat for a few minutes he did and Jackie immediately felt more at ease. From the touch of his hand, she knew Jack was more at ease as well.

Gene Moore came up from behind them with his girlfriend and a few friends who Jack knew vaguely. After introductions, they stood talking as people around them continued to make their way to the bus stop or toward the food spread. Gene was especially friendly to Jack and made a point of presenting he and Jackie to Mrs. Armstrong, Al's mother.

As the small group of them talked, Jackie mostly listened. Gene, his girlfriend and their friends were much like the MC in how effortlessly they flowed back and forth from hysterically biting commentary on the state of the city to angry outbursts against the police. It was informed in ways that lectures in social studies never were and full of raw insights direct from people's experience.

Jackie noticed the easy way Jack combined small bits of black English with his usual speech. She had seen him do something similar while talking to his hard-core white working class friends. The next time she spoke, she smiled to herself, noting the difference in her own speech.

The tension she had felt earlier was gone. She was proud of Jack for the easy way he moved among different kinds of people and of how respectfully Gene and his friends dealt with him. She also noticed the barely perceptible ways he made sure she was completely included. When he stepped back so a small space opened, she moved close and he put his arm around her as naturally as he might brush a stray hair back into place.

A part of her wanted to stay and partake in the barbecue and the day's music. She saw the chasm between the people around her and the world she inhabited, but she also saw the possibility of something else: not the erasure of differences but a day when differences would unite rather than divide people. Something about staying was too weird, though. Too difficult. There were differences, oppressive differences, and there was no wishing them away. No kid she knew had ever been shot by a cop and the people in her neighborhood did not wake up every morning to a power structure that despised them. People would welcome the two of them, even go out of their way to put them at ease, but they would still be two white kids in a crowd of black people surrounded by a large number of white men wearing blue uniforms and guns. Perhaps next time.

"Glad you came." Gene walked with them a ways from the crowd. "Nice meeting you."

"Nice meeting you, Gene," Jackie said.

"She plays some serious hoops," Jack said.

"God, Jack."

"Yeah?" Gene smiled.

"Don't listen to a word he says."

"I'm thinkin' point guard," Gene said. "Weavin' her way through the press smooth as can be."

"Smooth as can be is right," Jack said. "And she plays above the rim."

"Damn, girl. You should bring it around some time." Gene looked at him and then at her. "I do believe somebody's in love."

With barely a glance she saw Jack wince ever so slightly. "I hear you're a really good player," she said quickly.

"Yeah, well, on that note ... " Gene exchanged a soul shake with Jack. "Keep in touch."

Near the edge of the park, a woman approached and Jackie saw it was Miss Adele Williams. They put their arms around each other and Miss Williams gave Jack a big kiss on the cheek when Jackie introduced them.

"God bless and keep you, Jacqueline," Miss Williams said in parting. She didn't say anything about having lost her home.

On the way to the car, they spied a woman with beautiful brown skin who had addressed the crowd. She wore a black armband and was collecting donations to cover expenses so they detoured her way and put some dollar bills into the can she was holding. The woman smiled without breaking stride in the conversation she was having and handed them a flyer about a follow-up meeting at the community college.

The next day was the Fourth and they rode the train to Philadelphia with Susan and Walt for the Counter Bicentennial. It was the most diverse group of people they had ever been a part of and there was a revolutionary spirit amidst the industrial blight and poverty of North Philly that the rebels of 1776 would have appreciated. Among the historic buildings downtown that many North Philly residents had never visited, meanwhile, a significantly smaller, virtually all-white crowd attended the official celebration.

154

Susan ran into many people she knew and made a point of introducing almost all of them to Jackie and Jack. Walt was more inclined to deep conversation and he was engrossed for long stretches with several people they met. In the sea of humanity they came upon a group from NYU and, to their delight and astonishment, one from Keene State. Also present was a contingent of Puerto Ricans from back home who they recognized from the rally in Jefferson Park and spoke with for some time. Before moving on, they shared their addresses and phone numbers with a woman named Lourdes who was working on the march Mrs. Armstrong had mentioned the day before.

The rally and march through the streets of Philadelphia were inspiring and joyous experiences as well as an intense day-long seminar. Someone announced from the stage that they were fifty thousand strong and they gave their voices to the group's collective cries. Drawn by some spirited drumming, they fell in near a contingent of the American Indian Movement. Close by were Vietnam vets who led those around them in poignant and often hysterical anti-militarist refrains set to the traditional cadence chant. Throughout, the two of them took in a large collection of leaflets, newspapers and pamphlets.

Afterwards, when Walt announced that he was staying over, Susan's first thought was that it was a woman. He knew she was committed to getting back and she couldn't help but think that he had intentionally waited until the last minute to spring this on her. Whatever her suspicions, she wouldn't confront him in front of Jackie and Jack. She forced herself to believe that his story about "old friends" might actually be the truth and, after a late afternoon cloudburst, set out with Jackie and Jack for the train station.

Jackie was able to enjoy both the event in Philadelphia and the official spectacle in a way Jack and Susan envied. The evening before, she had turned an excursion in a huge crowd in sweltering heat to see the Tall Ships into a fun experience. Jack especially was taken with her zest, for he was in love and alive as never before. The enthusiasm she possessed was a rare and difficult thing to come by and so much better than the cool detachment that was so important to so many people he knew. He basked in her joy and even more in the fact that she wanted to be with him.

Something was smoldering inside her that had not been there when they were younger. Perhaps it was the coming of womanhood, perhaps it was a more generalized accumulation of wisdom. Whatever it was, she was overflowing with ideas and love and a desire to change the world and he was thrilled to be a part of it. It was all the more thrilling when she said she saw those things in him.

On the train to New York, though Susan answered their questions about the literature they had accumulated and some of the people they had met, she couldn't focus. Walt was not a last minute guy. In fact, his inability to deal with improvisation drove her crazy. That was one of the reasons she liked spending time with Jackie and Jack. Their spontaneity, their energy, their unabashed joy at being together – she remembered being like that. She drew on it so as not to let her gloom about Walt spill over onto them.

"How was Peter Frampton?" Amidst the other events of the week, they hadn't talked about the concert in Colt Park three days before.

"Oh my God, Susan." Jackie squealed with delight. "It was so good. Even Jack had a blast."

"You were a holdout from the Frampton bandwagon, Jack?" Maybe he still was. Susan understood. Sometimes the event was beside the point. A beautiful night shared with someone you're crazy about can be enough.

"It was so weird," Jackie said excitedly. "Frampton ran out to start his set and he fell right off the front of the stage."

"Poor guy."

"Nobody knew what was going on for like fifteen minutes," Jackie went on. "We were all wondering if they were gonna have to cancel. Then they started playing and they did a great show."

"Who's up next?"

"Jefferson Starship and Fleetwood Mac," Jackie said. "It's gonna be great. You guys should come. It's a beautiful venue in this really nice park."

"Jefferson Starship's doing a free concert in Central Park this week," Susan said. "We could see them there if you want."

"We can do both," Jackie said.

"*You two* can do both," Susan said and they all laughed. "And at the risk of sounding like an old foagie, Jackie, I've gotta say, as good as Jefferson Starship may be, Jefferson Airplane they ain't."

"Oh, my God, Susan." And, after she shot a smile Jack's way, Jackie was off on a detailed account of the night of her birthday.

It was easy for Susan to be in the moment in their company. Much as with them, music had really begun to matter to her in high school. In college, it was hooked into the upheaval all around until music and revolution became inseparable: Smokey, Dylan, Sun Ra, Joni. Keep on pushin' because the world's waiting to be seized. Freedom Now. It may not be televised but it will definitely be amplified. Nina Simone and Eric Burdon wailing in tandem toward liberation. And here were little sis and boyfriend madly in love with the music and each other and sure enough falling in love with revolution. How beautiful the future.

Philadelphia had been packed with people and activity, but it was nothing compared to New York. Much of the world appeared to be converging on the West Side for the Tall Ships and the evening's festivities, like V-E Day, the Central Park Mobe and the Miracle Mets all rolled into one. High without a drug, the three of them laughed and shouted as they made their way through the throngs at Penn Station to the subway. In seven years in New York, Susan had never seen anything like it.

On the way to the subway, they ran into a couple Susan knew vaguely from the neighborhood who had been at the rally and had ridden back on the same train. The ride downtown was like New Year's Eve. The main bulk of the riders were seeking a good place to view what was being billed as the fireworks display to end all fireworks displays. Others, hopelessly late and doomed to sit or stand far from the action, were heading to Battery Park for the symphony concert scheduled to precede the fireworks. People got off in droves at every stop and headed west. They were replaced by equal numbers heading further downtown in the hopes of getting as close as possible.

When Susan advised them that her neighborhood was undoubtedly so swamped with people that there was little likelihood they could get anywhere close to a good viewing spot, Jackie and Jack didn't hesitate. They exited at the next stop and set off at a rapid pace in the direction of the Hudson. The streets they traversed along the way were filled with music, people, firecrackers and motion.

It had been a long day, but Jackie's energy never waned. She pushed on, excited about what was to come while also in the now. He pushed on as well, excited about the big night but excited mostly because she was excited and because they were together. They weaved through, among and around hundreds of people, pressed close as one. The going slowed as they got closer to the river and the mass of humanity thickened. They tried different streets, probing and dodging drunks who thought it funny to throw firecrackers at passersby. Finding no openings, they were forced several times to backtrack and try elsewhere.

New tides of people kept coming and time was running short. The view from some spots was obscured by buildings, while other places with good sight lines were inaccessible because there were simply too many people. She was about to suggest they ditch when he led her to a row of wooden police horses lined along a fence on the other side of which was a large concrete construction barrier. Most of the barrier was behind a building but a small portion that jutted past it would make for an excellent viewing spot. The only problem was that there was no way to get to the top of the barrier. There was a ledge halfway up, but it was too high and too narrow to get to by pulling oneself up.

"We can hop that fence easily enough," he said. "If I boost you up to that ledge, you might be able to pull yourself up."

"How'll you get up?"

"I'll just listen from down below," he replied.

"Jack, no way."

She studied the layout. There was no way to go forward and get close enough to see anything. The music of the symphony concert had ended and it was just a matter of minutes before the fireworks would begin. Amidst the rising noise of the crowd, she explained what she had in mind. They each took a deep breath and shared a smile.

Figuring there was no sense in him struggling all the way up if she couldn't make it, she went first. Once he'd given her a boost onto the police horse, she stretched her left leg as far as it would go across and way, way up to the top of the fence. She stopped only long enough to bring her second leg up and then stretched it across an equal distance at an equally difficult incline to the ledge on the barrier. There was nothing to hold onto, no way to fully brace herself, yet she was able to pull her other leg along so she stood perfectly square on the narrow abutment. One inch the wrong way and she might fall the eight feet to the ground, so she pressed tight against the concrete slab.

A buzz surged through a portion of the crowd as people became aware of what she was doing. Getting to the top from the ledge would be as difficult as all she had done thus far, probably more so, for the distance was almost as high as she was tall. Watching from below, Jack didn't think it possible.

Somehow she was able to reach with her arms and pull so both feet came six inches up and swing her right leg all the way to the top. It was the only way, yet it still seemed impossible. Her anchor foot was hardly secure and should she fall from such an awkward position, she would have no control over how she landed. Jack started to climb the fence so he would be in a position to catch her but he froze, fearful that any move he made might startle her. Just when it seemed she was in a hopelessly untenable spot, she pulled herself up to the top with power that defied her slight frame. More than a few people applauded.

Jack was as amazed as any of them but he had no time to linger over how she had done what no one else in the throngs around them had even thought to try. Twice he slipped off the horse. On the third try, he was able to mount it and right himself. His balance wasn't as true as hers, though, plus his feet were almost twice as big, and three times he almost fell. Finally he steadied himself and the only thing he heard was her soft voice from above. Just before someone crashed into the police horse and sent it toppling, he stepped up and over just as she had. He overstepped crossing to the ledge, however, and just did pull his back foot across in time to keep from going down. The rest should have been easier for him because of his height but he struggled in a way she hadn't. Twice he had to let his feet back down to the ledge and start over. Finally, with great effort and utilizing every bit of his strength, he pulled himself up.

She welcomed him up with a hug and a goofy smile and they moved to the part of the barrier that protruded beyond the adjacent building. It wasn't as comfortable as the twenty-five dollar seats at Battery Park, but they had an unobstructed view of the Statue of Liberty and the fireworks. Others tried to follow, but no one was able to execute all the necessary steps. After one guy fell from the top of the fence, he and his friends took apart one of the horses, threw it over, re-assembled it and climbed on top. Even then, the first one only made it up with Jack's help. Subsequently, Jack and the first guy were able to assist two more guys and a girl up the same way until there was no more room. Everyone introduced themselves, Jack fired up a bone and just as the last traces of the sun disappeared, the city whose numbers seemed to have doubled for the weekend roared with delight as the first of the fireworks exploded against the night sky.

The pyrotechnic display was terrific as such things go, and the two of them remained well past the grand finale, soaking in the scene. Getting down was only slightly easier than getting up but they made it and, upon descending, fell in with the dispersing crowd. They walked downtown for blocks surrounded by animated conversation. Amidst the horde, the night people were out: freaks, partiers, slummers, whoever and whatever, people who didn't need a reason to get crazy and celebrate.

She rolled her hip into him and he made like he was going to fall until she laughed. She turned sideways and looked at him, forcing him to look at her. They had talked once before about how great Sunday nights were and this was the Sunday night to top all Sunday nights: nothing to get up early for, a flawless New York night, and a national celebration to boot. She took his hand, squeezed hard and swung their arms as she might have done had they been first graders walking home from school.

Many blocks later, they arrived at Susan's. She and some neighbors had decided on a street party and they were at work in a kitchen full of food. Susan's beat-up black and white television had been moved out of its corner hiding place and they had watched the fireworks as they worked. Jackie accepted a glass of wine and joined the talk while Jack showered, then the two of them exchanged places.

Susan and her friends remained behind when they ventured out to Prescott's. The overflow crowd spilled onto to the surrounding streets, drinking, dancing, and laughing amidst talk of the Tall Ships, the fireworks, the symphony concert, the Mingus concert across town, the Bernstein concert in Central Park and of street gatherings everywhere. It wasn't so different from any other wild night at Prescott's, yet different it was.

Susan and her friends arrived with food, wine and a grill. There was so much food that it took several trips to cart it all. Neither Jackie or Jack was much interested in the drink or even the pot that somebody broke out. Instead, they helped with the food and with making sure everyone who wanted some got some. They ate as they did and occasionally joined with those who were dancing. Though Susan objected, somebody set up a collection can and people threw money in as they ate.

Susan could get down and get down she did. She danced with Jack, she danced with Jackie, and she danced with a few of the stray guys who asked. She was all woman and utterly irresistible and every guy who wasn't with a woman, as well as some who were, wanted to be by her side.

When Prescott's closed at four, it became an exclusively outdoor party. Somebody got a tape player and the air filled with Jimmy Lunceford's rendition of 'Annie Laurie.' That was when Susan really got to it. Only a small portion of the crowd could jitterbug so much attention was focused on those who could, and Susan most definitely could. Jackie could, too, but she wasn't sure about Jack until he took her by the hand.

"You go and I'll help," and she went and he helped.

There was nothing left but to head for the roof. They grabbed the largest sleeping bag from Susan's hall closet and climbed up to a beautiful sky full of stars. There were taller buildings all around, yet they felt as though they were on top of the world. From the street below, 'Sing Sing Sing (With a Swing)' was up and they made love to Gene Krupa's tubbing. Afterwards they lay entwined, lost together somewhere between awake and not awake, their senses heightened. Exhaustion never felt so good.

It seemed only minutes later that they awoke to blazing daylight and a Manhattan cacophony. They craved sleep but the day was already too hot, too bright and too noisy. They lay sideways facing each other and she buried her face in his chest in a doomed attempt to evade the sunlight. He folded his legs and maneuvered the two of them deeper into the sleeping bag. When they were as far inside as they could possibly go, he pulled the flap over to keep the rest of the world out.

TWENTY

The job in New York provided Jackie good cover with her parents. There was no set schedule to the interview project so that gave her greater leeway and she was able to spend parts of some work days with Jack and many nights with him either at his place or at Susan's. They had to be on guard because of her folks, however, and in his ever inventive way Jack worked to lighten the tension. He arranged for the two of them to rendezvous in the last booth of a greasy spoon or beside the newsstand at the train station while pretending to have been separated for an unbearably long time. He never failed to play his part to the hilt. Once he appeared from the shadows with a fedora covering half his face, another time wearing ridiculously oversized sunglasses. It was corny and Jackie forgot their coded passwords more often than not, yet she couldn't help but notice how genuinely happy he was to see her every time.

They crashed an unbearably pretentious party at a loft on Spring Street one night and a boisterous kegger back home at the Point the next. They got familiar with the New York City subway system, memorized much of the schedule of the New Haven Railroad, and experimented with every possible vehicular route between Connecticut and Manhattan. As he was still working at the library as well as doing the interview project, Jack perfected the arts of catching an hour's sleep on the train and of making an hour's sleep enough.

They worked as hard as they played. After two weeks, Jackie's duties were expanded beyond interviews so that she was doing research and writing as well. She worked long hours in dusty archives and at the library on 42nd Street. The further she dove into the stories behind the women she interviewed, the less important days at the beach became.

She learned about sit-down strikes, slowdowns, flying squadrons, Don't Shop Wear You Can't Work, and women who went to jail fighting for their rights in the workplace. She read about the songs they sang, the skits they performed, and the meals they collectively cooked. She learned of the men they loved and fought with and loved some more, and of how the kids got looked after. She learned of the difficult, sometimes contentious and not always successful efforts of black women to get white co-workers to consider the world more broadly. She read about victories won and lessons learned, as well as of defeats that left some broken and others more determined.

She spent hours in poorly ventilated basements, lost in the past and the lives of women who became her heroes. The staffs at several libraries came to know her by name and offered tips that proved immensely helpful. When Susan hooked her up with colleagues at Columbia, NYU and the CUNY Grad Center, Jackie explored new gold mines of material. Along the way, she dreamt of writing and telling the stories of women whose lives were more interesting than the Queen of England's or Jackie Onassis's could ever be. She imagined what New York was like in 1933, what life and love and work anywhere were like in 1933. She had an eye for color as well as detail and without anyone caring that she was Susan's sister, funds were approved for her expanded hours as well as for an increase in pay. The work she did was worth every dime they paid her.

Since her folks insisted that she spend some time at home, she bunched her work hours, working from early morning until it was time to catch the midnight train. Jack and Susan were used to long hours even in summer, and many were the times that Jackie worked the last third of the long haul in an otherwise empty building alongside one or the other or both. Sometimes they pushed each other. Other times, overcome by the long hours, they cracked up laughing and gave up. Along the way, Jackie discovered she possessed analytical skills, an understanding of history and human behavior, and a passion for justice to a far greater degree than she had known.

They ate cheaply and remarkably well at the city's vast array of ethnic restaurants. They took in free concerts in Central Park, inexpensive high-quality plays on the Bowery, and traveled to Harlem with Susan for a jam-packed event marking the short, re-markable life of Ruby Doris Robinson. They walked wherever the streets took them in twilight, that wonderful time that was neither daylight or dark but both simultaneously, reveling in the heat, the endless asphalt and concrete and the mass of people. More than once they covered the four plus miles from the office to Susan's place, walking for blocks in silence, looking, exploring, studying a uniquely-shaped building or the intense way that old Puerto Rican men played dominoes. Other times they were engulfed in deliriously serious talk about Victoria Woodhull, Albert Ayler and everyone and everything in between. They went to demonstrations when the Democrats brought their sorry show to Madison Square Garden, meeting new people and discovering new organizations of resistance. And on many nights they went to Prescott's to dance for hours while drinking as little as they could get away with. Three songs for a quarter, fifteen for a dollar.

They explored their home city, the city they had lived in their entire lives, as keenly as they did New York, seeing it in a new way. They walked through woods they didn't know existed and amid the ruins of a huge amusement park. They walked in the surf of the Sound in a section where hardly anyone ever swam and crabs were so plentiful that virtually every step meant get-ting nipped on the foot. They discovered thriving machine shops in dead looking buildings in the unlikeliest places and rode their bikes past factory crews eating lunch in the outdoor heat, heat that everyone else complained about but which the workers found a welcome relief from the insufferable heat indoors.

Bicycle was the best way and whenever they rode Jackie took them through the small park near her house. Twelve years be-fore, her sister Veronica told her the park was a favorite haunting ground of the Headless Horseman and that to go there was to risk

being whisked away forever. For years, Jackie wouldn't set foot
in the park and she never forgot. If Veronica had meant to frighten
her, she succeeded – or perhaps Veronica had believed it, too?

No sooner had the sun set on the celebrations of the Bicentennial than fissures that couldn't be hidden erupted. Upheaval everywhere, in Seabrook, New Hampshire, at the AIM trial in South
Dakota, in workplaces, prisons and marriages. There were wildcat
strikes by Kentucky miners and militant strikes of rubber workers
in Akron, auto workers in Detroit and nurses in Seattle. Interna-
tionally, there was more revolt and repression and still more revolt
in the Soweto bantustans and a general strike in the Polish city
of Radom where Jack's paternal grandfather was born. Close to
home, Jack walked the picket line at the Westinghouse factory on
State Street with the rank and file network he belonged to. In many
other places, too – sometimes too many to keep up with – a steady
DRUMbeat of uprisings.

All the while, Jackie and Jack fucked like crazy. They fucked
early mornings at Susan's and evenings at his place. They fucked
at the beach, in the observatory, in the balcony of one of the
vintage movie houses on downtown Main Street, and in the ladies'
room at Fred's bar. She showed up at the library one afternoon
and fifteen minutes later, they were getting to it in the stacks. They
walked in an open door in their old grammar school and went at
in the seventh grade classroom. She bought a tattered copy of the
Kama Sutra for experimentation's sake, only to discover that it
was the edition without pictures. No matter; they didn't need help
figuring out how to experiment. Best of all, she had to admit, was
his eagerness to go down on her, again and again, and the fireworks that went off in her head made the Fourth of July's look like
amateur hour at the church hall.

They made sure that sex didn't sidetrack their friendship. And
they were friends. They talked for hours and felt as good as they
did making love. She took to brightening his apartment with plants,
dishware, framed prints, and a bookcase and asked him to make

her tapes she listened to while working around the house. Best of all was his favorite, a frenetic bootleg version of 'India' with Trane flying as though continued life on planet Earth was at stake. Fast as the speed of light. Free. Music to live by. She let it flow over her and came to know and love him even better from listening to it.

Other than the concerts at Colt Park, which they went to in a large group, they guarded their time together jealously. Other friendships sagged. Jackie especially noted a widening divide between herself and people she had been close to just months before. Just as Janet had been unable to understand the Counter Bicentennial, other friends could not get with interviewing old women who used to work in department stores and garment shops. There were many things like that, things that only Jack got immediately and in the same way she did. More and more, when she looked forward, Jackie saw school and she saw Jack. Other people and other parts of her life were rapidly receding in the rear view mirror. Rather than being sad, she was exhilarated. It was as though she had never really known another human being before.

She smiled to herself more than once at the realization that this is what Jack, the sexy sly devil, had predicted would happen. Not that she would admit yet to anyone she was in love, least of all to him, but there was no doubt that his prophecy had come true. He noticed that girls looked at him differently when he was with her and on the few occasions when he cared, he could only wonder that he was desirable in a way he had never been only now that he was insanely in love.

What neither of them realized was how much the glow within radiated outward. Love, desire, friendship – it was all of those things but it was more than all of those things. It was also the mutuality of what they felt. The desiring and the having were great but knowing, absolutely knowing, that each had the other's back no matter what the situation was unbelievably powerful. Even the friends of Jack's who thrived on intimidation and mocked the slightest sign of affection by any guy for any girl couldn't badger him into conforming to their code of behavior. She knew to be on guard about being too obviously a sexual being around guys like that, around any guy really, yet that was their problem. She had to watch that they didn't make their problem her problem, but she refused to suppress what was surging inside for anyone.

They weren't just a couple, they were a duo, and as July lengthened they came to believe they could do anything together.

TWENTY-ONE

"That was nice," Susan said as she and Walt rode the elevator up to his apartment. It was like many of the nights out when they first began going together: jazz, a good meal, and animated conversation without Walt's anger and without Susan feeling guilty. Perhaps the rest of the night would be more like the beginning than the recent past. Each time they were together was a potential turning point, Susan believed, after which they might be as they had been. Once, it had been common for them to pop popcorn and watch old movies all night. Other times, they put soft music on and talked more openly about themselves than either ever had. Often, they made love that was as intense as it was leisurely.

"Yeah, it was." He took her jacket and carefully hung it in the foyer closet.

"Thanks for dinner."

Walt's apartment in an old Upper West Side building was simple and not in any way ostentatious. Unlike many of the men in their circle, he walked the walk. Someone visiting for the first time would have been more likely to guess it was the home of a transit worker than a college professor.

Unlike Susan, Walt's idea for the rest of the night did not include popcorn, the Late, Late Show or lovemaking. Though he was tired from having romped away the afternoon with Mary, that was not the reason he would go immediately to bed. He would do so because he knew of Susan's burning desire for intimacy and he reveled in the power it gave him. He knew their nice night out had gotten her hopes up and he looked forward to her reaction when she discovered he had nothing more in mind than a good night's sleep. He smiled to himself, relishing the hold he had over this beautiful woman with the long litany of lovers and the endless number of men who would have her in a heartbeat – if only they could see her striking out yet again with her boyfriend on a Saturday night.

He moved away as soon as he realized she was going to put her hands on him. "I think I'm gonna wash up and hit the hay."

"So early?"

"I had a long day," he replied, still without looking at her.

"I know you did, honey."

"And I've got a long day tomorrow," he went on. "You know that."

"I know," she said. "That's why I thought … "

He went into the bathroom and closed the door partway. "What's that, baby?"

She leaned against the wall and listened as he brushed his teeth. Normally not one to live for weekends, she had been looking forward to this one ever since he had suggested going out. Now here it was, Saturday night, and he was turning in earlier than he did during the week.

"Nothing."

The affairs were a benefit of teaching Walt had not anticipated. After five years, they were about the only good thing left about the job and he looked forward to the beginning of each new term because of them. There was nothing quite as exciting as calculating during the first week of classes who among his eager female students he would end up making. The larger classes presented the most possibilities and his colleagues marveled at his willingness to teach Intro every semester and in both summer terms. As the semesters passed and he got comfortable with the routine, Walt was able to carry on with two and sometimes three Intro students at a time.

Not only were Intro classes far and away the largest, the women were younger and less likely to have developed a hard edge. Not that he minded the ones with hard edges – they knew the drill and generally got right to it. But a part of Walt despised them for their experience and their easy availability. Far better were the starry-eyed ones and the preliminaries that went with making them. He loved the way they flattered themselves that their brilliant professor had fallen for them and they for him. True, there was a greater risk of messiness with the younger ones; for starters, he always had to check the school records for any who might not yet be eighteen. But so far he had been able to get even the least experienced and most heartbroken among them to see that there were worse things in the world than trading several months of sex for an A.

"I'll be out in a sec, honey." Walt was certain Susan wouldn't press. Dinner and jazz were more than they had done together in two weeks and he knew all too well how she took progress in small increments. She might stay up for a while to brood, but she wouldn't push toward an argument on a night when they'd actually enjoyed themselves. Still, as he thought about Mary's lean young body and her invitation to fuck some more the following afternoon, he couldn't help sticking the needle in.

"Since we're going to bed early, we could go out for breakfast and then do something afterwards. Maybe go to the park?"

"Walt, I told you I have the women's meeting tomorrow."

"I didn't realize it was in the morning," he said innocently after he'd rinsed his mouth. "Can't you re-schedule?"

"We did twice already," she replied. "Can't you re-schedule what you have in the afternoon?"

"No." He went past her and got into bed. Even in the good times, Walt didn't like for her to initiate sex. She knew doing so now would make matters worse.

"Is it absolutely out of the question that you not go?"

"Absolutely," he said as he switched off the lamp on the night-stand. "Well, if you have to be up for your meeting maybe you should get to bed soon. Good night."

Susan stood peering into the dark bedroom for a long while, unable to see anything. "Good night," she said finally.

TWENTY-TWO

At ten minutes past seven, the twenty-two people sitting in a circle in a rundown classroom in the community college got down to the business of the evening. News had come down that Al Armstrong was out of the hospital. The early fear was that he might be paralyzed. Now, however, he was expected to make a full physical recovery.

Besides Jackie and Jack, ten of those in attendance were black and ten were Puerto Rican. Amani, the woman collecting money at the first rally at Jefferson Park, was chairing and she began with introductions, emphasizing that people should keep their remarks brief. Jackie was to Amani's left so she went second. She spoke briefly and a bit nervously about having attended both rallies at the park and, with a glance toward Lourdes, the Puerto Rican woman they had met in Philadelphia on the Fourth, about having gone with Jack to the Counter Bicentennial.

Jack was even briefer. He touched Jackie's arm to indicate that what she had said applied to him and then stated simply that he had been a union member at the Brass and was involved in the rank and file network. Most others spoke in greater detail, with Lourdes translating from Spanish to English as needed and Amani having several times to request that people cut their remarks short. Some in the circle took notes. Others read the leaflets and newspaper articles that had been left on a table at the entrance. Jackie, meanwhile, listened closely as a segment of the city's population that she knew little about opened up before her.

They moved on to a detailed discussion of the second rally that had been held in Jefferson Park. Overwhelmingly, it was hailed as a huge success. Of perhaps as much significance as the large turnout was the determined spirit of the day, a spirit manifested in the presence of seven new people at the meeting. The mood in the room was upbeat and there was a definite sense that the committee was making great strides, though everyone agreed on the need to keep the pressure on. For some, that meant increased outreach to churches and community groups. Several people thought a demonstration at police headquarters was in order while others emphasized the need to push black and Latino politicians to play a more active role. Most people thought they could and should do all of those things and no option was presented as mutually exclusive of any other.

Several people stressed the importance of organizing whites to get behind the committee's work and Jackie was sure they did so at least in part to help her and Jack understand there was most definitely a role for them to play. Amidst determination that sometimes boarded on anger and unequivocal condemnations of the white power structure, the two of them were never made to feel like anything but allies. As she listened, Jackie wrote down the names of friends of theirs and began formulating what she'd say to try and get them interested.

Neither of them spoke again until an hour in when Jackie asked if certain of the committee's goals were a higher priority than others. Several people nodded or smiled to acknowledge that it was a good question and a half dozen in all addressed the point. All were in agreement about the need for a civilian review board, but only a few people were enthusiastic. Several emphasized pushing for the indictment of the cop who shot Al Armstrong, plus those who had shot, beaten or otherwise brutalized a long list of Puerto Rican and black people in the recent past. Others emphasized movement-building and the need to get as many people as possible involved in ongoing efforts to both curb police violence and tackle some of the myriad other problems that afflicted the city's residents.

As the discussion deepened, the difficulties and triumphs of the work in progress came more fully to life. Juan, a Puerto Rican who worked in a factory that manufactured light bulb fixtures, talked of his efforts going largely ignored by the overwhelmingly white workforce while admitting that none of the few Puerto Ricans had shown much interest, either. Another Puerto Rican, a teacher at the community college named Roberto, talked of how he was constantly having to remind other Puerto Ricans that, while the two most recent victims were black, many others in recent years had been Latino.

Lourdes, who had said in her introduction that she was a GED teacher, underscored the importance of outreach to youth. Young people in her classes were outraged and ready to act if the right vehicle could be found to reach them. She suggested they think in terms of a series of events that could both build off each other and appeal to different constituencies. Amani picked up on that and spoke of how many of the black teenagers she worked with as a social worker at a youth center had come to the rallies.

One of the blacks, Morris, worked in the GE factory. He also spoke of needing to reach youth and thought the coalition should not write off those young men already organized into self-defense groups. Some called them gangs; the better term, he suggested, was common sense survival units. With the proper guidance, their deeply entrenched sense of solidarity and collective action could be expanded to include marching, picketing and perhaps even patrolling the police.

Two hours in, the first person got up to leave. When a second also got up, Amani stopped the discussion and asked about everyone's availability for another meeting. No decisions about actions had been made and it was agreed that, barring an emergency, none would be until they met again. The two people on their way out promised to come next time and the meeting resumed. Before many minutes passed, however, others got up to leave and Amani again brought the discussion to a temporary halt. Tasks were divviedup, all present vowed to keep getting the word out, and, after Roberto assured them that space was available at the college, another meeting was set for the following week.

They went until nine forty-five. Amani and Morris were the last of the blacks to leave. A core of the Puerto Ricans, Jackie, and Jack remained, talking on less formally but just as seriously. An energetic man named Carlos returned to a point he had made earlier, that no elected officials should be invited to whatever they decided to do. He switched midway through a sentence to Spanish and hesitated until Lourdes encouraged him to go on. He stopped every few sentences so she could translate, and several times she asked him to clarify something he had said. Others chimed in occasionally with their own interpretations until Carlos stopped and apologized in English to Jack.

"No, continuar," Jack said. "Hablamos espanol."

"Verdad?" Lourdes said.

"Si."

"No, *el* habla espanol," Jackie corrected and for the first time all night, there was laughter.

"Tu hablas muy bien." Lourdes smiled as she addressed Jackie.

"See, right there," Jackie replied, "you lost me.'

"She said you spoke your one sentence of Spanish very well," Jack said, and to everyone else he added, "Ella habla Latin muy bien."

"Latin?" Roberto said.

"Si. And Italiano." Jack smiled. "Tu hablas Italiano, si?"

"No, habla Italiano *no*," Jackie said to more laughter.

"But you do speak Latin?" Lourdes asked.

"Yes, unfortunately," Jackie said. "I wish I had taken Spanish."

"Don't be sorry about it, Roberto said. "It's a good skill to have. Besides, if you learned Latin, it won't be hard for you to learn Spanish."

"Well, I'm picking it up little by little from him," Jackie said, indicating Jack. He had been telling her for a month that Spanish would be a breeze compared to Latin and she poked him in the ribs with her pen.

As the seven of them filed slowly out of the room, they shared stories about the Counter Bicentennial. Lourdes was cautious in her appraisal until she heard how stirring it had been for the two of them. As she listened, Lourdes was transformed from one who had experienced the frustration of the event from the inside to seeing it through the eyes of two newly inspired people who had experienced it as the good thing it had been.

"We're going to Mimi's to eat," Lourdes said. "Would you like to join us?"

"Thanks," Jackie said, "we'd love to."

"Mimi's?" Juan said with a smile. "Great. Seaweed soup, coconut milk and raw corn on the cob."

Jackie looked at Lourdes. "Vegetariano?"

"Si. Tu?"

"Si," Jackie replied. "Los dos."

"Tu?" Juan said to Jack, surprised, and Jack nodded.

"Muy bueno," Lourdes said happily. "I knew it was just a matter of time before we were able to start a vegetarian caucus." She took Jackie by the arm. "You speak and understand Spanish better than you think."

"Grazie," Jackie said. Jack had taken to studying and speaking Italian to her that week and it came out by mistake but entirely natural.

"And Italiano, too, like I said," Jack said, and the four of them laughed.

TWENTY-THREE

"Hey, if it ain't the Great White Hope. Just the man I wanna see."

Frank O'Toole was a year older than Jack. They played football together in high school and had never liked each other. Frank had been a popular guy good with girls who relished reminding Jack that he was neither. He was also a linebacker. In the world of linebackers, most quarterbacks, even good ones like Jack, were pussies. Worse, Jack also played basketball. To Frank, that made him both a pussy and a nigger once-removed.

With Frank was his sister Cindy. She was a year younger and, like all of the O'Tooles, popular, and it was strange that the two of them would be hanging around the diner parking lot at that late hour with just each other. They spoke quickly and aggressively so Jack had little choice but to engage. They didn't bother to introduce themselves to Jackie and cut Jack off when he tried. Instead, they launched into a long spiel about their sister Peggy the relevance of which befuddled Jack. Finally, they came up for air and Cindy turned to Jackie.

"I know you, don't I? Where do I know you from?"

"Kindergarten."

"Holy crap." Cindy was ninety-five percent feral. Whatever she felt or thought, that's what anyone around her got. "Mrs. Barker. But you ended up going to Catholic school, didn't you? And high school."

Frank wasn't happy with the digression. "Hey, Miss America. Can we stick to the point here?"

"What exactly is the point?" Jack was about to walk away but they had said something about their sister Peggy, who he remembered well, being in trouble.

In scattershot fashion, they gave him more of it. Amidst the avalanche of words, five stood out: *Day three of cold turkey.* When he asked why they didn't take Peggy to a hospital, Cindy looked at her brother as if it was taking all of her strength to hold her temper. They explained again that Peggy had been in two hospitals already and came out worse each time because of perverts and lesbians who took advantage of her, talking slower so Jack would be sure to keep up.

"What do you even want us to do?" Jack said. "We don't know anything about scag."

"You don't have to do anything," Cindy said. "We just need a place to take her. We heard you got your own apartment."

Without Cindy or Frank noticing, Jackie had moved right up to their car. "Oh, my God. Peggy."

Peggy was twenty-two but could have passed for thirty-two. Propped against the door in the back of the car and seemingly oblivious to anything around her, snot ran from her nose. She was so thin and frail she could have been an advertisement for starvation relief.

"You know my sister?" Cindy asked in disbelief.

"She … from the swim team at the Girls Club."

Peggy as a twelve year old swimming and enjoying herself was far, far away from Cindy. Jackie might just as well have said they explored Jupiter together.

Frank eyed Jack. "Is Goody Two Shoes here gonna help?"

"Hey, we don't need this," Jack said. "Why are we supposed to even care what happens to your sister?"

"He didn't mean it," Cindy said, glowering at her brother. "Moron."

"Sorry, man," Frank said. "You gotta understand we're under a lotta strain here."

Jack knew they were being snowed. The question was how much. He could see Peggy was in trouble. Every other part of the story might have been a lie, but it was clear she needed lots of help, help that Cindy and Frank were incapable of providing. He wasn't as ignorant about scag as he claimed. His buddy Ed from work had gotten started with it in Vietnam and one day while they hiked in

Kent, Ed talked for hours about the war and his addiction as con-joined parts of the same nightmare. How killing other people and the prospect of killing more morphed into killing the pain and then finally to killing himself. His determined vow to quit upon coming home lasted four days. Saigon or Connecticut, the hell inside him was the same. The only difference was that the drugs in Saigon were better. It had taken dozens of tries before he finally quit, cold turkey, just as Peggy was apparently attempting.

"Peggy's no lesbian," Cindy was saying. "No way. It was the drugs and those freaks. Each time she went in, she came out ten times worse."

Jack was no longer listening. Neither was Jackie. Instead she moved closer, looking at him, waiting for him to look at her. Final-ly he did and without a word they decided what they would do.

Cindy eyed Jackie, trying by force of will to make Jackie's imagination take her to the parts of the story that went unsaid. In Jackie she saw a soft little girl, all pigtails, ribbons and bubble bath and likely to recoil in horror at the worst parts of Peggy's story, the parts about rape and trading sex for drugs. Cindy was sure Jackie could see it, could see herself in Peggy's place. She would be a sniveling, helpless piece of prime lamb fought over by nasty peo-ple should she ever be so unfortunate. Cindy knew they could get Jack if they got Jackie.

"You got sisters." Cindy was staring at Jackie. "Imagine that happening to one of them." She turned to Jack. "You got sisters, too. Would you send one of your sisters back to a place like that?" She knew he might think for a moment about his sisters, but that mostly he would think about Jackie.

"We just need your place for tonight," Frank said. "You two don't even have to stay. We'll handle it."

Jack looked at Frank and in a tone he'd never used even on the most vicious days on the practice field, said, "You responsible for this?"

"Fuck you talkin' about, Jackie Boy?" Frank used the name he and the other guys on defense used to taunt Jack.

Jack knew Frank wouldn't back down even while asking for a favor. He wouldn't back down because he didn't know how and never would. Though Frank wasn't as solid as he'd been in his linebacking days, he was still a big guy and Jack knew he'd have to move quickly. In a flash, he took hold of both of Frank's arms and pulled hard on the left sleeve of his shirt until it tore. Frank pulled back but he was too slow and Jack twisted his arm. Jackie and Cindy, uncomprehending until that point, stepped forward and gaped at the ugly track marks.

"What'd you do, turn your own sister on?" Jack said.

Cindy screamed at Frank as he tore himself free. "Is that what you did? All this time actin' like you didn't know anything."

"That was a big mistake, Jackie Boy," Frank yelled as he stormed off. "I know people."

"Let's go," Jack said as he moved toward Peggy. Cindy's reaction to Frank's track marks had been raw enough but Jack couldn't help but think maybe it was part of the show. It didn't matter. They would do this without her, either, if need be.

"Whatta you gonna do?" Cindy's voice was shrill but Jack ignored her as he looked over Peggy in a desperate attempt to determine exactly what they were getting into. He tossed Jackie his keys and opened the backseat of Cindy's car.

"I got a right to know what you're gonna do," Cindy said.

Jackie had started toward Jack's car. She stopped. "You want our help. We're helping. Don't ask so many questions."

"What the - "

"Follow Jackie," Jack said as he got in next to Peggy. "Gimme everything you got about this. And don't leave out the parts you don't want me to know."

Cindy got in the wind not long after they arrived, promising to return in the morning. Jack didn't even notice. He was thinking hard, trying to come up with something, but his thoughts were all over the place. He went forward, pretending, knowing that Jackie was afraid and trying not to let her see that he was, too. They turned the cable spool on its side and pushed it into the kitchen. In its place they laid out a quilt, blankets and pillows.

Peggy curled up in a mass in the fetal position. She had no idea where she was, nor did she give any sign that she knew who they were. She was shaking uncontrollably and no matter how many sheets and blankets they added to the pile, she couldn't get warm. Her skin was cold and clammy and beneath the blankets she rubbed her arms. Worse than the cold and the sweat and the itching and the snot was the intense pain in her stomach. It never subsided for very long and when it returned, she howled for relief. As she howled, she clutched her midsection as though she might exorcise the ache if only she could squeeze hard enough.

Jack toweled her face as best he could and spoke her name. There was no way to know what she could feel or sense, but he knew they had to communicate to her that she wasn't alone. When Jackie returned with more towels, she took his place and he moved more things to create additional space. There was too much about this he didn't know, however, so when he was done he put forward their other option: calling an ambulance.

"We can't do that," Jackie said. She looked at him the way she had at the diner. "Jack, I can do this if you can."

He started to say something but stopped. Five feet one and maybe a hundred pounds, and she was the toughest person he knew.

"That guy Ed you told me about – can you call him?"

He called Ed at a pay phone the graveyard crew at the Brass used and clinically summarized the situation. He looked at Peggy as he sat on the floor close by, absorbing everything Ed said. When he repeated what Cindy and Frank had said about Peggy's hospital stints, Ed confirmed that it was a common scenario. He also assured Jack they were doing the right thing and that nothing bad would happen if they kept their heads. Twice he said they'd be alright and Ed rarely said anything twice. When he did, people took it to the bank.

"Just don't let her fall asleep on her back and expect lotsa puke, lotsa fight and no sleep. And call me anytime during the night. I'll stop by in the morning as soon as I get outta here."

Jack turned to Jackie as soon as he hung up. "We should make a run to the store before it gets worse. I hate to ask you this but maybe you should go. She looks weak but she might be more than you can – "

"Make a list."

"Just score some shit for me," Peggy said looking at Jack. "You think I don't remember you. I know who you are. Little freshman, staring at me all the time."

"Just try and sleep, Peggy," Jackie said softly.

"Get a load of Little Miss Muffet." Peggy looked at Jackie for the first time. "You ever made it with a girl, sugar? I'll do things to you your boyfriend here hasn't even dreamt about."

"You probably won't hurt so much if you don't talk," Jackie said.

"I'll do whatever you want, muffin." The shaking started again and Peggy struggled to keep it at bay. "We'll get high together. It's like goin' to heaven. Nothin' can touch it. Sex, coke, speed – nothin'."

She was remembering it the way it was in the beginning, the magic that had long since worn off. It was good now only in short bursts. Mostly it was medicine to make the pain go away. No more getting high, she fixed to get straight. Back and forth between straight and sick, with a little rush in between that was no longer worth it. But it had its hands around her throat and it wouldn't let go.

"Whatta you say, muffin? I bet your muffin's sweet as candy."

"Peggy, stop with that already," Jack said.

"I heard you before talking about Frank and how he – " It was too painful for her to say out loud. She thought back over the last – how long had it been? So much of it was a blur and time no longer had any meaning. She had gone the usual route: snorting, skin-popping, then finally hitting the mainline. It was only when she was pretty far gone that she discovered Frank was able to keep it at chipping. Chipping became a challenge, something to live for: if he could do it, so could she. That lasted two weeks. Chipping. That was a laugh. Only she couldn't laugh. She surged up from the floor and Jack grabbed her from behind by the shoulders so she couldn't stand up as Jackie moved toward them to help.

"It's alright, I've got her." He lowered his hands so they were around her waist and her arms were pinned by his elbows. Jackie picked up the list.

"Aspirin," he said as Peggy struggled against him. "Something for diarrhea. Paper towels. We'll need food for her tomorrow. Soft stuff. Soup. Ice cream. And a can of coffee for us. Take money. You know where it is."

"I've got money," Jackie said

"Take it anyway so you can get plenty of stuff."

Peggy lunged forward. "Why don't you save yourself a lot of trouble and give me the money. Whatta you say, muffin? I'll eat you 'til you beg for mercy."

Jackie hesitated in the doorway as Peggy thrashed about.

"Jackie, we don't have to do this. You – "

"I'll be back as fast as I can."

Peggy fought hard but her determination could not make up for what she lacked in strength. She tried to spit in Jack's face but her mouth was as dry as a bone. Eventually, she lay back down. The pain in her stomach teased by subsiding just enough for her to think she was past it, only to return with a vengeance. Nothing had yet been invented that could bring relief except the drug itself, and that they refused to give. She squeezed herself tight and rolled up again, but there was no crushing the pain away.

For a moment, she slept. When she awoke, she had no awareness of having done so, unable as she was to understand time and place and sleep. The unrelenting pain in her stomach, that's what she knew. It had been hours, days, time gone by that she couldn't remember and still the ache was there. It would never end and she would rather die than put up with it any longer.

Jack wondered what her passions had been. He thought about the year they were in school together. She was right, what she had said about him. She was like many of the older girls, only more so: sassy, confident, breasts bulging through tight blouses, alternately amused and annoyed by the gaping of fourteen-year old boys like him. She shivered, oblivious to his presence, and he pulled several blankets up so they covered her.

Jackie walked through the room as quietly as she could. When she returned from the kitchen, she had a glass of water for Peggy and three falafel sandwiches. She set the water down, handed Jack two of the sandwiches and took over toweling Peggy's face.

"You used to be friends with my sister, you know."

Peggy looked at her blankly. "Oh, it's you. Who's your sister?"

"Veronica Gendron."

"You're Ronnie's sister? You're *that* Jackie?" Hell lifted and a look of wonder took hold. It lasted until she realized she was about to crap in her pants.

They got her to the toilet just in time. She went in torrents and made agonized noises while they waited just outside the opened door. The odor was rancid and lingered even after Jack sprayed the room several times. Peggy sat on the toilet for many minutes, still shaking and still sweating while they debated whether they should give her a shower. Her body odor was strong but they knew she would fight the whole way. Of greater concern than what she might do to them was that she'd hurt herself. They decided against it. They could live with her smell.

Jackie got clean clothes from the stash she kept in the bedroom and helped Peggy dress. Then she pulled Peggy's hair back into a ponytail so she more closely resembled the girl she remembered. Jack brought a comforter and every clean sheet he had into the bathroom and they positioned cushions near the toilet and the tub lest Peggy hit her head while thrashing about. In no time, she was back to shaking, sweating and swinging unpredictably from cooperative to combative. She recoiled when they gave her the anti-diarrheal, but they were able to get a good dose down.

The pain in her stomach never failed to return. The moments she clutched herself so tightly that they thought she might break were the moments they were most helpless. Between stretches where her only sounds were those of pain, she spoke in fast bursts. She still wanted to fix and, failing that, to die, though she stopped with the profanity and the propositions.

Jackie lit a scented candle and put it on the floor as far away from Peggy as possible. Jack sat close to Peggy with his back against the wall. They were sufficiently used to the shaking and the sweating and the way Peggy constantly grabbed at her stomach so that they could sip coffee while she did all those things. Bearing in mind Ed's warning that she might vomit at any moment, they took turns coaxing her onto her side and kept close watch.

"This could go on for hours," he said. "Maybe you should go before it gets too —."

"Can we stop with that already?" Jackie took a sip of coffee.

Jackie had drunk two cups of coffee in her entire life. The hazelnut made it easy going and in no time she was buzzed. When all seemed clear with Peggy, she went to the kitchen and returned with a refill and the clock radio.

"If it's like this tomorrow night, maybe we can go to the lake," he said.

"That would be nice."

"If you put on WCBS," he said, pointing to an outlet behind the door, "they'll have a report on the Olympics in a few minutes. Eight eighty."

"I thought you didn't care because of all the patriotism and the boycott and the lousy way they dealt with the African countries." She looked at him but he just shrugged and sipped his coffee. "Are you interested just because I'm interested?"

"Were there any gymnastics today?"

"No." She turned the volume up slightly when she found WCBS. "You think any of the Romanian guys you play baseball with are following it?"

"Don't know," he said. "So, yeah, tell me about Nadia. Is she really that good?"

She turned and faced him. "Oh, my God, Jack. She's unbelievable."

When the vomiting began just before four they moved Peggy back to the toilet. She hadn't eaten in days and it wasn't coming easy. She couldn't fight against it so she fought with Jack and almost hit her head on the toilet. When she was done, they maneuvered her into a sitting position against some pillows they'd propped against the wall and set a basin in her lap. No sooner had they relaxed than she started again. Some went in the basin, some on her shirt, and the rest went on the floor. They rushed her back to the toilet but all she did was dry heave. Exhausted and without hope, she lay on the comforter while Jack cleaned up the mess and Jackie fetched another clean shirt.

"Is that really worth it?"

Jackie ignored him and pulled the dirty shirt up over Peggy's head. Like much else about her, her breasts had shrunk and her bra hung loosely away from them. She was shivering more violently than before and Jackie put a shawl around her shoulders once she got the clean shirt on. The shivering stopped but her stomach began cramping and she clutched hard and rolled onto her side. When it subsided, she lay shivering and sweating, unaware once again of them or anything else besides the pain in her stomach.

They sat hoping against hope the worst had past while knowing somehow it hadn't. They turned the radio off and sat for long
stretches in silence as they drank coffee and waited. Jack was
ever curious, though, especially about Jackie, and soon he had her
talking about Paris, Venice, Copenhagen, Amsterdam and the other
places she had visited with her family. He listened with great interest as she talked of museums, churches, castles and architecture
but as with so many things, what interested him most was her – her
perceptions, her opinions, her observations, her insights. It was
great for her to re-live so many pleasant things, to share with him,
but eventually she stopped.

"I feel bad that I've been to all these places," she said, "while
you haven't had a chance to travel at all."

"I've been to Buffalo," he said proudly. "I bet you've never
been to Buffalo."

She laughed and loved him that much more for making light.
"Where would you go if you could go anywhere, with money no
obstacle?"

"Well, I'd be travelling with you so it would have to be somewhere you haven't been yet," he said. "Old cities in Europe that
aren't commercialized, where there's no McDonald's or Kentucky
Fried Chicken. Prague maybe or Budapest. Definitely Helsinki.
Let's start with Helsinki."

"Alright, we'll go to Helsinki first. It'd give you a good reason
to learn Finnish."

"Hey, I started to learn Finnish when I was going out with a
Finnish girl."

"A Finnish girl who wouldn't put out, I gather," she said, smiling.

He laughed. "A Finnish girl who wouldn't finish."

She laughed loudly enough that he had to shhh her. "Maybe it
wasn't her who wouldn't finish."

He shook his head in mock outrage. "God, that is ice cold."

"Poor girl," she said. "She's probably wondering to this day what she had to do to get some sex." She so enjoyed teasing him, particularly since he always took it so well. Sometimes he even seemed to encourage her. She was especially glad they were to a place where she could rib him about his prior ineptitude with girls. Looking at him, his face flushed red, her remaining doubts about Peggy vanished. She knew they would make it.

Peggy sat up shivering. As soon as they covered her with blankets, she began sweating. "Where am I?"

"Don't worry about that now," Jackie said. "Just try and sleep."

"How will anyone ever love me again?" Peggy was sufficiently aware to notice that Jack had gone to the kitchen to make coffee. "How will any man ever love me?"

She thought about some of the things she had done in the last year as well as about the things she had said to Jackie earlier. She had brought the ugliness that had come into her life to Ronnie Gendron's little sister, the young girl in the yellow bathing suit who had once admired her so. When Jack returned, she put an unsteady hand to her face so he couldn't see her clearly. This was the worst part so far, the self-loathing, worse than the smell of diarrhea and the uncontrollable shaking.

"Peggy, you're a beautiful girl," Jackie said. Though Peggy was thinking of how men would see her, Jackie knew she needed a woman's voice. "I always loved your hair. I wish I had red hair like yours."

Peggy smiled shyly. "You're just saying that because you feel sorry for me."

"No, it's true." As if to prove the point, Jackie stroked Peggy's ponytail. "Once when I asked Jack who he had the biggest crush on in high school, he said you."

Peggy moved her hand from her eyes and looked at him. "Is that true?"

"It is," he said. "And I wasn't the only guy in school who did, believe me."

"But you could never feel that way now." Peggy laughed but her voice contained ten thousand tears. "You know what guys will see? They'll see the same thing my father saw when he almost killed me. I sit in the bathtub for hours and hours and hours trying to wash it all away. But it doesn't go away. It never will."

Jackie moved closer. "You feel that way now, but it'll change when you're better. You'll see. And when you're better, some man will see what Jack and the other guys saw. And any of them that don't see it, well, too bad for them."

Peggy laughed. "I wish I could believe that, Jackie. But I don't think there's ... " Her voice trailed off. It wasn't sleep. Her eyes were open and she seemed on the verge of going on, but instead she looked off trance-like. Then the shaking started again.

He stood up and turned the radio off. "You're the toughest person I know, Jackie. You know that?"

"Doubt it."

"It's true."

Her coffee was lukewarm. "How in the world can you possibly say that?"

"Like with her," he said. "She used to be your sister's friend. Basically, that's it. So why do you care so much what happens to her?"

"Why do you?"

"Because I saw the expression on your face when you looked in the backseat of that car," he said.

There was more to it than that, she knew. There was no way they would be with Peggy except for him, yet he was giving it to her.

"Don't pay any mind to what losers like Frank say," he went on. "They'll find out the hard way how tough you are."

As tired as she was, Jackie forced her way forward. She had

decided several days before to tell him how deep her feelings for him were. "Jack, I want – "

"Goody Two Shoes one minute, Super Girl the next."

"Super Girl?" She tried again but she couldn't bring herself to say it. She'd have to save it for another time. "This Goody Two Shoes thing isn't gonna take off, is it?"

"You are like that, you know. Polite, friendly, always tell the truth, always eat your vegetables, then when you need to, you kick butt. Goody Two Shoes by day, Super Girl by night." He smiled mischievously. "With a muffin sweet as candy."

"God, Jack. Why don't you say it a little louder?"

"I don't believe it. The girl who never blushes is blushing."

"Yeah, right," she said as her cheeks darkened.

"Someday soon I'll make her mine," he sang softly. "Then I'll have candy *all* the time."

"Can you stop that?" He was irritable. She had been playing with the radio, running the dial from end to end over and over. "Just find something and leave it."

"There, how's that," she said as she turned it off. She was irritable, too. She was also about spent physically and on the down side of the caffeine.

"Sorry." He was sitting on the floor with the upper half of Peggy's body flopped across his shins. "Too much coffee."

Out of nowhere, Peggy began thrashing violently. Jackie knelt and pressed down on Peggy's legs as he carefully pinned each of her arms to her sides. He jerked back but not far enough and the top of Peggy's head slammed into his face. He squeezed her arms until she cried out.

"Come on, Peggy. You wanna fight?"

He had a good hold of her and he encouraged her in the hope she would tire herself. Peggy went along, struggling mightily. Her biceps were thinner than his forearms, thinner even than Jackie's forearms, so thin he could loop his thumb and middle finger around with an inch to spare.

"That's it," he said as she dry heaved and tried to get at him. "Fight."

Finally she threw up. Some of it went in the basin. More went on his leg.

"Don't tell me that's all you got," he said.

She continued to try and get free but she was less than ninety pounds and no match for him. She gave up, exhausted and utterly without hope.

"That's it? That's all you got is a little puke?"

"Easy, Jack." Jackie wiped Peggy's face with a wet towel. "Come on, Peggy. You've come this far. Get it all out."

She responded to Jackie's touch and to her voice by allowing them to guide her to the toilet. She heaved and heaved until she puked again.

"That's it," Jackie said softly. "Get it all out. You're gonna make it." She knelt and from behind pressed a hand to Peggy's forehead, remembering how her mother did that the first time in her life she had thrown up. Remembering how comforting it was.

"Please don't leave me. I don't wanna die." Even in her exhaustion and her terror Peggy remembered her manners. Her proper Irish Catholic upbringing. "Please. Please don't leave me."

"We're here," Jackie said after Peggy unloaded into the bowl. "We won't leave."

This time it was Jack who wiped Peggy's mouth with a wet cloth. Her skin was on fire.

"Please don't leave me."

TWENTY-FOUR

Ed came by after the last of the puking and helped them put Peggy to bed. He didn't fit the image Jackie had formed of either an ex-addict or someone who had been through the horror of war. He was earthy enough but he was also soft-spoken and had bright blue eyes. And though he knew more about Peggy's state than they ever would, he listened and asked an occasional question, mostly about Peggy's family and living situation.

Ed had to get to his other job but he waited until they were assured that he wasn't needed. Cindy arrived ten minutes later, without a plan and grateful that Jack was willing to let her sister stay. She handed Jackie a bag of Peggy's clothes and offered them money.

"For the groceries," Jack said and, again, just like that, Cindy was gone.

Ed had said it would be hours before Peggy would do anything except sleep so they piled a comforter, a quilt and what clean sheets were left on the floor of the living room. As tired as they were, it took forever to fall asleep. When they finally did, the bottom fell out. The next time either opened an eye, it was four-thirty. Jackie got up and looked through the cracked door into the bedroom where Peggy slept, oblivious to the day's heat and the noise from the street and everything else but her dreams.

Jackie hated to leave but she was walking a tight rope with her folks. They would never accept what she had with Jack as it was. If her father in particular discovered it as it was, he would destroy it and she was not about to let that happen.

"Just take my car," Jack said, unsure of what was so complicated about it. His bigger concern was where the day had gone.

"What'll I tell my folks when they ask me why I have your car?"

"I don't understand." Of course he didn't understand. He had his own place, his own car, his own money, his own life. "Do you want me to drop you off?"

He was lying on his back with his face under a pillow, wearing only boxers. She liked best the way he looked when he wore only boxers. She knew he was tired enough to fall back asleep at any moment. She was tired, too, despite the sleep, and in need of a bath. And she was stressed, though the stress had nothing to do with the long night with Peggy. It was the stress of her parents and the bigger world closing in.

"Can't you just take my car?"

It sounded childishly simple the second time. She knelt and put her hand on his stomach. He didn't remove the pillow from his face, but his breath quickened and then he stopped breathing altogether. She moved her hand so his heart beat into her fingers. She felt potent kneeling over him and knew her courage might dissolve if he sat up.

"I love you, Jack." A chill went through her. Neither of them had said it that way yet and she was thrilled to have said it that way and thrilled to have said it that way first.

He sat up. The intensity he saw in her face was as unexpected as what she had said. "I love you, too, Jackie."

It was as thrilling to hear as it was to say. She could deal with her folks no matter what with those words in her ears, and they would remain in her ears for a long time. She ran her hand through his hair. When he reached for her, she stood up. She had to go.

She dressed quickly, put her soiled clothes in a bag and checked the bedroom one more time. Peggy was snoring like a 747.

"I've been meaning to tell you I got that dog for my mom," he said. "Because of the break-in across the street I told you about? I finally convinced her."

"The husky?"

"Yeah. The girls named him King. Beautiful dog." He looked at her. "When I was there to drop him off, my mom invited us over for dinner again."

"What did you say?"

"I told her yes."

"Jack, that's great." She had been nudging him all summer to make peace. "Let's do it soon."

"She said something about tomorrow. They're all into the Olympics so we could – "

"It's the last night of the gymnastics," she said, relishing the idea of watching Nadia and the others with him, his mother and sisters. "Jack, let's do it. Only, what about Peggy?"

"With Ed on the case," he laughed, "I don't think we have to worry about that."

"You think he meant he could find a place for her that fast?"

"You don't know Ed." He was looking at her funny. "Wow. So Little Jacqueline loves me."

She wanted to stay. She wanted to put her arms around him and never leave. But she had to go. "Be sure to call if anything happens or if you need anything."

Ed was in the rocking chair when Peggy came into the room in her bra and panties. Though frighteningly thin, her overall appearance was better than it had been when she was last awake. Unsteady on her feet, she leaned against the door frame. It was only after Ed had been looking at her for a while that she realized he was there.

"Hi."

"Who are you?" She stepped back into the bedroom so just her head stuck out around the wall.

"I'm Ed. A friend of Jack's. And you're Peggy."

"Jack?" She struggled for a moment to put face and name together until Jack came out of the bathroom.

"This is Jack," Ed said. "Jack, Peggy. Peggy, Jack."

For the first time since forever, she smiled. "Very funny."

"That bag of clothes there is yours, Peggy," Jack said. "Ed found you a place you can stay, starting tonight if you want. I mean, you're welcome to stay her if – "

"Why don't we talk about that over soup," Ed said. "Do you like minestrone, Peggy? It's homemade."

"That sounds nice." She was having a hard time taking her eyes off Ed. "There was a girl. Jackie."

"She'll be back later," Jack said.

"I like your eyes." Peggy was still looking at Ed. "Bright blue, like the sky."

"Thanks," said Ed. "I love your hair. Vivid auburn, like nothing else."

The towels and the fact that he had told her to wear her bathing suit under her clothes were clues, but Jackie still had no idea where they were going even as they made their way down a deserted road not far from her house. She was still digesting Jack's remark about Peggy and Ed. A man was probably the last thing Peggy needed, but she certainly could do worse. Though Ed had seen Peggy ugly, Jack seemed to think he was interested. Oh, there was uglier. Peggy hadn't killed anyone. She hadn't really even hurt anyone besides herself. Perhaps it was because Ed understood what she had been through. But did he really? It was different for a woman, the way everything was different for a woman. Still, hopeless romantic that she was, Jackie couldn't help but hope that the sparks Jack swore he had seen were real.

The question that pushed forward until she could no longer ignore it was how Jack would react if he ever saw her ugly. Not strung out ugly or trading sex for drugs ugly, but somehow someway ugly. She thought about the night they roamed the streets of Manhattan and danced the night away, besting bouncers and cops along the way, the night she knew she was in love with him. The night he had flinched. She wondered if the other guys she had been with still bugged him and if it would ever go away.

There was no going back, after all. She would forever be his first and he would forever not be her first. Did he ever see that when he looked at her? When they made love? Was that her ugly, that she was forever stained for having been with others? She had seen enough and read enough to know there was something about that that drove guys crazy. And even if only briefly, she had certainly felt ugly that night. Slutty ugly. Dirty ugly. It had never come up again so maybe it no longer mattered. She had to hope so.

The surprise turned out to be well worth the buildup. After they parked and climbed a small embankment, they came upon a huge swimming pool in the back of the Embassy Condominiums. She had lived less than a mile away her entire life without knowing it was there, let alone that it was the largest outdoor pool for miles around and easily accessible to anyone daring enough to come in late at night through the back way.

They were as smooth in the water as on the dance floor at Prescott's. Every stroke, every movement, was just right as they swam, frolicked and dove. It was another first for them and she felt gloriously free with him by her side.

They fell into a race, one end of the pool to the other, and she won by three feet. They both swam her style, the forward crawl, and she won by the length of her body. Then they swam as he did, slightly sideways, and she won by the length of her arm. She wondered for a moment if not winning bothered him, knowing somehow that it didn't.

"You swam the forward crawl really well," she said. "You'd go faster if you did it that way all the time instead of Trudgen style."

She was sure he looked uncomfortable but then he said what she was dying to hear, words she wasn't sure he could say. "Teach me?"

"Alright," she said with great exuberance.

She encouraged him to concentrate on rolling while he swam. Then she had him watch as she swam the length of the pool and back.

"This time," she said, "really let go. Maximum roll is the most important thing."

He stuck his face in the water so she wouldn't see his smile and did as she instructed, up and back. By the time he reached her, he was rolling big-time while swimming as fast as ever.

"If you work it a little, you'll never look back," she said. He was no longer trying to hide his smile. "What?"

"You're a great teacher, Professor Gendron, but oh so serious," he said. "Sorry, I shouldn't have said that. It's great that you're serious. And thorough. Thank you."

His words were like soft raindrops and for the second time in twenty-four hours, she blushed. It was thrilling to be so wide open before him and this time she blushed without a trace of embarrassment.

"Wow," he said. "I've never seen you so lovely."

He moved toward her and she started toward him, then changed her mind.

"No matter how many lessons you take," she said, "you still can't catch me," and she took off. Three quarters of the way out, she plunged down. He followed and they descended to the bottom, rolling over each other without touching as they did. Then they shot straight up in unison to the surface and were swimming side by side, no longer racing or teaching or learning, when he nonchalantly rolled into a skilled backstroke.

"I thought you said that day at the lake you didn't know how to do that," she said, pretending to be angry.

"Did I? I guess I learned since then. Didn't I tell you?"

"Liar." She swam to him and pushed him under by his shoulders. She let him up, then pressed down again. The third time, she climbed up so she sat on the back of his neck. Gathering himself beneath the surface, he put his hands on her butt and pushed up as he launched himself from below with his legs. Though the weight of the water prevented him from ejecting her very far, she toppled away nonetheless.

"How is it that such a little girl is so strong?" She surged toward him but he stopped her with his arms. "Wait. Let's coordinate our efforts."

They went to deeper water so she could stand on his shoulders when he went under. After a few clumsy attempts, they got to where she was able to attain decent height when she jumped off. She couldn't control her body enough to avoid splashing, however, and they stopped after a few more times for fear the noise would attract attention.

"Think you can swim the whole way underwater?"

"Jack, it's over a hundred feet."

"Scared?"

"Let's see you do it ," she said. "We'll make it interesting. If you don't make it all the way, you have to dive naked off the diving board."

"Nice try," he said. "How's about we both do it?"

"Alright, we'll both do it," she said. "But those are the stakes. Loser has to dive naked of the diving board. And don't worry about me. You haven't won a race yet. Scared?"

They got out of the pool and positioned themselves. One more time he slowly said, "Ready. Steady. Go" and they both dove in. They were even until halfway when she began to lag. Twelve feet from the wall, she saw he was going to win, though he was too focused on the possibility that his lungs might explode to notice. She gave one last surge to cut the margin to a few feet, then they blew out of the water simultaneously, gasping for air.

When she was able she smiled and said sheepishly, "Tie?"

"Was it?" He was less interested in that than he was proud that they both had made it the whole way.

"Alright," she said once her breathing slowed, "backstroke. Same stakes."

"Yeah, right."

"Butterfly."

"You know, if you want me to take my bathing suit off and dive off the diving board, all you have to do is ask."

She watched as he peeled off his suit and walked the length of

198

the pool. The white of his ass was set off nicely against his tan and her heart skipped a beat at the sight of his lean and suddenly nude form. He did an okay dive and disappeared under the water. By the time he surfaced, she was slipping out of her suit.

"Jackie, don't."

She causally tossed her suit aside and hopped out. She knew he was watching her just as she had watched him and something about that gave her great confidence. The wiggle of her walk was freer and her damp skin glistened in the starlight. She climbed the ladder, stood naked before the world ever so briefly, then executed a flawless swan dive.

As she swam to him, his expression was stony. It didn't last, though, not in the face of her derring-do and her shy smile and eventually he smiled, too, until loud voices burst through the bushes beyond the far end of the pool. A pack of kids too stoned to understand or care about the noise they were making surged forward. Jack moved so he was between her and the others.

They were friends from grammar school, five guys and three girls. Jackie's immediate concern wasn't in getting re-acquainted, though, but with getting her bathing suit back on. The two of them drifted toward it but were still a ways away when the others spotted them.

"Who's that? Jack Simmons? My main man. Figured you'd be off playing for UCLA by now." "Yeah, Jack, what's this Keene State stuff?" "Are you naked? Look, he is." "Who's that with you? Jackie Gendron? I heard you guys were goin' out." "Hey, Jack. Where's the rest of your dick?" "You naked, too, Jackie? Wow, she is." "Will you guys cool it? You'll wake up the whole building." "Hey, Jackie. Stand up, will you?" "Yeah, Jackie. Give a guy a break. How's about a dive off the diving board?" "What're you, Wayne, eleven? Act like maybe you've seen a naked girl before." "Even if you haven't." "Yeah, Wayne. Even if you haven't." "The only naked girls he's ever seen are in magazines." "Hey, Donna. They really are naked." "Were you guys doin' it in the freakin' pool?" "Who's never seen a naked girl before? I've fucked more girls than all you homos put together." "Real nice, Wayne." "Look, that red thing floating there is her bathing suit." "Get it before they do."

From behind the forward contingent, a female voice of reason cut through the noise. "Will you guys shut up? They're gonna throw us outta here before we even get in the pool." It was Donna, a girl from Jack's class. Several of the guys snickered but they got quiet. "Everybody just come over here for a minute so they can get dressed."

The guys didn't go willingly but they moved far enough so the two of them could put their bathing suits on in a modicum of privacy. Then it was party time. The others jumped in and splashed about with no regard to noise or to the fact that it was past one o'clock. Everyone had come prepared with bathing suits under their clothes and the extra springy diving board was a big hit.

As they played, they got caught up. Other than Jack's assiduous avoidance of Steve, the ten of them talked randomly to, over and around each other about what they and others from school were up to. Very few girls from their grammar school went to Jackie's high school so she had been largely out of touch with the old crowd and delighted to hear about everybody. She had not seen June Whitmore, the one of the others she knew best, in three years and they stayed close in the water as they played.

Splashing about without a worry in the world evoked memories of carefree times. Jackie's class had been extremely tight and she knew from Jack that his was, too. She and June had gone eight years and even those who were older like Donna had always been friendly. Together again, they played just as they had on the best days in the old schoolyard.

Several of the guys insisted they all race. The girls didn't want to but Steve and Wayne wouldn't let it go. June didn't swim well and offered to serve as judge. Jack figured it would be between him and Jackie. From observing how everyone moved in the water,

Jackie thought Matt or Steve would win. With so much testosterone flying around, she also figured Jack would swim faster than in their one-on-one races.

She was right about Jack swimming faster. The testosterone must have affected her as well, for she also swam faster, though she was all wrong about Matt and Steve. She won, but she and Jack were six lanes apart and June missed that Jackie touched the wall a hair before he did.

"Tie!" A tie was the sweetest possible outcome once Jackie realized it was her and Jack. No one else was close. Wayne and three of the others were so far behind that they didn't bother to finish.

Eventually a guy tasked with patrolling the condo complex drove up in a golf cart. He had snuck in as a teenager to swim there himself, he explained, and he politely gave them five minutes to leave. When Jack asked Jackie to do one last dive, she was reluctant. She loved to dive, though, and the high, lively board was difficult to resist. She would pretend no one else was there but him.

She walked up the steps quiet as a mouse as most of the others drifted off, put something extra into her approach and soared through the air. It was exhilarating to do and breathtaking to see. For a moment Jack feared that the great height she obtained might throw off her descent, but she knew what she was doing – how could he have doubted that – and her execution was masterful, as good as any dive she'd done in her life. She smiled that shy smile again when she ascended and swam slowly toward him.

"Bravo," he said. He took the chain with the Francis of Assisi medallion he wore and draped it around her neck. Its color was silver but it was gold. It couldn't be anything but gold.

"Magnifico." When he was certain they were alone, he kissed her. Then she kissed him. She wanted to stay kissing him all night but Steve and Wayne had invited themselves and the rest of the gang to Jack's to party and their impatient voices cut through the still night air. One more time she kissed him and then they hurried out of the pool and grabbed their stuff.

The following evening they went to his mother's for dinner and to watch the last night of the women's gymnastics. Mrs. Simmons was overjoyed to see Jackie again and hard at work preparing a feast of rice golabki, Fozeleks, potato pancakes with homemade applesauce, and, best of all, mushroom onion spinach pierogies. The kitchen was an unbelievably exotic mix of aromas, led off most of all by paprika and garlic. Mrs. Simmons refused offers of help and Jack awkwardly presented Jackie to his sisters, then took their new Siberian Husky into the next room for some wrestling.

Penelope was surprised to learn that Jackie knew her kittens Jasmine and Ginger and they went upstairs so she could get reacquainted. Penelope looked more like Jack than his other sisters and she was like him in being infectiously enthusiastic – enthusiastic about her kittens, enthusiastic about her coming first year of high school, and enthusiastic about hosting her older brother's girlfriend. She handed Ginger to Jackie and held Jasmine close.

"Ginger scratched King's nose today," she said and the two of them laughed.

"Do you know we almost have the same birthday?" Jackie asked.

"Yeah, Jack told me." Hesitantly, Penelope added, "I remember you, you know."

"I remember you, too, Penelope. Such a pretty name." The twins Stephanie and Cheryl came into Penelope's room. "And I remember the two of you."

Eventually Lisa joined them and the four sisters vied for Jackie's attention. In addition to the kittens, they had turtles and art projects and books to show off. Jack gave Jackie an I-told-you-so look and took King out for a walk. When he returned thirty minutes later, the telecast was about to begin and they set up shop in the living room.

The girls got over their lack of enthusiasm for the all-vegetarian cuisine with their delight at being allowed to eat in front of the television. It didn't take long for Jackie to see that Mrs. Simmons was somewhat intimidated by her son. There was something jarring about that and Jackie was sure the Simmons girls saw it as well. Jack was unfailingly polite and informal, yet his presence had more the feel of a distant relative come for an awkward stay than the warm familiarity of a son and brother coming home.

Lisa was fifteen and the oldest of the girls. She had watched every minute of the gymnastics and was pleased to have someone besides her sisters and her mother to share her knowledge and excitement with. Once they finished eating, the twins drifted off whenever anyone besides Nadia was up. Their loyalty was to Nadia alone. Not Lisa. She only left the room during one commercial break all evening. Penelope's interest was in-between but she stayed throughout because of Jackie.

"I love Nadia," Lisa said when Jackie asked, "but I like a lotta the others. I feel bad for Olga. Some of the scores she got were lower than they should've been." Like Jackie, Lisa had a special place in her heart for Olga Korbut. Penelope and the twins had not been watching four years before when Olga captivated the world, but Lisa and Jackie were. They remembered.

"And don't forget the other Russian girl you like," Mrs. Simmons said, noting that Jackie was listening attentively.

"Nellie Kim," Lisa said. "I love her, too. She's the best."

"Really?" Jackie asked. "Better than Nadia?"

"Well, she's the best except for Nadia," Lisa said.

"Yeah," Jackie said. "The best except for Nadia," and the two of them laughed.

"Nadia's the best in the whole world," Penelope said.

Lisa and Jackie were hoping it would be true but Nelli and many of the participants were terrific and they cheered every one. Still, the night, like the first four days of the Olympics, belonged to Nadia. Some of the things she did were astonishing and she did them with a fearlessness that was equally astounding. And in the face of outstanding competition, she was utterly unflappable. There was nothing the commentators could say to amplify any of it. All that was necessary was to watch. Penelope was right. Nadia was the best in the whole world.

There were hugs all around when it was time to leave. Mrs. Simmons insisted that they take every bit of the leftover food and Jackie assured her they would be back soon.

"Will you be watching more of the Olympics?" she asked Lisa after the three younger girls had gone upstairs.

"Definitely the rest of the swimming," Lisa said.

"We're on our way to do some swimming of our own," Jack said.

"Can I come?" Though Lisa knew it was up to her mother, she directed the question to Jackie.

"I don't know," Jackie said, looking at Jack.

"You can come as far as I'm concerned," he said.

"Please, mom."

Mrs. Simmons saw an opportunity to get closer to her son and his girlfriend. Jack moving out and generally drifting away in recent years was one of the worst consequences of the upheaval in her marriage, one she had cried many tears over.

"I don't know." Mrs. Simmons looked from her daughter to her son and then to Jackie. "It's so late."

"You can come if you can change into your bathing suit and get back down here in two minutes," Jack said, and Lisa charged up the stairs before her mother could object.

"We can have her home by one," Jackie said. She wanted Lisa to come, for Jack's sake.

Mrs. Simmons turned to Jack. "You'll take care of her, won't you? And Jackie?"

He snickered. "Take care of Jackie? You shoulda seen what she did to a three hundred pound bum named Bluto."

"What did you do?" Lisa asked as she sped down the stairs and rejoined them.

"Last time we saw him," he replied, "he was lying on a pile of garbage."

"Nothing like that is going to happen tonight, is it?" Mrs. Simmons asked.

"No, Mrs. Simmons," Jackie said. "Right, Nature Boy?"

Mrs. Simmons' eyes brightened. "He is, isn't he?"

"Alright," Jack said with a smile, "that's definitely enough of that."

TWENTY-FIVE

Susan was staying overnight so Jackie knew there would be plenty of time to talk. First they enjoyed a pleasant dinner. Because of Jackie's tenacious loyalty to her sister, Mrs. Gendron had come to have a greater admiration for her oldest daughter. She had not previously acknowledged the difficulties Susan had overcome or appreciated how diligently she had worked to craft a career she was both passionate about and good at. Mrs. Gendron had worked most of her adult life and lately she had come to believe that she had helped open doors for Susan. And so it would be, she liked to think, for Jackie.

Jackie was talking about some of the department store clerks she had interviewed recently and the eloquence and conviction with which she spoke gave the stories added punch. Mrs. Gendron smiled, Jackie having apparently forgotten that she had worked in a department store for several years. She had been as hesitant as her husband about giving Jackie the okay to take the job, but doing so had been absolutely the right decision and she listened with great pride. It never stopped, this growing up, and Jackie was growing up faster than the others. There was no way to freeze the picture or call time out; it would go on relentlessly until one day too soon Jackie would be as smart and mature as Susan. So Mrs. Gendron listened to the beautiful young woman who only yesterday had been a girl and she savored.

When they were done with the dishes, Susan went in the yard. No one she knew in New York had a yard, let alone a sprawling, beautiful garden, and about the only time she ever was around trees was when she went to visit friends who lived near Prospect Park. She was thus more attuned to the serenity of the night air in the yard than her parents and sister, full as it was of the scent of flowers and the first stirrings of crickets and cicadas.

The swing set she had worn out as a girl was still up. Mr. Gendron had raised the seats incrementally as his daughters grew;

206

now two of the three were low again for the grandkids. The middle swing, however, was just the right height and Susan began to swing at a leisurely pace. It was a nice way to move, requiring little effort while creating a self-contained breeze that felt good against her face.

"I brought you a glass of wine," Jackie said as she joined her.

"How are things with Jack? Any more worries about all his previous girls?"

"No." Jackie had locked his secret away and would never share it with anyone, not even Susan. "I'm so crazy about him, none of that even matters."

"Wow, Jackie, that's fantastic," Susan said in great earnest.

They were off to a good start. Jackie knew that all she had to do was get it out and Susan would take it from there. She was great that way. She understood that the things that made people the most uncomfortable were sometimes the things that everyone had a natural, healthy curiosity about. Jackie knew, she just knew, that Susan would lay it out calmly and supportively and that she would feel better when they were done. And she needed reassuring, for this was one she wasn't sure about.

So many times she had seen Susan's students ask what they thought was a stupid question about an uncomfortable subject, and it was in those moments that Susan reinforced Jackie's belief that she was the best teacher in the world. She had seen Susan in action over the years, both in the classes she taught and in the workshops she led. She always had the group sit in a circle and she always began with introductions. That had been awkward for Jackie the first several times, a high school student among people much older than she, but she soon saw there was great value in it. Susan's classes were generally heterogeneous groups and structuring them that way facilitated togetherness and a common sense of purpose. Many attendees started out seeing only the things that divided them, yet most eventually came to see they had much more in common. Jackie was impressed at how seriously people in Susan's classes and seminars took concepts like solidarity and mutuality. She also came to understand, as many others did, that talking honestly about one's life, one's principles and one's dreams while listening to others do likewise could be very liberating.

Sometimes, Susan served mostly to convene discussion. Other times she spoke at great length, the way Jackie was used to teachers doing. Usually she did so only when the students asked her to. They keenly appreciated her respect for the expertise they possessed – some even confessed it was the first time anyone ever acknowledged their expertise, the first time they themselves really understood that they possessed expertise – but sometimes all they wanted was her expertise. Lecturing wasn't her favorite approach, yet she understood there were situations when it was the best way. Jackie relished those moments and secretly wished for Susan to lecture more frequently, for when she did she always sparkled.

"You know you don't have to get buzzed to say whatever it is you want to say," Susan said after Jackie swallowed two large mouthfuls of wine, one right after the other.

That was a nice thought but Jackie gulped another mouthful anyway, then blurted out that she and Jack had done anal sex several times recently and it had been great, better than all of the great sex they had had previously. Only when she finished did she look directly at her sister. She wanted Susan to tell her it was good and not dirty. She needed Susan to tell her she was good and not dirty for doing it and especially for liking it so much.

The reassurance she craved was not forthcoming. For the first time for as far back as she could remember, Susan was not supportive. She didn't reply at all at first and the silence between them dripped with disapproval. When Susan finally did speak, she didn't say Jackie was too young or that she should've waited. She didn't say Jackie should have come to talk to her first before doing it. Her disapproval was fundamental and she spoke rotely as their mother might have. There was no right time or right age or right guy.

There had to be more. Jackie stood there crestfallen, waiting, as the lovely camaraderie of the evening fell away to nothing. She stood alone and shamed before the one person she was certain would never shame her. She had crossed some line, obviously. In her need to know that she wasn't dirty, she felt dirtier than ever.

There was no more. Jackie changed the subject, hoping small talk would trigger something. They chatted amiably but never returned to the topic she desperately wanted to discuss. Her heart sank further when Susan finished the last of the wine and walked slowly toward the house. She walked along waiting, hoping, that Susan would smile and tell her she thought it wonderful. For the last hour before she turned in, she contemplated knocking on the door to Susan's room and forcing her to say what she wanted to hear or explain why she wouldn't. She couldn't. Silent abandonment by Susan was something she had no experience with and no antidote for.

They were as pleasant as ever to each other the following morning, yet something was different. Jackie didn't feel as slutty as she had when she went to bed, but the sense of shame remained. Worse, Jackie woke up hating Jack. Though the feeling quickly passed, the fact that she had even momentarily hated him deepened her shame. She didn't know how to press for an explanation, but she would not allow Susan to drive a wedge between them.

Jack and Jackie. She liked the sound of that. She had always liked the sound of that. What they had was pure and would not be made unpure by anyone. That Susan of all people would disapprove bothered her and she was stuck with the terrible sense of having to choose between two loved ones bothered her more. Two different types of love, perfectly compatible, as they had been all summer – why was she forced to choose? If she did have to choose, it would be her and Jack against the world. Jack and Jackie and no one else.

TWENTY-SIX

Jack made it all the way through July without having to work a single Sunday at the library. That took some doing, for people were always looking for Sundays off, what with barbecues and family excursions to Lake Quassapaug, not to mention plain old summertime flu. Audrey and the others pages teased him about organizing his schedule around Jackie. He never admitted it but they knew. Once word got out that he was working Sunday, they knew she must be out of town.

Audrey and Jack were a good team and he was glad she was working, too. Technically, the pages weren't supposed to help patrons but the librarians were always overwhelmed, even on Sundays. Teenagers who had recently graduated from the children's section of the library were by far the most interesting patrons. They were new to the advanced wonders of the library, and helping them go forth was the best part of many days.

Audrey and Jack didn't especially like to segregate their instruction, but they understood that it was often best to do so. The black kids were open to both of them but the presuppositions of the white kids were more fixed. They had already come to assume that no black female could possibly know anything better than a white male. Many were the painful times when a white teenager would be looking past Audrey at Jack for help while she was in the middle of an answer as informed as the library director might give.

"You're not Italian, are you?" Audrey asked in a quiet moment. Jack almost laughed. No white person would ever ask him that. He sensed she was trying to learn something, however, and that she'd never trust him again if he was dismissive.

"No."

"I thought maybe on your mother's side? 'Cause I know Simmons isn't Italian."

Whatever the real question, he would let her come to it in her own way. "No. My mother's Hungarian."

"I used to know a white family named Simmons," she said. "They were Irish."

"It's usually an Irish name," he said. "In our case, it's Polish. It was probably something like Syzmanski before my grandfather hit Ellis Island."

Audrey needed to know more. Whites could afford to think of black people as an amorphous group whose ancestors came from an amorphous Africa, but she would lump white people into one amorphous European mass at her own peril. Plus, she *wanted* to know more. Her teachers at the community college weren't much help. She loved Black Studies but she didn't only love Black Studies, the school's efforts to pigeonhole her notwithstanding. She wanted to know everything. And the white kids in her classes never said much about their ancestry. If anything, they seemed determined not to know. She asked him to explain the Ellis Island thing.

He picked up a box she had filled with books and answered as best as he could. The answer led to other questions and more answers, and he came up with questions of his own that no one had ever asked her. For an hour, they went on that way as they worked in the stacks moving dozens of boxes of books to a new area that had just opened and taking turns answering the buzzer to fetch books.

"Is it still an immigration center?"

"No," he replied. "It's a historic site. They started giving tours a coupla months ago. You take a boat over from lower Manhattan."

"You should go," she said.

"Audrey, it's just a bunch of run-down buildings."

"It's the place where your family touched down in America." As horrible as her ancestor's experience of America had been, she was encouraging him to better understand his. "The run-down buildings are a reminder of how hard they had it."

They talked about her summer classes, her boyfriend being pulled over again by the cops, the upcoming Earth, Wind & Fire tour and other things besides Ellis Island for the rest of the afternoon until just before quitting time.

"Seriously, Jack. You should go."

After a quick shower, Jack ambled out in that happy way of walking he had. Amidst the last vestiges of daylight, he strolled randomly through the neighborhood as a summer weekend was in lazy denouement: families arriving home from the beach, young people on their way out, others with nothing special to do sitting outside in the warm air. One block away hovering over much of the neighborhood was a chipped and peeling factory where chipped and peeling people worked making radios.

He walked under the railroad viaduct just as a train to Grand Central roared overhead. At a park nearby, the last game of a long day of softball had ended and men in colorful uniforms clustered to dissect the results. With the adults having finally relinquished the diamond, a trio of young girls took over. Their original race around the bases evolved into a game of tag and then into chaotic running with no evident objective other than Joy.

He made a point of taking a different route back and watched a woman on the top floor of a dilapidated three-story house haul sheets in off a clothesline. She was framed by the upper portion of a factory exuding clouds of white smoke that were as natural a part of the landscape as real clouds. Impulsively, he waved and the woman waved back.

He went past the door to his apartment and turned onto a street with five bars in a stretch of three blocks. The bars frequently hummed on weeknights but the nearby factories deployed skeleton crews on Sundays and the only people drinking were locals. He went in the last place on a hunch, sat on a stool and ordered a bottle of Pabst. Three men sat at the far end. In a booth to the side, a couple in their fifties who sounded like they'd been drinking since at least four o'clock sat across from one another.

He retrieved sections of the Sunday paper and debated while

he read whether it was to be a one-beer night. Then the bartender turned the TV to the closing ceremonies of the Olympics and Jack set the paper aside. Despite all the lies and hypocrisy, there was still something moving about seeing all the athletes gathered on the stadium field for the end of their brief moment in the sun. He ordered a shot of Stoli.

"No Stoli, but we got this." Gary the bartender held up a bottle of Finlandia. Jack smiled, thinking about the Finnish girl who wouldn't finish.

Though it had been ten days since she last performed, the Games were hailed everywhere as Nadia's Olympics. There was something wonderful about that and it became more wonderful after Jack downed the vodka. Of the thousands of athletes, a fourteen-year old girl with the ability to fly through the air stood tallest of all. Jack wondered if she was in the mass on the field and if she had any idea how great she was.

A commercial came on and he had just gotten back to the paper when two guys from high school walked in. Mike was two years older than Jack, Joe one, and their friendship back in the day consisted mainly of pot smoking, though he and Joe had also played some sports together.

"What's happening, man?" Joe said as he slapped Jack on the shoulder.

"Hey, Joe. I was hoping I might run into you. What's up, Mike?"

"Jack," Mike said. "Two Buds."

They fell into conversation and he was immediately struck by the fact that Joe and Mike seemed to be aging at a faster pace than most people he knew. Mike especially wore a perpetual scowl and his eyes were hard, but those paled in comparison to his voice. It wasn't that he was loud, or at least it wasn't only that he was loud, for he certainly was loud; it was the sharp, aggressive tone that made his voice like a weapon.

Joe was surprised that Jack was no longer at the Brass and asked if he'd put in a good word for him anyway. Jack skipped over the hiring freeze and the rumors he'd heard about coming layoffs, promising instead to make a few phone calls. He studied the side of Joe's face and saw that he wasn't beat up like Mike so much as he was beaten down – beaten down because he was working as a janitor, beaten down because he was living with his folks, beaten down mostly because life seemed to be passing him by.

"You still play basketball?" Joe asked.

"Yeah, once in a while," Jack replied. "Mostly at Jefferson Park."

"Jefferson Park?" Mike said. "Haven't you had enough of niggers by now?"

He talked on with Joe, trying to ignore Mike, but he wasn't easy to ignore. Just about everything set him off – talk of the fires around town, talk of the Bicentennial, even talk of old times together. Jack bought a round, hoping for the best.

"Fucking spooks," Mike said after Joe rattled off the names of a bunch of the guys – all black – that Jack had played with on the high school team. "Spooks and spics screw everything up. Trash everywhere, crime, all this arson."

"Hey, I heard you're goin' out with that girl Jackie," Joe said.

"How'd you pull that one off?" Mike asked. "I mean, her and you?"

"Be happy for the guy," Joe said awkwardly. "She sure is one fine chick."

"I can't believe he's hitting a nice piece like that, that's all. You are fucking her, aren't you?"

Jack glowered. "Hey, Mike. I would never talk about any girlfriend of yours like that."

"I knew it." A jagged piece of laughter shot out the side of Mike's mouth. "You're not gettin' any. Whatta you doin', waiting until the two of you get married?"

"Come on, man," Joe said uneasily. "Don't talk about his girl like that."

It only seemed to spur Mike on. "Haven't you nailed her at

214

least once?"

He knew Mike wanted a fight and he held back. When he got up to go to the rest room, though, either he moved too abruptly or else Mike was looking for any pretext and he lunged and grabbed two handfuls of Jack's shirt. Mike was soft and out of shape, however, and Jack had him pinned against the bar when Joe and Gary pulled them apart.

He sat down and drained a vodka Gary poured, the good feelings gone. He had come in search of old friends and he had found them. Before long, Joe started with small talk again as though everything was fine. So much of it was negative, though, this endless stream of stories about guys they knew who were strung out, in jail or in the army. Worse were the ones who had died of overdoses and those who were in mental hospitals or should have been.

When Joe rattled off a long list of people who had seemed to be on their way to doing okay only to see their jobs disappear in an avalanche of layoffs and plant closings, Jack repeated something Susan had said about how the only chance they had was to stick together. Joe's own father had been one of those who got thrown out when Singer closed up shop and moved – why couldn't he and the other eighteen hundred workers there have tried to take ownership of the plant? It wouldn't have been easy but with a little help from their union, the mayor and a banker with some local roots willing to take a risk, they might have pulled it off.

"They all ended up losing their jobs anyway," he said. "Wouldn't it have been better to go down fighting than to just quietly watch them padlock the place?"

"I guess," Joe said as Mike glowered and went to the pay phone.

"Who's he gotta call all of a sudden?" Jack asked after he downed another shot.

"Could be Ray," Joe said.

"Ray?"

Joe watched hopefully as Mike made his call. "Some guy we cop from."

"Joe, you really think you should be spending all kinds of money on drugs?"

Joe didn't answer for a long time. When he finally did, his tone was deadly serious. "You gotta understand, man. Sometimes, the loneliness is unbearable. I mean literally unbearable."

The raw honesty of it was so powerful that Jack didn't know what to say.

"Even worse is always being alone," Joe went on. "They say you can be with somebody and still be lonely, but there's nothin' worse than being lonely *and* alone. That's really unbearable. I'm talkin' put-a-.38-to-your-head-and-pull unbearable."

"You must meet some girls," Jack said delicately.

"No, not many." Joe was embarrassed but he had to get it out for the simple reason that there was no one in the whole world besides Jack he could get it out to. "Meeting them is hard but it's not the hardest part. The hardest part's getting any of them to like you. You know, to be interested. I'm telling you, the hurt of that is unbearable."

"Joe, come on, man. You - "

"Forget it." Joe had opened up too much and he moved quickly to shut down. "Forget all of it." He laughed bitterly and swallowed some beer. "Hey, Jackie have any friends?"

"Yeah, sure," Jack said. "I guess I could – "

"Forget it. Probably slick college girls like her. I mean, look at me, man. I make two fifty an hour. I don't even have a fucking car." He lowered his voice as Mike approached. "But good for you, bro."

He threw money into the kitty and agreed when they asked him to go home to get his car. Across town, he waited outside while they took care of business. Then they drove back across town to where Mike had a place in the back of an old house two flights up. Mike ducked out of sight into the kitchen and got busy with the stash. A mattress stood precariously against one wall of

216

the tiny living room and there were chairs that didn't match and clothes on the floor. It was ten degrees hotter than outside and Jack was drunker than he wanted to be. He tried to clear his head by talking to Joe but Joe was preoccupied.

"You first," Mike said to Joe as soon as he returned from the kitchen.

It was only then that Jack saw what Mike had been so busy with. He had cooked a bunch of the white powder into liquid and had the works laid out on a tray.

"You guys are shooting scag?" Jack surged out of his chair in disbelief.

"Listen to this guy," Mike said. "Fuck do we look like, a coupla niggers?"

"It's speed, man. Pure unadulterated pharmaceutical amphetamine." Joe spoke as if describing a beautiful woman.

"Are you crazy?" Jack said desperately. "Joe, come on, man. We'll go back to the bar and get drunk. You – "

"Sit down." Mike stood and glared until Jack sat. "You make me nervous."

Joe was eager to hit but Jack had rattled him. He took a breath to calm himself, regretting the things he had said at the bar. It was only his fourth time and he turned so Jack wouldn't see in the event he missed. He didn't miss. He barely got the needle out of his arm and the syringe on the table before he began to go up.

"You next. You want me to show you? Or I can hit you myself." The meaning of the leer on Mike's face was undeniable. He was dying for Jack to let him do it.

He felt sick. He wanted nothing to do with drugs at that level, yet here were two guys he'd known since he was six years old throwing their lives away. Joe especially seemed little more than a lost boy in way over his head.

Jackie would be home Monday night. He tried as hard as he could to concentrate on her and not on the stupidity of allowing himself to be put in such a bad spot. He got up again but he moved too quickly and the alcohol surged through him so that he staggered and almost fell. The door was locked and he fumbled with it unsuccessfully, feeling terribly exposed with his back to Mike.

"You leaving, pussy?" Finally the latch gave. "Hey, pussy, I did something you still haven't done. I fucked that slut girlfriend of yours. Fucked her silly."

He almost turned and went back but he was certain he would kill Mike if he did. Instead he forced himself forward, feeling sicker with each step. He stumbled down the stairs, missing some and almost falling. In the driveway, he crashed to the pavement when he had to veer quickly to avoid a row of garbage cans. He fought furiously to get up, knowing he had to get away fast. It was only after he started off in his car that he became aware that he was soaked with sweat and bleeding from three different places.

He berated himself for believing the connections to his past could be fixed. They were all killing themselves and he wanted more than anything to live. There had to be a way forward with Jackie because from now on it would be the two of them and Susan and Walt and whoever else was serious about life they met along the way. No more losers intent on dying. He had to make it so she loved him as much as he loved her, that she would no more leave him than he could leave her. She would be back tomorrow. He would talk to her and make her see.

He drove through two songs he despised without noticing. then switched to a sports round-up he cared nothing about. Even the report from the closing ceremonies in Montreal made no impact. That was somebody else's life. He cared about *his* life and being with Jackie and building a new world together. Tomorrow they would talk and kiss and maybe make love and most of all he would do everything in his power to make her want him more than anything in the world. There were five weeks until school. He would sleep and dream of her, dream of new ways of making her love him until she loved him so much she would never leave.

TWENTY-SEVEN

There was a large area around police headquarters reserved for authorized vehicles so Jack parked two blocks away on Elm Place. As they walked, they held hands for strength. They were encroaching on the police department's home ground in the middle of a busy downtown day and that was sure to infuriate more than a few people. The turnout was also likely to be far less than at either of the rallies in Jefferson Park so they would all be more vulnerable should the police get out of hand.

The call had gone out just two days before when Darrin McGee, a nineteen-year old black youth, was shot and seriously wounded by Officer James Larsen. The police brutality committee had decided on a weekday rally at police headquarters to disrupt business as usual. They knew in doing so that they would lose those not inclined to a more confrontational event as well as those who could not get away from work, and it was not an easy decision. Given the stakes, however, those who had attended the emergency meeting decided that something more than another rally on a Saturday afternoon far from the city's center of power was necessary.

There were twenty protesters in front of the four-story building as they approached. Police brass stood in a small cluster at a distance and eight officers guarding the building were lined across the steps. Gathered on the outskirts were off-duty cops in street clothes who had come to see the show, while upstairs in windows other cops and office personnel looked on with varying degrees of hostility.

The committee had done its media outreach well. A van with the call letters and channel number of a local TV station was parked front and center. Close by were a man with a TV camera and a woman with a microphone. Two reporters and a photographer from the local newspaper who had been at the second rally in Jefferson Park were also present. Slightly apart from the crowd were two men snapping photographs.

The demonstrators were forty in all when the rally began promptly at noon. Most carried placards as they walked up and down in an oval just to the side of the entrance to the police station. Speakers demanded the arrest of specific officers, an end to police brutality, the resignation of the police chief, and the creation of a civilian review board. There was chanting between speeches and at one point a strong-lunged woman led them all in singing 'Aint Gonna Let Nobody Turn Me Around.'

After twenty minutes, the chanting grew louder and more aggressive. Office workers on their lunch breaks wandered over to watch while some observers attempted to drown the action out with chants of their own in support of the police. The most persistent was a contingent of wives and brothers and fathers and mothers of members of the force. The number of cops on the premises – on duty and off, uniformed and non, some angry, none amused – grew steadily.

After the designated speakers finished, a decision was made to turn the bullhorn over to any member of the committee who wished to speak. Several of those who stepped forward were more assertive in their condemnations of the police. The most dramatic presentation was made by a woman who simply spoke the names of thirty people brutalized by cops in recent years. Two of the names she recited were of sons of hers.

The action was scheduled for ninety minutes and at exactly one-thirty, the rally chairs called everyone in for some final words. The hecklers persisted to the very end and the number of off-duty cops had swelled throughout until there were about fifty as the demonstrators began to disperse. The last words from the MC were that no one should walk alone to their car or bus stop or to wherever they were going.

They chatted with Lourdes and Juan for a while but, like the other demonstrators, saw the danger in staying too long. So after an hour and a half well spent with people they respected enormously, they set out through what felt very much like hostile territory. They squeezed their hands together and talked as they walked. Though several cops shot them angry looks, none said anything. A group of women who had led the heckling were not so restrained. They directed most of their venom at Jackie.

"Slut." "Nigger-fucker." "See how loud you yell for a cop when some coon rapes you." "I hope your spic friends burn your nice big house down."

Once they got far enough from the crowd, they were just two more people out for a walk on a summer afternoon. It was when they were ten yards from his car that Jack saw that the front left tire was flat. When he went around to the other side, he saw that the front right one was as well.

TWENTY-EIGHT

When she finished the last of 'Good Morning Revolution,' Jackie got up to check on the storm. The last traces of day were gone from the dark gray sky and she imagined herself walking many perilous miles in the driving rain because Jack needed her. It was past eight and he'd have left work so she said a prayer, hoping he would call as soon as he arrived home.

She opened her book of Shelley to 'Song to the Working Men of England.' She had been startled to see it referenced in a magazine she bought on the Fourth in Philadelphia and she read it aloud for the tenth time in a month. The words inspired her both because of what they said and because they made her dream of a day when she might pen something as powerful. Just when she finished, the phone rang. It was Jack. He wanted to go out.

"The storm's officially a hurricane, you know," she said. "Hurricane Belle."

"Gee, now I'm really scared," he said. "Would that be Tinker Bell or Clarabelle?"

"Neither," she said. "Just Belle."

"Jackie, I'm sorry," he said, "but there's just nothing very frightening about anything named Belle. Now Hurricane Jacqueline – *that* would be a force of nature that'd make the whole solar system tremble."

She laughed. "Seriously, it's supposed to get pretty bad."

"All the more reason to go out," he said excitedly. "Think how awesome the Sound will be. I mean, do you know how rare hurricanes are in Connecticut? I best the last one – "

"Nineteen Thirty-Eight."

He laughed. "There, see? This may be the only chance you ever have to do this."

"There's a curfew, you know," she said. "Last I heard it was ten o'clock."

"Are you serious? A curfew?"

"Turn your radio on."

"I believe you," he said. "That's gonna make things complicated. I'll have to duck in and out of alleys and cut through yards all the way to your house. Wait for me in the room upstairs with the balcony. We can get our own 'Romeo and Juliet' action going."

She laughed again, having thought many times about that very thing, and asked him to promise he wouldn't go out. He didn't answer right away and she knew he was caught in the powerful magnetic pull that existed between them.

"Hey," he said finally, shifting gears, "did your grandparents all come through Ellis Island?"

"My mother's parents definitely did," she said. "My father's parents came down from Quebec so I don't know if they did or not. Why?"

"We should go there. They re-opened it, you know."

"I'd love to," she said. "We could go Friday before work if you want. But no fair changing the subject. Promise you won't go out?"

He waited before answering. "Except for when you were at the Cape, I can't remember the last time a whole day passed when we didn't see each other."

She knew. She had the date memorized. "Think how great it'll be when we – "

"Yeah," he said. "Tomorrow?"

"Tomorrow. That's my promise. I love you, Jack."

Wind and rain, rain and wind. Slashing demonic rain and blood-curdling wind. Wind rain darkness. No moon, no stars, just black night and wind and rain. Gaea wailing, plucking, drumming like the mad woman she is. The real sound of music. A time for the magical people. Witches and sorcerers and naiads. Curfew for all others.

Wet. Wetness. Body wet. Gaea cleansing everything. Mommy, can I go out in the rain? Come in out of the rain, dear. Why don't more people like the rain?

Careful of falling trees. Friends most of the time, dangerous now. Trees pushed and bent to the limit. Mother Wind is stronger tonight. Shed a tear for trees that will die. But trees are tough. It takes a lot to kill a tree. Most can withstand even a hurricane.

She lowered herself into a puddle, naked. What a beautiful movement, to go from standing upright to butt-solid sitting – look, no hands. She stood up, no hands, and did it again. In love with herself. A naked force of nature like all that raged about.

Laughter as loud as a hurricane. Look at that. Three months of gardening blown away in one night. Hilarious. Like the end of 'The Treasure of Sierra Madre.' Guess Gaea didn't like my flowers. Or she liked them so much she took them for herself.

Eye of a hurricane, no joke. Such a beautiful night. Best night of my life – no. Jack. Any night with Jack. Is it strong enough to take me away? Take me up if you can, Belle. If you dare, Gaea.

Why do crickets go quiet in the rain? Why do people want the weather to be the same, always? No heat. No snow. No hurricane. No rain. Belle, Gaea, Hecate, whoever you are, I worship you. I am as strong as you are. Hurricane Jacqueline. I worship myself when I worship you.

Skin. Wet. The body electric. The body ecstatic. Rain and wet and wind so strong it makes my heart race. Better than love? Better than sex? Making love in a hurricane – that would be beautiful. Jack, you incredible boy. You incredible, delicious boy. Touch. Feel. Skin. It feels wonderful. She closed her eyes and honed in on the wind whipping through the trees. The sound of freedom.

She ran her hand through her hair. She loved the way her hair looked wet. Exotic. Primitive. What the future might look like. Beautiful. She thrust her arms upward, beckoning the wind to lift her up.

Thunder, too? Leaves blowing, tomato plants going home to heaven, and everywhere savage rain and wind and sound. A pot-pourri of mad beauty stronger than a million atom bombs.

She stood up. Must not awaken the authorities. Time to return to climate controlled backwardness. Modernity. Tyranny. Deathly unimaginative comfortable stuff. Good-night, Gaea. Hecate. And most of all, you, Belle. Rock on. Jazz on. Dance on. Love on.

TWENTY-NINE

Her hair was cut very short. It wasn't as short as his but it was short and it was set off spectacularly by the silver hoop earrings and her dazzling smile.

"Wow. Look at you." He stood frozen. "Wait. I flubbed my line." He closed the door and rang the bell again. When she opened it he said, with great exaggeration, the same thing she had the night of her birthday. "Oh, my God. You cut your hair," and he kissed her as if they were going down on the Titanic.

Along the Sound, remnants of the damage from the storm were all about – downed tree branches, overturned benches, sand blown into large piles far from the water. Still, the hurricane was already a memory. The weather had turned steamy immediately after it blew through and the city's residents were back to summer fun.

Though it was past seven, hundreds of people were on the four-mile long beach. A smaller but still significant number for that hour were in the water. Many were families enjoying a vacation close to home or taking full advantage of the Sound. Summer was fickle, after all. Those who spent July and August wishing the heat away always got their wish eventually, though many had second thoughts once it was too late.

There were no other cars at the far end of the Point near the rocky path that went out to the lighthouse. They had decided to walk to it again. There was no hurry, though, so they sat and watched a speedboat fly across the water with a man on skis in tow. Further out, other boats lolled lazily at a safe distance. They hadn't been parked five minutes when a figure approached on the driver's side and pulled open the door.

"Hey, what is this?" Jack said.

"Don't start the car." The form moved closer and opened a jacket to reveal a .38 tucked into a fat waist. "Out."

"Hey, come on," Jack said, "we got nothing."

"Jack." He turned to her. There was a form on her side of the

226

car.

"Nice and quiet, sweetheart," the second guy said. "We just wanna have a chat with your boyfriend."

"She's got nothin' to do with this." He had it figured out: Frank O'Toole's promise come to life.

"Get outta the car now and nothin'll happen to her."

He slid his left leg out. "It's gonna be alright. No matter what, just stay here."

"Walk." The guy with the .38 was white, maybe twenty-five and about six-one, two-thirty. The other guy was white, too, and bigger. He trailed behind, keeping an eye on Jackie. A Big Cheese waited, also white and a little older. At his side was a Latino guy. Not Puerto Rican, though. Probably Cuban. Smaller but muscular. Definitely more dangerous in a fight. He looked back at Jackie and whispered a prayer that she stay put.

"You put your hands on someone who works for me," the Big Cheese said. "That doesn't happen."

They were positioned between their two cars so no passersby were likely to see. Jack knew what was coming and that it was pointless to try and talk his way out. And though he was afraid, he was also somehow able to conjure up a weird kind of strength by thinking about Peggy, Joe, Al and others he knew and all those he didn't who had lost their way, all those who were in the clutches of people like these, and he felt the need to say something, to let them know even in a small way how pathetic they were.

"Hey, so if I turn one of my little sisters on to scag, do I get to join?"

The Cuban responded with a solid punch to the stomach. Then they took turns until they'd knocked every bit of breath from his body. As soon as the guy with the .38 let go of him, he fell to his knees.

"If you stay stupid and there's a next time, it's you and the girl," the Big Cheese said. "And don't ever get smart with me again, faggot." He wound up and kicked Jack in the ribs.

"She's a nice piece," the guy with the .38 said in a voice that was almost friendly. "We'll get you a good price for her if you ever decide to sell."

Before they were even gone, she dashed to where he knelt. He knew she was terrified and he tried to make himself presentable but the struggle to breathe was overwhelming.

"Oh, my God. Jack." She knelt and put her arms around him as if to give whatever of herself would make him better. Not being able to breathe got scarier the further into it he went and he let out some frightening sounds as he fought desperately for air. Finally, something cleared and he began sucking breaths.

"Oh, my God. Jack."

"I'm okay," he said as he drew deep breaths.

"I memorized the license plate numbers."

"Forget it. You didn't see anything or anybody. None of this ever happened."

"But – "

"Say it." He tightened the hold he had of her hand.

"I didn't see anything or anybody. None of it ever happened."

When he was able to stand, she helped him to the car and insisted they go to the hospital. He was having none of that, though he did accede to her demand that she drive. She almost sideswiped a parked car and at one two-way stop rolled so far forward into the intersection that a driver coming from the left had to blast his horn and swerve to avoid hitting them.

"Jesus, Jackie, I'm okay."

At the apartment, he put a record on and made iced tea just as he would have had nothing happened. She refused to relax, however, and again mentioned the emergency room.

"I'm okay," he said again. "Just a little sore. Besides, what are we gonna tell them happened?"

"That's what you're worried about," she said, "is what we're gonna tell them?"

"They'll probably call the police," he said. "I think that's a law or something."

"So they'll call the police." She went to the phone and began dialing 911 until he pushed down on the button to cut off the call. Refusing to give in, she dialed a second time and again he cut her off.

"Jack!" She yanked angrily so the phone crashed to the floor. "Either I call here or I'll go outside and find a pay phone."

"Alright, alright, we'll go. But I'm driving. If I pass out, you can take over."

She was near tears. "You think maybe this is one time it's not funny?"

On the way, he insisted that she had not been there and she helped him rehearse a story about a robbery pulled off by men with their faces covered. It was rush hour in the ER and they braced themselves for a marathon as soon as they saw the crowd in the waiting room. Brown and black people of all ages sat, stood and lay in the waiting room. An older man in a wheelchair wheezed badly as two women stood nervously beside him, while two young children wailed uncontrollably. A man not much older than Jack lay handcuffed to a gurney, dried blood from a gunshot wound coloring a makeshift bandage on his arm. A small phalanx of cops and paramedics stood to one side between the waiting room and the treatment area, filling out paperwork and talking idly about vacation plans.

They waited ten minutes until a registration clerk signaled them. After a few questions, the woman slid a clipboard of forms forward that Jackie intercepted and filled in as he answered more questions. When he explained that his driver's license and insurance card were among the stolen items, the woman typed on without missing a beat.

Their skin color enabled them to jump several spots in line and also got them a warmer welcome than those around them. The police were not notified and, though Jack offered no ID or proof that he lived on his own, no one ever said anything about having to contact a parent. None of the doctors and nurses questioned their story. And when he was examined by a specialist, Jackie was accorded her own private waiting space in the treatment area. Just over three four hours after arriving, they were on their way.

"Doctor's orders." She had kept his car keys and refused to give them up.

As soon as she started up, Frampton's voice filled the car. He made like he was going to turn it off but she pushed his hand away, cranked it loud and began singing. When 'Doobie Wah' rolled into 'Show Me the Way', she sang on, forcing the tension of the evening out through her vocal cords.

Six blocks from the hospital, they came to a stop behind a long line of cars. The road ahead inclined significantly and they could see that the cars traveling toward them were similarly stopped in place. People had exited their vehicles and stood, waiting, when the night suddenly filled with the sound of screeching sirens.

It was not a steady, low wail like so many times throughout the summer when she listened from her open window but rather an ear-splitting screech as four fire engines roared through the inter-section ahead. Two police cars zoomed past from behind, speeding the wrong way up the open side of the street and disappearing. From all around people emerged on foot, running, shouting, whis-tling, none of it joyous, much of it panic-stricken.

The unmistakable smell of burning wood descended and pen-etrated the air around them as a cop on foot ahead began waving cars forward. When she pulled forward out of the shadow of a three story building into the open space of the intersection, Jackie felt a surge of heat against the side of her face as bright orange and yellow flames enveloped at least three structures to their left. More sinister than the intense colors and even the heat was the sound the fire made as it roared out of control, a powerful, frightening sound that forced itself to be heard above the sirens and the screams of terrified people. Neither of them knew it was possible for fire to be that loud.

"Pull over," he said as soon as she was through the intersection. "Don't turn the engine off."

He was out and around the car before she could push the seat back and slide over. He cut a car off, raced to the next intersection and turned onto a street just before a cop pulled up to cordon it off. It was then that she saw they were close to a spot that sat above most of the city where they would have a good view. He drove along dark, forbidding streets neither of them had ever been on through a neighborhood that seemed to have died. Empty houses were missing large chunks, their jagged edges charred black.

They looked intently down each street, searching for a route they knew was close by. As they passed a vacant lot that had, until a recent fire, contained two homes, he saw the ridge they were looking for. With the fire temporarily out of view, she allowed herself to believe it wasn't real. When they came to a stop facing it straight on, though, it again became all too real.

Again they were struck first by the bright glow and then more ominously by the smell and the sound. The flames had spread and billows of ugly smoke filled the night sky, darkest gray on black. Even at a distance, they could feel its heat.

They watched in silence, shaken by the sight before them as well as by the inability of even an army of firefighters to get the inferno under control. Because the fire was so big and seemed to have sprung to its massive size very quickly, they couldn't help but believe that many people had been seriously injured and perhaps some killed. Besides the horror, there was a feeling of powerlessness, for though they were near enough to see what was happening with great clarity, there was nothing they could do.

It was sickening to watch, yet they couldn't pull themselves away. Despite the efforts of the police, dozens of people were gathered in front of the burning buildings, some of whom seemed dangerously close. Whether they were family, neighbors, friends or just onlookers, they, too, were powerless despite their numbers. Finally, enough was enough and he opened the door for her to slide across. As they went back along the dead street, the fire's power remained overwhelming. Worst of all was the sound, which was louder than ever.

THIRTY

When the door of Walt's apartment shut behind them, it had the sound of a prison cell closing and Susan knew she was sunk. Like all the other times, never once did she consider simply leaving. Instead, she slipped into the kitchen. Until the last month, on the rare occasions when she drank at all, Susan could make one glass of wine last a night. Now she needed alcohol. Walt either didn't notice or else accepted her need to numb herself as part of their new ritual.

Scotch was quickest and she swallowed a nasty mouthful of Dewar's. She gagged but poured another. She could hear him in the next room, seemingly in no hurry, and there was plenty of time to choose an alternative course. Instead, she forced down more of the Scotch. He had addressed one of their sorest points by reviving their sex life and acted wounded whenever she questioned him about what exactly it was they were doing. Here he was giving significant ground on a crucial matter and she was still pestering him – was that her idea of how to jumpstart their relationship?

When he went into the bedroom, she poured one more. She had no sense of having undressed until she felt his skin against hers. She stood before him, searching his face. Perhaps if she could make the first part as good as possible, the second part would be different. For a year, maybe more, he had been indifferent and during what little love they made, he was always rigid and detached. Now he wanted it all the time, though he was very strict in what they would do and how they would do it. The excitement he drew from forcing her to do what he wanted frightened her, yet things had gotten so twisted between them that she went along, validating the lie that he was giving her what she wanted.

"Please, Walt." Though she still never considered flight, it wouldn't have mattered at that late point. He would never have allowed it.

"Just relax, baby," he whispered softly in her ear.

"Please."

"Shhh."

Her resistance wilted in the face of his unbreakable determination and her last hope died when he rebuffed her attempt to put her arms around him. Instead, she again allowed him to turn her around. He gently caressed her hair, but there was no way she could make it so it felt good. Instead, she closed her eyes and focused on the music he had put on and turned up loud. The song was one more part of her humiliation, she knew, but as with the rest of it she went along. Much as she tried to concentrate on the crashing guitars, she could not escape the tale the singer told of his wildly successful efforts to transform one young girl after another into his personal slaves.

THIRTY-ONE

Jackie had just gotten home from New York with plans to stay for three days when the phone rang. It was Jill, a friend of Susan's she had met several times and Jackie knew immediately that something was wrong. The woman said that Susan was in the hospital and explained why.

"She said she didn't want you or your parents to know," Jill went on, "but I know how close the two of you are so I decided to call anyway."

"Thanks so much."

"She's in good hands and surrounded by friends, Jackie, and I know you just left, but my personal opinion is that she'd like you to be close by no matter what she says."

"I'll catch the next train." She wrote down the address of the hospital, still in a state of shock, both about what had happened and how it had happened. "So Walt – "

"Yeah, Walt," Jill said. "She's gonna be okay though, Jackie. Don't worry about that. And I know she'll be happy to see you."

She grabbed some things and set out for the bus stop without thinking or caring about what she would use as an excuse with her parents. She thought only about what Jill had said. *Injuries sustained from repeated incidents of violent anal sex.*

She had believed for a long time that Walt wasn't good enough for Susan and she of nasty names she would call him. But what had he done, exactly? Jill had said that the injuries were the result of repeated incidences. *Cumulative* was the word she used. That meant – she didn't want to think about what it meant.

She dozed on the train despite her anxiety and dreamt. Walt was having his way with Susan, laughing the whole time. Jackie tried to help her get away but was unable. Then Walt came after her and she couldn't get away, either, until she woke up. She looked at the people around her. The men all looked hideous. The good-looking ones, the ones with nice clothes, the conductor collecting tickets, the guy leering at her. All hideous.

Jack was holding her down. It was alright at first because she asked him to. Then it wasn't alright. She couldn't breathe. He turned hideous, too, and kept saying she must want it because she asked for it. She couldn't speak, couldn't tell him no. He laughed, not as Walt had but softly, the lovely laugh she had heard so often. She couldn't breathe – what was funny about that? The conductor's voice startled her awake. One Hundred and Twenty-Fifth Street.

At Grand Central, she went outside, avoiding eye contact. She'd skip the subway, for it, too, would be full of hideous men. Instead she'd take a cab. That way at least she could breathe.

Her mother was busy at the office when Jackie called from the hospital and didn't have time to question her about why she was in New York. Knowing how proud her mother was of the work she was doing, Jackie used that to her advantage when she called again that evening.

"You know how much I love this job," she said. "There's so much to do and we only have a few weeks left, plus some of the women are only available for interviews on certain days. Besides, I think I should stay because Susan's not feeling well."

"Is it anything serious?"

"No." Her throat caught. "She's asleep. I'll have her call you tomorrow. And mom, when Jack calls, will you tell him where I am and then call me right away? We had a fight and I don't want to talk to him right now, but I want him to know I'm alright."

Five minutes later, the phone rang. "I did as you asked. I told him you were turning in early but from the way he sounded, don't be surprised if he calls you there."

As soon as she started to draw a bath, the phone rang again. It could have been someone from the hospital or one of Susan's friends, and she thought about picking up and silently waiting until whoever it was spoke. But she knew it was him so she let it ring. It had been a long time since she had felt so alone, yet she refused to let Jack in. She would rather be alone.

No sooner did the ringing stop than it started again. When it stopped, she took the receiver off the hook and lay in the bath for a long time. Though Susan was cheerful, she had never looked so fragile and Jackie knew better than to press with questions. A dozen friends stopped in while she was there, smart professional women like Susan, and several times she almost took one aside so she might better understand. How could Susan have gone along with agreed something that put her in the hospital? And for a prolonged period, for one thing that was certain is that it had been going on for a while.

She put the phone on, grabbed some magazines and stretched out on the bed. None of the words she read registered, however, because she was troubled by images, just like on the train. They became clearer when she fell asleep and the action was always the same: Walt and Jack versus her and Susan. She tried talking to Jack but he refused to listen and sided with Walt on everything. Susan was afraid and that made Jackie afraid.

She slept badly and the quiet of the apartment exacerbated her aloneness each time she awoke. Susan's place, one of her havens all summer, suddenly felt dangerous. She got up and went cautiously into Susan's room. There was a cold ugliness that had been there all along, hiding, that was now out in the open. She touched the bed and thoughts of the things that had happened in it forced themselves on her. She thought, too, about the times she and Jack had had sex that way and shame swept over her.

She hated Jack. For a moment in the yard that night, Susan had made her hate him. Now she understood why. That moment of hatred was nothing compared to what she felt now, to what Walt had forced her to feel. Maybe Jack wasn't like Walt but he was of Walt so she hated him. When she awoke at seven-thirty, her thoughts were of Susan and Jack. She thought of her sister and getting to the hospital as quickly as possible and of Jack and how she hated him.

THIRTY-TWO

After eleven hours at the hospital, Jackie was drained. They had decided to keep Susan one more night and Jackie's day had consisted of lots of talking, lots of walking with Susan, and lots of reading while Susan slept. Through it all, she couldn't get past the fact that Susan did not blame Walt. She even used the word *we* instead of *he*, as though what happened was not something done to her.

The sun was setting as she made her way from the Chambers Street station. She was five paces onto Susan's street when she saw him. As he approached she began walking briskly toward him, not to greet him but to get past as quickly as possible. When he reached for her, she sidestepped his grasp and slapped his hand away.

"Jackie, what the heck is going on? What's the matter with you?"

"Nothing's the matter with me. Just don't touch me."

"Jackie!" He had dashed past her and was blocking the way.

"Whatever you do, don't touch me."

But he did, taking hold of her arm as she again attempted to pass. "I've been waiting two hours. Why did you tell your mother we had a fight? And how come you won't answer the phone?"

She freed herself and went toward the door. Something in his voice made her stop. "Susan's in the hospital. Walt forced himself on her and injured her."

"Injured her? What do you mean? Will you just stop and talk for one minute?"

"Just go home, Jack. She's coming home tomorrow. I'll call you when I can." When she turned with her keys and approached the door, he was beside her in a flash. He could easily have stopped her and when he didn't, for a brief moment she was grateful.

"Come on, Jackie, that's not fair. What happened? You know how much I care about Susan. You owe me more than – "

"Her anus is damaged from rough sex, okay? Walt – " She stopped, unable to say more.

He was as shocked as she had been. "He raped her?"

She turned to avoid his gaze and shook her head no. "Just go home, will you? I need to be by myself. I'll call you when I can."

She closed the door and gathered herself. Upstairs, she peeked out the window. He was standing in front, looking up at her. She splashed water on her face and ignored the phone when it rang. As soon as it stopped, she called home, intending to hang up if her father answered. She got her mother and told her she was staying for at least one more day because Susan had the flu.

"She took something for sleep and she's already in bed." Jackie couldn't take much more of the lying but she would not give Susan up. "Can she call you tomorrow?"

His car was still in front when she peeked through the blinds. Then the buzzer rang four times in quick succession, the last the longest, followed by silence. She stood completely still for what seemed like a very long time. She spoke aloud as if he was there, pleading that he go home. When she went back to the window, his car was gone.

That was when she lost it. The crying came on so quickly and so severely that she dropped to her knees. Before long, she was sobbing uncontrollably and she let it go without even trying to stop. It didn't feel good exactly but it felt necessary. She was too far gone emotionally and physically to bother with the bedroom so she grabbed a pillow from the sofa and lay on the floor. Still she cried and when she finally stopped, she slept.

THIRTY-THREE

No sooner was Susan home than she was smoothing things over for Jackie with their mother. And since there was no way around her having to stay in Connecticut for a while, Susan arranged with the head of special projects for Jackie to go to Yale and UConn later in the week to do the research they had been wanting somebody to do for months. It was Susan the organizer par excellence, and though Jackie hated to be away from her, she was comforted by how committed Susan's friends were to helping her.

Plus, as she was disturbingly aware, her need to be with Susan stemmed as much from her need to understand as for Susan's sake.

She put on a cheerful front for her mother and dodged two calls from Jack. The knot in her stomach made eating impossible and her books, her records and her journal all failed her when she needed them most. Without them, she lay on her bed for hours, her mind racing. When night fell, the quiet and the darkness dragged on interminably. She finally fell asleep at sunrise and awoke to the sound of falling rain.

Though she knew sleep would not return, she lay for several hours. Her folks had long since set out to begin another workday and the house was silent. She went downstairs when she couldn't stand her room another minute, only to find that the rest of the empty house was no better. She might have gone to what the hurricane had left of her garden but the rain had picked up so she went back upstairs and sat at her desk.

She stared blankly for many minutes at the fresh page of her journal before giving up in favor of a pile of scrap paper. Freed from the obligation of having to think or write sensibly, she doodled and drew pictures and stitched random words into incoherent sentence fragments for what seemed like hours. She made lists of every tape he had made for her, the concerts they had been to, every movie they had seen, their favorite records on the jukebox at Prescott's, of all the times they had made love. She wrote his name big and small, straight and diagonally, in block letters and as skinny as the pen would allow. She couldn't write her own name without writing his and she played with that, digging the synchronicity of it, of turning **j-a-c-k** into **j-a-c-k-i-e** and **J-A-C-K** into **J-A-C-K-I-E** over and over again.

She took a calendar out of her desk and charted the course of the summer by circling days significant and not and writing notes in the boxes about mundane as well as important things they had done together, except that none of it was insignificant or mundane, all of it was important, every day, from the afternoon in May when she opened the door to find him standing there to the last time she had seen him just two days before in front of Susan's but which now seemed so long ago. All of it was important and there was no way she could go on without him, no way it could be over, except she didn't know if she had it in her to do what might make it right or what it even was that might make it right or, worst of all, whether things between them *could* be made right.

There was no crying – she could no more cry than she could expunge the knot from her stomach. He'd be at work at the library until five and she thought about calling, but calling was all wrong. She thought about the possibility that he would again show up unannounced, just like the day in May and the night of her birthday, knowing somehow that she didn't hate him but rather that she wanted him more than ever, and when she went to the window just to see if he might in fact be there, she laughed for the first time in three days. No, this was for her to do and when the last agonizing hour was done, she called a cab, wrote a note for her mother and went out to wait in the rain.

When she didn't see his car, she was sure she had missed her chance. Waiting another whole day was a thought too unbearable to consider, though, so she started into Bandu's to wait, then stopped. Too many questions. No sooner had she bought a coffee at the store up the street and settled under the canopy than he pulled up in front of his door. She tossed the coffee and started to call to him but the rain was too loud. When she got to the door, she took a moment to think about what she would say.

She had come to love his apartment. The things they had shared there together were a big part of it, but it was more than that. It was a safe place in the same way Susan's had once been safe – more so, for she was more able to be herself with him than she was even with Susan. The apartment had also come to represent many of the things he was to her, his burning desire to live on his own terms most prominent among them.

She hesitated. In addition to the churning in her stomach, her heart was racing. Why was he obligated to love her just because she wanted him to? That was selfish, especially after the way she had behaved. But behaving badly was just a part of it, for she also saw that her need to hold back had hurt him. And, though it didn't matter so much at the moment, she also saw more clearly than ever that holding back had hurt her, hurt her even more than it had hurt him.

Just as she went to ring the bell, a gust of wind blew the door open. He was across the room and a look of surprise flew across his face when he saw her. She closed the door and the two of them stood facing one another. She was unnerved to see in his eyes and in the expression on his face something she had not seen before: fear. He had talked about being afraid but she had never seen any evidence of it. Now she did. He was afraid of her.

"You're soaked," he said. She wasn't really but he got a towel and tossed it to her.

"Thanks."

"I'll make tea." He hurried to the kitchen. As soon as he got the kettle going, he went to the bedroom and returned with a change of her clothes that he placed on the cable spool.

"Jack."

"Are you hungry?" His fussing was nice but she wanted him to just stand still long enough so she could explain. Even more disorienting than the fussing was the chattering, for if there was one thing Jack was not, he was not a chatterer.

"Jack, stop. Please?" He stopped only when he was all the way across the room, as if he was afraid of what was coming. "Jack, I'm so sorry. Can you ever forgive me?"

She took a hesitant step, hopeful but still uncertain how she'd be received. He moved too, and after just one more step she was in his arms. They stood silently, holding each other, as everything that had happened fell away. When the piercing whistle of the kettle approached unbearable, she felt him start to pull away.

"Don't go," she pleaded. "Don't ever go."

"Never." He held her tighter and she squeezed him for all she was worth. They were silent for a long time. Finally he spoke. "How's Susan?"

"Better," she said. "A lot better."

When she was no longer squeezing so tightly, he turned the two of them and they went into the kitchen with their arms around each other's waists.

"Peppermint?" She said. Peppermint tea was her favorite.

"Yeah," he said as she finally let go of him. "Why don't you change into some dry clothes?"

"I'm alright."

"Well *I'd* feel better."

She laughed and went and changed as fast as she could. They sat on the floor making small talk for a while but she knew he wanted to know everything she knew and that she owed it to him to tell. He flinched several times at some of the details and shook his head in disbelief. She mentioned the great friends of Susan's she had met at the hospital and how important their support was but, while that was certainly reassuring, he sensed there was something about it that troubled her. He had an inkling what it was but rather than say, he led her to it by coaxing and asking questions.

"I don't feel as close to her when her friends are there," she said. "Am I jealous of them because I want all of her friendship just for myself?"

244

"Is that what you think it is?"

"I don't think so," she said. "I hope that's not it."

"It's a really hard thing to understand, what happened."

"Oh my God, Jack, I know," she said. "I've been thinking about that over and over: Why? And she won't tell me and there's no way I can ask."

He suggested that she not be in a rush, that she be there for Susan and that being there would make it easier for Susan to open up when she was ready. "Focus on this great woman you love and not on trying to understand everything right this minute."

"With the way things are with my folks," she said, "there's no way I can go back to New York yet."

"Call. You know how she loves talking on the phone."

Liking the idea, she moved toward his phone.

"Keep her going with things you know she cares about. I'm sure she'd be interested in this, if it seems appropriate." He handed her a leaflet about a wildcat strike at the Hancock plant on Rakoczi Street he'd gotten from Lourdes. "In the meantime, I'll make supper. I have a turtle to pick up later. You can come if you want."

"Alright. But we'll have to stop at my house first."

"You can take the phone into the bedroom. There's a jack behind the nightstand. And Jackie?" He fumbled for a moment. "She probably doesn't want me to know about what happened but … could you figure out a way to tell her I care about her very much?"

It was the first time they'd been to the Sound since they ran into Frank O'Toole's friends. They avoided The Point altogether and parked near the middle of the beach. It was breezy and Jackie took her sweatshirt when they set out walking in their bare feet. The sand was smooth and they had to push off with each step, but they were in no hurry and it was a nice contrast to walking on concrete.

They had only gone half a mile when they became aware of sirens close by. A steady stream of cars were making their way along the seawall toward the exit, and the entrance to the park was blocked by a police roadblock. A cruiser pulled up near where they had stopped walking and a cop got out and announced through a bullhorn that the park was closed and that they were to leave immediately.

"Must be trouble at The Point," he said.

"Why are those other cops by your car?"

"I don't know." He smiled and looked out over the vast expanse of the Sound. "How's about we make a break for it and swim to Port Jefferson?"

"I'm afraid, Jack."

"Take a deep breath. We have to go over there." He took her hand and they set out toward the car. "A few years ago, I was at a game at Shea and at one point during batting practice I looked out to right field and saw that this pitcher for the Dodgers Andy Messersmith was playing catch with a kid about ten years old who was in the stands right near the field. It was a serious game of catch, too. I'd say they were at least sixty feet from each other and the kid never dropped the ball once and every one of his throws was right on the mark, and it went on like that for at least ten or fifteen minutes. Probably the kid just asked for an autograph and Messersmith invited him to play catch, and I thought it was so cool that he would do that."

"That *is* cool." She squeezed his hand as they stepped up onto the seawall. The cop near the back of Jack's car was Puerto Rican. The one near the front was black.

"Well, lookie here," the black one said. "If it isn't Abbie Hoffman and Patty Hearst."

"We just heard the announcement," Jack said. "We'll leave right away."

"Now that's mighty considerate of you, son."

The Puerto Rican was peering into Jack's car. "Whatta you got in that box?"

"I was wondering about that, too," the black one said. "Looks to me like a wild turtle."

"You poaching wildlife on public land, boy?" The Puerto Rican looked at each of them with contempt, Jack because he didn't know his place and her for being with a weakling whose acting out was obviously ineffectual and would always be. A girl like her should be with a man like him, a man close to the levers of power who no one messed with. All that was required for her to see it that way was for him to give her a good fucking.

"I'm a certified wildlife rehabilitator," Jack said. "I have paper-work in the car."

"Get it," the black one said.

As he did, the Puerto Rican stared at Jackie, trying to get her to look at him, but she was concerned only for Jack. The cops were armed, they had the entire weight of the law on their side, and there was no one within a mile except other cops. They could beat him for resisting arrest or shoot him for reaching for a weapon and everyone who mattered would verify it as justified.

"You know what happens to people who don't like cops?" The Puerto Rican moved toward Jack. "They end up in the joint. You know what happens to scrawny white punks in the joint, Booty Boy? Let me tell you something: it ain't pretty."

"We're leaving, okay?" Jack made sure to stand perfectly still.

"You'll be very popular inside, Booty Boy," the Puerto Rican went on. "Even her Jew lawyer father won't be able to help you."

In spite of himself, Jack smiled ever so slightly.

"Something funny?" The Puerto Rican stepped closer until he was just inches away. "I said, Something funny, Booty Boy?"

"You should be with us," Jack said, "not workin' for the man."

The Puerto Rican's face tightened and he put his hand on his revolver. Though she knew she shouldn't, Jackie took a step for-ward. "Please, just let us go."

"Easy, partner," the black one said. The Puerto Rican was staring, waiting, and Jack knew he shouldn't so much as breathe.

"You think you and your friends are gonna get away with this shit?"

"Let it go, partner." The black one moved closer, slowly, until the Puerto Rican took a step back and let go his grip. "I suggest you be on your way, son. I also suggest you watch yourself." He handed Jackie the document Jack had given him. "Have a nice evening."

They dropped the turtle off at his place and drove to the lake in silence, still shaken. From the parking lot they could see other kids on the beach. As she started toward the water, he lingered so that she turned around and walked back to the car.

"Jackie, maybe we shouldn't see each other for a while. You know, until – "

"What?" It was dark and she struggled to read his face. "Not see – "

"There's too much trouble. *I'm* too much trouble. If something happens to me, that's one thing. But if anything ever happened to you – "

She pushed him in the chest. "God, Jack. How can you say that? If something happens to you, it happens to me, too."

"I know, but – "

"You don't know. You don't think I can be there for you. That's it, isn't it?" She squeezed both hands into fists. "God, how can you say something like that to me? I love you, you know."

He turned away from her. "I know you do."

"You *don't* know. You say all this nice stuff but you're like everybody else. You think I'm some helpless little girl who needs protecting all the time." He moved toward her but she stepped back and went on. "Do you know how much I agonized over how I spoke to you that day in New York and how afraid I was that I had lost you? Maybe coming over to apologize wasn't some brave gesture like what happened with those cops or getting beaten up but I love you, Jack. I can't believe this. No, don't say anything."

Just a few words from him and she was thrown back into a pit of confusion. Maybe it wasn't love at all. Though she had never thought about what she had said before, maybe she was right: maybe he saw her the way so many others saw her, as a pretty but eminently breakable ornament. Nice to have around, nice to look at but not to be taken seriously because she wasn't up for the real stuff.

"Jackie, I love you, too. I just … I just don't want anything bad to ever happen to you." He was as confused as she was and he decided to make explicit something he was sure she knew. "It *is* different for a girl, the things that can happen. I mean, Jesus, Jackie, Susan's as strong as they come and look what happened to her."

"I think you should take me home," she said.

They had drifted while they talked and they walked back to the car five feet from each other. He drove aimlessly through the woods that surrounded the lake for fifteen minutes, backtracking and covering the same ground several times amidst a tense silence. She barely noticed the woods and the dark roads but thought only about how he had dared to suggest that they be apart.

"You always have to do everything the hard way," she said finally. "Even when there's an easy way staring you in the face, you choose the hard way."

Neither of them could look at the other and the silence returned and grew heavy. He didn't want them to be apart, not for all the trouble in the world. He knew there was little likelihood he could explain without making it worse but he had to try.

"I don't like for anybody to get pushed around, Jackie. I especially don't like for people I care about to get pushed around. You. Susan. Anybody. But you most of all." He knew it was inadequate but he went on. "I don't think for a minute that you're a little girl. Just the opposite. But certain things *are* more dangerous for you than they would be for me. I don't like it, you don't like, but it's true. Something happening to you would be worse than if it happened to me. You understand that, don't you? And you understand why I would feel that and be afraid of it? I know how brave you are because I've seen it and that's as good as it gets. With me, with Susan. With everybody. And you standing up for people makes *them* better. People in the committee have said as much, that they admire and respect you and are encouraged by you coming out. It's true with Susan, too, that you make her better. Especially now. And it's definitely true with me. You make me better in more ways than I could ever put into words."

She listened to every word. She didn't care about the cops or Walt or Frank O'Toole and his friends. They could overcome all of that and whatever else they had to face, but only if they were together. He was right about everything except he left out that he made *her* better. That's why the thought of them not being together upset her so much.

"Jackie, I'm sorry." He had pulled over and turned the ignition off. "About Susan. About everything. You know I don't want us to be apart. Not now. Not ever. It's just that things are a little messed up right now."

"Things are a little messed up, aren't they?" she said. "But that doesn't mean we can't make them right. *We're* not messed up. And even if we are a little messed up, we're better off being messed up together."

He laughed. "Yeah. And I meant it when I said you were brave. I was the one who was afraid."

She looked at him for the first time since they left the parking lot but he kept his eyes straight ahead. "It's alright to be afraid sometimes."

"Except this afternoon, I was afraid that you came over to break up with me."

"Oh, Jack." She continued to wait in vain for him to turn and meet her gaze.

"I feel like I need to show you that I love you, after the things I said."

"Like you have to do anything else to show that you love me," she said.

They were surrounded by trees and the air was full of the sound of crickets. He wanted to say more but there were no words for what he was feeling. Despite his joking, he had always wanted her to love him as much as he loved her. Now, here it was and it was scarier than all the cops and thugs in the world put together. All the bold proclamations of love and daring her to love him had been nothing but a cover for the fact that he was afraid to really give himself or to fully accept all she had to give.

"You're an amazing guy, Jack. You're the most amazing person I've ever known."

She knew he couldn't say it, to admit he was afraid to trust her unconditionally, and that was okay. She would say it, or at least say what she knew had to be said. All summer, whenever she had fallen, he was always there to catch her. Now he was falling and it was her turn. She was tempted to take him in her arms, knowing how much he needed her to hold him, but she also knew that it would be more complete, more lasting, if she gave voice to it first. That way, he would know that she knew and that it was okay. He had said so much that was just right, there was no need for him to say more. She would say it.

"There is one more way you can show me you love me. One way that you haven't yet."

"What?"

"Let me make love to you, Jack?" She turned and looked him in the eyes. "Surrender yourself all the way and let me make love to you. Tonight. At your place."

THIRTY-FOUR

"Are you sure you wanna go," Jackie said, repeating the question she had asked on the phone, "and that you don't need to sleep?"

"I'm fine," he said. "Are you sure *you* wanna go?"

"Definitely," she said. "It's exactly the kind of thing I've been reading and writing and talking about all summer."

The classroom was hot. Though it was hotter outside, all the windows were open because more than fifty people were packed into the small space. Most were workers from the Hancock plant and friends and community members there to see how they could support the strike in a more organized manner. Among the latter group were members of the police brutality committee including Lourdes, who the strikers had asked to chair the meeting.

She began with a quick recap: the workers had struck for two days in early August and returned to work believing they had won most of their demands, only to discover that the deal the union president had announced to them differed significantly from the actual deal he reached with the company. Within hours, the workers walked back out. Now the company was threatening to replace them and the union was refusing to support them.

Although Hancock employed two hundred people, both the initial strike and the wildcat that was now in its third day were largely invisible to the city's residents. The factory was nestled in an isolated corner of the city, bound by the highway, the elevated tracks of the New Haven Railroad and a much larger, long-closed factory and its billboard-sized declaration:

QUALITY PRODUCTS YESTERDAY TODAY TOMORROW

Once populated with Hungarian and Romanian immigrants, the neighborhood around the plant had been destroyed in the 1950's by construction of the Connecticut Turnpike and few people other than the Hancock workers traveled to it anymore. Where there once had been homes and shops and movie theaters there were empty lots and massive, impersonal storage facilities.

Hancock's black, Puerto Rican and Portuguese workforce was also largely invisible to the city's residents. There were twenty larger factories in town, after all, and only so much room in the local paper for news about contract negotiations, plant closings, strikes, and layoffs. When anything happened at GE, Westinghouse, DuPont, Sikorsky, Jenkins and the other big plants, people knew about it. Not so Hancock. The Hancock plant was even invisible in the voluminous coverage the paper's sports section accorded the Industrial Leagues, as it didn't so much as have a bowling team, let alone softball, baseball or basketball teams.

The strikers were far out on a limb and the atmosphere in the classroom was tense. Because the local's officers opposed the walk-out, none of the other unions in town would support it. Even the rank and file network that Jack belonged to, so enthusiastic in its support of the Westinghouse strike in July, was nowhere to be found. And the Hancock workers didn't have much time as company reps were working with agencies around town to recruit replacement workers.

While Lourdes spoke in English, those whose best or only language was Spanish or Portuguese sat in groups around two designated translators. And as soon as Lourdes turned the floor over to the strikers, their frustration spilled forth in three languages as one after another came forward with accounts of the troubles in the plant, the troubles with the proposed settlement and the troubles with the union officers. Amidst the heat, the anger, and the low hum of the translating, the strikers spoke about their jobs more than they ever had with anyone from outside the shop.

The meeting ended on a note of cautious optimism. Teams were formed to go to workplaces, churches, community organizations, the unemployment office, housing projects and social service agencies to counteract the company's recruitment efforts. Since the workers' place was on the picket line, others divided up the work to be done. Jackie, Lourdes, Jack and Juan constituted one team and stayed afterwards with several strike leaders to draft a new leaflet.

An hour later, the four of them went to Lourdes' apartment where Jackie typed, Lourdes worked on translation and Juan and Jack set up the mimeograph machine. Tomorrow they'd have somebody on the picket line translate the content into Portuguese; for now, they'd make do with English and Spanish. When all was ready, they began the task of reproducing several thousand leaflets, sharing wine and beer and mapping out the route they would cover the following day.

When the guys went out to buy ink, Jackie made a point of commending Lourdes on the job she had done chairing the meeting. She also expressed appreciation for the way Lourdes made everyone feel they had a place among the disparate group, herself included. There had been only ten women in the group, yet Lourdes was not the least intimidated, nor had she allowed the men to talk down to any of the other women.

From the moment the workers had begun talking about the difficulties of their jobs, Jackie connected to the strike in a way she wouldn't have just two months before, for people putting their livelihoods on the line was as real as it got. The workers' apprehension at the prospect of losing still more ground financially was also real, as was their anger at the union. Real, too, were their occasional bits of gallows humor. Perhaps most real of all was the intense way everyone enunciated the word *wildcat. Huelga salvaje.* And wild it was, and so very different from official strikes that were frequently orchestrated affairs following a predetermined course where those with the most at stake had little or no input. Supporting the strike certainly felt real and Jackie dove in, just as Susan would want, she knew – just as Susan herself would have – and over the next few days she worried less and less about her sister.

"Do you teach GED in the summer?" Jackie and Lourdes were waiting outside the bodega across from the Soundview housing project while the two men took a bathroom break.

"No," Lourdes replied. "The program coincides with the school schedule. In the summer I do a little bit of everything: tutoring, teaching English to Spanish speaking kids, teaching Spanish to English speaking kids. The kids are a nice change."

"I'm gonna learn Spanish one way or another, either in school or on my own."

"I went to NYU, you know," Lourdes said.

"Really?" Jackie immediately blushed in embarrassment at the surprise in her voice but Lourdes brushed it off. She had heard the same thing many times.

"Not bad for a girl from the projects, ay?" As she had once before, she put her arm around Jackie. "You're gonna love it."

"Alright, let's get to it," Juan said as he and Jack rejoined them.

"We should split up," said Lourdes.

"Why?" Juan asked. "He speaks Spanish."

"We should split up," Lourdes insisted. "Jack and I will start with this building, you guys start across the street. We don't have much time to spend at each door. The two most important things are the rally at the picket line and not to scab."

"It's just after three," Juan said. "Let's meet out here at five and evaluate how it's going. It may not be worth it to try and do the whole project."

Lourdes knew all of the housing projects in the city and her suggestion that they do Soundview rather than the Remington Apartments or Clark Terrace or Nathan Hale or any of the others was made with Jackie and Jack in mind. She had canvassed in all of them many times in the last seven years about other strikes, the free health clinic the Young Lords had helped establish, and the GED prep program she and other radical educators had forced the city to set up and Soundview was far and away the safest.

A crowd of boisterous kids, harried mothers and seniors struggling with groceries waited in the lobby for the only working elevator. Jackie and Juan took the stairs, ten flights to the top. On the tenth floor, they each took a door and knocked.

It took some practice and some eavesdropping on Juan before she got comfortable with her rap but once she did, she was able to get the basics out in a quick, friendly burst. If no one answered, they slid leaflets under the door. A few were curious at her presence, as eighteen-year old white girls so obviously from someplace else rarely came a-knocking in Soundview. Most of those they spoke to took leaflets and vowed that no one they knew would scab, and several promised to do what they could to come to the rally.

Lourdes had mentioned that Juan had done three years in Vietnam straight out of the same high school Jack had gone to, and Jackie asked him about it during what dead time they had – cautiously at first, then more comfortably once it was clear he didn't mind. Though the first year had been pretty bad, he spoke about it casually, as though it was a long time ago. The rest of the time had been fairly tame, he joked, because of the culinary skills he had picked up working as a teenager. Good cooks were hard to find in the army so the other guys kept him safe, and he'd be forever grateful that he had taken the job at the diner at sixteen rather than the one at the sporting goods store. He was now working at a restaurant that overlooked the Sound and was a semester away from getting his associate's degree at the community college.

"Soon as I got out of the army in sixty-nine," he said, "I joined the revolution. I met Lourdes and her cousin Carmen in the Young Lords – Carmen's my wife. We were founding members of the local chapter. Worked for a few years with some guys tryin' to get a local chapter of VVAW off the ground but that didn't last, unfortunately."

"VVAW?"

"Vietnam Veterans Against the War," he said. "I still go to New York for their events once in a while. I've met your sister a number of times, you know. Here and in New York. Fantastic lady. Smart as they come. You're a lot like her. You even look a lot like her."

From there on, Jackie doubled down with her efforts. More than ever, this is the kind of thing she wanted to do with her life and the kind of people she wanted to do it with. And so they made their way ten units per floor, unit by unit, floor by floor. At five o'clock, they had covered the top seven floors. After touching base outside, they decided to go until the two buildings were finished.

The four of them hit the DuPont plant on Barnum Avenue at six-fifteen the following morning. Afterwards, they picked up Juan's wife Carmen at the end of her overnight shift at the hospital and drove to the picket line. About seventy strikers were there, along with a dozen supporters. Though there were no scabs, there were lots of police and lots of talk of the rally scheduled for Tuesday. What went unsaid, though everyone knew, was that Tuesday might be too late.

"We shoulda stayed inside and took over the damn plant," one black worker said during a lull in the walking and chanting. "That's the way they used to do it."

"Man," another black worker said, "you know as well as I do that if we tried that, they'd be on us in no time with police dogs and billy clubs and fire hoses and all that mess. They would never let us get away with that."

"What we need is some brave brothers of the Caucasian persuasion to lead the charge," the first one said as he eyed Jack. "Whatta you say, my man?"

Jack laughed along with the others but behind the laughter was the depressing lack of support from the city's overwhelmingly white unionized workforce. The Hancock local's two thousand other members could hide behind the fact that the strike was in defiance of the union, but that was a dodge. Many of them knew better, for many of them knew all too well of how their Irish and Italian and Polish parents and grandparents had been on the other side of that deal. The strikers themselves, though embittered, took the

257

lack of solidarity in stride, for there was little in their experience to make them think support would be forthcoming from people who didn't look or speak like them.

Despite Jack's efforts, no one from the Brass came out to the picket line or pushed their local to support the strike. All of them – the workers at the Brass, the city's fifteen thousand UE members, the old-timers who went back to the sit-down spring of 1937 and had walked most every picket line in the city since – knew that the line the Hancock workers were attempting to hold was their line, too, yet the Hancock workers struggled on alone except for the support group who could not make up in spirit what it lacked in numbers and clout.

THIRTY-FIVE

When her long day of work at Yale was done, Jackie caught the train home. Just as Susan had foretold, Jackie's boss was full of praise and gratitude when she called in, much as she had been the day before when she called with an enthusiastic report on all the great material she had unearthed in Storrs. More than ever, poring through interview transcripts and old newspaper clippings was connected to that moment in Jackie's life, for the material was about people from factories throughout Connecticut just like Hancock including some *from* Hancock who had participated in strikes in 1913, 1934 and 1970. It was like a strong chain that ran through history as people struggled against long odds attempting to make things better, just as the current Hancock strikers were attempting to do, and she couldn't wait to get back to the picket line the following morning.

"Jacqueline?"

She had gone up to the third floor upon hearing her father arrive, hoping to avoid him until dinner. He was home earlier than usual and that was disconcerting enough. That he had come immediately to the door to the third floor upon entering the house was further indication that something was amiss.

"May I see you down here? Now?"

She went past him into his office, sat with one of her bare feet on the seat and waited as he went behind his desk. The two of them had not sat across each other in his office for several years, though it had once been a common occurrence. The room looked exactly as it did all those other times except the manual typewriter was gone, replaced by a new electric one. The windows were open and the curtains swayed softly as golden rays of sunlight cast rectangular images across the floor.

"I had a long meeting with an old friend of mine today," he began slowly. "Someone who has worked in numerous capacities in law enforcement for the last thirty-eight years. Knows everybody and most everything that's going to happen before it happens. Fortunately, he likes and respects me and he came to my office for a quiet, private talk so I would have the opportunity to handle matters myself."

There were four pieces of information that were of primary concern to Mr. Gendron, the first two the result of his friend's visit, the third the result of a phone call he made not long afterwards, and the last which he figured he could easily trap Jackie into admitting. Point one concerned activities Jackie had attended at which people who were or had once been members of the Black Panther Party, the Young Lords, possibly the FALN and other subversive organizations were present, and that among these activities were confrontational demonstrations denouncing the city's police department. Point two was a tip the police had received that an apartment rented by Jack Simmons was one where drugs were sold on a regular basis. Point three, one that he had suspected for some time, was that Jack was working with her at Susan's place of employment, the Center for Working Class Studies in New York. Point four, which he did not yet give voice to, was that she was spending nights with Jack at Susan's as well as at his place.

"I'll take your silence to mean that everything I've said is accurate."

"No," she said. "The part about Jack selling drugs is absolutely false."

"And you know this, how, exactly?"

"Because I know Jack." There was no longer any point in hiding what had never been bad when there was something new and ominous in the discussion. "And because I've spent a lot of time at his apartment the last two months."

He hadn't had to trap her after all. "You freely admit that?"

"Yes. And I don't know anything about subversives. All the people we've met have been good, serious people." She struggled to keep her voice strong. "But the most important thing, dad, is that you have to believe me. Jack has nothing to do with dealing drugs."

"My information may be wrong," he said. "Either way, you are forbidden as of this moment from having anything to do with him. Since I'm also going to assume that the two of you have been spending nights together at your sister's, effective immediately, you will quit your job in Manhattan and you will not travel to New York City for any reason until it is time to begin school. Should you violate any of these terms, you will not attend NYU and nothing Susan says or does will change that. Do you understand?"

Jackie blanched at the superior way he spoke her sister's name. That he could so smugly invoke Susan while she struggled as Jackie had never seen her struggle infuriated her. She knew, however, that she had to proceed cautiously.

"If I agree to everything you say – "

"We're not negotiating, Jacqueline. Everything I've said is in force right now. And if at any point from here forward I find that you continue to live in anything approaching the disgraceful manner you've been living in so far this summer, I will do everything I can to put Jack behind bars myself."

"You wouldn't." Of all that had transpired between them over the years, this was the first time he had said something that literally made her feel she was going to be sick. "But you can probably make it so it goes away."

"It would appear that the only way I can be sure you'll comply with my terms is to keep something hanging over your head."

"You can't do that to Jack." She was staring at him and struggling not to collapse to the floor.

"I'll be speaking to your mother about this tonight," he went on, "and I'd suggest you not lobby her or cry on her shoulder beforehand. And if I get so much as a phone call from your sister appealing to me on your behalf, I will go ahead with what I've said. Do you understand?"

"Yes," she said weakly.

He sat back in his chair the way he did whenever he was bringing things to an end. "I know you think I'm being hard on you."

"I'm your daughter. Doesn't that – "

"Precisely," he said. "You're my daughter. And if I mopped floors for a living and we lived in the Lincoln housing project, Jack and possibly you would be in far more trouble than you are. So you see, I'm the good guy of this story. And my ability to play the good guy comes from all the things that you and Susan and your new friends from the Black Panther Party despise – my position, my political beliefs, my connections."

A part of her wanted desperately to get away from him, out of that room away but also out of his life forever away.

"It's a cold world, Jacqueline, and sometimes we have to fight coldness with coldness in order to bring warmth. I note just for the record that you haven't asked and probably never will ask me to help any of the thousands of others you've spoken so eloquently about in the past. Or perhaps those tears you're trying to hold back are for all the innocent people not named Jack Simmons who are rotting away in prison?"

She staggered toward the door, thoroughly defeated.

"One last thing, Jacqueline." She stopped without turning to look at him. "A father's love sometimes comes in strange guises. When the cold thaws – and it most definitely will thaw – don't be surprised when you feel some warmth."

She almost made the bathroom before she threw up.

Her instincts were to call Jack. She wanted more than anything to see him and she knew if she called that he would come to her. But that was impossible. She wouldn't call Susan, either. The image of Susan in a hospital bed, fragile and vulnerable as she had never seen her, had not gone away. Even were Jackie inclined to disobey her father, Susan needed her more than she needed Susan and it was out of the question to ask her for help. She would have to be strong for the two of them – for the three of them.

She knocked on the open door. He turned quickly and surprise showed on his face.

"I'd like to talk to you again, dad, if it's alright."

"Come in."

"You said before we weren't negotiating," she said once she was seated. "With your permission, I'd like to say one more thing. Maybe it's negotiating, maybe it's not. I'll let you decide."

He hesitated, thrown slightly by her business-like tone. "Go on."

"In addition to all of your stipulations, which I promise to follow, I'll go to Harvard if you can still pull strings to get me in. I'll never complain about it, I'll never mention NYU again, and I'll be the best possible student I can be. In return, will you talk to your friend and do everything you can to make sure nothing happens to Jack? It's not true, the part about drugs. You have to believe me."

"I suppose you're going to tell me he doesn't so much as smoke pot."

"He smokes pot once in a while, the same way I smoke pot once in a while," she said. "Somebody is trying to get him in trouble."

"Why would you think that?"

"Jack had an altercation with a guy he went to school with last month," she replied, "and some of the guy's friends beat Jack up."

"Don't tell me you were there."

She nodded. "The first time was at the Seaport Diner. The second time was at the beach the day after the hurricane. Jack had to go to the emergency room. Well, the police … we heard that this guy got arrested a few days ago. He's a drug addict and a drug dealer and he probably made something up about Jack to save himself."

Mr. Gendron studied his daughter. "Is there anything else I'm better off hearing from you rather than from – "

"We helped a girl we know kick heroin." She said it simply and confidently, as an enormous surge of pride in Jack suddenly filled her. "Or Jack did, anyway. Ironically enough, she's this guy's sister."

"Jackie! Heroin?"

"Jack was great. You'd be so proud of him, dad. Peggy O'Toole. You remember. She used to be friends with Ronnie. Beautiful red hair. Jack saved her life." She wiped a tear from her cheek. "She'd be dead now if it weren't for Jack."

Mr. Gendron had half-expected the pot and the sleepovers. He had not expected hard drugs and beatings and cops. He was rarely flustered and whenever he was, his impulse was to resist.

"If you think you're helping your case, Jacqueline - "

"I promise to do everything you said. I won't appeal to mom. I give you my word I won't appeal to Susan. I'll go to Harvard the way you wanted all along." She cared about only one thing. "Will you please help him?"

She had never talked to him one adult to another, with no regard for her own interests. "What did you start to say earlier about the police?"

She drew a breath. "Two cops hassled Jack a few nights ago for no reason. I'm sorry, dad, but I was there for that, too. We were walking on the beach and they were clearing out the park. It wasn't intentional, but once they realized it was us they decided to scare him. You know, because of the rallies and everything."

"Did they do anything to you or bother you in any way?"

"No," she replied, "but they knew you. Or knew of you."

"What do you mean?"

"One of the cops told Jack to watch himself or they'd make it so even you couldn't help him. They didn't even acknowledge me. But they know I'm your daughter."

Mr. Gendron stiffened. Cops putting his daughter in a tight spot because of a few stupid rallies? Threatening her boyfriend? Jackie was right about more than she realized, only he couldn't let her know that.

"What's this strike I've heard you talking about on the phone?"

"The Hancock factory on Rakoczi Street. A wildcat? You know

more about that than me. But I know they're right. They work really hard for low pay and the company wants to cut their pay, only the union won't help. Just the kinda thing you always taught us to care about." Mr. Gendron turned away uneasily. "Isn't there somebody you can talk to about Jack?"

He waited a long time before answering. "I don't know."

She had allowed herself to expect more. "Is that all you can say to me?"

"Look, Jacqueline," he said wearily, "the police department is a totalitarian world. Nobody bucks them. You may think you're simply exercising your Constitutional rights by attending these demonstrations, but as far as the police are concerned – do you know anything about the Black Panthers? What they've done? How they operate? We're not exactly talking about Martin Luther King, you know."

"I know Jack knows one of the kids who got shot," she said. "He played basketball with him. Or maybe you believe all the lies in the paper about how the cop shot him in self-defense?"

"I know no one is helping matters by involving people who used to be in the Black Panthers."

"There's gotta be someone you can talk to," she persisted.

He shifted in his chair. "It's too bad you couldn't have just had a nice, pleasant summer and then gone off to school. Was that too much to ask?"

"Why do you hate Jack so much? You sat downstairs with him that night. Didn't you like him? Didn't you see that he's funny and smart and that he's in love with life?"

"Jacqueline, all these horror stories about – "

"Don't you care that he treats me exactly the way you would want a guy to treat me? That he has never so much as raised his voice to me? That when those cruds were beating him up, the only thing he cared about was my safety? I guess none of that matters because his father gets his hands dirty when he works and his mother's a secretary and because he can't afford to go to Harvard."

She studied him for a moment, trying to understand what he wanted of Jack. She knew they were done but she wouldn't go without saying one thing more.

"I'll be grateful to you for the rest of my life for anything you can do for him."

Upstairs, she scribbled furiously in her journal for a half hour straight, though she wrote nothing about the conversations with her father. Instead she wrote about Jack. She refused to believe they were over, yet she wrote as if documenting something for posterity. Eventually she stopped and stretched out on the bed. Though her room was bathed in sunlight, she immediately fell asleep.

"Jackie?"

"I'm lying down, mother." Too late. Her mother was on her way up the stairs.

"Jackie," her mother said when she entered, "the hall and the bathroom downstairs … you've been sick."

"I'm sorry," she said, sitting up. "I thought I cleaned it all – "

"I don't care about that. I care about whether you're alright."

"I'm fine," Jackie said. "Just a little tired."

As soon as she got a close look, Mrs. Gendron grew more alarmed. "Jackie, what is it? Your father's acting so strangely and you look so upset."

"Mom, whatever you do, please don't call him up here." Over the summer, she had moved upstairs from her room on the second floor because they hardly ever went to the third floor. It was her refuge and she would not allow the two of them to gang up on her in the only place in the house that still felt like home.

"Honey." Mrs. Gendron sat on the bed and ran her hand through Jackie's hair. She had not liked the short cut at first but now she saw that it accentuated her daughter's beauty more fully than any other. "What is it?"

"I promised dad I wouldn't say anything."

"Promised? Jackie, what is it?"

"I can't." She and Jack were so close to home free and it was all falling apart.

"Then *he'll* tell me." Mrs. Gendron rose. "Right now."

Her mother would take it better than her father but she would still be angry. Jackie had had enough of that kind of grief for one day so she did not follow. She would remain in her personal fortress and mourn the premature, disastrous end of the great summer.

Somehow, she slept again. Though it was warm in her room, she crawled under the sheets and even pulled a blanket up. She fell asleep praying that Jack wouldn't call. He would be home by eight-thirty and she was tempted to set the alarm so she could beat him to the punch, but she was too sad and tired and confused to do anything as demanding as set an alarm. Perhaps she could sleep until the first day of school.

When she awoke, it was again to the sound of her mother's voice. It felt like she had slept for hours, yet her room was still illuminated by the last bit of daylight. She heard her father's voice, too, and her parents' conversation went chaotically from barely audible to indecipherable and back as though they were talking while walking up and down stairs and going in and out of rooms. When she was sure they were both in his office, she went down to the second floor as quietly as possible.

"You knew about it?" Her father was incredulous. "Annamaria, you can't be serious. You knew he had his own place and that Jackie was spending nights there?"

"Yes," Mrs. Gendron said in a firm voice. "She told me the situation and I gave her my permission."

"You gave her your permission? Without speaking to me?"

"I didn't speak to you because I knew you would do exactly what you're doing now. She also told me beforehand that Jack had been hired with her for the summer at the Center where Susan works. I told her I thought it was wonderful they would be working together and from what I see, it has been." Mrs. Gendron hesitated ever so briefly. "I also told her it was alright if they stayed over together in New York."

Jackie listened tensely. Not only could she barely believe that her mother was lying to her father on her behalf, she had never heard her mother so unflustered in the face of her father's anger. She imagined where they were in the room and how close they were to one another. She stepped forward out of the shadows, less concerned about being discovered as that she might miss something.

It went on in the same vein as her mother proceeded to chastise her father for taking as gospel the bit about Jack selling drugs and for being weak-kneed about the demonstrations. Then she declared unequivocally that the punishments he lay down were rescinded and that he owed Jackie an apology. On top of all that, she said something Jackie did not think she would ever hear.

"This is a deal-breaker, Maurice. You say you're fed up? Well, no one around here is as fed up as I am. I think you've acted disgracefully. If you persist, you may find that Jackie is not the only one who leaves this house. You would think you were dealing with a homicidal maniac. I had allowed myself to forget what a bright, shining star she is. I will never forget it again as long as I live. If you've forgotten or can no longer see it, I pity you for what you're missing."

Jackie held her breath for a long time. Had she scripted a defense for herself, it could not have been as stirring as the one her mother presented.

"Many years ago we confided in each other that we both would have liked to have had a son," Mrs. Gendron went on in a dramatically softened voice. "If we had, we could hardly have done better than if he were like Jack. Even if you don't agree, at least keep Jacqueline's happiness in mind – not even her happiness as defined by her, though you should definitely consider that, but rather by some objective measure. If you can allow yourself to look at it honestly, I think you'll see she's happier because of Jack than she's

268

ever been in her life. Then think for a moment about what you're missing in terms of your own happiness by refusing to let her love you."

"Annamaria, this is too much."

"We're not negotiating, Maurice."

She started at hearing her mother use the same words her father had. She was so engrossed that the darkness that surrounded her didn't register, for there wasn't a single light on in the whole house save for the one in her father's office.

She wondered if her mother was sitting on the edge of the desk the way she had once years before. It was summer then, too, and her mother had been smiling radiantly. She was stunned by how flirtatious her mother had been with her father at the time and certain her mother was the most beautiful woman in the world.

"I'm sure you're tired and hungry," Mrs. Gendron said. "If you'd like, Jackie and I could go to Shanghai Delight."

Jackie knew her father would not come around easily. It would be great to sit around the dining room table and eat Chinese for a few hours, the three of them, but it would be tense. He never came around easily.

"You decide." Mrs. Gendron came out of the room so suddenly and quietly that Jackie had no chance to make a getaway. "Jackie. I was just coming to check on you."

"I'm sorry, mom. I - "

"How do you feel?"

Her mother was almost to her when Jackie surged forward and threw both arms around her and pressed her face to her mother's neck. There was a solidity to her that more than made up for Jackie's suddenly weak knees.

"Is it me," Mrs. Gendron said finally, "or is it dark in here?"

Jackie laughed. "You sound like Jack."

"Really?"

"He always says exactly the right thing to puncture all the tension." They took hold of each other and went about turning on lights. "I love you, mom."

"And I love you, honey. And I'm sorry to say I've neglected to tell you that I love your haircut." She ran her hand through Jackie's hair. "Why, Jacqueline Elaine. Are you a blusher all of a sudden?"

"Yeah. Isn't it great?" She laughed again. "Mom? What about dad?"

"Everything's going to be alright, honey. Trust me."

That was easy enough. She trusted her mother to the outer edges of the solar system and beyond. "He was so mad at me before."

"He'll pull through," Mrs. Gendron said. "He may need our help but he'll pull through."

"Will you show me ... how I can help him?"

"Absolutely. Is it alright if we eat first?"

Again Jackie laughed. She wanted to laugh until she was all laughed out. Laughing would wait, though. There was one more thing she had to know.

"Do you think he'll help Jack?"

"Yes, I do," Mrs. Gendron said confidently. "I'm guessing he'll have a plan ready by the time we sit down to eat. Speaking of which, how does Shanghai Delight sound?"

"Terrific. Is it alright if I call Jack before you call for the food?"

"Of course," Mrs. Gendron said. "Would you like to ask him to join us?"

It was one more unexpected in a whirl of unexpecteds. "Do you think it'll be okay? With dad, I mean."

"Yes." As though making up for lost years, Mrs. Gendron was again touching her daughter's face and hair. "Maybe I can help him with his Italian."

"He'd like that."

"You know your father took back everything he said earlier."

Jackie looked down. "Yeah, I know. I was listening."

Mrs. Gendron didn't care about that. She was concerned about something else. "What is it, honey? You still seem troubled."

Jackie wanted desperately to tell her about Susan. Never had she believed Susan was wrong about anything the way she believed she was wrong about keeping their mother out. She disliked that she had to choose between what she knew her mother would want and what Susan wanted, but she also knew she might regret saying something in a moment of great uplift. Her first loyalty was to Susan. She hated that just then, that it had to be one or the other, but there it was. She would wait. She would talk to Susan, perhaps even plead with her to let their mother in, but she would not give her up.

"Nothing. Just – are you sure it's okay to invite Jack over?"

"Positive. In fact, it's long overdue."

THIRTY-SIX

Jackie was the first to see the paper but she missed the article completely as she flipped hurriedly through the front sections in a vain search for something about the Hancock strike. Mrs. Gendron saw it, however. Sunday was the day a story that was somebody's idea of investigative reporting got published in the local paper. Often it was an expose of an eminently replaceable politician who had fallen out of favor in elite circles. In the world of journalism's version of closing the barn door after the horses were out, the expose served to let the public in on the joke.

This Sunday, however, people of some status were mentioned in a long article about the fires that had raged on the East Side all summer. No accusations of criminal activity were leveled and, since the word arson was never mentioned, it wasn't clear that any crimes had occurred, at least in the sense of law-breaking. Even if the prominent citizens named had nothing to do with the fires, however, they were now exposed as slumlords and for many around town, residents of the East Side most of all, slumlording was as least as serious a crime as arson.

It was all right there, beginning on the front page and continuing for a full page and a half inside. Barry Jensen, partner in the firm of Gendron and Jensen, was the first name – the only name, in fact – mentioned on page one. Though more prominent names followed, Jensen was the only individual listed who owned more than one of the properties that had been torched.

Mr. Gendron generally read the *Daily News* in the morning and the *Times* and the local paper after mass. There was no way his wife could let it wait, however, and her instincts were true. Once she showed him the story, Mr. Gendron decided to skip mass. It wasn't that anything wrong had been done. The only person in the world Mr. Gendron trusted more than his partner was his wife. Besides, that's what accumulated wealth was for: investing. Some people invested in GE, some invested in cheap property. But inquisitive looks from fellow parishioners was something Mr. Gendron did not need on a bright August morning. Without his having to ask, his wife also decided to skip mass.

The firm was mentioned three times and Maurice Gendron, unimplicated partner, was referenced by name. Though it was stated that he did not own any of the properties in question, the Gendron name had been sullied nonetheless, even if only by association. It did not make for happy Sunday breakfasting and the house was somber into afternoon.

While debating whether it was simply best to leave her father to his depression for the time being, Jackie was shocked to see Susan get out of a cab in front of the house and almost as shocked to discover that she already knew about the story in the paper. After a hug, Susan whispered that she was not there to talk about herself, not with their folks anyway. That was fine with Jackie. Her sister's presence was cause enough for happiness, all the more when she said she'd be staying the night.

"How's the strike?"

"We were there last evening," Jackie said. "They're trying really hard but they're all running out of money and new people have been hired and are set to start working."

"Maybe we can go over later," Susan said. "And you and I will definitely talk. But later. How is he?"

Before she answered, Jackie hugged her again.

THIRTY-SEVEN

The strike ended that week. The combined efforts of the Hancock workers and their small band of supporters were not enough to overcome both the company and the union. Six were fired. The rest returned under the same terms that had caused them to walk out, knowing they'd be stuck working for and being represented by people who had opposed them at the most critical juncture of their work lives, on indefinitely into the future.

In contrast to the strike itself, its conclusion was deemed newsworthy enough for the local paper to run three articles and a long editorial. There was much praise for the company for doing what it had to do to remain competitive and for the union for its responsible behavior. Concessions were essential, the editorial declared, to save jobs. If workers had to be disciplined into understanding that, then disciplined they would be. There was nothing but scorn for the strikers' failure to appreciate their employment as well as for the attempt by outside agitators to interfere for their own ends.

Some strikers and supporters, Lourdes especially, talked about the wildcat in positive terms: the workers had done the right thing, many of them had behaved courageously, they were closer than ever, they had new community ties. Still, it was a defeat and there was no getting around that. Her respect for Lourdes notwithstanding, Jackie couldn't see much positive, try as she did. When Lourdes suggested they write an article together about the strike, though, her thinking began to change.

"Some of the guys asked me to," Lourdes said. "Most of them think it's a waste of time but it could be good, helping them tell their story. It would mostly be based on interviews and that's why I thought of you, because of your job."

"Who would we write it for?"

"The guys think the *Telegram*," Lourdes said, "but I know from experience there's no way. Maybe the *Guardian* or *Claridad*."

"I don't think I'd be much help but I could try." Jackie grew more interested as Lourdes talked about the need to have one last meeting, persisting with the idea that it couldn't all be allowed to die in defeat. That was how people built relationships for the long haul, for the general problems they confronted were not going away and even a loose network of people could become something more substantial very quickly.

"But that takes work and people willing to do it." Lourdes smiled. "You in?"

"Sure," Jackie said, liking the idea more and more.

"One other thing came up," Lourdes said. "If Susan's willing and available, it would be great if she could come to the meeting and give an overview, exactly like all the things she was saying the other night at the Seaport Diner. She really nailed it."

Susan was her old self that night at the diner. Listening and asking questions at first, she eventually said something about similar strikes in other places until, prodded, she broke the Hancock strike down as representative of a growing national trend: increasingly belligerent corporations, pliant unions, workers who could successfully resist if and only if they stuck together across trades and worksites, a public that remained aloof at its own peril. As she listened and observed how Susan was regarded by the others at the table — street tough factory workers, people like Lourdes with graduate degrees, revolutionaries like Carmen, winter soldiers like Juan – Jackie had never been prouder to be her sister.

"The strikers would be the main speakers," Lourdes went on. "We'd also have somebody from the support committee, plus Susan. People know and respect her because of her job and her writings and she has cred because she's from here."

"I'll ask her," Jackie said, excited. "And I'll ask her for ideas about where we might get the article published."

THIRTY-EIGHT

Susan's visit had lasted all of twenty-four hours. By Monday afternoon, she was back home, working. When Jackie called Tuesday, she had been up since sunrise writing. Her career was one of the things Jackie most admired about her sister, but she had come to see that Susan kept other more difficult aspects of life at arm's length by burying herself in work. One more time, Jackie urged her to get away before summer ended.

"Actually, I'm going away Friday for a few days with Mindy and Sam," Susan said. "So I'm following your orders to the T, doctor."

Jackie laughed. Both the joke and the decision to get away were good signs. Susan was better, after all. Not all the way better but definitely better.

"It's been great working with you," Jackie said of the interview project that was ending the following week. "Thanks for making it happen."

"It's been great working with you, Jackie. But remember, you made it happen. We have never had anyone work as hard. All the extra research you did, your enthusiasm, your eagerness and all the great work you did made the whole project a rousing success. And sad though you may be, remember there'll be lots of other projects. Better ones. Plus, right now, you've got school to look forward to. Everything in time, Jacqueline."

"I know Jack's loved it," Jackie said. "So thanks from him, too."

"As a matter of fact, the florist delivered a beautiful coleus from him here this morning."

"Really? He didn't say anything about it."

"Does that really surprise you?"

"No, I guess not." She knew there was something more Susan wished to say. They ended up having no time to talk on Sunday night so she waited through an awkward silence, hoping against hope that Susan would say something about Walt.

"Jackie, that night in the yard," Susan said. "I'm sorry. I let you down and that's the last thing I meant to do."

"You didn't let me down."

"No, I did. And I'm sorry. I promise I'll never let you down again."

"I still think you should talk to mom," Jackie said. "Things have been so much better with her."

"I know they have," Susan said. "But not yet. And I'm sorry again about the strike. Remember, the best way to turn something like that into a positive is to learn from it. Hopefully, the workers will."

"Actually, Lourdes asked if I would write an article about it with her," Jackie said. "We're getting together when she finishes work to get started."

"I think that's a great idea. Where is she thinking about getting it published?"

"Well, she has a few ideas but we thought we'd ask you what you thought," Jackie said. "And she has this other idea for a meeting of the strikers and the support committee that we'd like you to come and speak to if you're feeling up to it."

It had been three weeks since Jackie was at that beach so when Janet called, she was eager despite the clouds. Janet had things to do first and suggested they meet there so Jackie took a ride along the Sound and parked near their meeting place fifteen minutes early. She scoped out the water, then sat in the car for a while. When it got so Janet was thirty minutes late, she thought about leaving. But it was a weekday and a cloudy one at that and long stretches of the beach were empty so, with nothing special to do, she set out for a walk along the water's edge.

She would be living in Manhattan close to Susan soon and thus in a position to really help, and that took some of the sting out of the prospect of being apart from Jack. Her latest plan was to ask

Susan about moving in with her. That would be better than the dorm for when Jack stayed, it would be better for her, it would be good for Susan and it would be easier for them to do things together.

Salt water was not Jackie's thing and she never considered going in for a dip, plus it was low tide and not great for swimming. Low tide was ideal for checking out horseshoe crabs and jellyfish, though, and she occupied herself while keeping an eye out for Janet. After another thirty minutes she gave up and was just about back to the car when the Puerto Rican cop from the other time pulled up next to her mother's car. He got out and stood by the driver's side so she couldn't get to the door without going right up to him. There was no one on the beach near them and traffic was light.

"No turtles this time," he said. "And no Booty Boy."

"Will you excuse me so I can – "

"What's your hurry?" He smiled. "Worried because none of your nigger friends are here to help you?"

"I haven't done anything so there's no reason for you to keep me here."

"How's about I keep you here because I wanna keep you here? You think there's anything you can do about that?" He was still smiling but his voice was menacing. "You think all this stuff with these demonstrations is some kinda game?"

"No, it's not a game."

He moved toward her and she took a step back. "Whatta you say me and you go somewhere and have us some fun. It'll be our little secret."

"I'd like to get in my car." She thought about running, back toward the water maybe or up to the other end of the beach but her legs were heavy and she couldn't, besides which she wasn't sure it was a good idea.

"Come on, girlie, show me what you got. What's the big deal?" He moved closer. "From what I hear, you've done it with just about every other guy in town."

She shielded herself from the words by thinking about Jack. She thought about how brave he had been last time despite his fear and about the blows and abuse he had taken for both of them.

"If you ever do anything to Jack, I swear, I'll dedicate my life to destroying you."

His face hardened. "Yo, girlie. Sounds to me like you're threatening a police officer."

"Whatta you gonna do, shoot me in the back?"

He hadn't expected her to accede to his overtures, but he had expected to be able to browbeat her without resistance. It took him a moment to recover.

"No, that'd be a waste," he said. "I'd rather fuck you to death. You'd be lying on your back as helpless as one of your turtles and if I wasn't able to kill you with my dick, I'd put my hands around your throat." He touched her neck ever so lightly with his finger. "Then, while you were coming, I'd squeeze as hard as I could. How do you think that would feel, girlie?"

Somehow, from somewhere, she found it in herself to slap his face. She was as shocked as he was and alarmed by the look that came in his eyes. Then she became aware of a second police car approaching from up the seawall. The black cop from the other time got out and another cop, a younger white guy, followed.

"Anything wrong, partner?" The black one said firmly.

The Puerto Rican looked at Jackie. "Everything's good. Just a little miscommunication."

"Anybody else around?"

"No, just her."

"Is she free to go?"

The Puerto Rican stiffened. "You tryin' to run my show?"

"I'm thinkin' of you, partner," the black one said as he moved closer. "Why don't you and me talk about this."

"Talk."

"Is she free to go?"

A passing car slowed and four teenagers stared. Fifty yards up the seawall, another police car approached.

"You're free to go, miss," the Puerto Rican said as he moved slowly away.

She looked at the white cop and then at the black one, their faces frozen in that official police look she had come to know. There was something about being allowed to leave that she didn't trust, but she knew it was more dangerous to stay.

"Sorry about the misunderstanding," the black one said.

"Hey, man, don't apologize for me," the Puerto Rican said.

Coolly, she got in and started the car. She found still another reservoir of fortitude and sat there longer than she should have waiting for the Puerto Rican to meet her gaze. He never did. The last thing she saw in the rear view was the black and the Puerto Rican in heated conversation.

She put on 'India' and turned the volume as loud as it would go. It helped but it wasn't enough so she called Jack at the library. He was too busy to come to the phone so she tried Janet and got no answer. Reluctantly, she dialed Susan's number.

"Twice in one day? How nice. Is everything okay?"

"Everything's fine," Jackie said, regretting she hadn't gotten through to Jack. Susan did not need this. She was still shaken despite 'India,' however.

"Jackie, this is Susan."

She took a sip of lemonade. "Why is it that guys care so much about who else you've had sex with?"

"Uh-oh," Susan said. "Did you have a fight with Jack?"

"Oh, God, no. It was just some loser at the beach."

"It happens, unfortunately." Susan could hear the fear that had come into her sister's voice. "Jackie, this is Susan. Tell me."

She saw an opportunity. "If I do, will you tell me about you and Walt?"

280

Reluctantly, Susan agreed. Feeling better already, Jackie related in a few minutes what happened with the cop and stopped, thinking they were done and that it was Susan's turn. But as she had so many times in the past, Susan drew her out, gave her space to talk through even her darkest, angriest thoughts, prompting here in just the right way and always honoring what she said and what she was feeling. Little of what she said had to do with the cop and eventually it was Susan who brought them back to that.

"Yeah," Jackie said an hour after she had started. "But the part I don't get is why some cop even cares about Jack and me. I mean, we're just two insignificant white college students. Shouldn't they be way more worried about the people in the committee who have been doing this work their whole lives?"

"Believe me, they are," Susan said.

"Me and Jack haven't even been able to get a single person to go to any of the rallies with us."

"You hit the nail on the head right there," Susan said. "Think about it. What is it that the powers-that-be fear the most in all this work we do?"

"I don't know," Jackie replied. "Lots of people in the streets?"

"Right. And the part of that they fear most and that's also most important is lots of white people in the streets standing against white supremacy and standing together with lots of black people in support of black liberation. Entire think tanks and magazines and university departments have been created and generously bankrolled for the sole purpose of preventing that from happening and the difficulty you've had getting any of your friends interested speaks to the difficulty of the task. Of course the black leaders of the committee are being monitored and harassed, but you and Jack represent a potential link that the powers-that-be do not want to grow, believe me."

"I hadn't thought about it that way," Jackie said, determined suddenly to do more and to do it better. Resisting, writing, organizing, learning, working with people, standing her ground. Everything. Including knowing how to be there when someone she loved needed her. Beginning immediately.

"Susan, I don't want you to talk about Walt because I blackmailed you into it so if you'd don't want to I – "

"No, I want to," Susan said softly. "Most of all with you. Because I owe it."

When she tried Jack again, she got through. "Busy?"

"Very," he said. "What's up?"

"Nothing," she said, surprised by the thrill the sound of his voice sent through her. "Just wanted to say hello."

"Well, it's nice of you to call just to say hello."

"I listened to 'India' earlier. The real frenzied version. It's so beautiful." She hesitated. "I finally heard that one part you were talking about."

There were so many parts to 'India', plus he was heavy with work. "Which part?"

"You know," she said shyly. "The orgasm part."

"Gee, Jackie, that's terrific, but – "

"Can we listen to it tonight? Together?"

"Sure," he said. "Is there something in particular you'd like to do *while* we listen?"

She laughed. "I thought you said you were busy."

"What are they gonna do, fire me? I'm quitting next week." He waited. "Are you okay?"

She smiled, marveling again at how much like Susan he was. "I had a long talk with Susan. She really opened up about Walt. And she loves the coleus. How come you didn't tell me?"

"How is she?"

"Much better. She's gonna speak at the meeting Lourdes and the strike leaders are organizing." She hesitated, knowing anything she said about self-defense would arouse his concern. "Hey, will you teach me some of the basics of martial arts?"

"Sure. Why, did something happen?"

"No, of course not." Susan had said she should tell him about the cop and she would, just not yet. "A lotta women are taking it up."

"Yeah, absolutely," he said. "And one of these days maybe you can teach me how to do a cartwheel into a back flip."

"Really?" She had never imagined he would want to know how to do that.

"You can't believe how cool you look when you do it."

"Alright," she said. "But you better go. I don't want you to get in trouble."

"Here's an idea," he said. "Why don't you go listen to more music?"

She laughed. "I will."

"Think how much fun we could have with Ravi Shankar," he said.

"Can't wait."

"Meanwhile, I get to spend the next three hours trying not to think about it," he said.

"Poor baby."

"Maybe concentrate on putting books away," he said.

"Good luck with *that*."

"God, you are so cold," he said, laughing.

"Don't worry. I'll be plenty warm by eight-thirty."

THIRTY-NINE

When Jackie and Janet finally went to the beach on the second to last morning of August, they went to the lake rather than to the Sound. She and Jack had done their last interviews on Friday and he was working his last day at the library. They would have the rest of the week all to themselves, together, yet Jackie could not help but feel a bit of sadness. Summer was dying.

Though she had watched from up close as all five of her sisters went off to college, it did not lessen what a big deal it was now that her turn was at hand. Everything was moving at lightning speed, her relationship with Jack most of all. Three months before, he wasn't even in her life; now, she hated to think about being apart from him for any length of time.

While she swam, she thought about her father. As her mother predicted, he had pressed further and discovered that the talk about Jack selling drugs was, indeed, a fabrication straight from the desperate imagination of Frank O'Toole. Mr. Gendron also expressed thanks several times for the support his wife and Jackie had given him during a very trying week. More difficult for him to express, to understand even, given their strained relationship, was his appreciation of Susan's tenacious, unbreakable solidarity. He owned to being floored by Susan's showing up at the house that Sunday for his benefit and realized not long afterwards that she most of all was responsible for his improved state of mind.

The change in Mr. Gendron continued as August gave way to September. On Tuesday, he took his wife, Jackie and Jack to dinner and fussed over Jack so much that Jackie would have been embarrassed had she not been so happy. For several days, he stayed home and put in long hours at his typewriter and on the phone as the newspaper ran additional revelations about Barry Jensen that never failed to mention the firm. Discreetly, Jackie overheard things, mostly what sounded like negotiations over Jensen's possible retirement. She didn't understand all of it and she didn't ask;

what she knew was that her parents were getting on better than they had in a long time.

One morning after breakfast, her father apologized. It was heartfelt and for the first time, she felt like an adult in his presence. The best parts were the nice things he said about Jack and Susan. The longest part was about NYU. He was genuinely proud and happy for her and vowed to do what he could to make her time there as good as it could possibly be. He was trying to make up for years of their lives, she realized afterwards, and though making things right would not be easy, it was a start.

FORTY

They went to Prescott's one last time on Saturday night. The bar was crowded and more festive than ever as people grabbed onto one last bit of summer.

"Let's do this," he said. Billie Holiday was up.

"Jack, nobody else is dancing."

"All the better," he replied as he guided her toward the dance area. "This way, I'll be able to show off the new moves I learned when you weren't looking."

It was fun and though he still wasn't much good, his moves were better than on the Fourth of July. Still, she was the star of the show. Dancing that way was more synchronized and that made it more intimate. Soon she forgot about the other people and focused on moving and on him. To the very last hours of summer, they were discovering new ways to grow closer. New first times.

"I guess that's our new theme song," he said when they were back seated. "Please don't talk about me when I'm gone." She laughed but it wasn't very funny.

They danced, got high and stayed high by dancing for much of the night, reveling in the joy of being together precisely as they had for three months. At two o'clock, they walked to the Hudson, hopped an iron fence and sat with their feet dangling ten feet above the river's strong currents. Amidst the good feelings, she searched for the words to tell him about the cop at the beach that day. She was positive he had never lied to her, not so much as a lie of omission, not about anything important anyway. She would honor that, show how important it was, by reciprocating. No matter that what had happened with the cop would upset him; not telling would upset her far more.

While she was working to get her nerve up, they went back over the fence and sat so they faced each other. Jack thought one more time about something he had been thinking about for weeks. He had waited and procrastinated and even considered letting what he wanted to say die altogether. Sitting under the stars, looking at her, he was seized by the urgency of the moment. There was no time left.

What he said was set off by the soft tone of his voice. She had anticipated that he would share his feelings again before the weekend was out, but she wasn't prepared for the things he said after he said that he loved her. He spoke about finding a job in New York and about the two of them getting an apartment. He had no commitment to Keene State compared to what he had with her. If he couldn't find a job in New York right away, he would use the money he had for school to live on until he did.

"Jack, you can't." Though she was not yet over her shock, she steeled herself. "You can't ditch all your plans now. You've already waited a whole year to start school."

"None of that matters, Jackie. You matter. Knowing you ... loving you ... having you love me ... it's changed my life. *You've* changed my life. I'm happier, I'm smarter, I'm involved in new things. I believe in people. I believe in the ability of the world to set itself right. The last three months of my life with you have been better than the whole nineteen years before that put together."

"Jack, don't."

"It's true," he said. "And it's all because of you. You changed my life."

"It's not because of me," she insisted. "You were like that the night we met at the library."

"Jackie, I'm so much better now than I was then." He forced himself to say it. "If I go off to school, I know it's just a matter of time before you meet someone better than me."

His words stung because of what they implied but she held back. "How can you say that?"

He knew he had gone too far but still he was glad he had said it. There was a part of him he had kept from view, even from her. He had to make her see.

"I know what I am, Jackie. A nobody who was never able to

find his way. Then I found you. I need you, Jackie. If I ever lost you, I think I'd … I don't even like to think what would happen if I lost you. I'd go crazy. End up like so many guys I went to – "

"God, Jack, you are so not a nobody," she said. "You're a great guy. You know that I love you. We can do this."

"There's one other possibility." He hesitated. "We … we could get married."

She knew he was serious. His voice, that's how she knew he meant it. He was asking her to marry him.

"Jack, we can't," she said. "I'm eighteen, you're nineteen. How could we live?"

"I'll do what I've been doing," he replied. "Susan will help me get a job."

"No." He was ruining everything, plus there was something cheap about it.

"I'll go to school, too," he said. "Maybe not right away but – "

"No," she said louder than she intended. "I won't marry you that way. I'm *never* getting married. Ever. Not that way. Not any way."

It wasn't fair that he would spring that on her. She looked at him gravely. She had known for weeks that parting would be hard but she had not expected this.

"I meant what I said that night at the lake," she said after a long silence. "You're the most amazing person I've ever known. And all I want is to love you."

She began with his hair. Then she worked every inch of his face with her hand and kept her eyes on his the whole time. She liked that he had to look away. She caressed his face until, finally, he smiled. Then, better, he blushed. No matter the hour, New York rumbled on, yet they were oblivious to all but each other. All of the city's great lights put together were nothing next to the majesty of a twenty-six day moon and they basked in its glow like two inno-cents who had never known moonlight.

"Jack, we can do this."

They were quiet for a long time and that was fine. Then he began to talk and that was fine as well. He talked about how crazy he was to say those things and about Freshman Day at Keene on Tuesday and about how great it was that they would soon have both New York and New Hampshire to share. They had talked at length about her classes but hardly at all about his, and she listened to every word as he did so because more than ever everything about him mattered.

When he caught himself, he moved so he was beside her. She was right. They could do this. They could do anything.

On the way back, he took them to the spot where they had stood on Memorial Day. Recognition filled her face when he stopped, though she said nothing. She simply gave herself over to his arms and mouth and ran her hands over every part of him.

"You're supposed to say, *Nice hands*," she said.

"Great hands."

"Great ass." She laughed easily and began to sing as they set out for the bar. "I know a guy who's oh so sweet. He's so fine he can't be beat."

FORTY-ONE

By the time he dropped her off, the sun was up and it was Sunday morning. There was little time for sleep. Though they would easily enough move her things to the dorm in increments, she filled two suitcases and a foot locker and went over her checklists again and again to make sure she had everything. At three o'clock, she showered for a second time to fend off sleep and took her mother's car to his place.

Peggy was taking the apartment. She would move in on Monday as soon as he left. He and Jackie had been carting items he wasn't taking to New Hampshire to his mother's all the past week, boxes of books mostly but other things as well like the big turtle tank. Since he didn't have any need for furniture in the dorm, most of that would stay. He and Peggy would figure out the details later.

The bed, the big cable spool and many of the other familiar things were just as they had been all summer. Still, Jackie detected a sense of emptiness in the apartment. It was cramped, it was noisy, and the heat was sometimes unbearable, but it was her favorite place in the whole world and she walked around trying to burn pieces of it into her memory. Peggy had come to regard them as friends and Jackie was certain she'd be back soon to visit, but it would be Peggy's place then. The same place with maybe even a similar look, but never the same.

He was leaning against the kitchen sink eating the last of a jar of his mother's applesauce, the only food left in the house. She no longer thought him unpredictable the way she had in the beginning and she had come to understand his wants, his desires and his feelings for her. She knew he was wanting to make love and that he could sometimes still be charmingly shy about starting. He was even more of a romantic than she, and there was something pure about the way he didn't confuse love and sex. She loved the way he led and she knew how much he liked to lead, so she would let him lead. But she would start.

As soon as she took his hand, he knew. It was exactly what he was hoping she would do and the fatigue and the sadness they were fighting fell away. He ran his hand along the side of her face, and though he had done the same thing dozens of times, it sent a tingle up and down her spine. It was even better when he switched to the other side of her face and she had to struggle to remain still. It was scary and wonderful and dangerous and safe all at the same time, what she felt, all rolled into one, plus other things too complicated and intertwined and overlapping to figure out. Besides which, she didn't want to figure it out. Not then.

They drove along the Sound and walked along the water's edge. There were cars and people and loud music all along the beach and they left, not because they were afraid or because of unpleasant memories, but because they did not want to share the beach or the Sound or the night with anyone.

They drove to the lake. It was pitch black and no one else was around. The parking area, the woods, the water – it was all theirs. They lay on the sand for a long time listening to the symphony of millions of invisible insects until it became possible to believe they were the only people alive in the whole world.

Jackie didn't want them to be the only people in the whole world, though. As never before, the friction that marred so much of life seemed a gargantuan waste of energy. Jealousy, one-upman-ship, egos, petty squabbling over things of no consequence, all seemed beyond silly. She knew she wasn't free of those things and probably never would be, but she was connected to something big-ger than herself and she vowed to work to deepen that connection – work, in fact, to make deepening it the foundation of her life.

She thought of Darrin McGee and Al Armstrong and of some of the women she had interviewed and written about. She thought of girls from school whose friendships she'd been too quick to dis-miss and the measures she would take to correct that. She thought of all the people she'd seen that summer plugging on despite the obstacles because there was nothing else to do but plug on. She thought of becoming closer to Peggy and Ed and of all the things she and Lourdes would do together, next month, next year and on into the future. She thought of her mother and of the evening their relationship changed so dramatically. And she thought of Susan and of how she would work as hard to be there for her as she worked in school or with Jack or in any other sphere of her life even to the point, if she deemed it necessary, of involving their mother against Susan's wishes.

"I saw a mink here a few years ago." His voice sounded as if he was far away.

"Really?"

"It had been hit by a car. People from the Wildlife Department had anesthetized it and were getting ready to take it so it could recover. They said it was hurt badly enough that it would die if they left it. Usually they bring it back to the same place."

"Then it's probably here in the woods," she said.

"Isn't that cool, though? I mean, raccoons, okay. Skunks, okay. But a mink? Who would ever have thought minks live right here, what, three miles from your house?"

They fell silent. The cicadas and crickets, their time soon to be gone, played on joyously all around them. Their sound had become so thoroughly a part of summer that it was difficult at that moment to imagine night without it. The two of them had grown accustomed to the lack of unnatural light and it wasn't so dark after all, for the pitch black sky was full of stars and a luminous moon that was almost full. Though Jack lay still, he was restless. He had hoped the story about the mink would make it easier but it hadn't, so he thought about the fact that they would be apart in twelve hours and forced himself to go on.

"Jackie?"

She had dozed for a moment and came dreamily back. "Hum?"

"I wanna tell you something," he said.

"Alright," she said. "And I have something to tell you."

"What?"

She felt him tense in the dark. "You first?"

He talked about Walt and things Walt had said to him about women and about relationships. He wished he had told Walt off and been more on his guard. He regretted not sharing more of it with her and of how if he had she might have figured out a way to warn Susan off of him.

"I can't help but feel that what happened to her might not have happened if – "

She put her hand on his. "No, Jack."

"But Jackie, you should've heard – "

"I told you I talked to Susan about it," she said. "I mean we *really* talked. I'll tell you about it some time. Not now. I'll just say this. It wouldn't have mattered if you had told me everything. And it wouldn't have mattered if I told Susan everything. Believe me, Jack. I know."

"Alright." He began playing with her hair. "It's good you're gonna be close by. You're as strong as she is, you know that? It'll be as good for her as it will be for you."

She told him about the encounter with the cop at the beach, leaving none of it out. He tensed at several points and stopped with his hand when she told him about slapping the cop's his face. When she finished, she lay her head on his chest and put his hand back to her hair.

He had said there were many things that were more dangerous for her. Though it was undeniably true, they had to live without him believing he always had to protect her. Only then would she have maximum room to grow. She was confident he knew that now. If there was protecting to do, they would protect each other as equals. Susan had once told her that the best way – the only way – people can navigate to higher ground was together and as equals. And so they would try.

The put on sweatshirts and huddled under a blanket. They

fought sleep, wishing to savor every minute until the end, but still sleep came. It was light, restless sleep and the slightest thing woke first one and then the other. When they did wake, they moved nearer, knowing that before the sun rose and set again they would be two hundred miles from one another. Without either of them having to say anything, without either of them understanding how it had happened, they were, for the first time, both perfectly okay with that.

FORTY-TWO

Monday broke warm and sunny and Jack met Jackie and her mother at the diner for breakfast. Though it was Labor Day, Mr. Gendron was busy with conference calls and emergency meetings at the firm that couldn't wait until Tuesday so Jack would drive, help get Jackie moved in and drive Mrs. Gendron's Buick back to the house before getting on his way to New Hampshire. Mr. Gendron would travel in later by train to join his wife, Jackie and Susan for dinner.

Jackie was happy things had worked out as they had. Jack was coming, for one. In addition, with her father absent, she would be able to talk to her mother in the car on the way.

"You have *lovely* hair, Jack." Mrs. Gendron leaned forward from the backseat where she sat with her daughter and stroked his hair.

"Yeah, Jack." Jackie ran her hand along the back of his head. "You have *lovely* hair." The women laughed together and Jack blushed without shame.

They had been on the road ten minutes when 'Baby I Love Your Way' came on. He caught her eye in the rear view mirror and his smile gave her the push she needed. She nodded and he turned the volume up so he would hear only the music and not the conversation he knew was coming.

Jackie drew a deep breath. "Mom, there's something I've been wanting to talk to you about. I'm sorry I haven't talked to you about it until now. I should have but I didn't have the courage, plus Susan asked me not to."

"Honey. What is it?"

"Susan needs you, mom." Her voice was strong and true. "She needs you like she hasn't needed you in a long time. She needs me, too, and dad and Jack and all of us. But mostly she needs you."

She didn't shirk from details she would have been unable to relate several months earlier as she told her mother about Susan having to go to the hospital. Mrs. Gendron stiffened, both at what she heard and also because the graphic words she was hearing were spoken by her youngest daughter. She recoiled at the description Jackie gave of Susan's injuries and felt shame that Susan did not trust her enough to come to her for comfort. It wasn't easy listening and Mrs. Gendron had to remind herself that Susan was thirty-one. So much time gone, so much wisdom and knowledge and experience, yet still so much trouble.

Jackie knew her mother would beat herself up so she emphasized that Susan was fully recovered physically. She knew, however, that Susan could not possibly be fully recovered psychologically, and that was why her mother had to know. Most importantly, she knew now that their mother had much more to give than Susan realized.

Though she had anticipated it might happen, she was still shaken when tears formed in her mother's eyes, for while her mother was beautiful and smart and strong, she was also fragile in the way all human beings are fragile. In a strange way, the fragility and the tears brought them closer. Her mother was a part of her in a way she had thought not long ago would never again be possible, in the same way Jack and Susan were a part of her.

Everything was not alright and certain things would never be alright. Jackie knew that but she also knew this: dissolve a part of yourself, open a door, and go in. It may not work but it's the only thing that can.

"Mom?"

They were mother and daughter, yes, but they were equals as well. Two human beings. Her mother refused to look at first so she waited. She was sure of herself as never before and even if she had to wait all the way to NYU, she would be ready with what she knew her mother needed. When finally her mother looked at her, they fell into each other's arms and Jackie felt warm tears on her neck.

Mrs. Gendron would stay in New York for as long as was

necessary, she said, either at Susan's if Susan would have her or at a hotel. She pressed forth with question after question because she suddenly wanted to know everything about her oldest daughter's life. And as she listened and marveled at how mature Jackie was despite her youth, at how smart and beautiful she was, she wanted suddenly to know everything about her youngest daughter as well. She had never imagined that Jackie possessed such dauntless spirit and she saw the sustenance she could gain from her daughters now that she was willing to accept it.

Jackie caught Jack's eye again and he turned the radio off. He was a part of her now, irrevocably and forever. There would be plays to see and Prescott's and NYU friends she would want him to meet. She had been reading up on things they could do in New Hampshire and the meeting about the strike was coming up, plus the police brutality committee was formulating plans for the fall. Never had she been so fully integrated into something greater than herself. She imagined herself a spectacular Redwood in a forest of spectacular Redwoods.

"Is there a reason we're going by way of Brooklyn?" They were across the Triboro Bridge and speeding along the Brooklyn Queens Expressway.

"Relax, mom. Jack knows what he's doing. Besides, where's your sense of adventure?" She looked at her mother and smiled. "There's only one way to come into the City and that's by way of the Brooklyn Bridge."

Summer was dying? Maybe that was all wrong. Perhaps there was no summer or fall or winter or spring. Perhaps summer and fall and winter and spring were as fluid as melting snow. At what point does the snow become water? At what point does the water change from being a stream on a mountainside to a part of the river to which it flows? Maybe there was a bit of summer in every January evening and maybe a part of the coldest winter day was there with them amidst the warmth of September.

What Jack had said was true of her, too: the last three months had been better than her entire life before that put together. She would remember the summer always, savoring and learning from it, perhaps someday even grieving over it, and it would never be fully past because it would always be a part of her. But as she looked out at the world that awaited her, Jackie thought not of the yesterday of summer but of today and tomorrow. There was much to do and some of it would be impossible. She couldn't wait to try.